The Dilemma

Also by Jenny Pitman

ON THE EDGE

DOUBLE DEAL

Jenny Pitman

The Dilemma

MACMILLAN

First published 2003 by Macmillan
an imprint of Pan Macmillan Ltd
Pan Macmillan, 20 New Wharf Road, London N1 9RR
Basingstoke and Oxford
Associated companies throughout the world
www.panmacmillan.com

ISBN 1 4050 0617 X HB
ISBN 1 4050 4120 X PB

5 7 9 8 6 4

A CIP catalogue record for this book is available from
the British Library.

Typeset by SetSystems Ltd, Saffron Walden, Essex
Printed and bound in Great Britain by
Mackays of Chatham plc, Chatham, Kent

The Dilemma

1

Jan Hardy leaned back in the passenger seat of Annabel Halstead's new BMW and closed her eyes. She shook her unruly mop of blow-away blonde hair and wondered why on earth she'd gone to all the hassle and expense of having it done. Immediately after she'd arrived home from Ludlow, with the two horses that had run there earlier in the afternoon, she'd driven like Michael Schumacher to keep an appointment with her hairdresser in Broadway. Now she was late for a date she wasn't sure she was going to enjoy.

'What exactly are you going to tell him?' Annabel asked, glancing sideways at Jan from the driving seat of the black convertible. She had sensed Jan's anxiety earlier and offered to give her friend a lift to what was likely to be a tricky evening.

'God knows!' Jan groaned. 'I don't even know what I think myself any more.'

'Come on, Jan. I've never known you stuck for words.'

'You know I like him; I like him a lot, but I don't want to give him any bullshit or scare him off for good.'

'Sometimes it's best, you know, being cruel to be kind,' Annabel said, although at times she gave the impression she was deliberately not seeing why Jan should feel ambivalent about Tony Robertson now Eddie Sullivan had come back into her life.

'Is this the place?' she asked as she braked.

They drew up in front of a cluster of golden stone cottages in the Cotswold hamlet of Middle Swell. One of the houses was invitingly lit and bedecked with hanging flower baskets. It had been converted a few years before into a tiny restaurant called L'Escargot.

'Yes, this is it,' Jan nodded, without making the slightest move to get out. 'Have you ever eaten here?'

'No; you need to take out a small mortgage first, don't you?'

'I've no idea; I haven't been back since Tony brought me here for a meal last November.'

'It's rather romantic of him to invite you again.'

'That's what I thought when he suggested it.' Jan sighed. 'Until Eddie turned up out of the blue. Oh well, here goes.'

Jan gave her friend a wry smile, opened the passenger door and climbed out of the car.

Annabel leaned across. 'Best of luck, Jan. I'll be thinking of you. Oh dear,' she went on, putting her hand guiltily to her mouth, 'I'm afraid Fred's been sitting on that seat.'

Jan looked down. 'I see what you mean.'

Standing in the gravelled car park, in the soft orange glow of the floodlights, she searched her smartest black dress for the long crinkly white hairs which her lurcher had deposited in Annabel's car. Then she gave Annabel a half-hearted smile and walked towards the entrance to the restaurant. On the way, she looked around until she saw Tony Robertson's car neatly parked by the side of the building.

Tony would *be early*, she thought. He was always so predictable.

Which was precisely why Mary Pritchard, her mother, was so keen on him, not to mention the financial security that a young unattached doctor could provide.

For the last few months Jan had been trying to persuade herself that she owed it to her children at least, if not to herself, to value that kind of security, particularly when it was set against the massive uncertainties of trying to train and win races with a yard full of inexperienced horses and a bent jockey.

Six weeks earlier, halfway through her first full season as a licensed trainer, Jan had begun to think that she might have to chuck in the towel. But suddenly, reacting to skimpy evidence but a strong gut feeling, she'd forced a harsh and very public showdown at Warwick racecourse, which had dramatically unveiled the treachery of two of her most important owners. She had been distraught at their betrayal.

However, her horses were soon winning again and on Easter Monday, just three days ago, and against the predictions of all the pundits, she had won the Irish National at Fairyhouse with Russian Eagle. The big, strong gelding belonged jointly to Annabel, who was her assistant trainer, and A.D. O'Hagan, one of the most influential owners in the British Isles.

It had been one of the most joyous days in Jan's thirty-three years. And to crown it Eddie Sullivan had miraculously appeared in the evening at her Dublin hotel. She hadn't set eyes on him for nearly a year, but within a few hours their friendship had exploded into something bigger and far stronger than it had ever been before.

Soon after the race Tony Robertson had rung her from England, bursting with excitement. He had just seen Eagle's dramatic win and Jan being interviewed on television; he had also asked her out for a celebration dinner later in the week. Jan had been only too happy to accept at the time, but when Eddie turned up Tony began to seem less important.

Outside the restaurant she shivered in the chill spring air and took a deep breath. All Tony wanted to do was buy her a celebration dinner, after all. With a resigned air, she turned the door knob and stepped inside.

The interior was warm and inviting, with shaded wall lights and small candelabra on every table. The silver cutlery gleamed and the crisp linen tablecloths and tapestry curtains glowed in the candle-light. The comforting smells of wood-smoke from an open fire, fine wines and expensive perfume filled the air. Jan didn't find it hard to feel more cheerful as she glanced around for her date.

Finally she caught sight of him, sitting at the same intimate table they had occupied last time they had been there. He was smiling warmly.

There was nothing really soft or weak about his smile, she thought, and his eyes revealed his affection and humour in equal proportions.

Tony, like Jan, had been widowed young. Soon after they were

3

married and before they could have any children, his wife had been killed at one of the big northern horse trials. Tony's main concession to his grief had been to move from Yorkshire to Gloucestershire, where, he'd told Jan, he hoped to restart his life with new friends in fresh surroundings.

When Jan's son, Matty, had become ill the previous spring with suspected though mercifully unconfirmed meningitis, Tony had given her far more support than a single mother of two could have expected.

As he got to his feet, Jan flashed him a smile.

'Hi,' she said warmly.

'How are you?' he asked, putting a hand on her shoulder as he kissed her lightly on the cheek. 'You look incredible!'

Jan couldn't help glowing for a moment. Maybe the trip to the hairdresser had been worth it after all. 'Thanks. I think I'm still on a high from Ireland.'

'I bet you are.' He drew back the other chair from the table. 'I ordered a bottle of bubbly to kick off with. Would you like some?'

Jan thought she must have drunk at least a case of champagne since Russian Eagle had thundered past the post just three days before, but she nodded as she sat down. 'That would be lovely.'

Tony sat opposite her and beamed as he poured. 'Here's to you,' he announced, 'the best-looking, most talented trainer in all England.'

Jan guessed she would never tire of telling the story and, as Tony had asked, she described the momentous race with almost total recall of the three miles, five furlongs and every one of the twenty-three fences over which the Irish National was run.

'The worst moment,' she said breathlessly, reaching the climax, 'was when he passed the post. He'd stood right off the last fence and put in one of the most spectacular jumps I've ever seen to land a good length in front, but the favourite just wouldn't let go. His jockey was riding him like a man possessed. It was agony – a bit like watching in slow motion as they gradually caught up with Eagle and

Murty. From where we were standing in A.D.'s box, fifty yards back from the line, everyone was sure we'd been robbed of the race.' Jan shook her head with a weary grin, remembering the pain of it all. 'Annabel came rushing up to me, looking like a ghost – she'd been watching on the TV. The camera angle was terrible; it wasn't in line with the winning post, so *she* was absolutely positive he'd been beaten. Then a photo finish was announced and we had to hang on for hours – well, about five minutes, actually – but I could hardly breathe; I felt faint, sick, everything. We'd all charged down to the unsaddling enclosure. The whole place was buzzing. Then, suddenly, the entire racecourse went so quiet you could hear a pin drop. When they announced Eagle had won, the crowd exploded and gave him such a fright. He tried to take off.' Jan chuckled. 'But that roar from the crowd was such a golden moment – a complete bonus!'

Tony was looking at her with undisguised admiration. 'It must have been fantastic! I wish I'd been there. I'll make bloody sure I am next time!'

Jan looked away quickly. 'Yes, well,' she murmured, 'if there is a next time.'

'Oh, come on, Jan! Don't do yourself down. You're on your way now! You've won a National in your first year as a licensed trainer – how many people have done that? And I see a lot of your other horses are firing well now, since your bust-up with the Sharps.'

Jan couldn't suppress a shudder. Angie Sharp, her closest friend last spring, whom she would have trusted to the ends of the earth, had turned out to be part of the massive fraud her parents had been operating, using the seven horses they'd sent to Jan's yard the previous summer. Through Jan's friendship with Angie, they'd wormed their way into her yard, corrupted Billy Hanks, her stable jockey, and lost her at least a dozen races she felt she should have won if they hadn't manipulated the results to match their predictions on their hugely subscribed telephone tipping service.

Now she said, 'They've all been arrested and charged, thank God.'

Tony nodded. 'I saw it in the papers at the weekend. No doubt you'll be called to give evidence.'

5

'I suppose so.'

'That won't be much fun.'

Jan didn't mind admitting she was dreading it. 'But it's worse than that,' she went on. 'The whole business has made me completely cynical. I used to believe almost everything anyone told me – you ask my dad. But after what's happened to me in the last couple of years, with Harold Powell, James McNeill that ghastly vet, and then Billy Hanks and the Sharps, my faith in human nature's taken a serious drubbing.'

'Who's Harold Powell?'

'The auctioneer who sold my late husband's farm to himself for half of what it was worth. Still, at least neither he nor the Sharps got away with it.'

'Sometimes I get the impression you don't entirely trust my motives either,' Tony said, with a slight change of tone.

She looked him straight in the eye and tried not to let her voice shake. 'Tony, please. It's not that I don't trust your motives, I promise. It's just that I don't know if I'll ever be able to give you what you want.'

'Not yet, of course. I understand that – you've lost your husband, I've lost my wife. There isn't a day that goes by when I don't think about her. It must be the same for you and on top of that you've got Megan and Matthew to constantly remind you of John. You're so lucky to have them.'

Jan couldn't stop the tears from welling up. She often thanked God that her husband lived on after his death in their two children. 'I know I am, but I do know too that one day I'll want to share my life with someone again.'

Tony looked encouraged. 'And I guess you'll want to share it with a true friend, someone you really get on with; someone who understands horses and what they mean to you; someone who understands you and what you've been through.'

'Yes,' Jan whispered, trying desperately to control herself.

'Jan, please, look at me. It could be me – you know that.'

Jan took a deep breath and glanced down at the table, where unconsciously she had been crumpling her napkin. 'Tony, please don't talk about it, not yet. I know it's pathetic not to be able to make my mind up, but I just can't at the moment.' She looked up at him and saw hurt and bewilderment on his face. She stretched a hand across the small table and gently touched his arm. 'Tony, please believe me – I really wish I could, and so does my mum. The trouble is I'm not sure I deserve someone as good or as kind and considerate as you. You'd let me have my own way all the time, and that wouldn't be good for me. I *do* care about you, Tony, and I'm grateful for everything you've done for me, but please don't push me, not now.'

Tony didn't reply, but Jan could see he understood what she was saying. 'I'm sorry if that's not what you wanted to hear,' she said softly.

'But Jan, what is it that's making you feel you can't commit yourself?'

'I really don't know, Tony. I just can't, I'm not ready to.'

The doctor sighed with a faint smile. 'Oh God, we haven't even ordered and already I'm getting the elbow.'

Jan put her hand on his again. 'Of course you're not getting the elbow, Tony. I'm just so sorry you're expecting more than I can give. You don't have to buy me dinner if you don't want to.'

'Of course I'll buy you dinner,' Tony said quickly. 'But can I just ask – because I really felt we were getting somewhere before you went to Ireland – does what you're feeling have anything to do with the fact that Eddie Sullivan's back?'

Jan winced. 'Where did you hear that?' she asked rather hurriedly.

'I know the chap who runs the King's Head in Stow. Apparently Eddie's turned up and is renting a room there.'

Jan looked away. She didn't want Tony to know how much this information had upset her. She hadn't seen Eddie since she'd left Dublin two days before. He'd rung later that day from Ireland and said he was coming to Gloucestershire as soon as he could. To her great disappointment, she hadn't heard from him since. She vividly remembered whispering to him in the dark, pre-dawn hours following her great win that he must come and see her at Edge Farm the minute he arrived back in England. And now it seemed he was back in the Cotswolds without even making contact.

'He said he was probably coming over.' She tried to speak lightly. 'He came to see the race in Ireland.'

This was evidently news to Tony. 'Oh, did he?' he said dejectedly.

'I didn't think you knew him,' Jan went on, aware that the two men had never met, although she had told the doctor about Eddie and all the help he had given her when she first set up her yard at Edge Farm.

'You know I don't, but your name cropped up in conversation with the landlord of the King's Head and he mentioned Eddie Sullivan. Anyway, if his coming back to Gloucestershire does have a bearing on your feelings about me, so be it,' he said, trying hard to disguise the disappointment he felt. 'In the meantime,' he went on in a determined attempt to be light-hearted, which impressed Jan, 'since we're here, we may as well order and enjoy François's excellent cuisine.'

2

The spring chill of the starry night produced a crisp, bright dawn and the day's work ahead helped to push any negative thoughts to the back of Jan's mind. Soon after six she followed the first lot from her yard to be exercised. There was a contented smile on her face as the big gelding she was riding pulled strongly up a long turf gallop towards the ridge above her farm. She was bringing up the rear of a string of eight horses. Between a pair of long brown ears, she could see Annabel's slender frame in front of her, perched high over the back of a nervous four-year-old filly.

Officially, Annabel was Jan's assistant, but she was also one of her best work riders, especially with the younger horses. Of the ten people now employed full time at Edge Farm Stables, Jan was closest to her and knew her far better than the others.

Annabel had worked with her for several years, since Jan had trained point-to-pointers on her late husband's farm across the border in mid-Wales. Before that Annabel had been a regular face in the gossip columns because of her eye-catching good looks, until she suddenly decided she'd had enough of London when a close relationship had gone wrong. She'd welcomed the chance to live in the country, where she could indulge her love of horses – she'd told Jan she found them far more dependable than men.

Despite, or perhaps because of, their different backgrounds and personalities, the two women had always got on extremely well. Jan didn't doubt that there would be a time when Annabel would decide to move on – after all, she was still only twenty-five. But their friendship had been cemented even more firmly since Annabel had bought Russian Eagle, seen him run spectacularly in the Foxhunters' at Aintree last season, and then win the prestigious race at Fairyhouse a few days ago. So Jan felt confident she would keep her assistant for at least another year.

Also riding out in the string with them was Joe Paley, a hardened young gypsy, who was devoted to Jan since she'd forgiven him for a serious lapse of loyalty for which most trainers would have had him arrested. There were also two local girls, Roz and Emma, who'd been with Jan for the past year, and two comparatively recent arrivals from A.D. O'Hagan's stud in County Wicklow. Dec and Con were a double act, a pair of uncurbed Irish lads who never stopped joking and teasing, but they rode beautifully and hadn't done much wrong since they'd arrived from Ireland the previous autumn.

What pleased Jan most about her staff was that there was very little internal bickering and no sign of the arcane pecking orders that blighted most other yards. They had a strong sense of being a team, and they all shared in the jubilation when one of their horses won a race. Even the malign influence of Billy Hanks, her former stable jockey, had done no long-term damage to the yard's morale.

Nevertheless, the circumstances behind Billy's departure had left a nasty scar. Jan had known Billy since he was a child. Like her, he'd been born less than a dozen miles from Edge Farm. As a small boy he'd admired her while out hunting as she jumped everything with the best of the field, and later, when she'd started riding pointers for Colonel Gilbert, her father's landlord, he'd always been there to cheer her on. When he started race-riding himself and began to show promise as an amateur, he had always given Jan priority. He'd ridden nearly all her point-to-point and hunter chase winners, and when he turned professional he'd ridden most of her winners during the early part of Jan's first season as a public trainer – that was, until the Sharps had arrived on the scene.

Thinking of Billy's treachery made her feel physically sick. With a determined effort, Jan pushed him from her mind and thought about the problem she was now facing – where to find a new stable jockey.

With barely a month of serious steeplechasing remaining that season, it wasn't vital to find anyone immediately, and besides, after his victory in Ireland on Russian Eagle, Murty McGrath, the champion jockey, had offered to ride for her as often as his retainer with a big Lambourn yard would allow. While she knew she couldn't rely on Murty to ride all her horses, she was hopeful that her track record in the final stages of the season would throw up a few other jockeys.

Jan's string trotted along the ridge and pulled up at the top of the escarpment that formed the western edge of the golden limestone hills. Although she didn't own it, she had access to a long, undulating stretch of grass just below the ridge. It was wide enough for three horses to gallop alongside each other and was a good testing ground to compare their abilities. Jan walked her horse past the others, issuing instructions to gallop up in pairs and to continue on past the point where she would be waiting three-quarters of a mile ahead. Twenty minutes later, feeling well pleased with the performance of her horses, particularly one who'd recently come back from a nine-month layoff, Jan hacked back down the hill with Annabel.

As they looked across the hazy Severn valley towards the jagged profile of the Malvern Hills, they talked a little about the two horses that would be setting off for Aintree as soon as the first lot got back in. They were nearly back at the yard when Annabel could curb her curiosity no longer.

'Jan, you haven't said a word about what happened last night.'

'That's because nothing "happened",' Jan retorted. 'Tony suggested I might like to share my life with him one day and I told him I wasn't ready to make that kind of decision.'

'Go on,' Annabel said when Jan didn't expand. 'What did he say then?'

'He asked me if it had anything to do with the fact that Eddie was back.'

'Who told him Eddie was in Dublin?'

'No one; he didn't know he was until I mentioned it. But the landlord of the King's Head told him Eddie's renting a room there.'

'Oh, no!' Annabel didn't disguise her surprise. 'I'd no idea he was here.'

'Nor had I,' Jan murmured sadly.

'Still, it's great news he's back, isn't it?'

'I suppose so.'

'Come on, Jan. You were really excited when we flew home on Tuesday.'

'I just thought he would have let me know he was here by now. After all, I really went out on a limb when I told him I wanted to see him at Edge the moment he got back.'

'Don't worry about it. Eddie's never going to do what you tell him – or anyone else, for that matter. He'll always want to do the opposite, so if you don't want to scare him off, I'd let him take the initiative. He's not one of your horses, you know.'

Jan understood what Annabel was saying. She found it hard not to say what she thought and, while some people were grateful, she knew that her straight talking could often put other's backs up. 'Yes,' she sighed. 'I know what you mean, but I just can't help it if I see talent being wasted through lack of commitment.'

'Don't I know it.'

'That's not fair, Bel. I don't nag you.'

'No,' Annabel agreed. 'Not any more, but it's your commitment that makes you so good at what you do.'

'Bel, do you really think Eddie will turn up here?'

'Of course he will, but in his own time and on his own terms. I saw the way he was looking at you at the party. And I saw you looking at him with big cow eyes. It must have been extraordinary, you two getting it together when you've known each other so well as friends.'

'Haven't you been down the same road with Eddie, though?'

'That was a very long time ago and it didn't last – I told you.' Annabel shook her head. 'I was much too young at the time and, besides, I just wasn't his type, though I must admit I was rather potty about him . . .' Her voice petered out.

Jan had often tried to discover what had gone wrong between Eddie and Annabel five years before she had met either of them.

'Anyway,' Annabel went on determinedly, 'if you want my advice, you'll just have to be patient, sit tight and wait for him to come to you. And in the meantime I suggest you don't let poor Tony go on thinking he hasn't got a chance.'

Jan was well aware that patience with humans was not her forte and so she hoped that it wouldn't be tested too severely by Eddie Sullivan. Luckily, she had a full day ahead of her, with runners in two minor races on the second day of the Grand National meeting at the famous Liverpool course. Jan thought both horses had a fair chance of winning. One, Tom's Touch, was her most prolific winner so far for A.D. O'Hagan. Her only regret was that, having run Russian Eagle in the Foxhunters' last year over a single circuit of the Grand National course, she didn't have a runner in any of the major races this time.

Two hours after Jan had watched Roz drive the lorry out of the yard with their runners, she said goodbye to her children and Fran, her nanny, before climbing into Annabel's BMW.

Annabel was still in the early stages of her relationship with her new purchase and liked to use it all the time. Jan was quite prepared to be able to take full advantage of it. 'If you want to drive everywhere for the next few weeks, that suits me just fine,' she said cheerfully. 'And, I must say, it's a great deal more comfortable and cleaner than my car.'

'Apart from your dog's hairs.'

'You shouldn't let him in,' Jan remonstrated.

'But I like taking him for his runs up on the hill,' Annabel said, 'and I always have a clothes brush in the glove compartment. Anyway, how do you think we'll get on today?'

'I'm more hopeful than positive, though Dingle Bay's race doesn't look too competitive.'

Dingle Bay was a competent and reliable chaser. He was never going to be a star, but Bernie Sutcliffe, his owner, had become very fond of him and liked to see him run as often as possible.

'Judging by his run two weeks ago and his work at home, I'd say he's still improving,' Annabel said optimistically. 'And I see half the newspapers have tipped Tom's Touch.'

'I don't know why; they haven't seen him run over three miles before and their tips certainly won't make him run any faster.'

'I suppose they think you wouldn't be running him over that trip if you didn't think he could do it; and after the Irish National they'll probably be thinking you've still got something to pull out of the bag.'

'Right now I just wish I had rather more in the bag than I have. Losing the Sharps' horses has made a bigger dent than I expected – I hoped we'd have replaced some of them by now.'

'Stop panicking, Jan. It's only been a few weeks. Now people know our yard's back on song and you took the stance you did, they'll soon start to realize you run an honest ship.'

'Yes, I suppose you're right,' Jan conceded. 'I've already got a few orders, but it's like I told Tony last night, I'm feeling far more sceptical now and I don't count my chickens till they're hatched. I've rather lost my faith in human nature.'

'But you know Miller's Lodge is definitely coming from Virginia Gilbert's, don't you?'

Miller's Lodge was a highly rated chaser who'd previously won the Cathcart Chase at the Cheltenham Festival. The horse belonged to Johnny Carlton-Brown, head of Brit Records, whom Jan's brother, Ben, had introduced to her. Johnny, usually known as JCB, already had two horses with Jan – August Moon and Supercall – but he had kept Miller's Lodge with Colonel Gilbert's daughter. Virginia Gilbert had been granted a licence the year before Jan but she had had only a fraction of Jan's success.

'Yes, so Johnny said, and I believe him, but I still wish Miller's Lodge wasn't coming from Virginia's.'

'Why? What does it matter? Everyone knows you two don't get on.'

'That's exactly why. I don't want people thinking I poached the horse out of spite.'

'We all know you didn't. Anyway, it's not important what anyone else thinks, is it?'

'Yes it is because it's the easiest thing in the world to lose your reputation and a great deal bloody harder to get it back once it's gone.'

Annabel shook her head at this excessive sensitivity. 'No one's going to blame you. Jan, you *are* still going to take him, aren't you?' she added sharply.

'Of course I am.' Jan grinned. 'I might be soft, but I'm not bloody stupid.'

'If we can get another good win out of Supercall this month, Johnny might even think about having a fourth horse with you. He told me.'

Jan shrugged. 'Well, let's hope so, but what we really need is a big owner with half a dozen or more to send us.'

'A.D.'ll send a few more now, won't he?'

'I'm not sure I want him to. I wouldn't mind swapping a couple of the moderate ones he's already got with us, but I really don't want him becoming too dominant in the yard, or he might start throwing his weight around.'

'But he's always behaved impeccably with you, hasn't he?'

'Yes, on the whole, but I get the feeling that as far as he's concerned he's the boss, and he'll let me do what I want only as long as it happens to agree with his own ideas.'

'I found, as a co-owner, he couldn't have been more cooperative,' Annabel observed. 'He was fantastic over Eagle's win – what about that party!' She shook her head in wonder, remembering the lavish impromptu celebration the Irish tycoon had organized for them at a few hours' notice.

'Of course,' Jan agreed, 'and bringing Eddie back from Australia to watch the race – that was just amazing. But maybe that's what I mean – he likes to control everything.'

'For God's sake, Jan! He knew he was doing you and Eddie a big favour. And it was such a nice thing to arrange.'

'All right,' Jan conceded, laughing. 'I'm really glad he did, but for heaven's sake, Bel, I just wish Eddie would stop arsing around.'

'You'll just have to be patient for once, Jan.'

3

Annabel and Jan drove into the busy trainers' car park at Aintree half an hour before the first race. Annabel had arranged to meet some friends in their hospitality box and left Jan to deal with the formalities.

As Jan approached the weighing room, she was spotted by several journalists. It was the first time she'd appeared on a big English racecourse since her triumph in Ireland and they all wanted to hear her version of events. Despite not having a runner in today's feature race, she soon found herself the focal point of a mini press conference.

She happily shared her experiences with the journalists, modestly attributing the win at Fairyhouse to the horse, the jockey and a certain amount of good luck. She was enjoying herself relating the story, until one of the hacks asked a question which stopped her dead in her tracks.

'Is it true that Mr O'Hagan is setting you up in a much bigger yard as a result of your success with Russian Eagle, Mrs Hardy?'

Jan froze. Although the racing world was always awash with rumours, occasionally some of them contained a grain of truth. Someone, somewhere, must have floated the idea, which was precisely the sort of scenario she wanted to avoid.

She managed a smile. 'I'm sure, if it was true, Mr O'Hagan would have discussed it with me first. And so far he hasn't said a word.' She could only hope none of them knew A.D. well enough to realize that he was quite capable of rearranging someone's future without the formality of consulting them.

'Would you like it if he did, Mrs Hardy?' another asked.

'I never answer hypothetical questions,' Jan said. 'Now, if you'll excuse me, I've got my runners to declare.'

🐎

Murty McGrath shook Jan's hand respectfully. Tough, intelligent and completely focused, he was very ambitious but didn't altogether conform to the standard image of a National Hunt jockey. Though not tall, he was a well-proportioned, good-looking man in his early thirties. He seldom drank alcohol, he'd never been known to cheat on his wife and he was paying for his three children's education at a private Catholic school. As far as he was concerned, his riding skills were simply a means of providing for his family; vanity and ego didn't affect his thinking. Jan knew that she was fortunate to have him to ride both her horses at this meeting, but she couldn't quite make up her mind if he'd taken the rides out of a sense of duty because she'd given him the winner of the Irish National, or because he truly believed in her as a trainer.

'Have you had a look at the opposition?' she asked.

'Of course,' he said in his soft Kerry accent.

'What do you think?'

The jockey shrugged non-committally. 'Tom's Touch has the class to pull it off if he's on song and gets the trip. The other one, I'm not sure. The horse is a great lepper, but the fella who rode him last time didn't make enough use of him. He doesn't have a lot to beat today, mind.'

'I'm sure Tom's as ready as he's ever been. He's freshened up since we gave him a bit of a rest in February. Dingle's taken a long time to get fit, but he's improving every day and, as you say, he's got a hell of a jump in him. By the way, Bernie Sutcliffe, who owns him, will want to know if he should back him. I'd rather you didn't over-commit yourself.'

Murty gave her a censorious look. 'Mrs Hardy, I've ridden for you before and you know I wouldn't venture an opinion on the outcome of a race – not to my own mother or even the parish priest. Is A.D. coming over to watch his horse?'

'No,' Jan said. 'He can't, but Jimmy O'Driscoll's coming.'

Murty raised a critical brow. Jimmy O'Driscoll, also from

17

Killarney, had been a leading flat jockey in his native land a dozen years before. For the last few years he'd been A.D. O'Hagan's racing manager. 'I heard word that A.D.'s sending you more horses, setting up a new yard for you.'

Jan laughed. 'I've just heard that myself. Several journalists collared me outside the weighing room and told me it's the latest rumour doing the rounds. But A.D.'s said nothing to me.'

Murty didn't say any more, but Jan could tell from his eyes he was thinking that if A.D. had decided to put his massive resources behind her, Jan could end up running a very important yard.

'I wouldn't get too excited, Murty,' she said quietly. 'Because it ain't going to happen.'

Since Jimmy O'Driscoll had been appointed A.D.'s manager, he seemed to think he was God, Jan reflected, as she stood with him in a small hospitability box in the main stand. At least A.D. pretended to listen when you talked to him, even if you knew he wasn't taking much notice of what was being said. But Jimmy didn't even pretend – he thought he knew it all.

'Looks like that horse is carrying a bit too much condition,' he remarked as they watched Murty canter Dingle Bay down to the start of the three-mile chase course.

'Jimmy, that's not fat; that's muscle,' Jan bristled. 'We've found the fitter he gets, the more he eats, and it suits him.'

'I never found a horse that improved by being overweight. The horse used to belong to Eamon Fallon, didn't it? Who's this fella, Sutcliffe, who owns him now?'

Jan wondered what business it was of Jimmy O'Driscoll's who her owners were, but she saw no harm in telling him.

'Bernie Sutcliffe's a wheeler-dealer from the Black Country – made a pile of money.'

'Doing what?'

'Various things – scrap originally, now mostly property, and he has recently bought a computer company.'

'Was that him in the ring with you just now – the hunch-backed fella in a mac?'

Jan nodded with a grin. In appearance, Bernie was an unlikely racehorse owner. Whatever he wore to the races, he never seemed to get it right. However much they'd cost, his clothes always hung off his shoulders below a long and slightly sunken face that made him look older than he was. 'He's probably not the best-looking owner in the yard,' she admitted.

'He's an ugly bastard,' Jimmy countered. 'Didn't he want to watch the race with you?'

'No. He's brought a gang of his mates along, so I said I'd see him after.'

'Does he bring his missus?'

'He's never been married and the girls seem to dump him as fast as he finds them, despite his money. They say he's very mean.'

'Does he pay his bills, though?' Jimmy asked sharply.

'I don't know if that's anything to do with you, but actually he's a very good payer. He checks every penny, finds it's all correct and pays by return each month.'

'You want owners like that,' the ex-jockey said. 'How did he end up with that horse?' He nodded towards the course, where Dingle Bay and the other runners were circling behind the starting gate.

'When Eamon Fallon got into trouble he told me to sell the horse for him. Annabel, my assistant, has money of her own so she bought him, mainly because she wanted to persuade Bernie to part with Russian Eagle and she thought he might be prepared to swap.'

'She got that right then, didn't she?' Jimmy said.

'Actually that wasn't the main reason she wanted Eagle. Though she felt he was potentially a good horse who just hadn't won when he should have done. Originally I bought Eagle for Eddie Sullivan, who wanted to ride him in the Foxhunters' here last year, but he'd got himself into a lot of trouble over his business – his father going under and all that – so he was forced to sell the horse.'

'A.D. told me about it,' Jimmy said with a nod.

'Eddie owed five grand in VAT, but he'd already used the money on a big bet with Cyril Goldstone.'

'A five-grand bet? What on, for God's sake?'

'It may sound incredible, but he'd backed himself to win the

Foxhunters' riding Russian Eagle, and Cyril had laid him at a hundred to one.'

'You mean he stood to win half a mil from Goldstone?'

'That's right, though it looked a hell of a long shot. In fact, he bloody nearly pulled it off.'

Jimmy nodded. One of A.D.'s horses had been lying right behind Russian Eagle when Eddie parted company with his mount at the elbow after clearing the last fence in the lead.

'Of course,' Jan went on, 'we all told him he was completely mad to have had a bet like that – he was very inexperienced and so was the horse. But Annabel's always had a soft spot for Eddie and she thought he ought to be allowed to have a go at least; she thought he might pull it off, but if he didn't line up it was inevitable he'd lose his money.'

'But why the hell did he have such a queer bet?'

'Well, it turned out not to be so queer. He was just desperate to help his old man out. Ron Sullivan was into some dodgy Italian bank for five hundred thousand and they were beginning to lean on him heavily – that's why the Sullivans disappeared last year.'

'So it was a case of shit or bust?'

'That just about sums it up. The problem was that Bernie had refused to let Eddie ride the horse, so Annabel cooked up a plan to get it away from him. Fortunately, he reckoned that Dingle Bay was a very good swap for Eagle.'

'I don't suppose he thinks that now. I bet he's really pissed off.'

'If he is, he hasn't shown it. After all, it was entirely his own decision, so he can't blame anyone else.'

Out on the course the horses were being called into line. The starter lifted his hand, pulled the lever to release the tapes and they were off. Dingle Bay was settled halfway down the field, where Jan had asked Murty to be for the first mile and a half.

'How come Eddie Sullivan fell off on the flat?' Jimmy asked nonchalantly with his eyes glued to his binoculars.

Jan didn't answer for a moment. Through her own binoculars she watched a small pile-up at the first open ditch, where two of Dingle's opponents were dramatically removed. 'His saddle slipped,' she said quietly.

Although she wasn't looking at him, Jan could sense Jimmy's eyes on her. 'Was that your fault?' he asked.

She lowered her binoculars and glowered straight back at him. 'No, it bloody well wasn't.'

'Ah,' the Irishman said with a faint lift of a ginger brow. 'And Cyril Goldstone saved himself half a bar.'

Jan didn't reply. Cyril Goldstone's foul play was well-covered ground for her. Joe Paley, racked with guilt, had confessed that Cyril had bribed him to sever the stitching on the girth, but there was no way she could prove it.

Jimmy turned his attention back to the track, where Jan's runner was putting in a performance worthy of a horse costing five times as much. His jumping was big and bold, and under Murty he was galloping on relentlessly between the fences.

A few minutes later Jimmy conceded grudgingly that he'd been wrong about Dingle Bay's condition, as the big horse crossed the line full of running two lengths clear of his nearest rival.

That's put you in your place, you arrogant little toerag, Jan thought happily at such a clear vindication of her training methods.

An hour later, when Murty brought Tom's Touch home first by a similar margin, Jimmy even bestowed a faint smile on her. A.D., Jan knew, would have been effervescent, showering her with congratulations and champagne. Looking at Jimmy O'Driscoll's bony profile, she was mightily relieved by his more restrained form of celebration.

🏇

Annabel, Roz and Joe looked ecstatic as their horse was accompanied by two mounted policemen down the long, hallowed walkway from the track. Joe clipped his lead rein onto Tom's bridle and led him under the famous veranda. Murty jumped off while Jan looked on with tears in her eyes. Today she'd not only had her first winner at Aintree, it was her first double for over five months.

Joe, as usual, had backed both horses. Dingle Bay had come home at twenty-five to one and once the horses had been washed down and were safely back in their stables, he went off jubilantly to collect his winnings.

Jan was beginning to tap her feet when he reappeared more than an hour later. 'Joe, where the hell have you been? I want to get these horses back home.'

'I'm sorry, Mrs H.,' Joe said, looking nervous. 'I wouldn't have been more'n twenty minutes, but . . .' He shuffled his feet sheepishly. 'I've just seen Mr Goldstone.' He winced at the bad memories he was opening up. 'He collared me as I was on the way to get my dosh. He said he wanted me to tell you he'd heard Eddie Sullivan was around. He said to tell him, if he was thinking of doing anything silly like, he better watch out.'

Jan felt as if someone had scoured her guts with a yard broom. It wasn't the mention of Goldstone that upset her, irksome as it was to think of him here at Aintree. It was the second revelation that hit her harder – that Eddie had been stupid enough to let Goldstone know he was back and that he had been such a jerk to let himself be seen and without even telling her he was coming here.

Eddie, you complete prat! she muttered angrily to herself.

Suddenly grasping a faint hope, she pulled her mobile phone out of her handbag to see if any messages had been left since she'd switched it off. There were a couple of routine calls and several of congratulation, but not a word from Eddie.

'OK, Joe, thanks,' she said, struggling to regain her composure. 'Did you get your money all right?'

'Yeah. I had to hang around for it 'cos he was taking bets on the next race, but I got it all right in the end.'

'That's something, then, isn't it?' Jan said, being careful not to let her anxiety show.

After such a successful day Jan should have been elated, but sitting beside Annabel on the way home she couldn't dislodge the image of Cyril Goldstone's brooding, lizard-like features from her head, nor the way the multimillionaire bookmaker had dealt with Eddie's challenge last year, like a man brushing away a fly.

🐎

Jan hadn't known how late it would be before the horses got back so she'd arranged for her nanny to stay the night. As it happened, the lorry had an easy run down the motorway and both the victorious runners were snug in their stables by ten o'clock. Jan guessed Megan and Matthew would be tucked up in their beds too, and fast asleep.

'As Fran's here, do you want to come down to the cottage for a nightcap?' Annabel enquired.

'No, thanks,' Jan said. 'I've got something else I need to do first.'

Annabel flashed her a curious glance, but didn't probe further. 'OK.' She shrugged. 'Anyway, well done! It's been a brilliant day. Please don't let this Goldstone business get you down too much.'

'It's not just Cyril.'

'I know,' Annabel said. 'But please, Jan, take it easy and don't do anything you'll regret.'

Jan felt a little ashamed of herself as she waited until Annabel's BMW was at the bottom of the drive before hurrying out and climbing into her old Land Rover, which rattled down the track to take the road back over the ridge towards Stow.

Stopping in the wide-open square amid the honey-stoned buildings of the old market town, Jan switched off her engine and sat in the dark for a while, trying to decide if she would be making a complete fool of herself if she went into the King's Head. A few moments later she'd made her mind up and climbed down from the vehicle.

She pushed open the door into the hubbub of the busy, smoky room and squeezed through the crowd to order a glass of wine before she started looking around. She took a sip and had just plucked up the courage to ask the girl behind the bar if she'd seen Eddie Sullivan when suddenly she spotted him herself.

He was sitting in a corner, half turned away from her but with his distinctive broken nose and handsome, craggy profile clearly visible beneath a mane of wavy black hair. He was talking to a small man in a grimy flat cap and a battered old waxed jacket. Jan watched him for a moment, trying to assess how she felt.

Suddenly both men burst out laughing. Jan took another deep breath and strode across the room.

'Hello, Eddie. I see you're back then,' she said, and immediately wished it hadn't come out so harshly.

Eddie wheeled round. Jan could hardly believe the flood of emotion that swept through her. It was extraordinary. For nearly a year, when she had first moved to Edge Farm, Eddie had been her closest male friend, as close as Annabel in many ways. They'd shared all their trials and setbacks, which had culminated in Eddie's disastrous but mercifully harmless fall in the Foxhunters'. When he had disappeared after the demise of his family's business empire, she had missed him terribly, but as a friend not as a lover. Now all that had changed – in the first few minutes of his arrival at the party in Dublin, Jan had felt an emotion she'd forgotten existed.

When Eddie saw her, he jumped to his feet with a slightly guilty and embarrassed smile on his face. 'Yeah, I got here the day before yesterday.' He leaned down and gave her a quick, soft kiss on the lips. 'Sorry, I had to sort out a few things before I came down to Edge.'

'So I hear, but I was talking about you getting back from Aintree.'

'Aintree?' Eddie looked blank.

'Yes, Aintree – that well-known racecourse where you fell off your horse like a sack of spuds last year.'

'I haven't been there since,' Eddie said with a puzzled laugh.

'I heard you were up there today; I had two runners. I'm sure you knew that.'

'Of course I did; I backed them – well done! But I watched the races here in Stow – in the betting shop around the corner.'

'He was in 'ere dinnertime,' the little man piped up, evidently thinking that Eddie's story needed corroborating.

It wasn't necessary; Jan believed him. Eddie, she knew, had his share of human weaknesses, but lying wasn't one of them.

'I'm sorry,' she said, suddenly meek. 'I was worried . . .' She stopped. She didn't want to talk about Cyril Goldstone in front of anyone else.

Eddie's companion sensed it and shuffled to his feet. 'I'll bugger off and leave you to it.' He picked up his pint and wandered off towards the bar.

'Who was that?' Jan asked.

'Dad's old gardener.' Eddie grinned. 'He's a lovely chap, always ready to lend a hand. God, it's so good to see you, Jan! Have a drink. Oh, sorry – I see you've already got one, but shouldn't you be on something a lot better than that awful house red after such a fantastic double? I'll get a proper bottle in a moment, but come on, sit down. Relax,' he ordered, waving at the empty chair opposite him, which Jan gratefully lowered herself into.

Eddie sat down too and looked at her with a puzzled expression. 'Something's worrying you, Jan. What is it? What's wrong?'

'Joe Paley bumped into Cyril Goldstone this afternoon.'

'That must have hurt.' Eddie laughed.

'Just shut up and be serious for once in your life. Cyril told him he'd heard you were around – I thought he meant up at Aintree. And he also said to tell you: if you were thinking of doing anything silly, you'd better watch out.'

'I'm glad the slimy old bastard's still got a guilty conscience about what he did – he could have got me bloody killed! I just wish to God we had some way of proving it.'

'If we were going to do anything about it, we should have done it as soon as Joe owned up.'

'But there was absolutely nothing for the police to go on – just the evidence of a twenty-year-old travelling lad with a bit of previous. I didn't want to deal with Cyril then, anyway; I wanted to lull him into a sense of false security.'

'So you said and that's precisely why I never reported Joe for it; but, Eddie, the man's not an idiot. By now he must realize we know what he did!'

Eddie looked at her with a rare show of anger in his dark brown eyes. 'But that isn't going to stop me getting even with the bastard sooner or later, and you may have to help me.'

'Me? How can I help you?'

'By organizing a really convincing coup with a couple of your horses.'

Jan screwed up her face and shook her head. 'Look, Eddie, you've got every right to want to get even with him and I'd love to see you do it. Of course I'll do what I can to help, but I'm not going to cheat and run my horses falsely for you, or anyone else for that matter. You need to understand that.'

Eddie's face softened and he sighed. 'That's what I thought you'd say. Still, there may be another way, but at this precise moment I'm tempted to go round and give the fat bastard a good thumping.'

'Rubbish.' Jan laughed and stretched across the table to take his hand. 'You couldn't punch your way out of a wet paper bag!'

'Yes, I could, if I was angry enough, but I'd probably get nicked and I still wouldn't get my money. Now,' Eddie went on, smiling again, 'it's time we had a bottle of fizz.'

Jan felt an unexpected tingle suffuse her whole body. She shook her head. 'Not here,' she said through a suddenly dry throat. 'A.D. sent over a case after the National at Fairyhouse. I've still got plenty left at home.'

Eddie didn't knock before he walked into the big stone farmhouse Jan had commissioned to be built beside her yard the previous year. She had moved into it just before Christmas and there was still some finishing to do, but Eddie was the first to agree that it was a lot more comfortable than his room in the pub. Jan also knew that her home held other attractions for him, but in the two weeks since he'd been back in England she hadn't let him spend a single night there. Part of her wanted him to – very much – but she was certain that she didn't want the children to find him in her bed in the morning – not yet anyway.

When Eddie pushed open the kitchen door, a three-year-old boy was sitting at the table beside a small blonde girl of eight, who was halfway through a bowl of Coco Pops. As soon as she saw Eddie, she leapt to her feet with a squeal of delight and ran round the table to fling her arms as high as she could around his waist.

'Sit down, Megan,' Fran Walters said, laughing, without the faintest hope of being obeyed.

Fran, forty-five, short, plump and permanently cheerful, had become devoted to Jan and her two children since she'd started looking after them last autumn and Jan was deeply grateful for her absolute reliability.

Jan had followed Eddie into the room, and tried to reinforce the nanny's instruction.

'But, Mum,' the girl protested indignantly, 'I have to help Eddie take his boots off!'

Since Eddie had come back to Gloucestershire, he'd driven over every morning from Stow in a borrowed old blue Morgan with a tattered black hood. He generally arrived around six-thirty to ride out and insisted on wearing long boots and jodhpurs, instead of the jeans and chaps favoured by some of the lads.

It had soon become a ritual when he came in for breakfast for Megan to straddle his calves and help pull off the skin-tight boots with a lot of teasing and laughter. While all the hilarity was taking place, Jan started cooking eggs and bacon for the rest of the staff, who would soon be gathered around the big pine kitchen table.

As always, while the others drifted in, the talk centred on the horses due to run that afternoon – three at Jan's home course of Cheltenham, two of which belonged to A.D. O'Hagan.

'Is the boss coming over to watch?' Dec asked, pouring himself some coffee.

'The boss is standing right here cooking your breakfast at the moment,' Jan replied sharply.

'Oh, don't take on so, Mrs H. I know you're my boss, but he's *the* boss, like.'

'If you mean is Mr O'Hagan coming to the races then, yes, he is. He's keen to see Wexford Lad run. He hopes we might go a long way with him. I told him Erin's Jet is starting to work really well at home, too.'

'Unlike that Emerald Isle of his,' Con added, frustrated that he had been unable to produce much effort from the gelding that morning.

'We can't expect them all to be stars, you know.'

'I expect he'll be sending us a few more now,' Roz ventured.

Jan grinned. They were always fishing for information, but she had learnt already that there were so many uncertainties in racing that it wasn't worth announcing things until they'd actually happened. 'Who knows?' she said. 'As long as we produce his horses looking as good as they can, and they keep on winning, I dare say he'll think about it.'

She glanced at Eddie, who was tucking into his breakfast. He winked back.

4

A.D. O'Hagan met Jan and Eddie in the pillared lobby of the Queen's Hotel with a broad smile, a firm handshake and a discerning gleam in his sharp blue eyes. Earlier in the week he had invited them both to join him for dinner at Cheltenham's leading hotel. Although he was in his late fifties, his dark, freshly groomed hair showed only faint hints of grey at the temples. Clad in a yellow cashmere sweater, checked trousers and suede loafers, he looked completely at ease in the grand proportions of the famous Regency building.

'It's great to see you both looking so well,' he said in a deep voice with the resonance of south-west Ireland. 'I'm sorry we didn't have time to talk at the races, but as you saw I had a number of people to entertain.'

'That's fine,' Jan said. 'We were busy ourselves and we knew we were meeting up again tonight anyway.'

'Well done with Wexford Lad; he ran far better than I'd hoped. I think we could possibly be looking at a Champion Hurdler, or maybe a contender for the Stayers', though I suppose he may still need a couple more years to show his true potential.'

Jan had been having the same thoughts, although she had kept them to herself until now. She nodded. 'I certainly hope you're right.'

'Pity about Erin's Jet, though. He didn't like the ground, did he? We'll put him away until the autumn.'

'I think he could still win a race this summer,' Jan heard herself say.

'But there it is,' A.D. said quietly. 'You can send him home, along with the other two, Emerald Isle and Anais Is Arish.'

Jan knew she couldn't let her disappointment show. While she didn't earn a great deal from her grass keep during the summer, it still kept some much-needed cash coming in. And she didn't disagree with her owners having their horses at home for their summer break, if they had good land and the horses were managed correctly, not just dumped out to fend for themselves.

'That's OK,' she said. 'When would you like them to travel?'

'In about three weeks when you've let them down, but in the meantime I'd like you to find a flat race for Galway Fox; twelve furlongs should suit, but nothing too classy. He doesn't mind a bit of a rattle in the ground.'

Jan was conscious that these were all decisions which, as trainer, she should be taking, but it was hard to take issue with A.D.'s pronouncements when he was in full flow.

'Sure,' she nodded. As it happened, she thought it was quite a good idea to run Galway Fox on the flat; the horse had lost some of his confidence jumping, but he was fit and fast enough to win if the right conditions in a modest race were on offer.

After a few minutes' discussion about A.D.'s sixth horse, Tom's Touch, they ordered their food. A.D. chose two expensive wines and Jan guessed each bottle probably cost as much as a meal for four. The Irishman encouraged Eddie into the conversation and talked enthusiastically about art. Eddie had specialized in equestrian paintings when he had run a gallery in Stow, although when the money had run out eighteen months ago he'd had to give it up.

As usual, Jan found the conversation with A.D. stimulating. But when Eddie left the table briefly, A.D. took the opportunity to lean across the table, so no one else in the crowded restaurant could hear him, and whispered, 'What's the score between you and Eddie?'

'How do you mean?'

'Where's it all going?'

'I just wish I knew!' Jan sighed. 'He spends a lot of time at the yard and he's riding out every morning. He's also promised to look after the building of my new stable block.'

A.D. jerked back in his chair. 'More stables? What for?'

'I reckon I could get another eight boxes along the open end of the yard, which would also close it in and make the whole place less draughty.'

'That would give you nearly forty boxes. Can you fill them? Do you really want all the extra hassle?'

'Yes and no. In an ideal world I'd rather just train ten brilliant horses, but you know it doesn't work like that. And I've had a lot of enquiries over the last month; of course, Russian Eagle's win helped.'

'But you haven't even replaced the animals those crooked tinkers had with you yet.' A.D. came straight to the point with his usual forthrightness, but Jan refused to be intimidated.

'I know that, but as it happens, I've just bought one of them back – King's Archer. I think Bernie'll have him.'

'You'll need more than the odd new horse to keep forty boxes full,' A.D. warned.

'But there's no point being negative about it.'

The Irishman laughed. 'You're right, but maybe you should hold your fire on this building work for the time being.'

Jan became wary at this first hint about A.D.'s proposals. 'Why?' she asked.

'Well, I've been thinking . . .'

'Here's Eddie,' Jan said, in a pointless bid to stop him, as if she already knew she wasn't going to be able to resist his proposal when it came.

'I don't mind talking business in front of him if you don't,' A.D. said quietly.

Jan had the impression he would almost prefer it. 'OK, that's fine.' She shrugged. 'We don't seem to have too many secrets from one another at the moment.'

A.D. shot her a searching glance which she couldn't quite understand. 'All right,' he said mildly.

Eddie sat down and drew his chair back up to the table, while A.D. filled his glass with an expensive Chablis.

'I've just been telling Jan,' A.D. went on in the same soft voice, 'that maybe she should think again before adding these new stables to the yard.'

Eddie leaned back in his chair. 'Why's that?'

Jan thought he looked disappointed, but was prepared to listen to whatever alternative was going to follow.

'Obviously, I've been impressed by Jan's achievements this season. I must admit I sent her the first few horses on a whim – I'd promised I would if she could train a great yoke like Russian Eagle to win a half-decent race; and I willingly concede he'd have won the Foxhunters' if you hadn't parted company with him . . .' It seemed as if A.D. was reluctant to refer to Cyril Goldstone's presumed guilt for Eddie's accident. 'Anyway,' he continued, 'she's gone on to achieve far more than I could have dreamed of, and has done better with some of my moderate animals than other, grander fellas have done with my best ones.' He nodded, looking proudly at Jan as if she were a fine oil painting he'd had the shrewdness to buy for peanuts at a country auction.

Jan glanced at Eddie, who, unseen by A.D., faintly raised an eyebrow, which seemed to say: *Just hang on and see where he's going with this.*

'I've had quite a few winners for my other owners, too,' Jan said firmly, trying to qualify her success.

'Of course you have.' A.D. laughed. 'I know I'm not the only pebble on the beach, but, assuming you want to expand, the problem you have now is that since your friend Angie Sharp and her parents were obliged to remove their custom, most of your owners have just shares or one horse apiece.'

'So?' Jan said. 'In some ways, a lot of small owners can be more manageable than one who dominates the yard.'

'Now then, Mrs Hardy.' A.D. came back with a smile that wasn't entirely humorous. 'I think you must agree that I've never taken advantage of my position.'

'Agreed. But I need to decide when and where I'm going to run the horses, so that I know exactly how to target their training. I live with them twenty-four hours a day, seven days a week, so I'm bound to know them better than anyone else.'

A.D. took a sip of wine. 'Well then, Jan, let me put it this way. While I don't disagree with you in principle, as the owner of many valuable horses and having a fair knowledge of the racing calendar,

I expect my suggestions to be taken seriously and I do like to have a say as to where and when they run.'

Jan couldn't argue with the manner or apparent reasonableness of what he was saying, and she felt she had already made her point. 'That's fair enough. I accept it's working well together as a team that's most important.'

'Right. Without beating about the bush, then, I'd like you to think about a proposition I have for you.'

'OK,' Jan said, feeling she knew what was coming next.

'I believe you have enormous potential as a trainer; your instincts and knowledge are as good as any in the business, and I think in the right yard, with the right horses, you could get to the top of the tree in National Hunt racing very quickly.'

This was an unequivocal endorsement of her skills from one of the most respected players in the game and Jan should have been feeling elated. But she really didn't want to lose control of her business.

'What do you mean by the "right" yard?' she asked.

'You need a bigger, more accessible place; you need facilities that are at least as good as your competitors' – all-weather gallops, schooling ground, swimming pool, horse walker, plenty of level paddocks.' A.D. paused and looked at Jan's rigid face before he carried on. 'And space to have a hundred quality stables and a hostel, so that you can entice top-flight staff.'

'I've got top-flight staff.'

A.D. shrugged. 'You need a professional assistant.'

'What's wrong with Annabel? She's been a brilliant back-up and she's totally reliable,' Jan said indignantly.

'There's very little wrong with Annabel,' A.D. agreed with a grin, 'but you can't really think a girl of her age, as beautiful and well connected as she is, will want to hang around a racing yard for much longer. And then you've got to realize that with a much bigger yard you'll need good people to take horses to the races when your runners are split, to instruct jockeys with the right degree of authority, deal with the owners and be responsible for some of the training when you're away from the yard.'

'But I don't want a hundred horses to train – around forty will suit me very well.'

A.D. leaned back in his chair and a quiet smile played across his lips. 'This is what you say now; but, come on, Jan, I know you're hugely ambitious. D'you think I'd have got behind you as far as I have if I wasn't aware of that already?'

Jan tried to confront the power in A.D.'s hypnotic blue eyes, but gave in after a few seconds and glanced at Eddie with an unspoken plea for help.

Eddie raised an eyebrow. 'A.D.'s right there,' he said. 'We both know how ambitious you are. Obviously running a bigger yard is tougher, but it would certainly increase your chances of hitting the big time.'

'Well, that's very kind of you both, but I'd prefer to get there gradually and in my own time.'

'Why?' A.D. asked bluntly, without blinking.

Jan stared back at him. 'Because I don't want to lose control of my career,' she said.

'No one's suggesting that you should. I'm just looking to speed up the process.'

'What precisely are you suggesting, then?' Eddie asked. Jan shot him a warning glance, but he waved his hand at her to be patient.

'I'm proposing that I put up the funds to find and, if necessary, equip a yard with everything or anything you may need to compete with the best in the country. And I'll back my judgement further by committing between thirty and forty horses of my own. I would also encourage the owners of another couple of dozen. With the firm commitments you already have, that would take you to ninety odd, and I would think you'd have no trouble at all filling any spare capacity you had after that.'

'You mean people will think, if you're spending all this money, I must be good?' Jan queried.

A.D. didn't rise. 'Up to a point, but, Jan, you've already built up a pretty impressive following of your own. Hasn't she, Eddie?' A.D. turned to him, addressing him directly for the first time since he'd unveiled his proposal.

'Of course she has. She knows that and that's why she thinks she can take it to the next stage on her own.'

Jan looked gratefully at him.

'Well, I understand that, of course. Jan, I always knew you were an independent woman and I'm certainly not suggesting you give up any of that independence.'

'But I wouldn't own the yard, would I?'

'No, but so what? There's nothing to stop you investing your profits in property elsewhere, and I'd be prepared to give you some interest in any appreciation in value that occurs as a result of your efforts.'

'That's all a bit woolly, though, isn't it? I tell you what,' she went on before A.D. could answer. 'I've listened to your proposal, but before you go into any further detail I'd like to think about the idea in general. When I have, I'll let you know if I want to take it further. Is that OK? Please don't think I'm ungrateful – I just need a bit more time.'

'Fine, Jan,' A.D. answered mildly. 'You think about it, balance up all the pros and cons and let me know your decision. But I have to tell you, if we do decide to go ahead, we'd want to aim at being moved before the start of next season.'

Jan had to drive Eddie's old Morgan home after he had got carried away by A.D.'s generosity and the Calvados at the end of dinner.

'I'm rather surprised A.D. didn't mind talking about his ideas for setting you up in a huge new yard in front of me.'

'Well, I'm not. He knew you'd be far keener on the idea than I would be and he's hoping you'll talk me into it.'

Eddie lay back in the passenger seat. 'Of course,' he said after a few moments' thought. 'You're absolutely right. He's as cunning as a fox, isn't he?'

Jan scowled. 'He's the smartest man I've ever met – apart from you, of course,' she added quickly with a giggle. 'And I think even you'd agree he's probably a bit better at business.'

'I'll concede that,' Eddie grunted, 'though he doesn't know you as well as he imagines if he thinks you'd take any notice of what I have to say, but I'll tell you one thing – I don't intend to mention A.D.'s proposal to you ever again. You must do exactly what you think is right. It's entirely your business, and it's got nothing to do with me. So you could say A.D. bought me all that expensive booze for nothing. Still, I'm not complaining.'

'I can see that.' Jan laughed. 'But actually I really would like to hear your opinion.'

'I'll tell you if you promise not to hold it against me.'

'I promise.'

'Well, I think A.D.'s plan is spot on. If he sets you up and sends you some of his best horses, you could hardly fail to be up amongst the top ten trainers within a few seasons. You'll have everything you need and no more cash-flow worries. You've got the ability and you'll have the staff and the confidence of the other owners. I'm sure A.D. wouldn't propose terms that didn't include a large incentive for you. He knows that you need to make enough money to support your children as well as yourself.' Eddie glanced at her to see how well his summary was going down. 'But I also think you shouldn't touch the deal with a bargepole because if you did you'd spend the next ten years, or however long it takes, telling yourself that you weren't your own person any more. You can't sell your soul – you'd hate it.'

Jan nodded slowly and then smiled. 'You're right; you know me far better than A.D. I hope you don't mind if I take your advice for a change.'

'Jan, please, don't do anything on my say-so; do exactly what your instincts tell you; if they happen to agree with what I've said, then all well and good.'

'Thanks, Eddie.' Jan took her hand off the steering wheel and squeezed his thigh. 'You're such a star,' she said, turning the car into the track that led past the yard and up to her house.

She stopped the car in front of the yard gate. The stables were in darkness; a single light glowed from an upstairs window in the house.

'Who's babysitting?' Eddie asked.

'Fran. I asked her to stay the night because I didn't know how late we'd be – you know what A.D. can be like once he gets going.'

'Oh,' Eddie said, sounding disappointed. 'Do you still want me to ride out first lot tomorrow morning?'

'Yes, please, I'm afraid I do, and that's not all. I want you to take me to my brother's party tomorrow night as well.'

'Oh no.' Eddie groaned. 'Just when I'd made up my mind never to touch a drop of booze again, you're dragging me out!'

Jan smiled, stretched out a hand and ruffled his wavy hair. 'Come on, you know you'd hate it if I went without you. But you can't drive home yet. You'd better come up to the house and I'll make you some coffee to sober you up.'

Eddie heaved himself up in his seat. 'Now there's a good idea,' he grinned.

In the drawing room a couple of embers were still glowing in the grate behind the fireguard. Eddie put more logs on and rummaged around for a romantic album to insert into the CD player, while Jan filled a large cafetière, which she carried in from the kitchen and placed on a long coffee table in front of the fire.

Eddie was already lounging with his feet up on the big sofa Annabel had given Jan as a house-warming present. He gazed at her with a long lazy smile as she curled up beside him on the squashy cushions. His lips gently brushed her forehead, then her cheeks, where they lingered, tantalizing, until they found her mouth.

Jan melted into the kiss and for a while all the tensions of the day faded away to the gentle sound of Eva Cassidy and the crackle of the fire.

'Eddie,' she whispered when his lips left hers for a moment. 'I'm so happy you came back.'

'God knows why,' he murmured with a display of the unexpected self-doubt she found endearing. 'I'm not much help to you.'

She lifted her head to look at him. 'Eddie, are you being serious? Don't you realize how much I lean on you? How much strength I get from having you around?'

He shrugged and shook his head. 'You never take any notice of what I say.'

'But I do!' she cried indignantly. 'I may not say so at the time, but what I get from you is the confidence to go on.'

He smiled and shook his head again. 'Frankly, I think you've managed pretty damned well without me here – you did brilliantly the year I was away.'

'But now you're back and it's fantastic!' Jan said breathlessly. 'You must know that.'

He looked at her without speaking for a moment. 'Yeah,' he said eventually, with a catch in his throat. 'Of course I do.'

❦

Later, as the last cinders glowed on the hearth, and Eva Cassidy had sung her way through her album several times, Jan propped herself up on one elbow and looked regretfully at Eddie. 'If you think you're sober enough, you ought to go. It's nearly two.'

'Oh God.' Eddie groaned. 'Do I have to?'

'You know you can't stay here, not with the children.'

'But I could sleep in your spare room and Fran's here to act as chaperone. I promise I won't do any corridor-creeping.'

Jan gave him a mischievous grin. 'OK,' she said. 'But I might!'

❦

Ben Pritchard was Jan's younger brother. Their parents often wondered how they had managed to produce two such highly motivated children. Both of them had shown an ability to succeed in careers that could scarcely have been more different. As a child, Ben had enjoyed fishing and ferrets as much as any lad in the village, but in his early teens he had discovered the guitar and rock 'n' roll.

By the time he left school, music had become his life and to his parents' dismay and bewilderment he'd gone off to tour Europe and the States with a moderately successful rock band. For a few years it seemed as though he had turned his back on his past and his family entirely, although occasional postcards from exotic, unheard-of corners of the world would arrive with brief but affectionate messages. From these his family had gathered that he was playing less and had found a niche producing records for other bands.

Last year, completely out of the blue, he'd arrived at Edge Farm from Australia and told Jan he was now the top producer for Brit Records, one of the biggest labels in the UK. Since then Ben had been to visit Jan and his parents every few weeks, occasionally bringing along the owner of the company, Johnny Carlton-Brown.

The day after A.D.'s dinner with Jan and Eddie in Cheltenham, Johnny Carlton-Brown was hosting Ben's thirtieth birthday party at the Manoir du Chèvre d'Or, a restaurant which claimed to be the most exclusive in the Cotswolds.

'Ben's really looking forward to meeting you,' Jan said to Eddie, as they drove through a blustery wet evening across the crests and valleys of the Gloucestershire hills.

'And I'm equally excited to be meeting him. I can hardly believe you've got a brother who's such a big cheese in the rock world.'

'That's what everyone says. We're very similar in lots of ways, except I can't play a note on the guitar and he can't sit on a horse without looking like a sack of 'taters, but our approach to life and our sense of humour's just the same.'

'Has he got a girlfriend?' Eddie asked.

'Not as far as I know, but he's been quite secretive so he might have. Last year I'd hoped he and Annabel might hit it off. I know he liked her, but when she met Johnny Carlton-Brown that went by the board.'

'Oh, is that who she's been seeing, then?'

'It's already petered out, probably because Johnny leads such a crazy life. He's away a lot of the time, jetting all over the world.'

'And Annabel's such a home bird,' Eddie observed.

'That's the reason she left London and came to work with me in the first place.'

'Yes, I know – remember?'

'I wish you'd tell me what happened between you two.'

'As far as I'm concerned, nothing too terrible; I was going through a bit of a wild patch, I suppose, and didn't really know the true meaning of the word "commitment". She was only nineteen then and couldn't cope with it. Then one night, when I forgot to turn up for dinner, one of my so-called friends tried to comfort her. He was very drunk – not that that's any excuse, but I wouldn't be surprised if he's put her off men for life.'

'Well, in your defence I think her father's the real cause of most of her problems. He's a small-minded, egotistical bully and he made her life a complete misery when she was a teenager. And yet, to me, she's the most fantastically loyal and hard-working friend I could have.'

'Out of adversity and all that,' Eddie said.

'She could have done without the adversity; it's left her feeling really insecure,' Jan said thoughtfully. She had often wondered what made her friend tick. 'I don't know if she'll be here tonight. I asked her if she was coming, but she said she wasn't sure.'

As it turned out, Annabel was almost the first person they saw when they walked through the huge oak door of the historic stone manor house. She looked like someone on a fashion shoot for *Vogue*, in an aquamarine silk-chiffon dress that floated around her thighs, showing off her long, tanned legs. She was talking to a tall, lean man in his thirties with long, very blond hair, who was wearing a light blue linen suit that hung off him in loose folds.

'Crikey,' Jan murmured to Eddie. 'That chap definitely isn't Annabel's type, but he's looking bloody eager. D'you think we should mark his card?'

'He'll find out soon enough,' Eddie said as Annabel caught sight of them.

'Hi there,' she called.

As they walked over to her, Eddie grabbed two glasses of champagne from a passing waiter's tray.

'You decided to come, then,' Jan said.

'Obviously,' Annabel said with an embarrassed smile. 'Johnny talked me into it. This is one of his business partners, Lord Lamberhurst.'

'Patrick, call me Patrick,' the tall man said in a deep, languid voice.

'This is my boss, Jan Hardy,' Annabel said. 'And Eddie Sullivan.'

Patrick Lamberhurst shook hands with Jan. 'Hello, I'm delighted to meet you: I've seen you leading in a few winners.' He turned to

Eddie lazily. 'Hello, Eddie, I heard you were back. Long time no see. Mrs Hardy giving you a few spare rides?'

Eddie pretended to ignore the double entendre. 'I suppose she may, if I perform all right on the gallops.'

Jan looked at Patrick coldly and sighed. 'I'm going to find Ben. I'll see you later,' she said to Annabel.

She walked from the entrance lobby into the great hall where the party was taking place. In front of a huge applewood fire Johnny Carlton-Brown was reluctantly holding court. Jan thought, not for the first time, that he looked nothing like her idea of a record company mogul. His prematurely grey, wavy hair fell almost to his shoulders, covering the collar of the cord suit he was wearing. He saw Jan, smiled and signalled that he was pleased to see her but couldn't talk to her right then.

Jan understood. Johnny was a man with many interests. Since she had first met him, he had bought two horses for her to train: August Moon, a dappled grey mare left to Jan by a former owner who had died, and Supercall.

Supercall was a seven-year-old novice chaser. In Jan's view he was a future Gold Cup horse and potentially the best horse in her yard, although soon after he had arrived in the autumn an injury to his foot had stopped him working and it had taken him several months to come sound. Johnny had been patient and hadn't tried to blame Jan as some owners might have done. He'd been justly rewarded when the horse had gone out and won his first race in early March. Now, before Supercall was let down for the summer, Jan hoped to give him another run in a competitive race at the end of the month if the ground softened a little beforehand. She really wanted to discuss this with Johnny before the end of the evening if she could.

In the meantime, she looked around for Ben and found him at the far end of the hall beneath the minstrels' gallery. With a deep tan and a crop of sun-bleached hair, he was wearing a broad grin. Standing next to him were two musicians, members of the Band of Brothers, whom Jan instantly recognized.

Ben suddenly saw her, leapt forward and wrapped her in his

arms in a huge bear hug. 'Hello, Sis! Great to see you! This is Mick and this is Darius,' he added, waving at the famous musicians behind him. 'This is my sister Jan, one of the greatest racehorse trainers on earth.'

Jan blushed at her brother's slightly drunken enthusiasm and shook her head disarmingly.

Darius Cooper was the band's lead singer and front man.

'We've heard loads of stuff about you,' he said. 'When we're in the studio Ben's always tellin' us what horses you've got runnin' and we often have a few quid on.'

'Yeah,' Mick said. 'We thought maybe we'd better get a horse – just to keep him quiet.'

'Yeah. Could you get us one called Half Brother or something?'

The two men laughed and wandered off, shaking their heads with pleasure at the idea.

Jan turned to Ben. 'Did they mean it?'

'Yes, I expect so; they've got money coming out of their ears right now. I'll follow it up for you, if you like. That was brilliant news about the Irish National. I just wish I'd been there, but I've been bogged down working in a studio in the Virgin Islands for over a month. It's great to see you!'

'It's good to see you too and thanks, I got your message.'

'I managed to get a nice big bet on him,' Ben said with satisfaction. 'Did you?'

'I told you before – I never bet; I couldn't stand the strain. If they win, I get my share of the prize money; if they don't, I haven't lost any.'

'It was a really fantastic achievement,' Ben said. 'I know that because all the papers said so. How have you been otherwise?' he went on with a twinkle in his eye and an Aussie twang he hadn't lost from four years working in Sydney. 'Mum said your friend Eddie's back, only she thinks he's a bit more than a friend this time.'

Jan nodded. 'Poor Mum, I wonder how she found out. She really wanted me to get together with Tony, the doctor who was so kind when Matty was ill last year.'

'I remember – steady, reliable sort of a guy.'

'That's him.'

'Whereas she thinks this Eddie's a bit of a Romeo and about as much use as an ashtray on a motorbike?'

'Ben, please, I know what she thinks, but I wouldn't call him either of those things. I showed you the video of him riding in the Foxhunters', didn't I? There's not many men who would have had the balls to do what he did.'

'OK, OK, message received. It's love then, is it?'

Jan felt herself blush. 'I don't know; maybe. All I know is I haven't felt anything like this since John died.'

'And does he feel the same?'

Jan looked at Ben and knew that he was genuinely concerned. 'I really don't know. I can't be sure,' she said truthfully. 'But since he came back he hasn't been seeing anyone else, I'm sure – at least, he seems to spend most of his time at my place.'

'Hasn't he got a place of his own, then?'

'He's rented a room in Stow – above the pub.' Jan raised her eyebrows. 'But he only sleeps there.'

'So now he's back, he's planning to do what precisely?'

'He was talking about starting up a gallery again. He really does know a lot about paintings, and if it hadn't been for that damned hassle with his dad, I'm sure he'd have been doing really well by now.'

'Such faith!' Ben chuckled. 'He's got a reputation for being a bit of a playboy, you know, not taking anything too seriously. Patrick Lamberhurst knows quite a bit about him.'

'Is that the skinny lord who was talking to Bel outside?'

Ben laughed. 'Yes, Viscount Lamberhurst, to be correct; I think one of his ancestors was Chancellor in the eighteenth century or something. He's a pretty odd geezer.'

'In what way?' Jan asked sharply, concerned for Annabel, whom the viscount had definitely been chatting up.

'Don't worry, he's quite safe,' Ben said. 'What I mean is there's more to him than meets the eye. He likes to put on the spaced-out, couldn't-give-a-shit attitude, but actually he's pretty smart. He invested in Brit Records at just the right moment. He made bloody sure he hung onto his shares and Johnny Carlton-Brown likes having him around. Patrick's no fool and appreciates lots of stuff – poetry, music, paintings, all sorts – he knows a lot of creative people.'

'I don't think much of his taste in clothes,' Jan remarked, seeing the man they were discussing enter the room behind Annabel.

'He looks mighty interested in Annabel.' Ben raised an eyebrow. 'Mind you, so was JCB, but he reckons he scared her off.'

'I'm afraid she scares rather easily, so I can't see his lordship getting very far.'

'Maybe not.' Ben shrugged. 'Anyway, let's get back to you. Where do you think this relationship will go between you and Eddie?'

'Ben, please. I've already told you I'm not sure, but he's helping me out and seems quite happy with the arrangement.'

'For the time being . . . I'm sure he is, as long as you don't start taking him for granted.'

'How do you know all this when you've never even met him?'

'Because I know you, Sis. Anyway, if you introduce me, I'll talk to him tonight and let you know what I think.'

'Oh thanks,' Jan said with a hint of sarcasm, although she knew she really wanted Ben's approval.

Jan stood under the arch of the massive stone porch at the Manoir du Chèvre d'Or, shivering a little in the chill that still lingered in the April night air. The roar of a half-blown exhaust and the rattle of ancient bodywork announced Eddie's arrival in the Morgan as it swept onto the gravel circle in front of the hotel.

He stopped the car beside her, sprang out of the driving seat and hurried round to open the passenger door with a big grin on his face to emphasize his rare display of gallantry.

Jan smiled at him doubtfully as she slipped into the low-slung seat and tried to make herself comfortable. When Eddie had climbed in beside her, she turned to look at him. 'What was all that for?' she asked. 'Are you sure you're OK to drive?'

'Such cynicism.' Eddie chuckled. 'And I've hardly drunk a drop; a fly wouldn't be plastered on what I've had.'

He certainly sounded sober, Jan thought, which was very considerate of him on her brother's birthday. She smiled as he put the car in gear and spun off, making the back end wiggle a little on the thick gravel.

During the thirty-minute drive home, they talked about the people they'd seen and talked to. Jan particularly wanted to know about Patrick Lamberhurst.

'I don't really know him that well,' Eddie said, 'but I think he's a bit of a dark horse.'

'In what way?'

'He's one of those men lots of people claim to know, but none of them seem to have any idea what he's really like or where he made his money after his father, the last viscount, died absolutely potless from bad investments and punting. Of course, Patrick's made a pile out of Brit Records, though he must have put up a lot of collateral in the first place. But he never gives anything away about himself: he seems to make a thing of being permanently aloof and he is inclined to think he's a bit special. Sometimes he completely ignores me, even though I've known him on and off for years.'

'Sounds a bit of a shit to me,' Jan remarked. 'I hope Annabel's seen that for herself.'

For the rest of the journey back to Edge Farm, Jan told Eddie about Darius and Mick from the Band of Brothers wanting to have a horse with her and Johnny Carlton-Brown's enthusiasm for those he already had. From there they moved on naturally to the other horses in the yard until, in what seemed like no time, Eddie was accelerating up her driveway.

Subconsciously Jan had been preparing for this, aware that Eddie might feel the time had come when he could stay with her in her own bed.

She didn't pretend that there wasn't a huge part of her that wanted him to. The night before, after their late return from dinner at the Queen's with A.D. when Eddie had stayed in the room next to Fran's, Jan had joked about creeping down the corridor, but even the idea of being in bed with him in the same house as her children was out of the question until she could be certain that what they had together as a couple would last.

In the meantime, Fran was again staying at Edge Farm, where she'd been looking after the children. And Jan had to admit Eddie had been very good about driving her to Ben's party. He deserved to be rewarded; she supposed it wouldn't do any harm if she allowed him to stay for a short time.

He had stopped the car and was already out, walking round to open her door. 'I see Fran's here,' he said solemnly as he gave her a hand up from her seat. 'Am I allowed in?'

Jan smiled. 'Of course you are, for a cup of coffee.'

'I think, since I've hardly had a thing all evening, I might risk a small Armagnac.'

Fran was still up knitting, and with damp eyes watching the end of *ET* on video, which Eddie had bought for the children.

'Oh, Jan, I'm so glad you're back,' she said. 'The children are both fast asleep – I checked about ten minutes ago. Do you mind if I don't stay tonight? I've got things to do at home first thing in the morning.'

'No, of course not,' Jan said, ignoring the quizzical expression on Eddie's face.

When Fran had finally gathered up her belongings and bustled out, Eddie looked at Jan. 'Am I still allowed my brandy?'

'Are you sure you should? You've still got to drive back to Stow.'

'OK,' Eddie said with a resigned dignity. 'I give in. I'll just have coffee.'

Later, as they sat on the sofa watching the residue of the fire, Eddie moved closer to her.

'Do you want another log on there?' he asked.

'No point,' Jan parried.

Eddie made a face. 'Jan, you know you want me to stay.'

'Don't be so bloody sure,' she retorted with a slight grin. 'You know damn well why I can't let you.'

'Tell me again.'

'Oh, Eddie, please don't keep badgering me about it. I really like having you around. I told you yesterday and I meant it. And, who knows, maybe there'll be a time when there isn't any doubt in my mind about what I want. The trouble is we're not a couple of teenagers or twenty-somethings just trying it out.' Jan looked away from Eddie and concentrated on the glowing apple log in the fireplace, still spurting small flickers of yellow flame. 'Believe me, once you have kids you're not a free agent any more, living only for yourself. My two have already lost one father; I don't want them thinking they've got another, only to lose him as well.' She looked at Eddie. 'So it's not just me you'd be taking on.'

'I understand that, Jan,' he said gently. 'I really do.'

Jan sighed. 'I hope you do; it doesn't feel that long ago since I lost John, which was so very painful, and I'm still not sure I want to make that sort of commitment to anyone else.'

'What sort is that?'

'The commitment I'd be showing if I let you stay the night here in my bed,' Jan answered abruptly before she softened. 'But, Eddie, I promise, when I *am* ready, you'll know about it.'

Now they sensed a barrier had come between them and they didn't cuddle as they had the night before. They sat in total silence for a while until Eddie drained the last of his coffee, jumped to his feet and kissed Jan thoughtfully on each cheek as he put on his coat.

' 'Bye, Jan. I'll see you in the morning for first lot.'

'I'm really sorry to chuck you out, Eddie,' Jan said, opening the front door for him.

'It's OK,' he said lightly, before adding with a grin and a mock threat, 'you'll regret it when I've gone!'

She watched him stride down the path through the cold, moonlit night. Just before he reached his car she called, 'Night, Eddie, and thanks for driving me.'

'Any time,' he called back and climbed into the car, which spluttered into life a moment later.

Jan watched it manoeuvre precisely round her parking area until it was lined up with the top of the drive, then it shot down to the road.

Standing in the doorway in the cold night air, she shivered with regret as the Morgan sped off up the lane, and a huge part of her longed for Eddie to wrap his arms around her, warming her through, body and soul.

Well, she *certainly approves of Eddie*, Jan thought the next day as she watched the new vet examine Nuthatch's leg while Eddie held him still.

Jan realized that she'd been a little nervous about Shirley Mc-Gregor meeting Eddie. When Shirley had become a partner in the veterinary practice near Broadway, Jan had quickly struck up a good relationship with her, bonded by more than just gender. They recognized a single-mindedness in each other that women usually attain when they set out to achieve in a man's world, and she quickly got into the habit of asking for Shirley when she needed expert veterinary advice.

But Jan couldn't help noticing, when it came to men, Shirley would behave like a hungry lioness; there was something menacingly predatory about her.

'You can put him away now,' Shirley said, tossing her long shiny black hair, which, Jan had noted, the vet only gathered into a tidy bun when it was a positive hazard in her work.

Eddie glanced at Jan with amusement and led the limping horse back to its stable as the vet stood watching, her hands placed on her hips, as though she was on a catwalk.

'You could line-fire him, if you don't mind doing that sort of thing. Otherwise he's likely to go on having trouble with that tendon.'

'I usually let the owners decide about firing,' Jan said. 'And if I tell this owner it's a choice of firing his horse's leg or taking him home as a pet, I know what he'll say.'

'Who is it?'

'Frank Jellard.' Jan frowned.

'What's wrong with him? He's got quite a few with you, hasn't he?'

'I know it's unprofessional to moan about owners, but we earn every penny we charge him just dealing with the hassle he gives us – always grumbling and telling us we're doing everything wrong – as if he knew! He'd never been near a horse in his life until he suddenly found he had more money than he knew what to do with and thought it would impress his wife's friends to own a "racer". But like a lot of new owners he became an expert overnight. However, we've managed to win quite a few races even with his moderate ones, so no matter how much he threatens to take them away, I doubt he will. Though, God knows, sometimes I really wish he would. People like him take all the fun out of the job.'

Shirley laughed at Jan's tirade. 'Professional frustrations – we get them all the time too. You know, some people will do anything to keep their horses on the road – bute them up to the eyeballs, or stuff other painkillers down their necks, when really they know the game's up. Anyway, I'm sure that chap will be fine with a bit of TLC and patience, which, of course, we all know is an owner's best asset. By the way, I like the look of your new lad – or is he your assistant? He seems a bit too smart to be a lad.'

'Hands off, Shirley. Don't go there. That's Eddie Sullivan, who rode Russian Eagle in the Foxhunters' last year. He's a really good friend who's helping out in the yard.'

'And in the house too, I wouldn't wonder.' Shirley chortled appreciatively.

Jan suddenly found she'd lost her sense of humour. 'There's one more I'd like you to look at. It needs a blood test,' she said brusquely and led the way to a box at the far end of the yard.

Over the next fortnight, as activity in the yard continued to wind down, Jan found she still couldn't come to a firm decision about A.D.'s proposal. Although her instincts were all against it, she knew she couldn't risk losing the support A.D. already gave her. So it was in a state of frustrating uncertainty that she kept a promise to visit her late husband's mother on the first free Sunday she'd had for some time.

She had just bundled Matthew and Megan into the Land Rover before setting off for mid-Wales when Eddie arrived from the village with the Sunday papers. He had already announced he was going to read them in the tack room until lunchtime.

He poked his head through the passenger window. 'Jan, would you like me to come with you? I could drive and you could chill out a little.'

Gratitude flooded through her. She had desperately wanted Eddie to be with her, but had thought it was too much to ask him to visit her notoriously difficult mother-in-law.

'Oh God, would you?' She turned to the back of the car. 'It would be a lot better if Eddie came, wouldn't it, kids?'

'Yes please!' Megan fluted with glee, as Eddie smiled back at her.

'OK, move over,' he said and walked round to the driver's door.

Jan repressed her instinct not to do as he asked, but slid compliantly across to the passenger seat.

'Are you sure you don't mind?' Jan asked as he put the motor in gear and moved off down the drive.

Eddie looked indifferent. 'Not really. Virginia asked me up to Riscombe Manor for lunch, but I didn't fancy joining the gang of Hooray Henrys she's got staying so I passed, and I haven't got anything else to do, apart from get drunk with a few old codgers in Stow. Anyway, I haven't seen the dreaded battleaxe for ages and I thought it might be quite entertaining.' He winked at Jan and turned into the lane.

'Eddie! She *is* the children's granny, don't forget.'

'But she is a battleaxe!' Megan yodelled gleefully, her already tanned face creased with laughter and her eyes dancing as her golden hair flew in the breeze from the open window. 'Though she always gives us nice toys. But she's got *really* wrinkly skin and a sort of beard you can feel when she kisses you.'

'Now I can't wait to see her again,' Eddie said with a grin.

'By the way,' Jan said, 'how come Virginia asked you to lunch?'

'She rang me . . .'

'At the house?'

'On my mobile. She said she'd heard I was back and did I want to come up for a drink, so I dropped in there Friday evening.'

Jan knew that the sudden surge of possessive jealousy overtaking her was totally unreasonable, but she couldn't stop herself. 'You never told me!' she blurted.

Eddie took his eyes off the road for a second to look at her in bewilderment. 'Only because I didn't want to bore you. It was pretty much a non-event, although I should have passed on Colonel Gilbert's message that he's planning to collect Wolf's Rock as soon as you've let him down after his race next week.'

'Oh. Did he mention anything about next season?'

'No, but I'm sure he's intending to send him back in time for the softer ground in the autumn.'

'Right,' Jan nodded, trying to pretend her earlier outburst hadn't happened. She knew she was going to have to keep a tight lid on her resentment if she didn't want to put Eddie right off. Somehow she would have to learn to trust him when he was out of sight, however difficult that might be.

But Virginia Gilbert, for God's sake! she thought.

Virginia Gilbert was a little younger than Jan, a racehorse trainer with a beautiful yard on her father's large estate and pots of money. She was, Jan conceded, quite attractive in a willowy, stuck-up sort of way, but her training record was unimpressive. Jan refused to treat her as a serious rival and was encouraged by the fact that Virginia's own father had Wolf's Rock, one of his best horses, in training with her at Edge Farm.

But if she saw Virginia taking a real interest in Eddie, then she wouldn't think twice about warning her off.

Jan shook her head and looked fondly at her companion as he drove the Land Rover with a frown of concentration. Eddie sensed her look and glanced back with a smile as he took his hand off the gear stick to squeeze her thigh.

'Jan.' He chuckled. 'The day I go off with Virginia, make sure you book my place at the funny farm.'

'Oh, Eddie, I know it's stupid, but I can't help it. I just feel every woman in Gloucestershire's hunting you down.'

'So? What if they are? I won't let them catch me. Not while you're around anyway,' he added with an enigmatic grin.

As they crossed Herefordshire and the Welsh borders, the scale of the landscape grew and the mountains stretched away in the hazy spring sunshine, leaving shadows in the deep valleys which Jan knew well from the eight years she had spent there with John.

'Do you miss it?' Eddie asked, reading her thoughts.

'Sometimes,' Jan said. 'Not in winter, though. The frost used to last so long in the valleys and the mist would come down like a curtain. Sometimes it stayed for days on end.'

'But it must have been heaven riding out across those hills on a fine morning.'

'It was. I loved the early mornings in August and September. There's miles of sheep-grazed turf between the heather and bracken, and gorse bushes to jump, which teaches the youngsters to pick their feet up. But, God, it was a different life then, keeping half a dozen pointers for a few old farmers who'd usually bought them for peanuts.'

'Jan, don't knock it; it's where you learnt your trade. I remember being terribly impressed when I came to see you after Eagle arrived here. I couldn't believe that a twenty-something widow of a hill farmer could be so confident and utterly on top of her game.'

Jan laughed. 'Is that really what it looked like? Anyway, I was already thirty-something then.'

They started the switchback descent from the high ridge down to the valley, where Stonewall Farm lay in a grassy combe scooped out of the hillside.

Jan gazed gloomily at the familiar scene. Even from a distance, the house and buildings looked sadly dilapidated.

'Hasn't anyone lived in the place since you left?' Eddie asked.

'No,' Jan replied grimly. 'Harold Powell has been trying to develop it, along with that massive caravan park he wanted to build, but since Toby's solicitors discovered the only access to it still belongs to me he can't do anything without my permission or until Olwen goes and I sell the bungalow.'

Olwen Hardy lived in a bungalow which had been built at the bottom of the drive ten years before, when Jan and John had married. When John died he left everything to Jan, with the condition that his mother could live in the bungalow for as long as she liked.

Although Jan didn't realize it at the time, the house and buildings had been bought by one of her owners, Harold Powell, a previously well-respected auctioneer who turned out to be little more than a thief in a tweed suit. But she'd had the last laugh when it became clear that, due to a cock-up in Powell's office, he hadn't, as he'd thought, bought a strip of ground beside the bungalow which was the only access to his property from the road. Harold had since been forced to pay Jan the sum he'd swindled her out of plus interest. As far as Jan could tell, he was still sitting on the project only through a stubborn determination not to lose face.

'What will you do with the bungalow when she does go?'

Jan frowned. 'I don't really know, but I certainly intend to have some fun with Mr Powell.'

Eddie turned the car into the drive and parked beside the small dwelling.

Jan let out the two small children and ushered them up to the front door beneath a rose-clad porch.

Three-year-old Matthew stretched up and rang the bell. A few moments later the door opened to reveal Olwen Hardy's upright and unforgiving figure. Her grey, wrinkled features softened as she saw her grandchildren and opened her arms in welcome.

'Hello, Matthew. How are you, Megan? My, you've grown,' she said fondly, in a lilting accent that had its origins on the far side of the Cambrians.

Once she had given them her customary hug and the hairy kiss Megan had been dreading, she looked at Jan sharply, quickly taking in Eddie, who stood slightly behind her.

Her lips tightened instantly. 'Who's that?' she asked unceremoniously, although Jan guessed she knew exactly who Eddie was and had a pretty good idea of their relationship.

'I told you on the phone, Olwen. This is Eddie Sullivan, who you've met before. He offered to drive us over. He used to have a horse training at the yard and now he's helping me out.'

'That's what it's called these days, is it?' Olwen observed. 'It was kind of you,' she said to Eddie with icy politeness, 'but she can drive herself, you know.'

Eddie shrugged, to show it was all the same to him. 'I didn't have anything else to do and I wanted to have a look at this beautiful country again,' he said mildly.

'Well, you'd better come in.' She shuffled – more than usual, Jan thought – into the front room, where she had some presents and new toys waiting for the children.

Matthew, normally an impulsive child, knew that in this house he had to ask before unwrapping presents or taking toys from their boxes, and that he had to do it tidily, not tear at it like a chimpanzee with a bag full of sweets.

'Please, Gwanny, can I undo that big parcel?' He gesticulated at a large package in the middle of the room.

'You know how to write your own name, don't you? If you read the label,' Olwen said, 'you'll see it's for your sister.'

Matty screwed up his small, earnest face in an effort to stop his lower lip from trembling at the gross injustice of his sister having the bigger present.

With great self-importance and her small tongue protruding between her lips, Megan carefully took the paper off the package to reveal, to Matthew's obvious relief, a half-sized sewing machine.

'Thank you, Granny,' Megan said steadily, without meeting the old woman's eye, 'but Fran makes all my clothes that Mum doesn't buy in Gap.'

'So now you can start to make your own, dear.'

Jan felt that this gift to young Megan was intended to pinpoint Olwen's view of her mother's inadequacies. Olwen decried Jan's modern practice of buying made clothes and factory jam, despite the fact that her daughter-in-law told her, if she sat about sewing and boiling fruit all day, she wouldn't be able to earn enough to keep herself and the children. But it was a battle Jan knew she could never win, so she decided to handle the situation tactfully.

'Meg, next time we visit, you must bring something you've made to show Granny. All right?'

Megan nodded in silent agreement. Now it was Matthew's turn.

As he doggedly unwrapped his package, Jan looked at his skinny frame and wished he were a little stronger. While Megan was now loving every minute of her riding and spent hours grooming Smarty, her pony, the more Jan tried to encourage Matthew to ride the more he seemed to back away. She knew it was perhaps selfish of her to want her children to share her love of horses, but, she reasoned, it would be an immense help in the future if they did.

⚘

As they ate a lunch of overcooked lamb and roast potatoes, Jan was eager to catch up on the continuing saga of Harold Powell's efforts to recoup something from his investment in Stonewall Farm.

'Has Harold been doing anything with the buildings lately? They're beginning to look pretty knackered.' As far as Jan knew, all Harold had been able to do was to let the grazing to neighbouring farmers who could get their stock on the land without having to use the access by Olwen's bungalow.

'I told him he could let some builders through so they can tidy up the roofs. That front gable should have been done years ago – I just can't bear the sight of it. But I reckon it's likely he'll try and do a lot more than that if I don't watch it.'

'Well, it doesn't much matter to us if he does because the minute he tries to sell the place or let it, we can always refuse access.'

Olwen cackled. 'We've certainly got him by the short and curlies,' she said with uncharacteristic vulgarity. 'I saw in the *Brecon & Radnor Express* that he's applied for planning permission to build one of them so-called courtyard developments.'

'What?' Eddie laughed. 'Yuppie hutches? Out here in the middle of nowhere? He'll be pushed to find punters for them.'

Jan shook her head. 'Well, it's irrelevant at the moment anyway, isn't it?'

'He's just keeping everything ticking over,' Olwen said knowingly. 'Even if they give him permission, he's got five years before he has to do anything with it. Meantime, I reckon he's just hoping I'll leave this place, he won't care whether it's on my feet or in a box.'

Just before lunch, a few days after their visit to Olwen, Eddie strode into Jan's kitchen with an enigmatic smile on his face.

'I've brought someone to meet you,' he said.

Following him was a slight, auburn-haired man of about twenty. The visitor stood in the doorway, staring at the floor as if he had a guilty conscience.

'Who is he?' Jan asked, curious about the young man's obvious discomfort.

'Finbar Howlett. I found him in the King's Head.'

'You're always meeting people in the King's Head, but you don't usually bring them back here,' Jan said, wondering what Eddie was up to.

'Don't you know who Finbar is?' Eddie asked with a hint of disbelief.

The man raised his head, and Jan was struck by the bright blueness of his eyes, like A.D. O'Hagan's but without the steely edge.

'No. I'm sorry, I haven't a clue.'

'I mentioned him to you the other day when I was reading the *Racing Post*. Finnie's come over from Ireland to be Virginia's stable jockey.'

Jan's eyes instantly focused more sharply as she tried to assess the diffident young man. On the face of it, he didn't look as if he had the physique or the tenacity to make a good jockey, but she had already learnt that jockeys, like other athletes, could only be judged by their performance. And apparently the most docile men could be transformed once they were in the saddle. She remembered Eddie saying that Finbar already had an impressive track record in Ireland, so Virginia must have offered him a very attractive retainer to entice him to her relatively poor-performing yard.

'Don't stand around in the doorway, then. Come in and have a drink.'

Finbar Howlett came in and pulled a chair out from the table to sit down. 'Thanks, I'll have a cup of tea,' he said in a soft brogue.

'Nothing stronger?' Eddie asked.

'No thanks; I never touch alcohol.'

Eddie looked amazed. 'Why? Did you take the pledge?'

'Nope. I just never liked the taste of the stuff and since I've been riding I've seen a lot of fellas turning up the worse for wear.' He shrugged. 'It's a tough enough job as it is without raising the odds against yourself.'

Jan was impressed. Jockeys who took their calling seriously enough to forgo drink were very rare creatures indeed. She turned to the Aga and slid a big, flat-bottomed kettle onto the hotplate.

'What were you doing in the pub, then?'

'That's where you hear all the gossip – you don't *have* to drink, you know.'

'Do you think you'll do all right at Virginia's?'

The jockey shrugged. 'I know she's not had the greatest season, but she has some good horses; and that Miller's Lodge will definitely win a decent race, I'd say.'

Eddie closed his eyes and turned away.

Jan wondered if Virginia had deliberately failed to tell her new jockey that her star horse was going, or if JCB hadn't got round to telling her, or, much worse, if he'd changed his mind. 'Yes, I think he will,' she said cautiously. 'Now you're here, do you want to stay for lunch?'

The young jockey lifted a quizzical brow, before letting a broad smile spread across his face. 'I'd be delighted.'

🐎

Jan had no runners that afternoon and, since Megan was still on holiday from school, she took both the children across the hills to the small village of Riscombe, where her mother and father still lived in the cottage they had occupied for the last forty years.

Although Reg Pritchard had retired, Colonel Gilbert, his land-lord, had allowed him to stay on in the small house. The estate no longer needed it since modern machinery had allowed them to run the farm with fewer staff. So Reg had been left with just thirty thin-soiled acres, on which he still ran forty ewes with the aid of a one-eyed dog and a stick.

As Jan drove her Land Rover between the leaning gateposts, down onto the cobbled forecourt in front of the honey-coloured stone cottage, a host of happy memories of her childhood in the tranquil valley came flooding back to her.

As soon as they had clambered down from the vehicle, her mother appeared in the open doorway. Mary Pritchard, five-foot four with curly white hair, was wearing an ancient floral cotton apron exactly like the ones she had worn for the last thirty years. The children were already running flat out down to the house. Jan knew that, while they respected their other grandmother and enjoyed her regular supply of presents, they absolutely adored Mary. The old woman produced a couple of sweets from her apron pocket and flung her arms around Matty and Megan.

Jan followed, smiling at the scene and tried to envisage Megan's children one day rushing up to hug her in the same way.

Inside, beneath a low-beamed ceiling, the kitchen table was already laid for tea.

'But Mum, we've only just had lunch,' Jan protested gently.

'I know, I know. It's for later. Your dad wants to show you something he's got for Matty first.'

'Gran, what is it?' Matthew squealed in anticipation.

'Here's Grandpa. He'll take you out and show you,' Mary said.

Reg had entered the room quietly and stood just inside the door, beaming proudly at his grandchildren. 'Now, now, don't get too excited,' he warned the little boy. 'It's just for you to try, mind.'

'What is it?' Matthew demanded insistently.

'Follow me. It's in the paddock at the back.'

Reg led a small procession through the house and out the back door. They followed him past a tidy kitchen garden and through a gate in the picket fence into a small field of permanent pasture.

'There he is!' Reg announced, waving his hand at the far corner, where, in the shelter of a high hedge, a sturdy black pony about twelve hands high stood looking at them. 'He's called Rocket and he used to go like one as well,' he grinned.

Jan's heart sank. She was sure she had told Reg about the difficulty she'd had teaching Matty to ride but, typically, the stubborn old man must have decided he knew best.

'He's a bit long in the tooth now but fit as a fiddle, mind. If you can jump two foot on him by the end of the summer, he's yours.' Reg turned and looked at Matthew's doubtful face.

'But, Grandad, when I fell off Smarty I hurt my arm,' the boy whispered to him.

Smarty was the pony Reg had given to Megan two summers before – a talented but wilful chestnut.

'This ain't no Smarty. I knows what you need. That's why I found Rocket for you. He's not got an ounce of badness in him. Don't look like that, Jan; the pony can stay here, and if you bring Matty over a couple of times a week, I'll take care of him.'

'But, Dad,' Jan protested, 'I've already told you – since he's fallen off, he doesn't want to ride. Every time I try to put him on the pony at home, he runs off and hides under the table.'

Reg shook his head. 'I've told you before not to put him on Smarty; that pony's too sharp for him. And I've got my own way of doing things. Don't forget, I taught you and Megan. You trust Grandad, don't you, Matty?'

The small boy looked at the old man. After a few moments' doubt, he made up his mind. 'All right, Grandpa, but if he chucks me off, I won't do it again.'

'Don't worry, m'boy, he won't. Now, I've got a good little saddle for him, so we can start right away. You come with me. Megan, you go with your Grandma; she'll find something for you to do.'

Reg led Matty back to one of the ancient stone buildings, where he still hoarded a collection of old farm implements and tack.

Jan took her cue, sighed and went back into the house.

'I wish Dad hadn't got that pony without asking me,' she said to Mary.

'Your dad knows what he's doing, Jan. And sometimes kids will do things for their grandparents that they won't for their own mums. One thing's for certain, your dad wouldn't have got the pony if it wasn't right for the job.'

Jan couldn't deny that: when it came to judging and dealing with any livestock her father had a wealth of experience and knowledge. She had often taken him with her to the sales to get his opinion of any horses that had taken her eye. 'All right,' she sighed. 'I suppose it was a bit ambitious to try and get him started on Meg's pony. But, Mum, is Dad up to the job physically?'

'He may be a bit slow on his pins, but he's still strong and fit. Anyway, it'll give him something to aim at, if you know what I mean.'

'You mean besides growing bucketloads of tomatoes and beans?'

'Well, let's face it,' Mary replied, 'teaching kids to ride takes time and patience – and you haven't got a lot of either at the moment.'

'Why do people keep telling me I've got no patience, I wonder?' Jan asked rhetorically.

'Now you're here, sit down and have a cup of tea and tell me what's going on. Meg, you can do some drawing for me in the parlour. The crayons are in the drawer.'

'Where do you want me to start?' Jan asked as Megan disappeared.

'Tell me what's happened with that nice doctor friend of yours.'

Jan could see from her mother's expression that she knew Tony Robertson's chances had been moved to the back burner in the last few weeks.

'Mum, I know you like him a lot and so do I. I know he's really nice and he's very kind, but I'm just not sure he's for me.'

'But, Jan, this other chap, Eddie whatsisname – what's going on there?'

'Mum, you know perfectly well he's called Eddie Sullivan. And, if you want the honest truth, I don't really know where I am with him myself. But it's the first time since John died I've really felt something more than the cosy feeling I have with Tony. I admit that Eddie's unpredictable, but I quite like that.'

'That's all very well in a teenage girl, Jan, but you're a mother now. And that Eddie comes from such a different background.'

'Not that much different from the doctor actually, and anyway, so what? He may have been to Harrow and all that, and know a lot of so-called grand people, but his dad was just a London builder who made pots of money; the Sullivans are no better than us, Mum. Besides, this background thing isn't so important now. It's not like the old days when everyone round here went about tugging their forelock to Colonel Gilbert just because he was born with a silver spoon in his mouth. Things have moved on since then.'

'The colonel's been very good to you, Jan.'

'Only because he knows I'm good at my job. I'm not knocking him, mind. But it proves my point when he's sending his horse to me to train instead of using his own daughter.'

'I don't want to argue, Jan. But I can't help worrying about the future of those children if you take up with some man who may be very nice, but is always drifting around.'

'Mum, he's not drifting around now,' Jan said, trying to keep her voice under control. 'He's being very helpful and supportive to me. It's really good for me to have someone to talk things through with.'

'But you can always come and talk to us. And what about Tony? You've often said what a good listener he is.'

'Yes, I *do* feel at home with him – I can almost see myself with him sometimes, but he doesn't make me laugh like Eddie. Anyway, Mum, I *do* come and talk to you as well, but it's not quite the same.'

Mary sighed. 'No, I suppose it isn't. But just keep in mind what I'm saying and don't write the doctor off.'

'I haven't, Mum, I promise. I know what you mean and, believe me, if I did give up what Tony's prepared to offer, Eddie would bloody well have to come up trumps!'

Mary seemed satisfied that her daughter hadn't completely lost sight of her priorities and changed the subject with a smile. 'Now, you will let your dad have a go at teaching Matty to ride, won't you?'

'Yes, of course I will, but if he wants him twice a week, he may have to come over and get him, especially if I've got horses running all over the place.'

Now the tricky subject of her love life had been dealt with, Jan was able to relax and the two women settled down for a gossip until Reg and Matty reappeared about an hour later.

'How did you get on?' Jan asked Reg.

'Ask him.' Reg nodded at Matty.

Matty sniffed to show he was reserving judgement. 'All right. He's a kind pony,' he conceded.

'What did you do?'

'Walked around the field a couple of times on a leading rein,' Reg said.

Jan turned to him sharply. 'But he's off the leading rein.'

Her father held up a hand. 'You just leave it to me, Jan,' he said patiently.

Jan smiled. Patience. That's what Reg had in abundance.

'Anyway,' he said, settling down in his big elm carver, 'how are all your horses looking now?'

'Not bad. I hope to have a few more by the end of the summer. I've had a lot of enquiries, winning the Irish National hasn't done us any harm. As a matter of fact, when I saw A.D. three weeks ago he told me he wanted to buy a much bigger yard for me, with all the trimmings and enough boxes for a hundred horses, including thirty of his own.'

Reg leaned forward with a look of concern on his ruddy face. 'Did he, by God? Why didn't you tell us before?'

'I needed to work it out on my own. It's a very tempting proposition. With the sort of backing he can give me, I could get to the top of the tree very quickly.'

'That sort of thing don't always work,' Reg growled. 'So what have you told him?'

'I haven't said anything yet. But he's coming up on Saturday, after Lingfield, and I'm going to tell him then that it's a no-go.'

Mary nodded. 'I'm sure that's the best thing. Then, when things go wrong, you've got no one to blame but yourself.'

'Or when they go right,' Jan added with a laugh.

'How will he take it when you tell him?' Reg asked, still anxious.

'You never know how he's going to react.' Jan shrugged. 'But so far he's always been very fair with me.'

'Well, let's hope things stay that way and he doesn't just "up sticks" and take away any of the horses he's already got with you.'

6

Three weeks after A.D. had put his proposal to Jan, she still hadn't given him her answer. Like Reg, she was worried that if he didn't like what he heard he would take away the six horses he already had in training with her.

She had spoken to him on the phone a few times since their dinner in Cheltenham, but they'd only talked about routine matters until the last time when he had said a little tersely, 'I was hoping we might have come to an agreement regarding my proposition by now.'

She promised to give him her answer when he next came to England to watch one of his Irish-trained flat horses, which had been entered for the English Derby and was due to run in the trial at Lingfield on the second Saturday in May. But, as the day of the meeting drew nearer, she was finding it increasingly hard to totally justify her decision to turn him down.

Before A.D. had left the Surrey racecourse, Jan was driving her lorry back from Worcester races with the two Irish lads for company. She had woken that morning still unsure about her resolution to turn down his offer. Now, with four runners in the back of the lorry and not a winner amongst them even in mediocre fields, she wouldn't have been surprised if A.D. decided to withdraw anyway.

Jan now felt desperate that Eddie wasn't with her, but he had gone to tack up another runner at the evening meeting in Warwick. She had deliberated, before finally deciding it would be best to deal with A.D. on her own. Now she was regretting her decision.

As the sun slid down through a golden sky towards the northern crest of the Malvern Hills, Jan looked through her kitchen window and saw its rays reflected on A.D.'s long black Mercedes gliding along the lane. The car turned off the road and cruised up the long tarmac track to where her yard and house stood on the hillside in the shade of a cluster of swaying Scots pines.

The large car stopped on the gravelled circle which had recently been laid in front of the house. A.D. stepped quickly out of the rear door without waiting for Daragh, his chauffeur, to open it. The Irish tycoon looked cool and spruce in a beige cotton suit, cinnamon suede brogues and dark glasses.

Jan knew that his Derby prospect had run disappointingly that afternoon. She also knew that if A.D. felt let down by a horse's performance he never let it show.

As he made his way up to the front door, she ran her eye over the room, especially tidied by Fran, and smiled at her scrubbed and shining children.

She took a deep breath and waited for the knock; mustering up her best smile she opened the door.

'Hello, A.D. How nice to see you. Come on in,' she said brightly.

'Good evening, Jan. You look great!' The Irishman took off his dark glasses and gave her a quick, habitual kiss on each cheek. 'Hello, Megan. How *are* you?' he asked with easy, infectious charm. 'And Matty, my, you look so well! I think you must have grown two inches.'

Jan couldn't help glowing. Matty *did* look well. He and Megan had spent several afternoons swimming with Fran and running around in the sunshine.

'Thanks, A.D. You say all the right things.'

A.D. gave her a searching look, as if he was already assessing her intonation and body language before they got down to the real business later on. 'I do, when I can.'

'Now, are you staying for supper?'

'If I may.'

'It's all laid on – two of the best fillet steaks my butcher could produce.'

'Great! Hang on a moment.' A.D. turned and stepped back

outside. 'Daragh, would you ever bring me a couple of those bottles?'

The young chauffeur rummaged in the boot before walking up to the house with a smile and a nod to Jan, whom he had driven several times. He handed two bottles of red wine to A.D., who in turn passed them to Jan. 'My contribution,' he said. 'Daragh, you nip down and get yourself something to eat in the pub and call back here for me in an hour and a half. I want to get to the ferry by midnight.'

He turned to Jan. 'I've promised my wife I'll be at Mass tomorrow morning for the christening of our butler's first child. These things are very important where I live. I've a cabin booked on the three o'clock ferry to Rosslare, but they'll let me on board around midnight. That way I'll get a good night's sleep and be home in plenty of time.'

Jan was constantly surprised that someone as dynamic as A.D. should be so averse to flying. His domestic commitments were even more surprising, given the punishing timetable he set himself, with not a minute wasted. Although it was a popular pastime in the racing world to guess A.D.'s wealth and how he had accumulated it, no one ever suggested he used it to pursue other women. At times, when Jan saw him smiling at her children, she wondered how much he regretted his own childlessness.

'So Eddie's not here?' A.D. queried, sitting on a sofa in Jan's drawing room, with a glass of mineral water beside him.

The children had gone to bed, meekly for once.

'No,' Jan answered. 'He's taken a runner to Warwick for this evening's meeting, I've been to Worcester this afternoon.'

'So I saw. No luck, then?'

'I wasn't expecting much. Still, none of them ran badly.'

'My fella did,' A.D. said without expression. 'It's the first time I've had a horse entered for an English Classic.' He shrugged lightly. 'I don't think we'll be able to risk running him in the Derby now. Maybe I should follow my instincts and stick to jumping.'

This was as close to an admission of failure as Jan had ever heard from A.D. She took it as a sign of his trust in her, which was going to make their conversation even harder.

'What did he think about the proposal I've put to you?' A.D. asked casually.

'Who?'

'Eddie, of course.'

'He didn't say exactly. He feels I must make my own decision.'

A.D. put his head on one side. 'He's quite right, naturally. But I had the impression he was getting rather more involved here than that.'

Jan shook her head. 'He's a help and he likes riding out, but I think he really wants to get back to his picture dealing.'

'An independent sort of a chap, you could say.'

'I suppose so.'

'Well now, what have you decided?'

Jan was sitting in an armchair opposite A.D. and immediately tensed. She leaned back and took a deep breath before she unconsciously closed her eyes for a second. She gathered her composure, sat upright, then looked at A.D. as steadily as she could. 'I realize that if I say no to the very generous proposition you've made, you probably won't increase the number of horses you have with me and you might well take away those you've already got here.' She paused without meaning to, as if some inner guide were telling her not to jump. Struggling to clear the lump in her throat, she went on. 'But I'm sorry, A.D., I've decided not to take you up on your offer, I just can't.'

The Irishman didn't speak for a few moments. The only sign of emotion he gave was a sharp intake of breath through narrowed nostrils. 'Right,' he said quietly, picking up his glass and taking a mouthful of water. 'That really is a great pity.'

'I'm not saying it doesn't make sense . . .'

A.D. held up a hand. 'There's no more to be said on the subject, Jan. I presume you've given the matter careful consideration; you've given me your answer; that's fair enough.'

Jan wondered wildly what to say next. 'Oh, would you like another glass of water?'

'I'd prefer a small Black Bush, if you have it.'

Jan got to her feet, grateful for the distraction, and walked to the drinks cupboard, where she knew there was a full bottle of the Bushmills whiskey, which Sean McDonagh had sent the first time Supercall won for her.

When she had poured out a large measure, she turned and handed it to A.D., who had got to his feet.

'Thanks,' he nodded, and took a short, sharp gulp of the pale liquid. 'All I will say is you're a very brave girl. If you had said "yes", I would have sent another two dozen horses to you. As it is, I'll still be keeping the six with you. However, the two who haven't performed well, Anais Is Arish and Emerald Isle, won't be coming back. But I will be sending you a couple of better ones.' He smiled and winked over the top of his glass, and Jan knew the danger had passed. For the time being at least.

🐎

'This is *the* most delicious fillet I have ever eaten,' A.D. declared later, as he savoured the first mouthful.

She smiled gratefully. 'The wine's pretty good, too.'

'So it should be,' A.D. said. 'It's from the best year and the best vineyard in the Médoc.'

'It's lucky you don't have to drive yourself.'

'That, Jan, is not a matter of luck and, anyway, I never drink more than half a bottle.'

Towards the end of the meal, A.D. deliberately brought the conversation back to horses. 'I see you've entered Supercall to run at Perth on Thursday.'

Jan nodded. It would be the first time she had sent a runner north of the border. 'I wanted a reasonably competitive race which he had a chance of winning, and his owner was happy for him to go – he loves Scotland.'

'That's your music man, Carlton-Brown, isn't it?'

'Yes, he's my brother's boss, sort of.'

'You did well to get that horse. A lot of people in Ireland are keeping a close eye to see what you can do with him.'

Jan chuckled. 'I bet they are.'

'I'd like you to look at a few horses with me at the end of June. You'll be coming over to Fairyhouse, won't you?'

'Oh yes,' Jan said. She was looking forward to it. This year the 'Derby' sale would be a very different ball game from the last time she'd been. 'I wouldn't miss it for the world.'

🐎

Jan had suggested to Ben that he should drive down from London for a traditional Sunday lunch the next day. He had been only too happy to accept and she wasn't completely surprised when he turned up with an extra guest.

'I hope you don't mind,' he said, jumping out of his car. 'I've brought Darius with me. His girlfriend's thrown a wobbly and he wanted to get out of London.'

'No, that's fine,' Jan smiled, shaking hands with the sleepy-eyed rock star. She wondered what the girls in the yard would say when they knew the lead singer of the Band of Brothers was having lunch up at the house.

They stood outside for a few minutes while Darius, like most first-time visitors, drank in the spectacular view. They were just turning to go inside when Eddie appeared in jodhpurs and brown boots, walking up from the yard with Jan's old lurcher, Fred, close on his heels.

'Morning, Eddie,' Ben said in greeting. 'What's my sister been making you do on such a lovely Sunday morning?'

'I'm not sure I should answer that,' Eddie grinned, 'but right now I've been exercising the stable star.'

'Which one?' Ben laughed. 'This yard's full of stars.'

'My favourite and the one least likely to notice my weight – the bold Eagle.'

Ben nodded and turned to Darius. 'Russian Eagle won the Irish National for Jan at the beginning of April, but when Eddie tried to win the big amateur race on him at Aintree last year he fell off unfortunately.'

'Well, that's not the whole story.' Eddie grimaced.

'You can tell Darius all about it,' Ben said. 'He and the rest of the band are going to have a horse with Jan, so he wants to have a bit of a look around.'

'Fine, we can go now,' Eddie suggested. 'Unless you want to, Jan.'

'It would be a great help if you did,' Jan said. 'I've got things to do if you want any lunch. Ben, can you come and give me a hand?'

'They'll be fine,' Ben said confidently as he followed her into the house.

'Yes,' Jan agreed. 'Eddie's very good at that sort of thing and he more or less knows what he's talking about now. By the way, you still haven't told me what you really think of him. It's a while since you met him at the party.'

'I think he's great,' Ben said. 'He's one of those guys you can't help liking – great sense of humour; knows a lot about music and all that, but Patrick Lamberhurst did say he's never had a regular girlfriend. He just takes 'em out a few times, has a bit of fun, then moves on.' He looked thoughtfully at his sister.

'He admits that,' she said. 'And though he spends a lot of time here, he still likes to go off and see his other friends.'

'Don't you mind that, Jan? I know what you're like, don't forget.'

'Well, maybe I'm growing up a bit. It was different with John. We never went anywhere much socially and he never ever went out without me, but Eddie's a great deal more sociable and I wouldn't want to tie him down.'

'I get the impression, the minute he felt you were, he'd be off like a shot.'

'Don't say that, Ben,' Jan said fiercely. 'I know him better than most; he loves hanging around the yard and dealing with the horses. Anyway, he's admitted to me that he used to be a bit of a grass-hopper, but he's growing up too, you know.'

Ben smiled at Jan's vehement defence of Eddie and held up his hand in submission. 'I only said he's got too much independence for you to expect him to always be there when you want him.'

'I know that, and I prefer it that way. One of the reasons I can't really get excited about Tony Robertson is that – well, he's too nice, actually, and he's always willing to do whatever I want.'

'Fine then. As long as you're sure and you know what to expect, I certainly don't object to Eddie hanging around.'

'That's really big of you, Ben,' Jan said with a hint of sarcasm. 'Seriously, though, thanks for telling me what you think. It's important. I just have a gut feeling Eddie's going to stay and make me really happy. He's been a fantastic support, listening to all my problems, and he's very balanced about them.'

'What did he say about O'Hagan's offer, then?'

'He said if I took it, I'd be one of the top trainers in a couple of seasons. And also that I shouldn't touch it with a bargepole.'

Ben grinned. 'He was right there. Well, good luck, but if he lets you down or hurts you, you just let me know and I'll sort him out, OK?'

When Eddie and Darius came back to the house, Ben told Jan they were going to pop down to the village for a pint. 'Do you mind? Darius loves a country pub when he gets a chance to be in one.'

'That's fine. Julie the barmaid will be delighted.'

'Oh no, man,' the singer groaned. 'I'm incognito today.'

'Not for long down there, you won't be.' Jan laughed.

The men arrived back in good time for their roast beef and Yorkshire pudding and even Darius seemed to have woken up enough to talk about the horse the band wanted to buy.

'If you really want to get involved,' Jan said, amused by the thought, 'you should come over to Ireland at the end of June and look at some of the horses in the Derby Sale. I could show you a collection of more good, young, jumping-bred horses in one place there than anywhere else on earth.'

'Dublin? Yeah, great. I love Dublin. I'll be there.'

'Have you decided how much you want to pay?' Jan asked, more casually than she felt.

'Yeah.' Darius nodded. 'JCB said if we wanted to be sure of getting something really good, we'd need to spend a hundred grand.'

'Well, in this game no amount of money will give you a cast-iron guarantee of a good horse, but a hundred thousand should certainly shorten the odds in your favour. You will just need to make sure your management people get in touch with me and confirm it all before we go.'

'Right,' the singer said. 'It's done.'

She crossed her fingers and hoped he wouldn't forget.

⚘

As Jan walked down from the house to the stables, it seemed to her there was always more noise in the yard on Thursday mornings, when Shirley McGregor paid her routine weekly visit.

Shirley had a big, lusty laugh that matched her personality, and now it was echoing from the recesses of the old barn where the hay was stored. There were also four stables inside – the first Jan had built at Edge. Shirley was in there checking Dingle Bay's foot, which was showing signs of a soreness that Jan had been unable to identify.

Jan smiled at the sound as she crossed the yard to check if the vet had uncovered the problem, but she was stopped in her tracks when she heard Eddie's answering laugh. She knew it was absurd to be jealous when it was just part of his nature to flirt, but she couldn't help it.

Her antennae were hypersensitive as she walked from the bright sunlight into the gloom of the barn. In the second or two it took for her eyes to adapt to the darkness, they had heard her. Eddie was looking straight at her, alarmed.

Jan felt instantly sick. There was no way she could stomach the idea of anyone, especially this randy vet, touching up her boyfriend – Eddie *was* her boyfriend, for God's sake, she knew that!

'What the hell are you doing?' Jan blurted.

Shirley took her hand from Eddie's leg and stood up.

Eddie bent down and quickly pulled up his trousers, then leisurely zipping the fly he turned back to Jan.

'Nothing,' he said with a grin. 'She hadn't started.'

'What?! What are you doing right here, in my bloody yard . . .'

'Hang on, Jan.' Eddie frowned. 'Don't get your thong in a tangle. Shirley found a lump on Dingle's leg; I told her I had one on my thigh, and she said she'd have a look at it – that's all.'

Jan closed her eyes tight. She didn't believe it; she wanted to, but she couldn't – it sounded too ridiculous – too pat.

'Did you have to drop your trousers?' she spluttered.

'I'm sure Shirley's seen a man's leg before.'

'And a pair of Calvin Kleins,' Shirley added with a grin. 'You don't seriously think I was about to do something with Eddie here in the open barn, for Christ's sake? Give me a break, Jan.'

Jan looked at them both, painfully aware she couldn't dismiss the thought that there must have been a sexual undercurrent in what they claimed to have been doing. She closed her eyes to hold back the tears.

When she opened them, Eddie was standing in front of her with a fixed smile on his face. 'Come on, Jan, get real.' He gave her a quick peck on the cheek. 'I'll leave you with Shirley so she can tell you why Dingle's lame.'

An hour later Jan's fury had subsided a little and she had managed to push the upsetting scene to the back of her mind. She was driving Colonel Gilbert's gelding, Wolf's Rock, to run in the fifth race at Hereford that afternoon. It was to be the horse's last race before his summer break and, as the colonel was going to be there, Jan wanted Wolf's Rock looking as well as possible.

She was giving him a final polish before putting him on the lorry when Eddie wandered into the stable.

'Why don't just me and you take the Rock to Hereford?'

'Because I've already asked Con. He wants to see how the horse runs – he's been worried about him.'

'Why, what's wrong with him?'

'Nothing, as far as I'm concerned. But Con seems to think that he's blowing too much after a couple of miles. And it's two six this afternoon.'

'Murty's riding, isn't he?'

'Yup.'

'He'll soon tell you if there's a problem,' Eddie said.

'Yes, I'm sure he will. Anyway, I'm just taking Con with me, if you don't mind.'

'You're not still pissed off about this morning are you? Because you shouldn't be. On reflection, I admit it was pretty stupid of me to drop my trousers right there and then, but it seemed like a bit of a fun thing to do at the time. And you know Shirley – she did rather egg me on.'

'Don't pretend to be so bloody naive, Eddie. She'd have done a lot more than egg you on if you'd given her half a chance.'

'All right, all right. I'm sorry – I know she's a bit of a fun-loving girl, but she makes me laugh and even you have to admit she's a damned good vet.'

'That's precisely one of the reasons why I put up with her.'

'What are the others?' Eddie asked curiously.

'Frankly, this business is so masculine, it's quite nice to deal with a woman for a change.'

'Good heavens – women's lib hits National Hunt racing! Come on, Jan. Most of the people who work in this yard are women.'

'And ninety-nine per cent of the decisions in racing are taken by men, most of them wearing sodding blinkers.'

Colonel Gilbert was waiting for Jan by the lorry park at the racecourse. He raised his trilby and, with a pronounced limp that was a legacy of his own point-to-point career, walked over to greet her with a friendly smile in his bright blue eyes. 'Mind if I come in with you and have a good look at him?' he asked.

'If they let me sign you in, that's fine,' Jan replied. 'He likes seeing you, I'm sure he still recognizes you.'

'D'you know, I think he does. Of course, I saw him more or less every day for the first four years of his life and I don't really think he's ever forgotten.'

'Some don't,' Jan agreed.

They followed as Con led the horse into his stable, where he was greeted warmly by several lads from other yards. She'd noticed that Dec and Con seemed to be very popular and got on with anyone; it was a natural gift a lot of the Irish seemed to have.

There were still two hours to go before they had to saddle the horse for his race, so the colonel invited Jan for a drink and a light lunch in the busy members' bar. They watched the first two races, chatting happily; they'd known each other for a long time and, despite being her father's landlord, the colonel always treated Jan as an equal.

'How's Virginia getting on?' Jan felt compelled to ask.

Colonel Gilbert shrugged his neatly tailored shoulders. 'Not bad, considering, but I'm afraid she's still only playing at it. I wish you'd been up and running a year or two sooner, and I could have persuaded her to go and work with you for a while before applying for her own licence.'

'Well, she wouldn't do that now.' Jan grinned.

'No, more's the pity.'

'I met her new jockey last week. He seems a nice chap.'

'He's a damned good jockey, too. I can't see him getting enough winners with Virginia, but she's offered him a good retainer and I suppose it'll give him a chance to get known in England.'

'Not if he hasn't got anything good to ride he won't.'

'Oh, I don't doubt there'll be plenty of other trainers ready to give him a try when Virginia doesn't need him. By the way, I'm really pleased we've got Murty on board today.'

'So am I,' Jan said. 'To tell you the truth, Con says the Rock's a bit thick in his wind and this trip might be too far for him, so I'll be glad to hear Murty's opinion.'

'Well, I hope Con's mistaken. I've always fancied this horse as a three-mile chaser.'

'What do you want to do with him after today?'

'I mentioned to Eddie that I'll have him back for a couple of months. I've got masses of grass at home and I'd far rather give it to him than waste it on sheep with the price they're fetching at the moment.'

'A bit of spring grass will do him the world of good. I'm looking forward to getting the rest out too. The development of the young horses can be astounding through the summer.'

'But you're keeping a few going, I gather, and running a couple on the flat for A.D.?'

'Yes. I've entered Galway Fox to run at Newbury in a fortnight.'

'Have you got any new horses to replace those dreadful Sharps' yet?'

'Possibly,' Jan said guardedly. She didn't want to mention that Miller's Lodge might be moving to her from Virginia, and most of her other client enquiries were at too early a stage to be definites.

'I would imagine you want at least thirty now, with the set-up you've got. It's not as though you can afford to subsidize the operation like my daughter does.'

Jan often wondered about Colonel Gilbert's attitude to his daughter. She thought that perhaps, too late in life, he realized he had over-indulged her as a child.

'Jan, you must let me know if you think you might be short of horses,' he went on. 'I could send you a couple more. By the way, talking of daughters, how's Megan getting on with that smart little grey pony? Last time I saw her she looked very impressive.'

'She's done really well, actually,' Jan said proudly. 'Smarty's a beautiful pony. He's not an easy ride, but she's learnt a lot from him. The trouble is, she's getting a bit too big for him now and Matty's not up to riding him. In fact my dad's got Matty another pony and he's taken over teaching him up at his place.'

'I bet he's enjoying that.' The colonel beamed. 'I'll look out for Megan. I might just have something I'd like her to try for me – if that's OK with you.'

Jan nodded. 'You know Meg, she'll certainly give it a go.'

❧

Later, after Jan had been round to the stables to tack up Wolf's Rock, she and the colonel walked over to the parade ring – where he knew all the local stewards – and watched as Con led the horse around.

'He certainly looks well,' Colonel Gilbert remarked. 'And I'd say he's the fittest of this lot.'

'He's fit all right,' Jan murmured as Murty and the other jockeys filed out of the weighing room alongside the ring.

As Murty stood between owner and trainer, Jan gave him brief instructions. 'He should travel well for the first couple of miles, but you'll have to try to keep a bit in the tank for the last six furlongs. I need you to listen to his wind – if he's really struggling you'll have to pull him up. OK?'

The Irishman nodded. 'Sure thing, Mrs H. I'll do my best.'

Ten minutes later Jan was watching anxiously through her binoculars when the jockey, following her instructions, eased the horse up. As the rest of the runners went on to take the last plain fence on the back straight, Murty swung his mount away and walked it slowly back towards the stands.

Colonel Gilbert, standing beside Jan in the members' enclosure, sucked his teeth regretfully. 'Perhaps your lad was right. Ah well, there it is. A good two-miler is better than nothing.'

Two days later Jan doubted that she'd have come all the way to Perth if she'd known what a marathon drive it would be. She'd driven up in the lorry with Roz Stoddard, who was Supercall's groom, arriving the evening before the race so that the horse could have a well-earned rest after such a long journey.

Johnny Carlton-Brown arrived by helicopter the next day in time for lunch.

'Are you seriously telling me you set out yesterday lunchtime?' he asked, impressed that his trainer would go to such lengths for one horse.

'Yes, I am. I didn't want to drive him up this morning. It's too far and too demanding, you couldn't possibly expect him to run up to his form without a decent break. But, I have to say, I think I'll come in the chopper with you next time.'

'Why don't you let me drop you back then, at least?'

'Because I really wouldn't expect Roz to drive all that way on her own.'

'Well, let's hope it's all worth it. It was clever of you to get Murty McGrath to ride.'

Jan gazed out across the unfamiliar course, which she had walked for the first time that morning. 'Actually I asked him to ride the horse as soon as we decided to run here. The ground is just soft enough and Murty's no fool. He knows a star when he sees one, and he'll expect to go on riding him when he can.'

'Tell me, Jan. Just how much difference does the right jockey make?'

'That's a big question. For a start, not all jockeys suit the same horse. And a really good horse can often win with a moderate pilot. But what a good jockey brings is an understanding of the horse he's riding, an appreciation of just how much pushing the horse needs, whether the stick will help or hinder. He also needs to understand the tactics of the race and how his opposition are travelling and likely to play it. And a good jockey will do his homework and will also know the way a course rides; where the better ground is and how not to get boxed in, which is what often happens to younger jockeys. He also needs to be able to relate information to the owners and trainers afterwards.'

Johnny was looking at her keenly, taking in everything she said. 'So it can make a real difference?'

'Without a doubt, but then again good horses also make good jockeys.'

'So what are you planning to do about a stable jockey next season?'

Jan looked sharply at her owner. She hadn't realized that this was where the conversation was leading. 'Whoever my stable jockey is,' she said, 'if I think I can get a more suitable one for a particular horse or race, then I will and frankly, after some of the results we've had recently, it won't be so hard to persuade the majority of them.'

'I see Virginia's got this young Irish chap, Finbar Howlett. What do you think of him?'

'He looks pretty good. I've met him, as it happens, and he'll probably ride a few for us.'

'He can do that, can he, with his retainer?'

'Yes, if Virginia hasn't booked him for the same race.'

'Good. I'd rather like him to go on riding Miller's Lodge when he comes to you.'

'Have you told Virginia that Miller's coming to us?'

'No, not yet, but I will.'

Murty rode a near-perfect race to bring Supercall home first in a field of fifteen well-rated novice chasers.

'He didn't win by much,' the horse's owner remarked as he and Jan walked down to the course to meet it.

78

'He could have won by twenty lengths if Murty had let go of his head,' Jan said, 'but that wouldn't have helped anyone really. Like I said, the game is to win races, and half a length is just as good as winning by twenty lengths.'

'You know, it's much more enlightening going racing with you than it is with Virginia. She never tells me anything.'

'Oh?' said Jan, trying to sound surprised.

7

On the long journey home from Scotland with Roz that evening, Jan felt their trip had been well worth the effort. JCB was clearly delighted with the result and had put her mind at rest about Miller's Lodge moving to Edge Farm.

The only event of the day to leave a sour taste in the mouth had been the widely reported appearance of the Sharp family at Bristol Crown Court for a pleas and directions hearing. Their full trial, at which Jan would almost certainly be required to give evidence, was scheduled for September. Inevitably, the subject had cropped up while she and Johnny Carlton-Brown were having a drink to celebrate their win.

'You must still feel really sick about what those crooks did to you,' he said.

'It was what Angie did that hurt most. Right from the start she set me up. She pursued me, knew exactly how to gain my trust and then stitched me up like a turkey! I feel such a bloody fool for being so completely taken in by her.'

'Jan, from what I hear they were real pros. Just don't let any of the bad publicity rub off on you. In fact, my advice is that you go through the whole thing with our media people to make sure you get the best possible press coverage, then you can put your side of the story if necessary.'

'I must admit I wouldn't mind having someone to hold my hand when we do get to court.'

'Did I hear on the grapevine that you bought one of their horses after they were arrested?'

Jan nodded with a grin. 'Yes, I managed to get the best of them

– King's Archer – but I won't be running him again until the late autumn.'

'Have you found a buyer for him yet?'

'I've got one in mind,' Jan said, thinking of Bernie Sutcliffe.

'Well, let me know if it falls through.'

Jan nodded. 'I think I can get at least one more big win out of him,' she said. 'Then he'll be worth loads more,' she added with a satisfied smile.

Roz drove for the first leg of the journey home while Jan caught up with the news from Annabel via her mobile. She learnt, to her delight and somewhat to her surprise, that the Band of Brothers' management had officially underwritten her expenditure up to £100,000 at the Fairyhouse sales and confirmed that they would lodge funds in her client account three days before the sale began.

Another potential owner had firmed up and Bernie had rung to say he definitely wanted a new horse. And, thank God, A.D. had also confirmed which six horses he would have in training with her next season.

When Jan took over the driving after an hour, Roz needed little encouragement to keep up her constant chatting, which was designed to stop her boss from dropping off, she said.

'So,' Roz asked, relishing the excuse for a good gossip, 'how's it going between you and Eddie?'

Although Roz wasn't too sophisticated, she was surprisingly perceptive, and in the two years they'd known each other Jan had got into the dangerous habit of confiding in her almost as much as in Annabel.

'If you'd told me after Eddie did his bunk a year ago that he was going to be back here, living in Stow and hanging around my place again, I'd have laughed at you – though I suppose it had crossed my mind occasionally.'

'But now he's here, what d'you think will happen?'

Jan wasn't at all sure if she should be talking to her staff so intimately, but right now Roz was much more a friend than an employee.

'Well, I suppose it could happen,' she said with a lazy grin.

'What? You and him – marry?' Roz gasped.

Jan turned to her. 'It wouldn't be that surprising, would it?'

'No, no, course not, but, you know, I wouldn't think he was the type to settle down.'

'They all have to come down to earth sooner or later and he really likes being around the yard and the horses.'

'And at least his riding's got a hell of a lot better.'

'Exactly.' Jan chuckled. 'A good work rider I'd never have to pay – that'd be worth having! But listen, Roz, please don't tell anyone I said so.'

'Hasn't he asked you yet, then?'

'No, but I think I can see it coming. I don't know – perhaps I'm kidding myself. I know the longer he's around, the more it'll hurt if he lets me down. Maybe I should just forget about Eddie and pursue the doctor.' Jan sighed. 'So please don't start gossiping about it. I don't want Eddie to know how I feel – not until he's well committed anyway.'

Having stopped for a short break, Roz offered to drive the final leg home. Jan soon fell asleep, although uncomfortably propped against the door of the cab, when they finally turned into the entrance at Edge Farm. It was half-past two on a thick black night, but there were lights on in the yard when there shouldn't have been any. She held her breath as she climbed down from the lorry, until she heard a set of firm footfalls.

'Eddie?' she called into the dark.

'Hi, Jan. Well done – fantastic result! I meant to ring you but I couldn't find my mobile and that's the only place I've got your number.'

'Some excuse. I suppose it didn't occur to you to ask Annabel. Still, never mind. Did you see the race?'

'Of course I did. Murty is a maestro, there's no question about that, and you'd trained the horse spot on.'

'Why are you down here, then? Is there a problem?'

'No, I was waiting for you to get back. I reckoned you'd both be totally bushed, so I thought I'd deal with the horse while you go and run yourself a nice hot bath.'

Jan glanced meaningfully at Roz, who had climbed down beside her. 'Isn't he an angel?' she giggled.

'He's a bit too muscular for an angel if you ask me.' Roz looked him over. 'They always look a bit poofy to me, but I know what you mean.' She laughed. 'I'm that knackered, I don't know if I'll stay awake long enough to drive home.'

'Stay up at the house,' Jan urged her. 'We've got two bathrooms working now, and the kids are down at Mum's.'

'No thanks. I think I'll get off. I don't sleep well in strange beds. Not on my own, anyway,' Roz said, with a cheeky grin that Jan couldn't misinterpret, and she trudged across the parking area to her car. The sound of her feet crunching across the stony surface seemed to hang in the stillness of the clear summer's night. As Roz started the motor, Jan glanced at Eddie and found him looking at her with a transparent tenderness.

'What are you after?' she asked with a playful dig in the ribs.

Eddie opened his eyes wide with feigned innocence. 'I just wanted to help – like I told you,' he protested.

'Then I suppose you want a nightcap?'

'That'd be great – if that's OK?' he added with exaggerated diffidence.

'Yes, of course it's OK. And thanks for waiting up for us.' She stretched up to plant a soft kiss on his cheek before turning and striding up towards the house. 'Don't forget that warm mash and to put some hay in his rack,' she called over her shoulder, smiling good-humouredly to herself.

Jan awoke the next morning to find Eddie beside her. She gazed at the unruly dark curls framing his peaceful face and longed to wake him. She glanced at the clock beside the bed. It was five forty-five. He deserved the last quarter of an hour before the alarm went off, she thought. She looked at him fondly, shaking her head in disbelief that she had allowed him to stay the night – still, the children would never know, and if the rest of the staff noticed his Morgan when they arrived, she would just tell them he had turned up early and they might do well to follow his example.

Careful not to wake him, she slipped out of bed, tiptoed from the room and down the stairs.

In the silent kitchen, she slid the heavy-bottomed kettle onto the hotplate of the Aga and reached into a cupboard for a couple of mugs. While she waited for the kettle to boil, she looked sleepily out of the large window that faced west across the broad valley, where the hills beyond were beginning to glow in the early sun.

She was reflecting how natural it seemed to wake beside Eddie, and how perfect it would be to have him permanently in her life; suddenly she was jerked from her thoughts by a shrill version of the *Mission Impossible* theme coming from Eddie's mobile phone. Automatically, she looked up at the mahogany clock that had travelled with her from Stonewall and now stood on the mantelshelf above the range. It was still only five to six. She wondered who on earth would be calling at this early hour. At first she couldn't pinpoint the source of the sound but, making an effort to focus, she narrowed it down to the big oak dresser, where an assortment of papers and other objects always accumulated. Lifting a stack of newspapers, she found the telephone still trilling urgently.

She snatched it up, pressed the green button and grunted a hoarse 'Hello.'

'Eddie? Hello – Eddie?'

Jan was suddenly wide awake. The voice was a woman's – a youngish woman and Australian, Jan guessed from the few syllables she had uttered.

'This is Eddie Sullivan's phone,' she confirmed in a clear, terse voice. 'Jan Hardy speaking. Can I help you?'

'Who? Who are you?'

'Jan Hardy.' She hesitated for a moment. 'A friend of Eddie's,' she added. 'Who's that?'

'Whoever you are, I don't know why you're answering his phone, but is he there?'

There was a distinct note of hysteria in the woman's voice, not far below the surface.

'It's before six in the morning here. He's still asleep – he was up very late last night.'

'Oh God, sorry! It's still early evening here – I didn't think . . . Can you get him? I've *got* to speak to him . . .' She didn't need to add that it was urgent.

'I'm sorry,' Jan said, with a stab of guilt, 'I'm not going to wake him now. If you tell me who it is, I'll ask him to call you as soon as he's up and about.'

'*Shit!* For Christ's sake . . .' The girl – she sounded quite young and desperate, Jan thought – was crying now. '*Please* ask him to call me back as soon as he's up. It's Louise.'

Louise, Jan thought, *who the bloody hell is Louise?*

'All right,' she said, a little more gently. 'I'll tell him.'

The connection was cut and Jan switched the phone back to standby. Tears welled up in her eyes as she took a long, quivering breath. This person, whoever she was, had demanded to speak to Eddie as if she had sole right to his time. She sounded, Jan thought, very much like a lover at the end of her tether.

'Not again,' she whispered to herself as the lid on the kettle was beginning to rattle and steam spewed noisily from the spout. Mechanically, Jan slid the cast-iron vessel off the hotplate and with shaking hands tipped boiling water into the two mugs she had already primed with tea bags.

As if in a trance, to keep at bay the significance of what she had just heard, she added a spoonful of sugar to Eddie's mug and half a spoonful to her own, and topped them up with milk. She stirred hers slowly and took a sip; the hot fluid quickly coursed through her and helped to stimulate her into action.

She picked up the other mug and carried it upstairs to the bedroom. She put it down on the table beside Eddie and drew back the curtains, letting the early morning light flood in.

'God,' he groaned, 'is it time to get up already?'

Jan nodded. Her throat felt tight and she didn't trust her voice just yet.

Eddie grinned philosophically. Propping himself on one elbow, he picked up his mug of tea and took a gulp.

'Thanks,' he said. 'I'm not sure I'm going to be much use riding out first lot, though.' He patted the bed beside him, still smiling lazily.

Jan looked back and pictured him waking up with Louise.

'Someone just rang for you,' she managed to say.

'Oh,' Eddie said indifferently, taking another mouthful of tea before glancing at the clock again to confirm the time. 'Bit early,' he observed.

'She was ringing from Australia – it's the middle of the afternoon there apparently.'

Comprehension and unease clouded Eddie's eyes before he looked away. 'Ah,' he said, putting his mug down and leaning back against the headboard with his eyes closed.

'Someone called Louise,' Jan added coolly.

Eddie nodded. 'Yeah, Louise.' He opened his eyes and looked at Jan, puzzled. 'I wonder how the hell she got this number.'

'She didn't. She rang your mobile. It was under a pile of papers on the dresser in the kitchen.'

'Oh.' Eddie nodded again. 'Did she say what she wanted?'

'She sounded very distressed. I said I'd get you to call her back. I presume you've got the number.'

'Yes, I've got the number and, before you start grilling me, I'm going to have a shower.'

'Do I take it you're also going to ride first lot, then?'

Eddie sighed and swung his legs over the side of the bed. 'Yes, you do,' he added churlishly.

🐎

Jan was always disciplined about her work. She managed to ride out two lots and eat a little breakfast with the rest of her staff before she spoke to Eddie about Louise. In fact it was he who took the initiative.

He walked into the office next to the tack room and looked around to make sure no one else was within earshot.

'I've just spoken to her.'

'Who – Louise?'

Eddie nodded. 'It's a bit – ' he paused, seeking the right word – 'tricky, actually.' He winced, confirming the understatement.

Jan gazed at him and felt completely numb. Before Eddie she had never been jealous of anyone in her life; she'd always felt utterly secure in her relationship with John. The idea that this man, for whom she had been prepared to lower all her defences, whom she had allowed to become an integral part of her life, had even the vestige of a commitment elsewhere was making her feel physically ill. Her head was spinning alarmingly and something mechanical seemed to be stirring her innards. She closed her eyes.

'Eddie, please tell me. What's been going on?' she asked faintly.

'Louise was a girl I knew in Australia, in Sydney. She worked for one of the big art auctioneers there – I was doing a bit of business with the family.' Eddie shrugged. 'Her dad's a big collector and I spent a lot of time with them. She's a very good-looking girl. I had no plans to come back to the UK, no commitments back here – you wouldn't have expected me to live like a monk, would you?'

Jan glanced at him. She felt the tears surging up her body and clamped her eyes tightly shut. Now Eddie's hand was on her shoulder, gently squeezing. Feeling drained and empty, she slowly pushed it away.

'Come on, Jan. I didn't know what was going to happen in Dublin any more than you did. You and I were just good friends. We'd never been lovers, or even thought about it, really.'

'You'd thought about it, you bastard.' Jan sniffed.

'Yes, I suppose I had in an academic sort of way, but I never really saw us in a long-term relationship then – and you certainly didn't.'

'But why haven't you mentioned this Louise before? You haven't, not once, since you've been back.'

'What good would it have done?' Eddie asked simply. When Jan didn't reply, he went on, 'After Dublin everything changed. I rang Louise and told her I was trying to set up a new business in England and I wouldn't be coming back to Oz for a while.'

'Did you tell her you'd got a new lover?'

Eddie sighed. 'No, but she's been around; she knows the score.

I suppose I thought she'd pretty soon forget about me and the whole thing would die naturally.'

Jan stood up and walked across the small, timber-lined room, in the hope that she might be able to think better standing up. 'Apparently it hasn't, though.'

'No,' Eddie admitted.

'She sounded like she needed to talk to you pretty desperately. What did she want?'

Eddie straightened his back and looked directly at Jan. 'She told me she's pregnant.'

Jan felt the force of what he'd just said as if she'd been kicked in the stomach. She sat on the desk, clutching the edge with white knuckles.

'Pregnant?' she whispered. 'Please, please, tell me it's not yours, Eddie.'

He nodded guiltily. 'I'm sorry, Jan. It looks as if it is.'

'Oh my God, Eddie! What are you going to do about it?'

'I've got to go to Sydney and see her.'

'But why?' Jan asked, knowing what a dumb question it was as soon as the words came out.

'Oh, come on, Jan! I can't just ignore her and pretend it hasn't happened.'

'Why can't she just . . .?' Jan despised herself for half suggesting it. She knew it wasn't an option she would ever have chosen.

'It's too late for that and, anyway, she wouldn't – she couldn't, she's a Catholic. I'm so sorry, Jan, but I've got to go and face up to my responsibilities. Believe me, I really don't want to, but I've got to sort my life out before I can even think about us with a clear conscience.'

'But, Eddie,' Jan whispered, feeling herself dissolve in a way she'd never done before, 'does that mean you will be coming back . . . or not?'

Eddie stood in front of her, as she sat on the desk like an adolescent schoolgirl. He took her chin in his left hand and tilted it until her eyes couldn't avoid his black pupils shining in circles of dark coffee.

'I don't know, Jan,' he whispered as he kissed away her tears and brushed her nose with his lips. 'I honestly don't know.'

🐎

Annabel stood beside Jan, watching the taxi that had arrived a few minutes earlier from Cheltenham creep back down the drive to the lane and turn left towards Winchcombe.

'Where on earth is Eddie going with that massive rucksack?' she asked.

Jan didn't look at her. 'He's getting a train from Cheltenham to Heathrow Airport.'

'And?' Annabel asked impatiently.

'He's flying to Australia.'

Despite her resolve not to let it show, Jan's voice began to crack. Annabel heard it too.

'Jan, why, what's the matter? What on earth's happened?'

Jan turned and looked bleakly at her closest friend. She knew there were tears in her eyes, but she didn't try to wipe them away. 'Come on, walk down to the bottom of the drive with me? The others will think we're going to look at Eagle.'

'Sure.' Annabel agreed at once. With Fred and Tigger the terrier trotting along beside them, they began to stroll across the parking space in front of the yard and down the long slope towards the paddocks on the level ground by the road.

Annabel said nothing, letting Jan take her time.

'I knew I wouldn't be able to keep it to myself,' Jan said, sniffing. 'I just don't know how I've got through today without breaking down altogether, though I bloody well wasn't going to do it in front of him and be accused of emotional blackmail.'

'I sensed there was some kind of tension between you, but I didn't think it was anything really serious. After all, you've been getting on brilliantly; I've never seen you as happy as you've been for the last few weeks; you and Eddie, you can't have broken up?'

'Not as such.' Jan sniffed again. She tried to calm herself and tell the story as reasonably as she could.

'As the kids were with Mum and Dad, I let Eddie stay with me last night.'

'Was that the first time?' Annabel asked gently.

'In my bedroom? Yes. But this morning, just before six, while he was still asleep I was in the kitchen making tea when his mobile started ringing. Normally, he turns it off because he hates getting calls at odd hours, but he'd lost the bloody thing, obviously, hearing it, I found it and answered it.'

'That was asking for trouble,' Annabel observed.

'I wouldn't have normally; anyway this was bound to come out sooner or later. To cut a long story short, it was a girl called Louise who'd apparently been an item with Eddie in Australia, and – this is the awful bit – she'd rung to say she's pregnant.' Jan paused. 'And he's the father.'

'Oh, my God, Jan, how awful!' Annabel gasped. 'I'm so sorry. No wonder you're feeling miserable. But Eddie had to go, didn't he – it's for the best?'

'I suppose so.' Jan sighed.

'Jan, of course it is! He'd be a total bastard if he just told her to get lost – and, whatever else he is, Eddie is definitely *not* a bastard. So poor you, you've had to live with this all day, riding out, working in the office, doing the entries? I thought you looked a bit peaky a couple of times, but I put it down to that marathon trip to Perth.'

'It hasn't been easy trying to keep it all under wraps and, to be honest, I'm really relieved you know about it, but I'd rather the others didn't. Oh God.' Jan groaned. 'I did let my guard drop a bit yesterday on the way back from Perth – I told Roz I thought Eddie and I were going to get married. There's no chance of that now.'

'Why? Eddie's gone out to see the girl and help her cope with the fact that she's pregnant. That doesn't mean to say he's going to marry her, for God's sake!'

'I know, logically, that's right, Bel, but Eddie's such a good guy. If this girl really wants him to stay around, I can't see him chucking her, no matter what he feels deep down.'

'He's not that soft, Jan, and I know from the way he's behaved with you he's really, really fond of you.'

'But he's never actually said he loves me.'

Annabel made a face. 'He's not the type to say that, he suffers from emotional constipation. You've got to have faith in yourself,

Jan. I mean, you're a good-looking, talented, dynamic woman with a strong personality. A lot of men would think you were a hell of a catch; so don't go putting yourself down the whole time.'

'Maybe,' Jan said, as the tears began to trickle down her face once more. 'But how would I ever be able to trust him again? Or anyone else for that matter?'

'You can try and I'm sure I'm right. Eddie will be back sooner or later, you'll see, and in the meantime you've got to get on with your life. And that may mean letting the doctor take you out now and again. I tell you what, I was thinking of having a few people over for dinner on Saturday – to christen my new conservatory. Why don't you come and I'll get a crowd together? You'd enjoy it.'

'OK, that'd be good,' Jan said, trying to smile at her friend's efforts to cheer her up.

'After all, it's not as though Eddie's walked out or there's anything wrong between you. It's only a bit of his past catching up with him, and you'd find a man without a past a very boring proposition – I know you, don't forget.'

Jan was beginning to feel better already. 'Thanks, Bel. It's great having you on my side.'

They leaned on the gate of the lower paddock and talked for a while to the horses, who wandered across the field to see them. As they fondled the animals, Jan automatically checked them over with a careful eye; she was extremely grateful for Annabel's understanding and sympathy.

They had begun to walk back up the drive when they heard a car turn off the road behind them. Jan looked back and saw her father's well-worn Daihatsu rattling noisily towards them. They stood to one side to let him pass, but Reg pulled up to greet them.

'Hello, Jan,' he said. Then he looked at her sharply and asked, 'Are you all right? Your eyes are a bit bloodshot.'

Jan wished her distress wasn't so obvious. 'I'm fine, Dad. Nothing serious. A bit of a bug, I expect.'

'Ah well, you're in good hands.' He smiled at Annabel. 'I've just come to pick up our boy again to take him for another session with the pony – is that all right?'

'Yes, of course. I told Mum it was, if you really don't mind having him back so soon. That would be great.'

'You know I enjoy it,' Reg said. 'We would have kept them at home all day if Megan hadn't had to go off to school. Where is he?'

'He's up at the house with Fran. Have fun.'

Reg nodded and trundled on up the hill.

'You're so lucky with your father,' Annabel said. 'He accepts you as you are, and just . . . loves you, I suppose.'

Jan nodded. 'I love him too. He's such a good man, very fair and straightforward.'

'I wish I could say the same about mine.'

They watched as a delighted Reg came back down the hill with his grandson and drove away with a cheerful wave.

'Come on, let's get back to work. I want to have a look at Supercall,' Jan said. 'He looked a bit peaky this morning; I don't think he liked all that travelling.'

Annabel followed her across the yard and into the young chaser's stable. Jan took off his rug and looked at the big handsome horse. With his coat dull and his belly tucked up, he was hanging his head and shivering slightly.

Jan reached up and hugged him, burying her face in his neck and sucking in the horsy smells she'd always loved. 'Come on, old chap. You ran a brilliant race yesterday. What's wrong with you now?'

She stepped back, opened his mouth and peered inside his lips. Finding no obvious symptoms, she closed it, patted his nose and felt each of his legs.

She stood back and shook her head. 'I don't know. I guess he's just a bit knackered. We'll give him some more electrolytes and lead him for a couple of days before we exercise him properly again.'

Hoping that she wouldn't have to get the vet in to look at him, Jan and Annabel had just walked out of the stable when Shirley McGregor strode across the yard towards them.

'Hi!' she called. 'I was just passing and I promised Eddie I'd drop something in for that lump on his leg he was so worried about.'

'That was very thoughtful of you,' Jan said quickly, trying to stop herself from sounding too sarcastic, 'but I'm afraid you've just missed him.'

'Doesn't matter,' the vet said. 'I'll just leave it with you.'

'I'm afraid he won't be able to use it for a while.'

'Oh?' Shirley asked, echoing Jan's lack of warmth. 'Why's that?'

'Because he's gone to Australia, that's why.'

Shirley hadn't quite reached them, but she stopped short. 'Oh, I see.' It was obvious that she realized Eddie's exit was completely unexpected. 'I'm sorry,' she added more gently.

Jan stifled her scowl and sighed. 'Yes, so am I. I'll have to shell out for another work rider now.'

🐎

'Who would you like to sit next to?' Annabel asked Jan on Saturday evening as they laid the table in the large conservatory she'd had built on to her pretty house in the village. Annabel had formerly rented the cottage from the late incumbent of Stanfield Manor, Victor Carey, who had also been one of Jan's owners. After his death Bel had bought the freehold from the estate and had immediately set about enlarging and improving it to suit her own needs.

'What men have you got coming?' Jan asked her.

'JCB, Patrick . . .'

'Patrick? Is that Lord Lamberhurst or whatever he's called?'

'Yes,' Annabel said a little guardedly. 'Do you want to know who else is coming?'

'Go on, then.'

'Toby Waller and, just to add a little Irish flavour, guess who else?'

'Not A.D.?'

'That might have been fun, but no. Finbar Howlett.'

'Oh good,' Jan said after a moment's thought. 'I'd like the chance to talk to him a little more; he's been riding so well for Virginia, considering the dross she's sending out.'

'Actually, it was JCB who suggested it.'

'He's a crafty bugger!' Jan laughed. 'Anyway, stick me between Finbar and Toby.'

'As long as you promise not to get poor Toby too excited,' Annabel teased.

'It's you he's interested in, not me. Toby's a lovely guy, but you'd have to say he's not exactly my type, is he?'

Toby Waller was a successful merchant banker and one of Jan's most loyal and supportive owners since he'd first sent her a horse the previous year. He had several horses of his own and had persuaded some friends to form syndicates to buy a couple more. He had also appointed himself Jan's professional adviser. It was he who had galvanized his London lawyers into dealing with Harold Powell's skulduggery, and had forced reparation from the dishonest auctioneer under the threat of protracted legal proceedings and the resultant bad publicity.

Toby, though rich, popular, likeable and clever, was not a physically attractive man and Jan felt slightly sorry for him now, having to meet the undoubtedly good-looking, if somewhat bizarre, Lord Lamberhurst as a rival.

'So much for your male guests; what about women? Or are you and I supposed to handle this lot on our own?'

'Good lord, no. There's the terrible twins, Lucy and Victoria Thorndyke – they could look after a roomful of men on their own. And I hope you don't mind, but I've also asked George Gilbert and his sister.'

'Annabel!' Jan gasped. 'You've asked Virginia? You can't do that to me.'

'Why on earth not? You've got to get used to the idea that in racing everyone mixes whether they like each other or not, and sooner or later you're bound to bump into Virginia at social gatherings. You'll just have to learn to carry it off, as if there were no animosity between you. I know you'll think it's a bit two-faced, but that's the way it is.'

🐎

Johnny Carlton-Brown was the first to arrive, carrying a freezer box containing several bottles of vintage champagne. He kissed Annabel lightly on the cheek and asked her for glasses while he opened the bottles. He had just filled half a dozen glasses when Toby Waller walked in.

On the face of it, Toby and JCB were from completely different moulds. Toby's idea of good music was Gilbert and Sullivan rather than the Band of Brothers. They had, though, already met several times at the races and, in the end, they knew that they were both in business to make a profit and each respected the other's territory. The two men were also united in their admiration and support for Annabel and Jan, so they chatted together comfortably in the understated but stylish drawing room.

Annabel had become Jan's unofficial caterer, as well as her assistant trainer; she really loved putting together dinner parties and did it with great flair. 'I may as well enjoy it while I can, before I have a husband to get in the way,' she had previously told her friend.

Jan had to admit that the arrangement suited her very well. Time allowing, it was all she could do to produce a plain, old-fashioned Sunday lunch, never mind a full-blown dinner party on any other day of the week. Anyway, she'd decided Annabel's house was much better suited to the job than her own, which, however much she tidied, always seemed to be strewn with toys and bits of horse tackle.

Jan asssisted Annabel in the kitchen for a while, before going back into the drawing room to check out how their guests were getting on. She was mightily relieved that Toby was already there when George and Virginia Gilbert arrived.

Although Jan had known them all her life – insofar as the daughter of a tenant farmer could ever really know the children of her father's landlord – she had always found it difficult to connect with either of the Gilberts. George, she guessed, probably wasn't too bad, or he wouldn't be such a good friend of Eddie's and Toby's, but his sister was a completely different story. Virginia had been looking down her 'beaky' nose at Jan for as long as she could remember.

It was obvious as soon as Virginia walked in that she hadn't been expecting Jan to be at the party and she wasn't at all pleased to see her. But her annoyance was doubled when her new stable jockey walked in seconds behind her. Sharing leisure activities with her staff was not her idea of enjoyment.

Jan had no idea Bel hadn't mentioned to Virginia that Finbar would be there, but she sensed Toby had quickly picked up the hostile vibrations as she saw him move in smoothly and greet them both with equal charm.

But, despite Toby's best endeavours, Virginia continued to look foul-tempered until Lord Lamberhurst arrived, when she perked up instantly. For Virginia, the presence of anyone who appeared regularly in the gossip columns easily outweighed any undesirables, even though it was clear that Patrick Lamberhurst's preference lay elsewhere.

As she chatted to Johnny Carlton-Brown, Jan was fascinated to see the tall, languid peer lean forward to kiss Annabel with feeling, and noted Annabel's look of amused pleasure at his warm greeting.

Shortly before they were asked to take their seats, Patrick made a point of coming over to chat to Jan.

'Hello, it's good to see you again,' he said with spurious friendliness. 'I've been watching your horses more closely since I met you at the Chèvre d'Or. Is it my imagination, or do they seem somehow glossier and better fed than their competitors?'

Jan was flattered by his interest. 'I don't like sending my horses out looking like hat racks,' she said with a chuckle. 'Whether that makes them stand out from the crowd, I wouldn't like to say. Self-praise is no recommendation, my dad says.'

'They never seem to come last, though.'

'I really do try not to send my horses racing until I know they're well and ready for the job in hand!'

'It sounds a bit like our business, don't you think, Johnny?' Patrick said with a vague wave of his hand. 'Our bands have to be in good shape before we send them on the road; they have to be trained and well schooled if they're going to give a decent performance. A lot of people think bands can't play or sing properly these days and just mess around with drugs the whole time. Of course, every so often between gigs or recording sessions they can go off the rails a bit, but I can tell you most of the class acts work very hard, very hard indeed, and they're totally dedicated. Some of them are highly talented, clever guys.'

Jan nodded. 'Of course, you're right, most people don't see them like that. They couldn't begin to understand what goes on behind the scenes. Darius came up here the other week to talk about buying a horse, and he was a lot more knowledgeable about it than you could possibly imagine. So he must have done his homework.'

'Having said that, some of them put on a bit of an act, thinking back to the rebel bands of the sixties and seventies,' Patrick mused. 'But on the whole kids aren't so rebellious these days – their mums and dads did all that. Most are a great deal more professional and want to look after what they earn.'

'I never did much rebelling, nor did my dad,' Jan said.

'No, well, you're proper country folk – you haven't got time for that sort of thing. I bet your friend Annabel hasn't been much of a rebel either,' he said, subtly changing the subject.

'Actually, she is, in a way, She's had to make a positive stand against her father. Apparently he's a real tyrant.'

'Is he?' Patrick nodded with interest. 'That makes sense.'

Jan noticed that as Patrick talked he looked her straight in the eye, concentrating on her, not allowing anything going on over her shoulder to divert his attention. He seemed to be absorbing and weighing up everything she said and, she had to admit, it was rather flattering. His sparkling blue eyes hardly moved and it was hard to ignore what he was saying. Now she was beginning to understand what her best friend saw in him.

'What makes sense?' Jan asked.

'In a lot of ways Annabel seems extremely naive. When I first met her with JCB she reminded me of a startled fawn who would run away at the first bark of a dachshund. I could see she needed careful handling, but underneath all that I bet she's quite tough and has a lot of guts. I suppose she's had to build up some kind of resistance to her father if he's the little Hitler you say he is.'

'I guess you're right,' Jan replied. 'There's a great deal more to Bel than you see at first glance. She's an incredibly good friend to me, a perfect assistant and she's nobody's bloody fool either. She will always stand her ground if we disagree about anything, but she doesn't make a personal battle out of it, so, more often than not, we end up with the right solution.'

Patrick nodded. 'I know she's had a great time at your place and learnt a lot that'll be invaluable when she moves on.'

'I don't think she's planning on going elsewhere for the foresee-able future,' Jan said, with a hint of coolness.

Patrick gave her an easy smile. 'Sorry – didn't mean to tread on toes, but obviously she's not going to be working as your assistant for ever. There are other things in life to be considered.'

Jan bit back a riposte. Patrick was right, of course, but Jan had always avoided the question of what would happen when Annabel decided to move on. Besides, it was up to her to decide and was no one else's business. 'One thing's for sure, Bel's got the racing bug and that's very hard to shake off,' Jan confirmed.

At dinner Jan sat beside Finbar Howlett, as she had requested. It turned out Finbar was excellent company; if he thought there was anything strange about sitting down to eat with two wealthy owners and two rival trainers who were known not to be on speaking terms, he didn't show it. Jan couldn't be sure whether he was simply too innocent to be aware of the tension or sophisticated enough to see it and take it in his stride.

He talked openly about riding for Jan and from time to time she caught Virginia throwing suspicious glances down the table.

'Mr Carlton-Brown tells me Miller's Lodge is coming to you – is that right?' he asked, wide-eyed.

Jan glanced at Virginia, who thankfully was totally absorbed in conversation with Patrick. 'If that's what he's told your boss.'

'I think he has, Mrs Hardy. I was hoping I might be able to go on riding him.'

'JCB's already mentioned that and of course, if you're free, I'll make sure you do.'

'There's a lot of other horses in your yard I wouldn't mind a crack at.'

'I expect there are and maybe we could give it a try, but I have to say it will probably be inviting all-out war between our yards if you start riding out for me. Virginia and I are not the best of friends, you know.'

Finbar frowned at her, as if she'd just told him how to tie up his shoelaces. 'So I've heard – before I left Ireland even.'

'Ah,' Jan said, thinking she ought to be used to the way information travelled around the incestuous world of racing. 'Who told you?'

'Sean McDonagh; he's an old friend of my dad's. He thinks I would be a lot better off riding your horses.'

8

As usual, Reg and Mary knew Eddie had gone away before Jan and the children arrived for lunch at Riscombe the next day. The rural grapevine always signalled bad news from village to village as fast as hilltop beacons.

At first all their attention was focused on Matty riding his new pony. Since Rocket had arrived, Matty had been over several times for sessions with Reg, who treated the young boy with infinite patience and demanded minimal progress. As a result, Matty was beginning to gain confidence and found he was actually enjoying his new-found sport.

'Keep your heels down!' Jan called across the paddock.

Her father spun round. 'For heaven's sake, leave him to me, Jan! It was all those bollockings you gave him that put him off before. He's doing fine; I'll worry about the little details as and when he's ready for 'em.'

'All right, Dad, keep your hair on,' Jan said remorsefully. 'I'll leave it to you. At least he seems to have fun when you're around.'

'The thing is, Jan, he can't cope with his fear of losing control of the pony, and you bawling instructions to him ain't no good until he's settled.'

'I don't bawl,' Jan said indignantly.

Mary nodded. 'You do sometimes, dear, a bit. I know you don't mean to, but it's probably because you're having to deal with all those horses outside in the strong winds and such.'

After the reprimand Jan kept quiet, but she was secretly delighted by Matty's growing confidence.

Over lunch Mary asked her tentatively why Eddie had left. Jan guessed her mother had already heard several versions of the story, and thought it best to tell her exactly what had happened.

🐎

In spite of their best efforts, her mother's genuine sympathy and Annabel's well-meant party had achieved little in raising Jan's spirits after Eddie's abrupt departure for Australia.

By Sunday night, after she had tucked her children into bed and read them both a story, Jan sat down in front of the television and tried to pretend she wasn't missing her lover. Alone and full of emotion she switched on the TV set, but she could see nothing as her eyes filled with tears. She wondered what she had done to deserve such a blow. She felt betrayed and abandoned. 'God, please tell me why this had to happen,' she whispered to herself.

She hadn't asked Eddie to come to Dublin, but he had; everything had been magical for the few short weeks that followed. Suddenly it had all been whisked away from her, now she wished A.D. hadn't bothered to interfere in her personal life. 'This whole, bloody, tragic mess is all down to him,' she muttered.

Jan leaned back on the sofa racked with a mixture of emotions – betrayal, rejection and battered pride. Unexpectedly the telephone on the table beside her rang.

Gritting her teeth, she snatched it up.

'Hello?' she grunted brusquely.

'Jan, Jan, is that you?' The deep, soft voice oozed sympathy. 'I'm *so* sorry to hear young Eddie's flitted off again. But I'm sure he'll be back as soon as he's sorted out his troubles.'

'Are you really sorry, A.D.?'

'As a matter of fact, Jan, I am. But,' he paused, 'the problem seems to be how long is the piece of string?'

'Look, A.D., if you'd never got him over for the Irish National, I wouldn't be in this position now. And I'd be no worse off than I was three weeks ago, which wasn't too bad, despite what some people might think.'

'And now you feel like the kid who's had her birthday cake taken away.'

Instantly Jan's hackles rose. 'Please, don't patronize me, A.D. This situation's a bit more important than a bloody birthday cake.'

'I know, I'm sorry – bad metaphor. But you're tough, Jan, and I do know how you're feeling. I always thought young Eddie was the perfect foil for you because, in many ways, he's exactly your opposite, a real counterbalance. But don't fret, I'm positive he'll be back before long.'

'Well, maybe I'll have moved on by then. Anyway, A.D., whatever happens, I don't want it to be because you've . . .' she paused, not wanting to be rude.

'Interfered?' he suggested.

'Let's say "taken the initiative". I do realize the reason Eddie's back in Australia is because, whatever else he is, he's not a complete bastard.'

'Yeah, I'll buy that. And don't worry, I have no intention of getting involved in your love life ever again. But I am over in the UK next week – business in London. Could you ever get up there to meet me for dinner? I'll send a car, if you like.'

Jan's mind went blank. The idea of a tête-à-tête with A.D. at this particular moment did not appeal to her, but he was still the biggest owner in the yard and business was business.

'I expect that'll be OK. Which day?'

'Is Galway Fox running at Newbury next Friday, as we planned?'

'Unless we have a torrential downpour or something goes wrong at home, which can happen, as you know.'

'Good. I won't be able to come and watch, but I'll have a car pick you up from there after racing and run you home later. I'll see you then. God bless, Jan. Take care.'

🐎

Late on Friday evening, following Galway Fox's race at Newbury, the driver of the Merc A.D. had sent to collect Jan pulled into the heart of Mayfair and parked outside Harry's Bar. He leaped out swiftly and pulled open the car door for her.

Inside the discreet but bustling establishment, which seemed to smell of money, Jan was expected. She had the impression that no guest of Mr O'Hagan's would be allowed to feel insignificant or uncared for.

Mr O'Hagan, she was told, had not yet arrived, but she was shown to a large table laid for two beneath a fine painting which, from the knowledge Eddie had given her, looked like a Munnings.

I wonder if that's real, she thought, as she glanced round at the other tables and their apparently wealthy occupants. She mused on the odds against a small tenant farmer's daughter like her ending up being cosseted and treated with deference in a place like this.

When A.D. arrived, calmly moving through the room like the bow wave of an ocean liner, he motioned to her not to get up, then leaned down to kiss her on both cheeks. The next moment he was sitting down opposite her, regarding her with proprietorial fondness.

'I was just wondering,' Jan said, continuing her train of thought, 'if the reason I'm sitting in this restaurant at an important table with a famous billionaire is because I've been lucky or because I've been clever.' As A.D. was about to answer, Jan smiled and put a hand up. 'And don't tell me it's all thanks to you because I know you don't do favours for nothing.'

'I was only going to say, Jan, that you're here for both reasons. And I'm a firm believer that you can improve your luck with dedication and hard work. But before we talk about that, let's order. The grills here are the best in London.'

Jan was always slightly amused at the way A.D. treated her as though she were an equal, and at the same time as though she were his slightly wayward daughter. It was charming and, as he no doubt intended, quite disarming. During the year or so that she had known A.D. O'Hagan Jan had studied him closely and she felt she was beginning to understand how he operated. She knew, for instance, that he always preferred to bring people round to his point of view rather than use his authority or buying power as a blunt instrument. Unless someone clearly understood the reasoning behind a particular order or instruction, he didn't believe he could rely on them to perform it correctly.

Therefore, Jan had concluded, if people did as he asked only out of fear of disobeying him, rather than from the conviction that it was the right thing to do, he quietly dispensed with their services. And this was the reason Jan had been so worried that, when she turned down his offer to back her, he would drop her as his trainer. The fact he hadn't done so showed her how much he valued her contribution to his racing activities.

For the first part of the meal, they talked about Galway Fox's victory in the low-grade ten-furlong handicap that afternoon. Albeit a modest win, it was the first on the flat for both the horse and Jan, meriting, in A.D.'s eyes, a minor celebration. It wasn't until Jan was halfway through her tender steak that he brought up his proposition again.

'Jan, you know I feel sure Eddie will be back. My grounds for saying this aren't because I have some vast intelligence network that allows me to see into the inner workings of Eddie Sullivan's mind. It's simply that I know he is very, very fond of you. And, you said yourself, he's a decent fella. I just think he feels he must sort this situation out in an honourable way. But I do have cause for thinking, in time, he will feel he's done all he can and return to you. However, time marches on – a year lost now could have a significant effect on your long-term career.'

'A.D., if you're going to try and persuade me to move to this bigger yard, forget it. Eddie's got nothing to do with my decision. He didn't want to be involved in the first place; he's got his own career. Obviously I was glad to have his help – it was free for a start – but I wouldn't want to be his boss or his business partner, either. My reasons for not accepting your generous offer are the same now as they were two weeks ago.'

'But, Jan, please don't be so hasty; think about this. Building up a successful training establishment on your own in the very competitive world of racing is always going to be a hell of a challenge: there'll be highs and lows; triumphs, for sure, but disasters too. To shoulder that emotional burden alone won't be easy, and that's where Eddie comes into the equation.'

'Well, I was doing fine before you brought him back into my life and I'm determined I'll do it again. I'll cut the grass verges with nail scissors if I have to.'

A.D. took a mouthful of claret before leaning back in his deeply upholstered chair. 'God, you are a fighter, aren't you, Mrs Hardy,' he said admiringly. 'You know I want to send you more horses, but I'm just not prepared to until I feel you have the set-up you need to do them justice. And yet – ' he raised an eyebrow – 'do you really value your independence more than the security my money can provide?'

'A.D., I really do, and that's a fact.' Jan grinned at him. 'But will you promise me that if you ever come to my yard and think it's finally reached your high standards, you'll send me some more?'

A.D. nodded. 'Jan, you know I will. And that's a firm promise.'

Jan didn't doubt that if she ever found herself with an equine swimming pool, a horse walker, plus an all-weather gallop of her own and the capacity A.D. seemed to consider essential for a yard to be entrusted with a dozen or so more of his horses, he would send them to her, provided of course they hadn't fallen out over something else in the meantime. Now as she reviewed the list of horses she expected to have in training the following August, even allowing for the Band of Brothers and the other firm orders for new horses, she calculated she'd still be short of the thirty she needed for the yard to operate viably in its present form.

She reflected dolefully that A.D. had been quite right when he'd intimated she still needed Eddie's shoulder to lean on from time to time. On a gloomy Monday morning, with little racing for the month ahead, and even less prospect of a winner, she was feeling his absence keenly. If Eddie had been there, she would have shared her worries with him, and he would have told her to be more patient and stop fussing – autumn would be here soon enough and the yard would be alive and bustling again.

Only six horses had been exercised that morning, and Jan's despair hadn't dissipated one iota when, shortly after ten, she looked up from her desk in the office and saw an unfamiliar car pull into the parking area.

Her first reaction was that the long, thin, balding man didn't match the red Porsche from which he had just emerged. It wasn't that he was too old – in his early forties, Jan guessed – more that he looked far too serious and conscious of his own importance to be interested in anything as trivial as driving fast cars.

As usual, Jan stored the impression at the back of her mind as she walked out of her office to greet him.

He shook her hand mechanically. 'Mrs Hardy? I'm John Tanner. I represent Gary West.'

Neither name meant anything to Jan. 'How can I help you?'

Tanner was evidently affronted that she wasn't expecting him and she obviously hadn't heard of his principal. 'I phoned earlier,' he said a little peevishly. 'I told the paddy who answered I was on my way to Worcester for a business meeting and I'd be calling in. He said fine and he'd tell you. I hope your communication system is usually better than this.'

Jan rolled her eyes up at the blotchy sky. 'I'm sorry. Declan suffers from chronic memory failure and he's not really supposed to answer the phone. But,' she went on with a smile, looking directly at her visitor, 'he's a brilliant work rider. Anyway, you're very welcome.'

Tanner pursed his lips. 'I'm glad to hear it,' he grunted. 'Maybe I'd better enlighten you. Mr West is one of the biggest individual shipowners in the southern hemisphere and is a major player on the Far East stock exchanges as well as London. He doesn't spend a lot of time in the UK and I am his personal representative here.'

In other words, Jan thought, *you're a rich man's gofer.*

'I see,' she said out loud, 'that's interesting. And why have you come to see me?'

'As you may well know, Mr West has a large amount of bloodstock in Australia . . .'

The mention of Australia pitched Eddie right to the forefront of her mind, but the man's pomposity was beginning to aggravate her. 'I'm sorry, I didn't know,' she said. 'I'm afraid I don't know too much about foreign flat racing and even less about it in Australia.'

Tanner looked scornful at her ignorance. 'I see,' he said. 'That's disappointing, but it probably needn't concern us too much.' Despite his expensive clothing and flash car, he had the mannerisms of someone who had started on the bottom rung of the ladder and was now anxious to jettison cumbersome social baggage from his earlier days. But despite his best efforts, he'd been unable to lose completely his Liverpudlian twang.

Jan had always been proud of what she was and where she'd come from and she wasn't at all impressed.

'Although he's not here very often, when he does come over in the winter months Mr West likes our British National Hunt racing and he's decided to invest in some top-class horses, including mares to breed from eventually.'

'Is he doing this because he thinks he'll make money out of it?' Jan asked, clearly implying how unlikely that was.

'No, of course not. He knows all about that side of things from his extensive operations in Australia.'

'I see, so he just wants to enjoy the sport? Is that the nub of the matter?'

Tanner inclined his head and allowed the hint of a smile to stress the understatement he was about to make. 'He does rather enjoy having a bit of a financial interest when they run.'

'If that's the case, I don't know why he's sent you here. I run a totally straight yard and I won't fiddle a race for anyone.'

'Mrs Hardy, he doesn't expect or want you to do anything like that.'

Jan looked him straight in the eye for a moment, summing him up. 'Hmm,' she murmured. 'You'd better come into the office.'

As he seated himself on a rickety bentwood chair on the other side of Jan's desk, one leg crossed fastidiously over the other, she pulled out a pen and a clean sheet of paper, on which she wrote 'Gary West'.

'What is Mr West's full name?' she asked.

'Garfield Ernest West. You'll find most of his particulars in the *International Who's Who.*'

'What precisely would he like me to do?'

'By and large he's left the details up to me,' Tanner said importantly, 'and for practical purposes you can think of me as the owner, although the horses will be registered under the name of a Jersey company of which I'm a director.'

'That shouldn't be a problem.'

'If I decide to use your services, we shall want you to buy us one or two youngsters and four or five good-quality, proven horses ready to run next autumn, preferably already qualified for the bigger races in the jumping calendar.'

'Both chases and hurdles?' Jan asked.

'Yes. Obviously, we're interested in successful young hurdlers who might develop into top-class chasers.'

'Seven top-class horses could easily cost you a million pounds, maybe more. Does the company have that sort of money available?'

'Of course,' Tanner nodded. 'We did do a little homework before coming to see you,' he added sarcastically.

Jan looked at the man more closely. There wasn't much about him that appealed to her, but she was beginning to like what he was saying. Nevertheless, her natural cynicism held her in check; the few years she'd already spent in this business had taught her never to treat an order as confirmed until the money was safely lodged in the bank.

'It might take some time to find that many really good animals. But there are a couple of sales coming up, and we could ask around. Maybe we'll have to use a bloodstock agent, which will add five or ten per cent to the cost, depending on which one we choose.'

'The ultimate decision must rest with you,' Tanner said firmly. 'We could have placed our order with an agent in the first instance, but it's your judgement and expertise we want.'

Jan couldn't help feeling gratified, but she tried not to let it show. Tanner, she guessed, was an accountant and would have to be handled like one. 'OK, that's fine. There'll be a lot of work involved sifting through pedigrees, form and so on, and I don't intend to spend any of my scarce time without a firm commitment and a reasonable deposit to cover my costs. If I've spent a lot of time working on your behalf and then you or your Mr West suddenly change your mind and decide to go in for ballet dancers or something, I'll still send you a bill for my services. I'm sure you'll find that acceptable.'

Tanner was shaking his head. 'Listen, Mrs Hardy, let's get one thing clear. I haven't driven all the way out here because I've got nothing better to do or to tell you a fairy story. We know what we want to do and we've got the money to do it.'

'Who else have you asked? I'm sure I'm not the only trainer you've considered.'

'No, of course you're not, but we wanted a smaller yard; we felt that we'd get more personal attention and more loyalty, you might say, than we would with one of the very big trainers.'

Where have I heard that before? Jan said to herself, thinking of the Sharps and all their promises. 'As long as you remember loyalty's a two-way street,' she said. 'So let's recap: five to seven horses of varying ages, let's say four to nine, and a couple of females. As I've already said, I can't guarantee that I'd have that many suitable horses by August, though obviously I'd try my hardest. What's more, I can't promise to perform miracles, but I can promise to give you a square deal and do my best for you, Mr Tanner.'

'That's all we want, Mrs Hardy, but before I confirm my instructions in writing, I'll need to have a look round your set-up and see the facilities for myself and that you've got enough space.'

'That's fair enough; in fact, I always insist on it myself. We're not racing today. As you probably know, jump racing begins to quieten down a bit now, though we like to keep a few on the go. We had a runner on the flat last week.'

'Yes, I saw – Galway Fox for A.D. O'Hagan, wasn't it? It ran really well.'

Jan shrugged. 'Well, it wasn't much of a race, to be honest. Still, at least he was the best of a bad bunch. We may run a few more during the summer. It keeps the place ticking over and gives the staff a bit of an interest.'

Getting to her feet, she led her potential client from her office, warming to his proposal, while remembering that owners came in all shapes and sizes. She reminded herself what they'd all thought of Bernie Sutcliffe when he first came to the yard and how eventually they'd become rather fond of him. Although, she had to admit to herself, Tanner looked a different proposition altogether.

As they went round the yard, Jan stopped to introduce him to any staff who were around. Annabel wasn't there, though; she'd gone to pick up supplies from the vet, and the two Irish boys were having a fortnight's holiday back in Wicklow.

Jan and Tanner were just making their way back from the gallops and schooling grounds when Annabel's new convertible shot up the drive. She leaped out and jogged down to meet them.

'This is Annabel Halstead, my assistant. Bel, this is Mr Tanner, who's considering buying six or seven horses.'

'Or maybe more. Pleased to meet you.' Tanner offered her his pale and beautifully manicured limp hand. 'I hope you don't mind me saying so, but you look very young to be left in charge of all these valuable horses when Mrs Hardy's away at the races or the sales.' As he spoke, he reddened slightly.

Annabel noticed and took it in her stride. 'I don't mind at all. It's always a treat when people think we're younger than we are.' She smiled serenely.

'Annabel is the mainstay of my yard,' Jan said firmly. 'She's worked with me for years and I should tell you, Mr Tanner, that trainers have to be as good at judging people as they are at judging stock. It's no good having a yard full of beautiful horses if you've got a bunch of plonkers looking after them.'

'I was only thinking of her experience,' Tanner said hastily, trying to justify himself. 'She looks so frail.'

'Was there anything else you wanted to know about our set-up, Mr Tanner?' Jan said curtly.

'Well, yes, a couple of things. How do you operate during a wet winter without an all-weather gallop?'

'We've managed without one so far.'

'Maybe, but you'll have a lot more horses using your grass gallop if we send our new purchases to you. Which brings me to my next point: unless you're going to remove some of the horses you had here last season, you're going to need more stables as well.'

'That's in hand,' Jan said. 'We're putting another building across, there.' She waved her hand at the near end of the yard, currently enclosed only by a post-and-rail fence. 'Eddie . . .' She stopped herself. 'Gerry, our builder, is planning to do it right now.'

Tanner nodded. 'OK, fine, but I think we'd prefer it if you also installed an all-weather gallop. Will you be able to do that?'

'Well, we have been considering it,' Jan replied, 'but like everything else, Mr Tanner, it's a matter of finance.'

'Bear in mind, you'll be getting substantially more in training fees over the next few years. So it makes financial sense and would also be an asset,' Tanner added, with a smile which Jan guessed was deceptive in its blandness.

🐎

Roz came out to join Jan and Annabel as they watched the sleek red car creep down the track to the road.

'Cor, what a complete dickhead!' she exclaimed, voicing the others' view.

'Do you think he's serious, though?' Annabel asked more practically.

Jan shrugged. 'I dunno. You occasionally get these Walter Mittys who go round pretending they are a big cheese and getting a kick out of it, but he openly admitted he's the organ grinder's monkey.'

'Well, he wasn't behaving like the monkey.'

'That's because the organ grinder's not watching, presumably.'

'What the bloody hell are you two talking about?' Roz asked plaintively.

'I've heard ducks fart under water before,' Jan chortled. 'He says he represents an Australian shipping tycoon called Gary West . . .'

'Ooh yes, I've heard of him! It was in the papers – he's been going out with that American film star.'

'Oh God,' Jan groaned. 'That's all we need. A billionaire Aussie Romeo.'

'Sounds a bit of a challenge.' Annabel grinned.

'Still, having just told A.D. I don't want him to move me into a new yard, we desperately need someone to replace the Sharps and help out with our finances. So if this bloke wasn't talking complete bullshit, I reckon Mr West could be just what we need. But I think I'd like to meet the man himself before we all get too excited.'

🐎

Toby Waller came to see Jan at the weekend. It was another quiet Saturday with only two runners going to the afternoon meeting at Stratford, one of them a talented mare called Gale Bird. Toby had bought her from Jan the year before and she had got off to a good start novice chasing, with a second at Worcester in Jan's first race of the season, followed by a win at Chepstow soon afterwards. By Christmas it had become clear that the mare didn't like too much give in the ground, so Jan and Toby decided to keep her ticking over and bring her out for some summer racing.

The race at Stratford was a qualifier for one of the big novice chases and it included a number of well-rated horses, who also liked fast ground, running for a prize of ten thousand pounds.

Toby was in ebullient mood as he drove Jan to the race track in the comfort of his new leather-seated Range Rover.

Once they had settled into the journey, he asked her about A.D. 'What was the outcome of your session with him last week?'

'I still said "no".'

'Was that wise?'

Jan chuckled. 'I suppose I'll be able to tell you in ten years' time, still I feel a lot better for making the decision – rightly or wrongly.'

'Are you sure you won't have an awful struggle to keep the numbers up, though?'

'If you'd asked me that a few days ago, I'd have said we were going to be fine. Last Monday we had a visit from a strange, bald bloke driving a Porsche, who told me his boss wanted me to buy several good-class horses for him. Against my better judgement I was beginning to feel quite excited about it. Unfortunately, I haven't heard a squeak from him since.'

'But that's only five days ago,' Toby said. 'Presumably this chap had to report back to his boss. Who was it by the way?'

'Someone called Gary West.'

Toby took his eyes off the road long enough to turn and look at Jan in amazement. 'Gary West – the Australian Gary West?' he exclaimed.

Jan nodded. 'That's the one. Do you know anything about him?'

'Not a lot; mostly what I've read in the newspapers, though a couple of friends of mine have had some dealings with him. He's a heavyweight in the shipping world – what the tabloids call a "colourful" character, which usually means somone who has a pretty high-profile sex life and runs his businesses in a fairly unconventional manner.'

'Is he rich?'

'Oh yes – he's rich all right. Only God knows how much he's really worth. It probably varies by several million from day to day. He started out when he was twenty, inheriting a small shipping company which ran ferries from Melbourne to Hobart. Now he's got a fleet of supertankers; he owns several massive marinas in Australia and the States – he's one of those guys who seems to be into absolutely everything. How the hell he keeps tabs on it all I've no idea, though he must employ some very high-powered people as well.'

'Don't you think it's rather odd he's interested in owning a few jumpers over here?'

'No, not really. I think he's quite an anglophile and he probably thinks National Hunt racing epitomizes the English way of life and its sporting values. I'd say he'd be a pretty good owner.'

'Well, that's great, except this chap Tanner hasn't been back since. I haven't even had a phone call from him.'

'I'm sure it would take time to sort it all out. But I'll do some research on Mr T and Gary West's horses in Australia if you like. Jan, I do hope if you take him on, and with A.D. already having at least six with you, we small-time owners aren't going to get ignored.'

'Oh, don't be silly, Toby, of course you won't. That's one of the reasons why I didn't want to go along with A.D.'s great scheme. I like paddling my own canoe.'

'And you also don't like being told what to do,' Toby added with a wry smile.

🐎

As Emma led the beautifully groomed Gale Bird into the pre-parade ring at the small Midland course, Jan looked on proudly. She knew the racing public expected to see her horses among the best turned out.

'She looks great,' Toby said appreciatively.

'Handsome is as handsome does,' Jan answered cautiously. 'But I'm fairly sure she's going to like the track here.'

He nodded. Earlier they had both been out onto the course,

where Toby dug in his heel and noted it had only penetrated the first half-inch of turf. 'She wouldn't want it any firmer than this, would she?' he had asked.

Danny Morris, the bright, up and coming young jockey Jan had booked in Murty McGrath's absence, strode up to them in the parade ring and touched his helmet politely.

'Have you seen this mare run before?' Jan asked.

The young West Countryman nodded. 'I looked at the video you told me to. I saw she made all the running at Chepstow and won very comfortably.'

'Right. Don't bustle her, though. Just let her reach the front in her own time. You may need to give her a reminder once you're over the last, though, as she may try pulling your leg.'

Jan was feeling quietly confident as she watched the compact bay mare bounce out onto the course.

Gale Bird jumped away from the start and settled in the middle of the fifteen-runner field. Danny Morris held her there, travelling comfortably for the first mile of the two-mile race. Passing the stands just before the next plain fence, she had closed on the leader.

The first horse fumbled it, letting Gale Bird move easily into the lead. She was still in cruise as she approached the home straight for the second time, and landed three lengths clear over the last, but the jockey on the following horse seemed to sense that Gale Bird was beginning to idle and decided it was worth making a final assault.

Jan had been keeping her fingers crossed that this wouldn't happen, but Danny Morris was ready when the other horse's head drew alongside. He gave Gale Bird a neat backhanded slap along her rump, without any effect. He gave her another.

'That's enough!' Jan hissed between clenched teeth, knowing it would take a moment or two for the mare to realize what it was she was being asked.

Danny raised his whip higher and gave her a strong forehand swipe, and then another.

'For Christ's sake!' Jan hissed. 'He'll be for it. Oh no!' she groaned as the jockey hit the mare vigorously, twice more, even as they were pulling away from the challenger. She looked at Toby.

'I'm really sorry. I told him to give her a reminder, not a thrashing. I'll bloody kill him!'

Toby nodded grimly. 'Jan, I don't want him riding her ever again, even if they do win today.' His voice rose a few notes. 'And they're going to! There's a good girl, Gale Bird!' he yelled gleefully at the top of his voice as his horse passed the post a length in front.

Once the initial excitement of the win had passed, Toby turned to Jan. 'God, she ran well, but I'm sure she didn't need all that whipping. If the stewards punish the jockey for excessive use, will they take the race away?'

'No, no, they won't, but I'm really sorry about the way Danny rode her. He's normally a very competent jockey and hungry – a bit too hungry, perhaps. But listen, Toby, don't get involved. I'll deal with it. He probably doesn't even know how many times he hit her. I'm sure he simply got carried away in the heat of the moment.'

'Even so, he's a professional – he *should* know exactly what he's doing every second of the race.'

'OK, but don't let it spoil the win for you. I'm sure she's fine, she ran a super race and Danny Morris will probably be in a lot worse shape when I've finished with him.'

The jockey was given a three-day ban by the stewards for his over-zealous riding, but Gale Bird was confirmed as a worthy winner of the competitive chase.

'What do you think?' Toby asked in the car on the way back to Stanfield. 'A potential Champion Chaser?'

'We've a long way to go before that, but as a matter of fact, I think she could go at least another half-mile, if not more. You saw how easily she was going today after two miles.'

'That would be fun. Gosh, I'm glad I let myself get talked into having these horses with you, Jan. It made the winter go by so much faster, for one thing. Flamenco's come on wonderfully and I think we'll have some real fun with him next year. Look, I've decided, I do want another youngster, and I'm thinking we might get something else at Fairyhouse this year. Only up the ante a bit.'

'Suits me,' Jan said, lightly. 'What sort of money do you want to spend?'

'Fifty maybe? What do you think?'

'We should certainly get something good for that,' Jan nodded with a grin. 'Mmm, I'm rather looking forward to my second trip to Fairyhouse.'

9

Jan sat beside Annabel in the deep tapestried recesses of a large Knole sofa in the flagstoned hall of the Manoir du Chèvre d'Or.

An expressionless waiter walked silently towards them.

'What would you like to drink, *mesdames?*'

'I suppose a pint of bitter's out of the question?' Jan said, trying to keep a straight face as Annabel started to giggle.

'I am sorry, we have no beer,' the waiter answered solemnly in a strong French accent. 'Champagne? A cocktail?'

'A vodka and tonic for me,' Jan replied innocently.

'And I'll have a Campari and soda,' Annabel said, trying to be demure.

The waiter nodded and they watched him glide away through a distant gothic arch.

'Jan, why did Tanner want to meet us here for dinner?' Annabel asked.

'When he phoned me on Monday, he asked which was the most expensive restaurant in the Cotswolds. I said this place, as far as I knew; he didn't even ask what the food was like.'

'I thought it was fantastic when JCB had that party here for Ben.'

'It was,' Jan agreed, 'but it just shows what type of man Tanner is, if all he cares about is how much something costs. Still, it's not his money he's spending, I suppose.'

'Come on, Jan, at least he got back in touch with you. You were worried he wasn't going to, weren't you?'

'Yes. Now I'm not so sure I'm pleased he did.'

'What are you talking about? You *need* an owner like Gary West. Does it really matter if his sidekick is a bit of a shonker.'

'No, I suppose not. Then again I don't want someone coming in the yard who thinks they can push us around and I didn't like the way he implied you were too young and frail to be my assistant. If he tried to force me to get an older bloke in, I'd tell him to take his horses and stuff them where a monkey stuffs its nuts.'

'I'm sure he'd wouldn't do that, but if someone gives you an order for six or seven horses, you have to expect them to be a bit uppity – and, frankly, you'll just have to learn to handle it. You didn't go into this business because you wanted a few nice friends to play with, did you?'

'OK, OK,' Jan conceded, grateful, not for the first time, that she had Annabel to keep her feet firmly on the ground and give her another perspective. 'Anyway, things are looking up with or without Mr Tanner. Supercall's much better and even our old friend Bernie's given me written instructions to find him another horse.'

'You're going to be awfully busy.'

'I know. If Gary West comes up trumps, I'm definitely going to have to get on with the extra stables.'

'You've been saying that for months, though.'

'Maybe I have,' Jan admitted. 'It's just that I'm worried about borrowing more money and finding I'm out of my depth, which is all too easy these days. Look how many racehorse trainers and other small businesses go under each year.'

'If you want more horses, you haven't got much choice – that is, unless you take up A.D.'s offer.'

'Bel, you know I'm not going to, so why keep bringing it up? But – ' Jan paused as the waiter returned with their drinks – 'it just all seemed a lot easier when Eddie was here.'

'Jan, don't give me that. Now I know you're exaggerating. All Eddie ever did was listen; he refused to voice his opinions, which I always thought was a cop-out. Besides, he was only back here for six weeks, and you did manage to get through the previous years pretty damn well without him.'

'Well, that's your opinion, but he was going to look after the building project while I concentrated on training the horses. I don't want to get my arse caught between two stools.'

'You know Gerry can do that just as well – better probably, considering he's actually a builder in his own right.'

'All right, all right.' Jan frowned at Annabel's persistence. 'Let's just listen to what Tanner has to say first. Though, I must say, I'm not impressed with his time-keeping.'

🐎

When Tanner eventually arrived, nearly half an hour after he'd arranged to meet them, he made no attempt to apologize.

He walked through the front door into the medieval hall and handed his car keys to the doorman without looking at him. 'It's right outside,' he said curtly, already turning away to the two women, who were watching him intently.

'Hello, Jan.' He shook her hand as feebly as he had last time. 'And Annabel.' His body language conveyed as clearly as if he had bellowed it across the room that he found Annabel very attractive. 'Oh good, I see you've got a drink – you chose whatever you wanted, I hope?' he asked, as if they were small children he was treating to an ice cream.

'Yes, we did, thank you,' Jan said politely. 'We've been here quite a while.'

Tanner ignored the implicit rebuke. 'Nice place this,' he said, looking around with approval at the stags' heads and suits of armour which the owners had used to add grandeur to the surroundings.

The waiter reappeared like a genie from a lamp and hovered beside Tanner, who sat down heavily in an armchair near the sofa and put his feet on the oak coffee table. 'Can you get us some champagne?' he asked.

Without asking him to specify which label, the waiter nodded and melted away.

Tanner looked at his guests with relish, almost licking his lips. 'I always like a bit of champers before business,' he said, evidently in an attempt to impress.

'I'm rather more cautious, I'm afraid, and usually wait until everything's agreed and signed,' Jan remarked.

'I'm sure we won't have any trouble there, Mrs Hardy.' Tanner grinned confidently.

'But before we get down to the nitty-gritty,' Jan replied firmly, 'we'd like to know a bit more about your boss.'

Tanner winced slightly. 'Gary West isn't my "boss".' He scratched the quotation marks in the air with his forefingers, then leaned towards his audience. 'We're more like associates. I was a young bloke working on the Baltic Exchange, dealing in oil tonnage, when he came along and asked me to join his operation. That was twenty-five years ago, and since then Southern Star Line has grown about a hundredfold. I was in on it almost from the start and I've done very nicely out of it, thank you. I've got a beautiful home in St John's Wood, a lovely villa in Sotogrande right next to the golf club and a top-of-the-range Sunseeker cruiser in Puerto Banus. You'd both be very welcome to visit them any time,' he added with an ingratiating smile. 'I've also got two beautiful girls at Roedean.' Jan sensed from a slight change in his tone that his children weren't currently giving him as much satisfaction as the villa and the boat. 'So obviously I'm more than just the office boy. Gary relies on me a great deal to look after his activities in Europe, including his racing interests – and he gives me carte blanche to make all the decisions regarding those matters.'

'But Mr West, what does he actually do?' Jan enquired.

'Gary's got fingers in more pies than you've had hot dinners,' Tanner continued. 'Mainly he's into shipping – oil tankers and cruise lines. He's also got interests in mining around the world, TV stations, shopping malls – oh yeah, and yacht marinas. He's got a string of holding companies, which he uses to buy and sell large chunks of equity in anything that takes his fancy. If you read your *FT* regularly, you'd know he's recently been involved in a few mergers and acquisitions of British companies.'

'Is that what they call asset stripping?' Annabel asked innocently.

Tanner laughed. 'Yes, when we get the chance – but people got wise to that when it was all going on back in the seventies and there aren't the same opportunities now.'

'So why is Mr West so interested in getting involved in National Hunt racing here?' Jan persisted.

'Like I've already told you, he's been to the races a lot here in England as a guest, and he likes the way it's done. And he likes a flutter too; so he wants to take a better position himself. He'll happily spend up to a million on it.' Tanner shrugged. 'That's petty cash to us, but you must understand we do like value for money.'

Toby had assured Jan that, as far as he knew – and he'd asked around extensively – Gary West was a very wealthy man indeed. Nothing Tanner was saying conflicted with what she had already heard, but Jan had a gut feeling there was something about him that didn't quite fit.

Nevertheless, she wasn't in business to make new friends, and if Toby thought these people were sound for the money, she had no choice but to believe it.

As Tanner finished his eulogy, the waiter returned with a bottle in an ice bucket and three tall champagne flutes, which he filled and placed on the table. Tanner reached forward, picked one up and raised it as though the deal was done.

Annabel remained sitting primly, legs neatly crossed, and made no attempt to respond.

Jan ignored the drink and leaned forward to look more closely at her prospective owner. 'I guess you've made a decision. So what have you decided you want us to do?'

'I'm prepared to give you an order to buy six horses on behalf of Harlequin Holdings Ltd, who will be responsible for all training fees, and the running of the horses; the company will receive any prize money they win. As discussed, you'll have a bank guarantee for up to a million pounds to purchase them, but I'll need to approve each one in writing beforehand.'

'That could be a bit tricky,' Jan said quickly. 'If I'm at a sale and you're not there, or if an agent rings me and tips me off before an animal comes on the open market, they're bound to want a quick decision.'

'All right,' Tanner said testily. 'I may give you carte blanche – I'll have to let you know.'

When you've asked the organ grinder, Jan concluded to herself.

'I will also need you to put in a proper all-weather gallop, and I want assurances that you'll have sufficient quality stabling for these extra horses by the time they arrive.'

'Do you still want me to get an older, male assistant trainer?' Jan asked dryly.

Tanner laughed. 'You're very touchy women, you two, aren't you? No, I've reconsidered and I'm more than happy about that side of things.'

'That's good of you,' Jan said more lightly than she felt. 'The stables are certainly going to be built, I've had a lot of enquiries and several firm orders so I will definitely need the space. But I'll have to let you know about the all-weather. I'd also like to meet Mr West before I start spending all his money for him. Then I can assure him that I'll spend it as wisely as if it was my own.'

'That won't be necessary.'

'Maybe it isn't to you, but it is to me.'

Tanner leaned back in his chair, evidently annoyed but inclined to be impressed that someone he was offering so much to was still putting barriers in his way. 'All right,' he said. 'I'll try and see if Gary has the time, but he's a very busy man.'

Jan fixed him with a gimlet eye. 'And I'm a very busy woman,' she retorted.

When Jan let herself back into the house, completely exhausted, just after midnight, Megan was still wide awake in the drawing room watching a video with Fran, who had stayed on to babysit.

'Mummy, Mummy!' the little girl whimpered sleepily, climbing off Fran's knee and rubbing her eyes. 'I was worried about you!'

'What on earth for?'

Megan looked at Fran, who stood up.

'I'll be off then, Jan. They've both been ever so good, and when Megan said she had to stay up for you I thought she might sleep in front of the TV – which you did a bit, didn't you, darling?'

'Not really.'

'Say thank you to Fran,' Jan instructed her daughter.

'Thank you, Fran – for being so kind,' Megan said truthfully.

When Fran had left, Jan sat down on the sofa and Megan jumped onto her lap.

'So, why were you worried about me?' Jan asked.

'Because . . .' Megan started, 'because you seem so unhappy, Mummy.'

'Why should I be unhappy?'

'Because you liked Eddie and now he's gone, just like Daddy,' Megan blurted quickly, as if she had to get the words out before she changed her mind.

Jan was shocked. 'Oh, Meg! My darling Megan, it's not the same. Daddy died. Eddie's only gone away for a while, I'm sure he'll come back.'

Megan shook her head. 'I don't think so, Mummy, I heard Roz and Emma talking in the tack room. They didn't know I was there, and Roz said Eddie's got a girlfriend in Australia and she's going to have a baby and he's going to marry her.'

Jan screwed up her eyes, desperate to hold back the tears.

Of course everyone knew, she told herself. She was only kidding herself when she thought they didn't. Even if she had only told Annabel – somehow details would always slip out. Maybe Eddie had confided in someone at the pub before he left.

'Darling,' she tried to say gently, 'he may have to, but I'm sure he'll come back and see us.'

'But, Mum, don't *you* want to marry him? You don't want him to marry someone else, do you?'

'If that's what he *really* wants to do, then that's what I want,' Jan answered, half truthfully. 'Now come on, Meg, bed. And don't you worry about a thing. Bel and I have just had a lovely meal with a man who wants me to buy some more horses! So we'll need our sleep.'

'Yes,' Megan said gloomily. 'And then you'll be even busier.'

Jan felt a sharp stab of guilt. It seemed she was always being torn apart by her need to earn a living to support her children, and her need to be a mother to them. 'I'll make sure I've got just as much time for you, I promise. By the way I forgot to tell you: Colonel Gilbert says he's got a pretty pony he'd like you to try. Years ago, when I was a little girl, he lent me my first pony and he was very good; he jumped like a stag.'

As Jan had anticipated, Megan's eyes lit up like stars. 'When can I ride it?'

'Soon. Colonel Gilbert says he's going to watch you riding Smarty next time there's a show.'

🐎

Satisfied that she had put Megan to bed in a happier frame of mind, Jan lay in her empty bed and tried to come to terms with the harsh decisions she had to make in her life.

Both A.D. and Eddie had already told her that, if she was as ambitious as they thought, it was essential for her to accept good horses from whoever offered them, provided they were going to pay their bills. She really couldn't afford the luxury of just picking and choosing owners whom she liked.

She had learnt to put up with Frank Jellard's foibles, and at least Tanner had taken her and Annabel to a top restaurant and hadn't stinted on the hospitality. Toby had done his checks and was confident that the set-up Tanner represented was good for the money.

Jan wondered what it was about her that made her so reluctant to trust people like Tanner.

Eventually, by about three in the morning, she'd made up her mind that she had to go ahead, and now she began to get excited about the project, which had the bonus of pushing her heartache over Eddie to one side – at least for the time being.

If it meant putting in the new gallop, which could cost her twenty-five thousand pounds or more, depending on how much groundwork had to be done by the contractor, then she would just have to borrow the money – sink or swim, she decided. After all, half a dozen more horses represented a gross income of over six thousand pounds a month. And at least Tanner hadn't quibbled over her training fees. She'd been expecting him to try to beat her down, like the Sharps had: he wouldn't have got anywhere, she thought, especially after her ghastly experience with them.

🐎

By the next weekend, after more soul-searching, Jan had made all her decisions. She had taken the bull by the horns and been to see her bank manager. She was amazed when she met no resistance to her application for a large loan to pay for the installation of an all-weather gallop and the additional stables, the main stipulation being the bank wanted a second charge on her home.

If you can make one heap of all your winnings/And risk it on one turn of pitch-and-toss, the Rudyard Kipling poem that hung in her office constantly reminded her.

She had phoned Tanner to tell him she was prepared to put in the additional facilities he had asked for, and repeated her request to meet Gary West.

She had also contacted Finbar Howlett and established that he wasn't riding for Virginia on Saturday, so she booked him to ride A.D.'s horse, Erin's Jet, in a two-mile hurdle at Worcester.

Jan took Emma with her in the lorry to the racecourse as Connor, who normally looked after the Jet, was keen to spend the afternoon in the pub watching the Epsom Derby on television with the rest of her staff. This year Jan found she couldn't work up much enthusiasm for the nation's premier flat race, especially now that A.D. had withdrawn his runner.

Erin's Jet was a small brown gelding by an Irish Derby winner out of a flat-winning dam, but A.D.'s principal Irish trainer, Dermot O'Hare, had declared early in the horse's career that it was unlikely ever to be fast enough to catch a cold.

When he'd first arrived at Edge Farm, Erin's Jet had become anorexic and it had taken Jan several months to get him ready to run, although she had managed to win a minor race with him the previous November. On his next two runs she felt sure Billy Hanks had stopped him, but she knew the Jet had enough pace for the good-to-firm ground which the riverside track offered. In the parade ring before the race Jan was quietly confident, but she didn't let it show. Finbar was manifestly delighted to be riding a horse from her yard and fixed his bright blue eyes on her as she gave him his instructions. When she had finished, he nodded in agreement as he watched the horse being led round by Emma.

'That's a very handsome little horse,' he remarked. 'And he looks like you've brought him here fit enough to win.'

'If you can make it happen, Finnie, I'm sure there'll be more chances on him – as long as Miss Gilbert can spare you, of course,' Jan said, tempting a comment.

Finbar picked up the undercurrent in her voice and glanced sharply at her but said nothing. Emma stopped and turned the horse in towards them, holding its head firmly while Jan legged the jockey into the saddle.

Finbar, though modest and self-effacing on the surface, was like a Tartar tribesman on a horse. Watching his determined manner, it was clear to Jan that if he thought his horse had a ghost of a chance, he would do everything possible to make it win. He rode with a very short stirrup, so he could position his weight over the horse's withers and drop his hands lightly on its neck.

Coming off the final left-handed bend, Finbar was lying in third place with three flights to jump. Between the obstacles, he rode like a flat jockey in a five-furlong sprint. Erin's Jet flew the last and, easing down, won by six lengths.

Jan shook her head in sheer delight that her judgement of Finbar Howlett had been so clearly vindicated. He was absolutely her type of jockey in every respect. It was just such a pity he was locked in to Virginia for next season.

The next day was Sunday and, with so few horses in, Jan was able to take a break from her work and spend some quality time with children. She packed a picnic lunch and told Megan to give Smarty a thorough brushing and to oil his feet. When the pony was ready, Jan plaited his mane and loaded him into the trailer to take him to a show a few miles the other side of Broadway, where she had arranged to meet Reg and Mary with Rocket.

It was a beautiful, blue-skied day and the show was being held in an area of manicured parkland dotted with huge, spreading oaks. As Jan had really hoped, Colonel Gilbert was there to help with the judging, along with another of her owners. Lady Fairford was a well-known, old-fashioned grande dame of the county who was besotted with her horses. She owned an old chaser called Young Willie, which Jan had trained to win a couple of good races during the previous season.

Young Willie had returned home to start his summer break and Lady Fairford, a large, enthusiastic woman, was keen to tell Jan exactly how he was doing.

'To tell you the truth,' she admitted reluctantly as they stood talking beneath the shade of one of the ancient oaks, 'although I love having him at home, he's getting rather rotund and I think he's bored too. Maybe he's missing his horsy friends.'

'You can send him back to me if you like, but I won't start doing any work with him for a couple of months at least. I don't think there's any point in running him before November.'

'Oh well, he can stay where he is then and jolly well like it! I'll just have to put him in Alcatraz, the little paddock where I keep my fat horses. Now, is your daughter going to ride that smart little chestnut pony today?'

'Yes, but I'm afraid this'll be her last summer on him; she's a little too big for him already.'

'I hope you find something good to replace him; these girls can so easily get discouraged if they're not enjoying the pony they're on, you know.'

Colonel Gilbert joined them, hearing the last part of their conversation. 'Hello, Jan. I think I mentioned to you the other day at Hereford, didn't I, that I might have the very thing for her? I'm looking forward to seeing how she goes this afternoon.'

As Jan helped Megan to tack up and Reg prepared Rocket for a leading-rein class with Matty, she reflected on the public-spiritedness of people like Colonel Gilbert, who gave so much of their spare time to the encouragement of young riders simply because they cared about the future of the sport.

Once Smarty was spruced up and ready, Jan sent Megan off to work him in for a while, to loosen him up and pop him over a couple of practice fences. She watched with obvious pride as her daughter sat with a straight back and kind, neat hands, which kept a gentle contact with her pony's mouth. There was no doubt that if her interest survived her teenage years and boyfriends, Megan had all the natural characteristics that would make her an exceptional horsewoman.

❧

Smarty and Meg performed superbly in the Working Hunter Pony class, and the judges awarded her second prize. Colonel Gilbert was apologetic to Jan as they shared the picnic later on.

'Personally I thought Megan and her pony were easily the best combination, but we felt little Fiona Mattingley needs all the encouragement she can get. I hope you don't mind – I'm sure you don't, having won so many times before.'

Jan did mind; it just wasn't fair. If Megan and Smarty had won, they'd won. When horses finished second in races they didn't get placed first just because their jockeys burst into tears. She did, however, appreciate the colonel's point of view and knew the decision hadn't been taken out of malice – quite the opposite, actually. 'We'd better not tell Megan,' Jan said to the colonel quietly.

'No, better not, but you can tell her I was very impressed indeed with her riding and I really would like her to have Monarch for the rest of the summer, to see how she gets on with him.'

'Is that the lovely brown job I saw in your paddock?'

'That's the one. He's thirteen-two in old money, I don't know what that is in new measurements – I haven't caught up with all this new-fangled Euro stuff yet. Anyway he was broken in very carefully, but I feel he still needs a good strong rider, which, of course, your Megan is.'

❧

The following Saturday morning, as Jan and her staff were finishing breakfast, Roz's cousin, Gerry Harris, drove up in his van, followed by a small lorry from the local builders' merchants, which was loaded to the gunwales with materials for the new run of stables. The concrete base had been laid at the beginning of the week and now it was dry Gerry was anxious to get on with the job of building.

Gerry was twenty-seven, single and still living at home. His main incentive for working at Edge Farm Stables was the opportunity it gave him for being close to Jan. Mistakenly, he thought nobody knew about his private obsession. He had been responsible for almost all the building work and repairs Jan had undertaken on the site since she had moved there. When she had asked him to complete the fourth side of the yard with more stables, he seemed delighted, particularly now Eddie Sullivan was out of the way.

Shortly after nine, Jan was watching the start of the work with Matty and Megan and was amazed to see Colonel Gilbert's jeep towing a trailer up the drive. She had deliberately not said much to Megan in case the pony didn't live up to the colonel's description, but she called out to Meg as he turned the Jeep into the parking area and pulled up beside Gerry's van.

'Quick, Meg! Colonel Gilbert's here with the pony for you to try,' she said. 'He told me he would last weekend after you did so well on Smarty.'

Megan looked up at her mother as if she was completely mad. 'But, Mummy, I didn't do well, I only came second.'

'Out of eighteen,' Jan reminded her. 'That's not bad. Anyway, this one's a bit bigger for you; he's a thirteen-two.'

'What can he do?'

'Not too much, yet. He's young and he's only just been broken in.'

The colonel climbed down from the Jeep and walked towards them. 'Good morning, ladies. I see you weren't joking when you said you were expanding the yard,' he said, looking around with approval at the activity. 'Anyway, if you've got time, I've brought Monarch over for you to see. I thought perhaps Megan could jump up on him so I can see how he goes?' He kissed Jan's cheek and patted the girl's blonde head.

'Would you like to do that, Meg?'

'Can I see him first?'

'Of course.' The colonel walked across to the trailer, where he lowered the front ramp, untied the head-collar rope, and unhooked the breast bar before leading the pony down.

'He looks really nice,' Megan conceded as the neat brown gelding pranced energetically at the end of the rope.

'He's no slouch, as you can see,' the colonel warned. 'Jan, his tack's in the back of the Jeep, if you wouldn't mind grabbing it.'

He led the rather spooky pony past Gerry's materials into the yard and tied him to an iron ring on the wall in front of one of the stables. Jan made sure Megan went through the full routine of grooming and hoof-picking before they tacked him up, then she untied the pony and legged the small-framed girl up into the saddle.

Colonel Gilbert took Monarch's head and led the pair out of the yard towards the paddock below, where there was a small area of level ground which Megan used for jumping.

Satisfied, the colonel gave them both a pat before letting them go. Megan rode into the small field and walked quietly around the edge, as Jan and the colonel propped themselves on the gate to watch.

'She knows her stuff, all right,' he said with a chuckle. 'Knows how to work him in slowly.'

'She's had it drummed into her often enough,' Jan replied.

'I'll bet she has. That's nice,' he added as Megan gave the pony a reassuring pat, then gently drew its head towards its chest, giving it a nicely arched neck.

They carried on watching in silence for several minutes, until the colonel spoke again. 'George is up for the weekend and he was hoping he might ask Annabel over for dinner this evening. Is she around?'

'Nope. I'm afraid not. He's been beaten to it and in some style, I may add. I gave her the weekend off as there isn't much happening here at the moment. Apparently Johnny Carlton-Brown sent his helicopter to pick her up yesterday, and she's gone off to France for the weekend to see the Prix du Jockey Club at Chantilly.'

The colonel laughed. 'Has she, by God? Lucky girl. I used to love racing at Chantilly – it was one of the prettiest racecourses in the world, in front of that beautiful chateau. So Mr JCB, as you call him, has his eye on her, does he?'

'I think he had for a bit, but it didn't seem to be going anywhere, and then he introduced her to his business partner, a chap called Lord Lamberhurst – I expect you know him.'

Colonel Gilbert shook his head. 'His father was in my regiment, but I really don't think Patrick was cut out for a military career.'

'Not if his taste in clothes is anything to go by,' Jan said, giggling.

'You've met him too then, have you?'

'Yes, Johnny gave a birthday party for my brother and Patrick was there.'

'What on earth will you do without Annabel if she takes up with that chap permanently?'

'Well, it's a big jump from a weekend in Paris to getting married or actually shacking up with someone; and no one in the yard is indispensable – not even me, if I've been doing my job properly.'

The colonel raised an eyebrow at the intensity of Jan's delivery. 'I'm sure you're right, but you can't expect to hang on to her for ever, you know.'

'I suppose,' Jan answered, not wishing to contemplate the future.

In the paddock, Megan had asked the pony to trot on and he was moving as smoothly as silk.

'What a lovely pony that is,' Jan murmured approvingly. 'Does he jump?'

'Only loose so far. He's not been ridden over anything.'

'In which case, once she's got used to him on the flat, she'll have to start trotting him over poles to see how he gets on.'

'There's no need to rush him,' Colonel Gilbert added. 'It's not as though there's a race for him next week.'

As they talked, Megan was concentrating all her budding skills on getting the pony to move in a controlled and balanced way, something she had already learnt to recognize and feel.

Jan watched proudly and felt a surge of gratitude towards Colonel Gilbert for showing such faith in Megan. She knew it would mean just as much to her for her daughter to grow up enjoying and excelling in her riding, as it would to train the winner of the Cheltenham Gold Cup.

10

The warm clear weather of the weekend carried on through into Monday. Just before lunch Jan was in the yard, thinking about taking the afternoon off to be with the children, when she heard the throbbing sound of an engine coming over the top of the ridge. She looked up and saw a small, compact, black helicopter sweep down the face of the hill before it swooped back up and circled, as the pilot looked for somewhere safe to put down.

'Is that Bel?' Roz shrieked.

'I expect so, but I bloody well hope they don't try to land here or the horses will go mental.'

It soon became clear, if they had planned to land at Edge Farm, the pilot had changed his mind. The aircraft swooped back into the sky and carried on towards Stanfield, where Jan watched it drop out of sight behind a stand of Wellingtonias in the open parkland beyond Annabel's small garden.

Ten minutes later Annabel's new BMW swung through the gate and raced up the drive. She jumped out, beaming with excitement.

Jan couldn't help returning her smile. 'You look like the cat who got the cream,' she said.

'I've had such a brilliant weekend!' she said. 'You really should have come – Johnny and Ben were upset you didn't.'

Jan shook her head. 'It was nice of him to ask, but it's not my scene really. Anyway, I never like leaving the kids at weekends – I don't see them enough as it is.'

'To be honest, I was dreading going without a friend for support – the chopper flight, a whole weekend with JCB and everything – but your Ben was fantastic, he really looked after me.'

Jan opened her eyes a little wider. 'My brother? He's not known for his chivalry. Don't tell me you and he . . .'

'No, no, calm down. We're just good friends, but he's so funny and a really thoughtful guy – not a bit like you,' Annabel added with a teasing grin. 'Actually,' she said, immediately full of remorse, 'I didn't mean it like that, but he's just so – sort of easy-going. Nothing seems to faze him.'

'It's OK, Bel. I know what you mean.'

They started to amble back towards the house, with Fred and Tigger leaping around Annabel's legs as if she'd been away for years. 'Anyway,' she said, 'we had an absolutely *amazing* time! And the clothes were to die for.'

'God, don't tell me you've turned into a shopaholic?' Jan groaned, as if Annabel had undergone major personality surgery.

'No, don't talk tosh. Actually, I couldn't wait to get back here and start shovelling horse shit again.'

'Well, the good news is there's not much to shovel at the moment. What was the race like?' Jan already knew it had been won by a French horse – a twenty-eight-to-one outsider ridden by a top English jockey who'd picked up the spare ride, much to the jubilation of the English supporters.

'It was a great race but an extraordinary finish. We had dinner with the owners afterwards – Patrick knew them.'

'And how did you get on with Lord Lamberhurst, then?'

Annabel put her head on one side with a small, private smile. 'Not badly, I suppose. He didn't try to pounce on me or anything, which I thought he might.'

'So you didn't . . . ?'

'No, Jan, I didn't,' Annabel said sharply. 'I hardly know him. What about you?' she asked, taking Jan's hand. 'Any news?'

Jan shook her head.

'Eddie hasn't phoned?' Annabel pressed.

'Nope,' Jan answered through tight lips.

'Oh, Jan! I just don't believe it! There must be a reason. Maybe he's planning to come back as soon as he feels he's done all he can or maybe he doesn't want to get your hopes up just yet.'

'Yeah.' Jan sighed. 'There are an awful lot of "justs and maybes", Bel.'

'God, I'm so sorry! Have you been OK?'

'Not great, but now I'm even more determined to get a move on. I've agreed with Tanner to put in those extra things for Gary West's horses and Gerry's already made a start on the new stables.'

'I can see that.'

'And,' Jan admitted, 'it's quite nice having him around, gazing at me like a lost sheep; it certainly keeps the girls entertained.'

'Poor Gerry.'

'Oh, I don't know. I'm sure if I suddenly turned round and said, "OK, Gerry, you're on," he'd run a mile. I think he's a bit of a mummy's boy really.'

'How about Tony Robertson?'

Jan shrugged, showing a little more indifference than she felt. 'He phoned yesterday evening, as it happens. He asked me out, but I couldn't do the dates he suggested.'

Annabel looked at her intently. 'Jan, don't put him off completely.'

Jan shook her head. 'I won't. Actually, I am very fond of him.'

As they reached the house, Jan heard the phone ringing. She dashed in and picked it up, desperately hoping it might be Eddie.

It was John Tanner.

'Hello, Mr Tanner,' she said, trying hard not to let her disappointment show.

'Morning. I was just calling to let you know I've arranged everything. You'll be getting confirmation of our order, and the money can be lodged with a day's notice from you.'

'Thank you,' Jan said, with genuine appreciation. 'That's great.'

'And Mr West will be more than happy to meet you next time he's in the UK, though he's not sure when that's going to be. He says he'll make a special trip if he has to,' Tanner added, as if he were arranging for God to drop by.

🐎

The following evening a bank of low pressure drifting across Wales from the Atlantic had enveloped the British Isles in intermittent but heavy downpours that lasted for the next three days. The gloomy, overcast weather did nothing to improve Jan's mood and the excruciating pain she felt over Eddie's departure, but at least it allowed her to give two of Frank Jellard's horses the run he'd insisted they should have before they were turned out with the others for their summer holiday.

There were fewer options now the proper season was almost over, but a meeting was scheduled to take place at Newton Abbot, a popular course for locals and holidaymakers alike, which included a three-mile chase that would suit Cambrian Lad, and a two-and-a-half-mile hurdle for Rhythm Stick.

The previous day Jan had phoned Finbar Howlett at his lodgings to see if he was available to ride.

'Yes, I'd love to,' he'd said joyously. 'There's nothing much else going on at the moment, so I'm going back to Ireland for a month next Tuesday.'

'I don't blame you,' Jan remarked. 'But as far as my two runners are concerned, I'm afraid I'm not too hopeful that either of them will win, so you'll have to pick up some other rides if you're looking to fill the coffers before you go.'

'I have a chance of a couple – I wasn't going to go, though, because my old car's poorly and I'm not sure she'll make it.'

'Don't be daft! Someone will give you a lift. You're welcome to come with me if you like, and it'll be a lot more comfortable than last time – I'm picking up my new vehicle this afternoon. So if you decide to, be here by three tomorrow.'

Jan's 'new' Shogun was three years old, but it seemed state of the art to her after years of driving old pick-ups and the ancient Land Rover.

She had told Terry Clarke, the landlord of the Fox & Pheasant, that she was considering buying a new four-wheel drive to cheer herself up. Two days later he had phoned to say he'd been at an auction and bought a Shogun on spec. It was in perfect condition and was knocked down at half the book price. He just hadn't been able to resist it, he said, and did she want first refusal?

When she and Annabel had been to view it, they noticed it had a petrol engine and would use considerably more fuel than her diesel Land Rover, but Annabel had persuaded her with fewer and cheaper servicing costs it would quite likely balance out.

'Come on, Jan! For God's sake, you haven't bought anything just for yourself in years. You deserve something after what you've been through; this is lovely, it's quiet and comfortable and one thing's for certain – you'll get to the races a hell of a lot quicker.'

After Terry had arranged for the vehicle to be thoroughly checked over, Jan, feeling extremely irrational, asked Annabel to drive her down to the pub to collect it.

With the deal completed, the landlord offered Jan a large drink to celebrate.

'Not this time,' she said. 'I'm driving.'

'Maybe you're right,' Terry agreed. 'I've often noticed how for some reason or another, the more booze a driver pours down his throat, the faster it makes his car go – it's very strange.'

Jan couldn't help feeling pleased as she drove out of the yard in comfort the following afternoon, despite the prospect of an evening with Frank Jellard and running two of his horses that were unlikely to win.

With Finbar Howlett perched on the passenger seat beside her and a clear view over most of the roadside hedges, she felt more in control of her own destiny. Even when they were cruising almost noiselessly down the motorway, and Finbar asked her about Eddie, she refused to let herself be downhearted.

'Eddie's been a good friend to me,' she said. 'The fact that he's attractive to women and has a bit of a past isn't altogether his fault.'

Jan glanced at the Irishman. She wasn't sure she should be having this sort of conversation with him, but his concern seemed genuine and since she'd first met him, the day Eddie had brought him back for lunch, she'd instinctively felt that she could trust him.

'But if he turned up here again, would you have him back?' Finbar asked.

Jan looked back at the road ahead and the stream of holiday

traffic heading for the coasts of Devon and Cornwall. 'I don't know. I'm not so sure now,' she answered untruthfully. 'Anyway, that's enough about my private life; I'm a racehorse trainer and you're supposed to be a jockey, not an agony aunt.'

'Oh, don't you worry yourself about that, I'm used to it.' Finbar laughed. 'I've four sisters back home, two either side of me, and they're always asking me what they should do about their fellas.'

'How are they coping without you then?'

'They're not. They're forever ringing and writing to get me to go back – that's why I'm going home for the summer.'

'Will you definitely be going back to Virginia's in the autumn, then?' Jan asked lightly.

Finbar nodded. 'I've given my word – she'll be expecting me.'

'Aren't you worried that she won't have enough runners – or at least not enough good ones?'

'Nope – I reckoned by tying myself to a smallish yard, I'd have a little security as well as the chance to ride for others – and that's what I really want . . . to start with, anyway,' he added, tantalizingly.

As they drew nearer to their destination, Jan's sense of well-being was marred by the knowledge that the two horses she was sending out to race were doing so against her better judgement. Although it wouldn't do either of them any harm as they were fit enough, she felt they were both completely outclassed. However, it seemed Frank Jellard thought he only had value for money from his training fees if his horses ran a certain number of times each season. There was no real logic to it, unless he measured his enjoyment by the hours he actually spent as an owner at the race track – which, Jan guessed, was precisely what he did.

He was waiting just inside the racecourse gates and greeted her in his usual, proprietorial way. He was a big, hard-faced man, who towed his wife around like a dog on a lead. Jan often suspected he wouldn't mind slipping a collar over her head as well.

'I hope we're in for a sound result today, Jan,' he growled threateningly, as if she was suddenly able to do something that could influence the result of the two races he had runners in. 'It's a bloody long way from Evesham.'

'I know,' Jan nodded. 'It's about the same from Edge.'

'I see you brought that Irish jockey with you. Is he all right?'

'Yes, Frank. He's absolutely fine. I think he'll do very well over here.'

'Why's he riding for that snotty cow, Virginia Gilbert, then?'

'Who knows?'

'You should have got in there first,' Jellard rasped.

Jan really wasn't looking forward to a whole evening of this barracking and Frank hadn't brought his usual gang of impressionable friends, so he would expect her to stay around and answer his inane questions. 'You'll have to excuse me for me a while, Frank, I've got to go and make my declarations. I'll see you in the parade ring just before Cambrian Lad's race.' She walked away quickly before he could start grumbling again, although she knew she'd pay a high price later on.

First, Jan went to check the horses. Con and Dec had travelled with them and they were both in the stables, grooming their charges before oiling their hooves the way Jan liked. As she looked over his stable door, Dec gave Cambrian Lad's gleaming rump a pat.

'This fella's in great shape,' he said. 'He's been working real well on this better ground.'

Jan really didn't want to dampen his enthusiasm. 'We'll be asking Finnie to have a crack at it,' she confirmed, without much inner conviction.

She had a long look at Rhythm Stick, as he scraped his feet over the floor impatiently.

You're looking uncooperative already, she thought. He wasn't her favourite horse and, although he hadn't cost a great deal since he'd arrived at her yard, he had produced a couple of wins in the lowly races she'd found for him. But today's was completely out of his league, she thought.

Jan really disliked sending out horses when she didn't think they had any chance whatsoever. Feeling despondent, she made her way to the weighing room to make her declarations.

Maybe, she thought, *with Gary West's horses, I won't have to go on training for bullies like Frank Jellard.*

On the other hand, she reminded herself, she was a professional trainer and it was her job to train her clients' horses to the best of her ability, despite what she thought about their personal failings. She had no doubt that Frank Jellard wouldn't be the last owner in her yard to think he knew best. Today even he noticed how well his horse looked in the parade ring.

'He looks better than when I saw him last week,' he observed grudgingly. He clearly hadn't forgiven Jan for abandoning him.

Jan nodded. 'His lad's quite bullish.' She turned to Finbar, who had just approached them. 'This horse'll get the trip OK, but try and keep him off the pace early on. If he's there or thereabouts at the last, you can get after him,' she said quietly to Finbar, before turning back to the owner. 'There's a lot of quality in this race for the time of year, Mr Jellard, so we could be up against it, but Finbar's really going to do his best for you.'

'He'd bloody well better,' Jellard growled menacingly.

🐎

Newton Abbot was a small left-handed track, clearly visible from the main stand, where Jan stood beside her owners. Jellard talked loudly about his horse as it cantered past the stands on its way to the start. A few punters had taken notice of the horse's obvious well-being and decided to put their faith in Jan's reputation.

'I've got a grand on him at eight to one,' Jellard half whispered to Jan.

She stifled a groan: she thought she'd already made it clear to him that the horse was outclassed. A small bet might have been justified, but Jellard was one of those men who thought small bets implied small balls.

Jan already had her binoculars up to her face and was studying her runner down at the start. 'He'll be doing his best,' she answered lamely, without taking her eyes off the horses.

Finbar rode shorter than most jump jockeys, sacrificing safety for greater speed on the flat, he claimed. He wasn't particularly small, so he stood a little higher above his horse's back than the rest of the jockeys. After the tapes had flown up, Jan watched him quickly settle the large horse in midfield, and they were soon passing the stands for the first time.

'He's jumping well,' Jellard murmured beside her.

'He is,' Jan agreed with pleasure. She had never seen the horse travel so comfortably. Perhaps, she thought, this is one of those occasions when the jockey was absolutely suited to the horse. But there were still two more complete laps to go, and Jan was forced to let out the breath she'd been holding since the tapes went up.

The favourite, a renowned front runner, had made all the running so far but as the field passed the stands for a second time, with another entire circuit ahead of them, his lead was diminishing rapidly. There were six horses in the following bunch, including Cambrian Lad. Having watched the first part of the race with no real hope of success, Jan now found herself gripping her binoculars with white knuckles and breathing in short gasps. With just four fences to cover, Frank Jellard's distinctive colours were beginning to move even closer, and the long-time leader had almost come back to the pack.

Cambrian Lad put in a huge jump at the open ditch and landed in third place. Now he was looking like a real contender. Jan could hardly believe her eyes but she still didn't think they could win. She was expecting at least two of the runners to make a challenge once they rounded the final bend to head up the home straight and faced the last two plain fences.

Jan thought her whole body was about to explode when she realized Cambrian Lad still had enough left in his tank to crank up the speed and Finbar, with his powerful, driving style, fists pumping like pistons along the horse's neck, urged his big mount on to surge past the two jockeys in front of him.

'First number twelve,' the announcer said as soon as Finbar had crossed the line, half a length ahead.

Cambrian Lad's win was the best Jan had achieved for Jellard, with a purse of twelve thousand pounds, and another eight thousand he had won from the bookies. In a rare moment of warmth, he turned to Jan, beaming, and hugged her like a long-lost lover. Jan wanted to wriggle free, but she thought he would take offence, so endured the embrace until he released her to give his wife a less extravagant squeeze.

When the jockey had weighed in and the all-clear was given, Frank was presented with a small trophy from the race sponsor. He then insisted that Jan should join them to celebrate in a bar crowded with holidaymakers from the local resorts. This time she was telling the truth when she said she had to get away quickly to saddle up Rhythm Stick for the hurdle race.

In the saddling box, she noticed the tough little horse was still behaving in a moody and uncooperative way. She talked to him and patted his neck, trying to reassure and humour him.

In the paddock she told the jockey about her fears. 'He's probably going to be a bit tricky today, Finnie. I'm afraid he's likely to try and fight you for the first mile, then he'll probably start to run out of steam. There are only eight flights to jump, and he does have a bit of speed, so make use of it in the straight if you can.'

Finbar nodded and looked at Rhythm Stick thoughtfully.

Jan's foreboding was confirmed from the off. There was nothing any jockey could have done to settle the wayward horse as he ran the first circuit with his head high in the air, tossing it from side to side.

He never saw the second flight in the back straight and hit the top bar, completely flattening the panel. The horse stumbled and crashed to the ground, flinging Finbar clear of the field. Rhythm Stick struggled to his feet and tried to stand. Jan knew immediately his off-fore leg was badly injured. Through her binoculars she could see it hanging loosely below his knee.

Her blood ran cold. She had seldom had to deal with these moments, but the certainty that one of her horses would have to be despatched made her want to retch. Without realizing it, she clutched Jellard's coat sleeve. He turned to her, alarmed.

'What's up, Jan?'

'He's broken his leg,' she choked. 'They'll have to put him down.'

'Shit!' Jellard gasped. 'I never renewed his insurance when it came up last week; I was going to shop around.'

Jan was shocked and stared at him, disbelieving. 'Is that all you can think of?' she asked bitterly. 'That poor sod's about to be put down, for Christ's sake! He may only be a possession to you, Frank, but he's an individual to me. He might not be the easiest horse in the yard, but we'll still bloody well miss him.'

Jellard was silenced for a moment by Jan's outburst in front of other racegoers, who were eavesdropping on the conversation.

Mrs Jellard took his arm. 'It's all right, Frank. But don't let's stay here and watch,' she pleaded.

In an angry daze, Jellard let his wife lead him away as Jan gazed through clouded eyes at the St John Ambulance first-aiders arriving to deal with the stricken jockey.

Finbar was quiet as they drove home. Jan guessed he felt as bad as she did about losing the horse. 'I always think it's such a terrible thing they can't save them.' He shook his head.

'They do quite often,' Jan said, 'but it's nigh on impossible to set a horse's leg when it's so badly broken. I saw one at our local vet's once. She had spent six weeks dangling from the ceiling of her stable in a vast sling with a leg in plaster. The poor animal looked dreadful, but she did survive. More often than not, though, the pressure on the gut stops it working, so it's a no-win situation and only causes more suffering.'

Finbar shook his head with a sigh. 'Sometimes I feel we humans have let them down because we ask too much of them, though I guess horses and ponies break legs out on the mountains and moorland, and they don't have anyone to put them out of their misery.'

'Exactly,' Jan agreed, 'and they don't have anyone feeding, grooming and tending to all their needs every day, either.'

Finbar asked to be dropped off in Cheltenham, where he was meeting some friends. He said he would get one of Virginia's lads to drive him round to pick up his car the next morning, so Jan left him in the centre of the town on the busy summer's evening and drove out past the racecourse. She suddenly felt terribly sad and alone.

After Rhythm Stick's death, her excitement about the new car had completely melted away. Although she had lived on a farm all her life, she found it extremely hard to deal with the death of another living creature, especially one for whom she was responsible. On top of this, Frank Jellard's attitude had sickened her. In the end, he had readily accepted that although Rhythm Stick had died uninsured, Cambrian Lad had earned him a great deal of prize money, without taking into account his large winning bet. Once he had persuaded himself that he could show a substantial net gain on the day, he was completely happy. As Jan was going, he had turned to her with an imperious wave of his hand. 'I suppose I'd better get a replacement,' he said loudly. 'See if you can find me another good youngster in Ireland. Not too much money, mind.' Jan left him laughing and joking in the bar with some new-found friends, while his more sensitive wife looked on dejectedly.

Philosophically, Jan tried to come to terms with the day's events as her car climbed to the top of Cleeve Hill. To the north-west, the sun was setting in a blaze of pink and flaming orange over the distant Welsh hills where she had started her training career. The sight helped to clear her head of the many things she couldn't change and to focus on what she had to do the next day.

She thought about the horse she was sending to run at Bath and found she could never quite muster up the same enthusiasm for flat racing as she did for National Hunt. She didn't know too many of the people involved, just a few of the officials and a couple of trainers; somehow there seemed to be less of the camaraderie she found in jumping and she had never even met the jockey she had booked to ride tomorrow.

As the road dropped down towards the ancient stone town of Winchcombe, she was musing on the uncertainties of getting too involved in a new, unfamiliar field when her mobile phone trilled. She picked it up from the seat beside her.

'Is that Mrs Hardy?'

It was a deep, male voice, with a strong Australian twang.

Jan's heart gave a flip as she immediately thought of Eddie, who was never far from her mind. She guessed wildly. Perhaps it was the girl's father, checking on Eddie's circumstances. 'Yes?' she answered guardedly.

'This is Gary West.'

Jan quickly made the mental leap from her private persona to her professional identity.

'Hello, Mr West. I'm very pleased to hear you.'

'Congratulations on your win today; I caught the race on satellite. I'm sorry we haven't spoken before, but John Tanner has kept me up to speed with the arrangements he's made with you, and I must say I'm delighted we've reached an agreement. But I would like to see you and view your set-up for myself. I'll be in the UK on Monday night. I won't be able to pay you a visit this trip. Would it be asking too much for you to join me for dinner in London?'

The invitation was issued with a panache that took Jan completely unawares. 'Well, yes, of course,' she blurted out. 'That'd be fine.'

Gary West gave a throaty chuckle. 'Sorry to hit you with it at such short notice, but I did want to finalize this deal with you myself. I hope you don't mind? I intend to drop by your place later in the year, once all my horses are installed.'

'Whenever,' Jan agreed, relieved to be dealing with the man himself and not his insufferable sidekick. Just the sound of his voice had dispelled all the lingering doubts caused by Tanner's abrasive self-importance.

'And I hear you have a rather pretty assistant. Would you like to bring her with you?'

'As she's a key member of my team,' Jan said, wanting to focus his attention on Annabel's skills, rather than her looks, 'I would probably have brought her along anyway.'

'Fine! That's settled then. Monday, eight o'clock at Crockford's. Is that OK?'

'Where is that?'

'Mayfair.' Gary West laughed. 'Your cab driver will know.'

'Have you ever been here before?' Jan asked as Annabel carefully parked her BMW near Curzon Street between a Bentley and a Porsche. They were less than a hundred yards from the entrance to the large white stucco building that housed the gaming club established by Mr Crockford in 1828.

'No, most of the people I know go to Aspinall's or the Claremont.'

They let themselves out of the car and in the balmy evening air walked along the street in the most suitable evening wear they had been able to find in Annabel's wardrobe. A liveried doorman smiled his appreciation as he stood to one side to allow them in.

'Haven't you got *any* idea what he looks like?' Annabel whispered as they tried to look composed in the lobby, where designer-dressed women floated through an atmosphere charged with cigar smoke and expensive perfume.

'No,' Jan whispered back apprehensively. 'But look,' she went on, relieved. 'It's OK; there's Tanner.'

John Tanner was looking more than usually uncomfortable in a shiny, dark blue tuxedo.

Annabel shook her head. 'That definitely is *not* OK,' she said with a quiet giggle.

Beside Tanner a stocky man rose to his feet, no taller than five feet nine and aged about fifty, Jan guessed, with short-cropped blond hair. Tanner saw their guests and quietly said something to the other man, who looked across at them. His deeply tanned face lit up and Jan couldn't help feeling the charisma it gave off.

The men approached and the blond man held out his hand to Jan. 'Hello, I'm Gary West, I'm very pleased to meet you,' he said intimately, but still loud enough to be audible to most of the people around, who, recognizing the famous name, lowered their own conversations as they turned to look.

Gary shook hands with Jan, then Annabel, looking deeply into their eyes as if they were the most important people he had ever met. 'I'm so glad you could make it. Come and have a drink. John, I'll see you after dinner. There's a big game at Aspinall's tonight and I want to be there.'

Gary nodded without expression at his lieutenant, before turning to usher Jan and Annabel through to a room where a low table with three chairs around it had evidently been reserved for him. Champagne appeared as they settled around the table.

'Now then,' he said, leaning forward and gazing at Jan with brown-black eyes beneath his golden brows. 'You *are* going to get me some good horses, aren't you? I want you to tell me what you'll be looking for and what you hope to do with them.'

It was, Jan knew, too broad a question and too susceptible to unknowns for her to give an accurate answer, but at the same time she understood that Gary West wanted a firm idea of her own aspirations as a trainer.

'John Tanner has already told me how much you like our National Hunt racing, which probably means you're interested in top-class steeplechasers.'

'Yes, though I can appreciate the talents of a really quick hurdler, too.'

'That's great!' Jan said, boosted by his attitude. 'It makes my task much easier if you're keen on all aspects of the jumping game and you've got enough patience to wait for a good young hurdler to mature into a high-class chaser. That way we should have some real fun, especially with the budget you've committed.'

Jan settled into her well-rehearsed strategy for acquiring a string of talented racehorses. She explained the merits of the different auction sales they could visit, the bloodstock agents they might have to use, and the studs where she could deal direct for the younger, well-bred animals.

The Australian interrupted only when he asked her for clarification, otherwise he listened intently to what she was saying without taking his eyes off her as he sipped his champagne.

When she had exhausted her repertory, he leaned back in his chair before questioning her about the prices that were being paid for the sort of horse they were aiming at. Eventually he seemed satisfied that he had as good a grasp on the details as was possible for the time being.

'Right,' he said, getting to his feet, 'let's pay a quick visit to the tables and work up an appetite, then we'll stroll round to the Gavroche and have a bit of tucker.'

He put his hand into the pocket of the dark suit he was wearing and pulled out a pair of gambling chips, which he handed to Jan and Annabel. 'Here's something for you girls to chuck around while I have a quick raid on the chemmy table.'

Jan had never been inside a casino or seen a gaming chip before; she looked at it closely. Engraved on the surface in gold was the figure '£500'.

She quivered slightly at the thought that she had been given such a huge sum simply to chuck away if she chose to. It seemed bizarre. She looked meaningfully at Annabel as she thought about all the useful things she could do with that much money. Her friend shrugged, unsurprised by what the tycoon had just done.

Gary West was already marching towards the first gaming room like a soldier on a parade ground. Nervously Jan and Annabel followed. Inside the cavernous room, beneath a cascading crystal chandelier, dozens of people were jostling around green baize roulette tables or sat perched on stools at blackjack games being dealt with weary detachment by glamorous women. Gary West bypassed all of these and carried on towards an archway on the far side of the room.

Here the atmosphere was markedly quieter and more serious. There were just two tables, where the players were concentrating as if they were in a trance and it was clear that huge stakes were being played for.

Gary found a space at one of the tables and barked, 'Bank!' The other players looked up, acknowledging his presence; most of them seemed to know who he was.

Jan watched him join in the arcane rituals of chemin de fer. She couldn't begin to understand what the game was about, as players called their bets and croupiers dealt the cards, then scooped up large piles of losing chips to rattle them down a slot in the table's green baize surface. But Gary was committed. With his pile of chips growing rapidly, he was hunched over the table, absently fingering his plastic wealth, and appeared to have forgotten his two guests even existed.

Jan glanced around for Annabel and saw her hanging back in the shadows on the far side of the table. She walked round to join her. 'What shall we do?' she whispered.

'There's a man playing here,' Annabel nodded at an impeccably clad pair of shoulders in front of them, 'who I really don't want to meet. Come on, we may as well go and do something with these.' She waved her £500 chip with the grin of a naughty child. 'If we can turn it into a few thousand, you and I could go out and do a bit of shopping without feeling guilty.'

'Some chance! I don't even know what to do.'

'Well, I do; my life in London wasn't wasted, nor was it entirely innocent.'

A minute or so later the two friends were standing at the edge of one of the roulette tables in the main gaming hall. Annabel threw her large chip to the far end of the table, where one of the black-tied men operating the wheel was scooping up the bets.

'Fivers, please,' Annabel called. A moment later, five tall columns of smaller plastic tokens were being pushed across the table at the end of the croupier's rake.

'What I like to do,' Annabel said in an undertone to Jan, so as not to show her up as a total novice, 'is to pick a couple of numbers and then put every kind of bet around them – the whole number, the column, the colour, odd or even, the halves and the quarters.'

Jan watched bemused at the amount of money that was being tossed about with complete abandon and she soon cottoned on to Annabel's method as she deposited chips around 36 and 21 on the numbered grid, and the various boxes for side bets, although there seemed to be no clear logic to it. At the last minute, as one of the croupiers was beginning to spin the wheel prior to flicking the little silver ball in the opposite direction, Annabel called, 'Zero, one,' and flipped a chip to the top of the table, where one of the men placed it on the line between the boxes marked '0' and '1'.

'No more bets, please,' he called as he flicked the ball into play. The friends watched hopefully as it rattled and jerked around the rim of the wheel, deflected by the obstacles in its path, dropping towards the centre as the wheel slowed, bouncing on the ridges between the numbers around the hub and hesitating almost, before moving on until, with a sudden cessation of its busy rattling, it dropped into a slot and stayed put.

It was on a number which lay next to one of Annabel's. She'd won several of her side bets at lower odds – enough to cover all her losers, which were swept away.

'Bad luck,' Jan whispered.

'There was nothing wrong with that,' Annabel said. 'I think I might even have gained one or two.' She leaned forward over the table and busily placed the same bets.

The next spin paid her out on only the colour and the odd/even bet. She placed her original bet all over again.

The spin that followed seemed to take longer, with the ball bouncing in and out of several slots before making up its mind to settle in the '0'.

Jan felt herself getting caught up in the tension and drama the process was designed to create and she shrieked with pleasure as it paid Annabel a stack of eighteen chips, while leaving most of the side bets undisturbed.

Annabel grinned and leaned over the table to double the size of her original bet.

Neither of them could stop themselves from whooping even louder a minute later as the little ball dropped into '36'.

'Come on, Bel, you're on a roll now!' Jan urged gleefully, as she watched Annabel double up her stakes again.

For a dozen spins, Annabel had a full number up twice, and several of the higher-paying fringe bets on the balls in between.

Then the ball that followed this run of good luck took away every chip she had just placed on the table.

'Right!' Jan declared, with a tingle of excitement; she now felt she was closer to understanding how a racecourse punter must feel when he is picking winners. She also had a feeling she had got the measure of the game. 'Now your roll's over. Let's see what you've won.'

Annabel nodded and looked gleefully down at the stack of chips in front of her. 'I'll cash them in,' she said.

Carefully they carried the stacks of tokens to a cashier's window at the end of the room, where Annabel exchanged them for a little over fifteen hundred pounds. Stuffing the notes into her bag, she looked at Jan. 'Right, I've done my bit. Now it's your turn.'

'OK,' Jan nodded, 'but I've decided I'm going for sudden death. I'm going to put my chip on one of the columns. If it wins, I'll have made a grand like you. If it loses, I'll have saved a lot of time and stress.'

They walked back to the table where Annabel had triumphed. Jan watched the play for a couple of spins before putting her chip on the middle column. She watched breathlessly as the ball teetered on the edge of a number that would earn her a thousand pounds, before it dropped into the next slot.

Jan sighed, limp from the experience, but relieved that it was over. 'I knew I wasn't a born gambler. Actually, I'm really glad I lost or I might have been tempted to try it again.'

'Jan, let's face it, you haven't lost anything,' Annabel chided.

They were making their way back to the room where the chemmy was being played when they an ebullient Gary West on his way out.

'I hope you girls were lucky,' he boomed.

'We made a small profit between us,' Annabel said quickly. 'Thanks for staking us. Do you want it back?'

Gary looked at her as if she were mad. 'Good God, no. And I wouldn't want it back even if I hadn't just won a fifty-grand bank. I tell you what, though, I'm as hungry as a hunter. Let's go eat.'

With the same single-mindedness with which he had ignored Jan and Annabel while he was playing chemin de fer, Gary West let nothing distract him as he escorted them to dinner.

They walked a short distance through the uncrowded streets of Mayfair to the famous French restaurant, where they were shown to a large, discreet table. Jan wasn't surprised by Gary's broad knowledge of food and wine, and found herself enjoying the meal more as he told them where the wine had come from, and exactly how the food had been cooked.

She found the unexpected variations in his behaviour fascinating. The two extremes seemed rather extraordinary in the same person. By the end of dinner she was left in no doubt that here was a man with such charm and personal magnetism that it was going to be fun and, without doubt, a challenge to work for him.

The fact that she didn't mind seeing her relationship with him in those terms was in itself an indication of his character. And by the end of the evening all her reservations about Gary – which Tanner's behaviour had inspired – were totally dispelled.

After their meal, Jan was feeling satisfied, not overfull, and pleasantly relaxed. As the evening ended Gary ushered them outside and into the back of a Bentley Mulsanne, which seemed to have appeared from nowhere.

'There's no way I'm going to let two pretty women like you drive home alone. It must be at least a hundred miles.'

Oh no! Jan thought, *Here we go!*

'My driver, Mac, will run you both home and I'll have another of my people deliver your car to you; they can get a lift back with Mac. So you just tell him where you want to go and he'll do the rest.'

He stepped back from the car, grinning with pleasure at his own gallantry.

'But how are you going to get home?' Annabel asked with instinctive thoughtfulness.

'Don't you worry about me. I'm walking round the corner for a little more mental exercise – and a bit of profit too, I hope,' he winked. 'Jan, you have a great time at the sales in Ireland. I wish I could come over with you, but I can't. I'm already committed elsewhere, though John will be there to ratify any purchases. The money'll be in your bank tomorrow, in case you see anything you think I should definitely have, but just two youngsters for the time being, OK? I really do want us to have a crack at the big time. Good luck – it's been a pleasure meeting you both.' He poked his head back into the car and winked again at Jan. 'And one thing's for sure, I'm bloody certain I've already backed a winner.'

Ten minutes into the journey Jan leaned back into the soft

leather seats, slipped off her shoes and buried her toes in the luxuriously deep-piled carpet. She closed her heavy eyelids.

'Bel,' she murmured, 'is someone having me on or am I bloody dreaming?'

11

Twenty minutes after A.D. O'Hagan's garrulous chauffeur Daragh had met Jan and her father at Dublin airport, he turned his boss's Mercedes into St Stephen's Green and pulled up in front of the Shelbourne Hotel. He leapt out of the driving seat and opened the rear door with a flourish. Jan stepped out, followed by Reg, and blinked in the bright afternoon sun as they walked up into the hotel lobby, with Daragh lugging their suitcases a few paces behind.

The receptionist at the desk in the busy lobby recognized Jan immediately. Jan wondered if the staff there had been briefed by A.D.'s office, until she detected a genuine warmth in his welcome.

'Mrs Hardy, it's good to see you again! That was a grand night you had here after Russian Eagle won the National!'

It had been – Jan thought wryly – the night Eddie had reappeared after a whole year away.

'It was, wasn't it,' she agreed with a smile, hoping that the reddening of her face wasn't noticeable and busied herself introducing her father.

'Mr O'Hagan left a message for you,' the receptionist said. 'He'll be round in an hour or so, about sixish.'

Once Jan had made sure that Reg was settled in his room and she was alone in her own, she found a bottle of Ballygowan in the fridge and took a long sip. She kicked off her shoes and lay down on the big carved bed beneath a high ceiling, trying hard to expunge from her memory a vision of the last time she had stayed at the hotel in a very similar room.

Instead she reminded herself how very different this second visit to the Derby Sale at Fairyhouse was going to be from her first foray across the Irish Sea the previous year.

She had brought her father along then, driving onto the ferry in her old Land Rover, which had broken down before they'd even got ashore. She recalled her first day, checking into a simple B and B in one of the narrow streets north of the Liffey, and her lift out to the sales ground with a minibus full of grooms and old retired jockeys.

It was almost impossible to believe that she had been so naive then. She remembered vividly how uncertain she'd been that her judgement would have any relevance and how she had worried about overspending. It seemed more like a century ago.

Now, just one year on, she had orders to buy horses that would have excited any National Hunt trainer. She had already had a few good winners at home, a new gallop was being laid, more stables built, and she had a good working relationship with the Irish champion jockey.

Nevertheless, on the plane and now, lying gazing at the mouldings on the ceiling high above, she thought of the people she'd left behind. Of course, she was thankful for her dad's presence, for his knowledge and support, but she missed her children, she missed Annabel, and – damn it – she missed sodding Eddie.

She was worn out after such an early start and the long journey. A few moments later she was sound asleep. She woke with a jolt when the phone on her bedside table rang noisily. Rubbing her eyes, she peered at her watch to find she'd been unconscious a mere twenty minutes. She grabbed the phone and croaked into it.

Mr O'Hagan was in the Horseshoe Bar, Mr Carlton-Brown had phoned and, the girl on the switchboard added with breathless envy, 'Darius, the singer with the Band of Brothers – he's coming here tomorrow. He left a message to say he would like to have dinner with you tomorrow evening and can you call him back.'

Jan sat up. 'That's fine. Can you let me have Mr . . . Darius's number, please, and could you also let Mr O'Hagan know that I'll be down in about fifteen minutes?'

She replaced the receiver, lay back on the pile of big, squashy pillows and took in a few slow, deep but controlled breaths.

All these people were demanding her attention and they would assume that she was going to be around for them alone, whenever they wanted a view on a horse, or just her company.

Jesus, she thought, *how on earth am I going to manage?*

She'd had no idea that Darius was planning to come over so soon. Tomorrow was only the preview day, after all; the selling – the important part, which the owners usually liked – didn't start until Thursday.

A.D. hadn't yet asked her to buy a horse. He was, she thought, still irritated by the scale of Gary West's commitment to her yard. Nevertheless, he would still expect her to be at his beck and call. She knew she was going to have to be firm and stand her ground with him and the others, especially John Tanner.

Not for the first time since Gary had kissed her on the cheek outside the restaurant in London, Jan really wished the Australian was coming to the sales in person and not sending his obnoxious sidekick.

'Come on, you'll have to shake yourself,' she said decisively, swinging her legs over the side of the bed and making her way through to the big marble shower. She ran her fingers through her hair and sighed. The hassles had not gone away as she'd become more successful; they'd just grown bigger.

Once she was dressed and satisfied with her make-up, Jan padded along the deeply carpeted corridor to her father's room.

Reg was sitting up with a big smile on his face, his legs stretched out in front of him on the huge bed. An Irish TV channel was blaring and, Jan noticed, there was a good measure of Irish whiskey in a glass on the bedside table.

'You OK, Dad?' she asked with a grin.

'Couldn't be better, pet.'

'Just pick up the phone and ask the receptionist if you need me, or anything else. But don't go mad, mind.'

'Don't you worry; I won't be touching any more of that stuff.' The old man nodded at the glass of whiskey. 'It's took the roof of my mouth off.'

'Take care, then. I'm off to see Mr O'Hagan.'

Downstairs, amid the mirror-lined walls of the Horseshoe Bar, Jan was surprised to find that A.D.'s wife had accompanied him.

Jan had already met Mrs O'Hagan several times, but couldn't help being a little overawed by Siobhan Fitzgerald, a tall, auburn-haired singer who was one of Ireland's leading sopranos. Jan had always considered her an unlikely partner for a man like A.D., although she'd never heard the slightest murmur about any marital discord.

When Jan had finally wended her way to their table, A.D. rose and kissed her on both cheeks. She shook hands with Siobhan, who enquired politely about Megan and Matthew. As Jan was halfway through answering, they were interrupted by the arrival of a leading member of the Irish Dáil. A.D. introduced him as Padraig Feahy, an important figure in the Treasury. The politician didn't disguise his irritation that A.D. was entertaining a racing colleague and made it very clear that he neither knew nor cared about horses of any description.

Jan found the Irish were either totally committed to and passionate about horses and horse racing, or they were quite the opposite and resented the assumption that they should be.

If A.D. was aware of his new guest's lack of interest in racing, he ignored it and carried on the conversation with Jan as he would have done whether Feahy had been there or not. Eventually, though, he apologized. 'Jan, please bear with me a moment. I have a few things to discuss with Mr Feahy.'

Jan guessed that A.D.'s wife was used to dealing with the awkward situations that arose in the life of a man with as many interests as he had. Siobhan looked at her with one eyebrow slightly raised and, moving her head almost imperceptibly, suggesting they leave.

As the women rose to their feet, A.D. acknowledged their departure with a slight wave of one hand. Once they were a few yards from the table, Siobhan said, with a tilt of her head, 'I'm sorry. I don't imagine they'll be long, but I thought you might like a turn around the Green after a being cooped up in a plane all afternoon.'

They made their way through the lobby and the revolving mahogany doors onto the broad front steps. The late sun was still warm and reflected the air of permanent carnival that seemed to embrace Dublin in the long summer evenings. In the square outside the hotel there was a constant coming and going. Siobhan took Jan's arm and guided her across the road into the comparative tranquillity of the twenty-acre park.

'I do hope my husband isn't putting you under too much pressure,' Siobhan said as they strolled through the gates. 'I know he has a tendency to completely take over the lives of people who act for him,' she added apologetically.

Jan couldn't tell if there was a hidden agenda in what A.D.'s wife was saying. 'No, not at all,' she answered, wondering if her response would get back to A.D. 'Obviously he's a really important owner in my yard, but not the only one and he won't even be the biggest once Gary West's horses arrive. Anyway, I consider all my owners to be equal.'

'How many does Mr West intend having with you?' Siobhan continued lightly.

'Five or six to begin with, he says. I may buy one or two this week, then I'm travelling down to County Wexford to see a contact who has a few for me to look at.'

'Then you must come and stay at Aigmont, if you have the time. It's on your way and I'm sure A.D. would want you to. Did he tell you we're leaving first thing in the morning?'

Jan had had no idea that A.D. wasn't staying for the sales. Her first thought was she didn't know if she was relieved or not, but on reflection she admitted that she was disappointed. There was no doubt that his presence and support, even in the background, gave more weight to her as a buyer.

'No, actually, he didn't. I assumed he'd be staying for the sale.'

'I'm performing at a concert in Geneva and he has meetings with some financiers there.'

'Oh, that's a shame – for me, that is,' Jan added quickly. 'When will you be back?'

'Friday evening. Come down then, if you like; I'll tell them to expect you. And please stay for the weekend. I expect the break will do you good.'

Jan considered her options. Perhaps this would be better than having A.D. at Fairyhouse, especially if she wasn't buying anything for him. 'Thank you, Siobhan. If you're sure I won't be in the way and it suits your husband, I'd love to spend a day or two at Aigmont.'

'It will be fine by him, I'm sure. Now, when Paddy Feahy turned up, you were just about to tell me how your daughter's getting on with her show-jumping; I'd love to hear more.'

The two women returned to the hotel half an hour later, just as the politician was leaving. A.D. looked preoccupied for a minute or two, although he quickly reverted to his role of attentive host.

'I've invited Jan to Aigmont for the weekend,' Siobhan informed him.

'Perfect! Did my wife tell you we're away to Switzerland tomorrow?' he asked.

Jan nodded.

'So, how'd it be if you joined us for dinner tonight at No. 27, the restaurant here? It's the best in town.'

Jan had been intending to spend the evening going minutely through the three hundred and eighty odd entries in her sales catalogue, but this dinner could be important, particularly as A.D. wasn't going to be around for the rest of the week. 'I'd like that very much, thank you,' she said, knowing that she would have to complete her research on pedigrees well into the early hours of the morning. 'You know I've got my father with me, don't you?'

'Of course – we'd be delighted to see him, if he'd care to join us.'

In the restaurant, which was part of the hotel, half a dozen other people A.D. hadn't mentioned earlier turned up to join them at the large round table he'd booked.

Jan had noticed before how this tended to happen with A.D.'s parties. Often the guests had little in common other than knowing A.D. But he always made a point of talking to each of them on whatever matter had brought them there. Sometimes he spoke in a discreet undertone to his neighbour; at other times he liked to address the table in general.

When dinner was nearly over, a space opened up beside A.D. and he beckoned Jan from across the table to join him.

'I imagine you'll be wanting to get away and have a read of your catalogue,' he said, in a politely phrased instruction rather than a question. 'If you see a couple I would like – animals that look as if they might take a bit of time to grow into chasers – would you get them for me? Spend whatever it takes, just ring my office for the money when you need it.' He was looking at her with his clear blue eyes quite motionless. 'You would like to do that, wouldn't you?'

Jan took a sharp breath. 'But won't you want to know the details before I commit you?'

'No. As long as you think they're nice individuals. You know the kind of horses I like. I know I can trust you to get the right type.'

Daragh was driving his boss over to England to catch the train to Geneva, so another driver in A.D.'s organization had been allocated to ferry Jan and Reg to the sales each day.

As they sped out of Dublin, Jan was again reminded of her first journey along the Navan Road in the minibus, when Micky Byrne, a septuagenarian ex-jockey who had befriended her, had given a running commentary on everything they'd passed and regaled her with stories of jockeys jostling their way around the tight, narrow bends of the now defunct Phoenix Park racecourse.

But by the time the car reached the octagonal building and the huge complex of barns that made up the sales ground on the opposite side of the road to the scene of her Grand National triumph three months earlier, she was ready to put aside her nostalgia and focus on the three days of very hard work that lay ahead.

With A.D.'s last-minute and completely unexpected request for two new horses, Jan now had orders to buy eight or nine youngsters, with funds to purchase several at the top end of the price range. From the details in the bulky sale catalogue, she had already eliminated some of the animals on offer on the strength of their breeding and their declared flaws, but that still left her with around three hundred to look at in the flesh.

She had no doubt there would be some non-runners for one reason or another, usually because they had failed the pre-sales veterinary examination, and she would drop more after one glance through the grille on the stable door, but there was still an enormous amount of work to do if she was to have a thorough look at the rest.

The horses to be sold were housed in stables in a series of long barns which held between forty and fifty each. Jan had dog-eared the pages of the lots she wanted to examine physically and planned to do them one barn at a time, taking a short break between each block to appraise what she'd seen. She hoped that by the time her owners arrived the next day, wanting to see the animals she was recommending they should buy, she would have a good list of quality horses to show them.

Jan and Reg had reached Fairyhouse just after nine o'clock and by mid-morning they had seen around fifty horses. Twelve of them she noted in her catalogue while trying to disguise her interest from anyone else who happened to be in the vicinity. She'd learnt on her previous visit and at subsequent sales in England that the more you liked the look of a horse the less wise it was to let on, but her father still had to admonish her a couple of times when she'd voiced her approval a bit too loudly.

Soon after twelve Jan and her father made their way to one of the tea bars alongside the sale ring. Although the selling wouldn't start until the next day, a large number of people took the preview very seriously, and the place was already crowded with trainers, breeders, agents, a few owners and the usual farrago of the racing fraternity.

She carried two mugs of tea and a slab of fruitcake for Reg to an empty table in the corner by a window, which overlooked one of the walkways. She sat down, took a gulp of her tea and smiled at her father. 'OK, Dad. So what do you think?'

'There's a few I need to go back and have another good look at before I could recommend 'em,' he answered, taking his function seriously as always, and fidgeting in his seat because he wanted to get on with it. 'Mind you, when they're all together like this, the milkman would probably have as much idea as anyone which will turn out the best.' Jan smiled at his dry sense of humour.

'It's a good job we don't have a milkman, then. Now you have your tea and a bit of cake or you'll flake out otherwise. It's very tiring slogging round this place all day.'

'I'm all right,' Reg replied sharply. 'Don't you fret.'

He looked relieved when he'd finished his tea and had picked the last crumb of cake from his plate. 'Right, I'm off.'

Jan shrugged. 'All right, Dad, but I want to recheck the print on the ones we've seen so far. You can tell me what you think later.'

Reg nodded and walked off as briskly as his old legs would carry him. Jan looked after him with gratitude. She knew that whatever conclusions he came to they would be equally as valuable as those of the famous bloodstock agents.

She sighed at his independence, resigning herself to her own counsel and carefully going through all the comments she had written on each of the horses they'd already seen. One – a large, late-developing individual by a stallion she'd always admired – she had earmarked for A.D.

She had seen another that might suit Johnny Carlton-Brown, or possibly several other prospective owners, for that matter. Apart from A.D., she realized, it wasn't essential to see each potential purchase in terms of a specific owner now that she had a sheaf of orders for quality horses.

As she was trying to concentrate and get her impressions together, before checking the details of the next batch of animals she wanted to inspect, several agents and breeders called out cheerful greetings. This time last year, she thought, they wouldn't have known her from Adam. A number stopped and, in view of her growing reputation since the Irish National, as well as her connection with A.D., one of the biggest heavyweights of the jumping world, they were eager to know what sort of animals she was looking for.

She was friendly and cheerful with them all, but brief and uninformative as she tried to get her head back into the pages of her catalogue. She didn't allow herself be distracted again until she heard a well-remembered, soft Wexford voice speak over her shoulder.

12

'Sh'jaysus, Jan! It's great to see you.'

Jan turned and found herself looking into the twinkling eyes of the man she most trusted in this land of mercurial yarn spinners, and the one person she really needed to talk to.

'Sean! I was praying I would meet you today.'

Sean McDonagh was in his late forties, lightly built, with a copper-beech complexion, a thick crop of wavy grey hair, luminous blue eyes and an encyclopaedic knowledge of thoroughbred bloodlines. He was also alive to most of the rumours that did the rounds at major bloodstock sales. More importantly, though, he could identify where the smoke reflected genuine fire, and those started by arsonists with vested interests. Sometimes, he'd told Jan, false rumours were started by rival breeders, but more often by rival bidders.

'You should have phoned me as soon as you arrived, but here I am anyway and at your service.' He smiled. 'Hell, you're looking great!'

'God knows why.' Jan brushed the compliment aside. 'I've been working my balls off. Have you got time for a cup of tea – or would you sooner have a Harp?' she asked, knowing that twenty minutes spent with Sean and the catalogue could save her several hours of fruitless search.

'A Harp. That's why I'm here,' he declared, licking his lips. 'Another cup for you?'

'Please,' Jan said. She watched him thoughtfully as he made his way across to the self-service counter. When she had met him this time last year, it had been in very similar circumstances; it had

162

also been the day Angie Sharp had attached herself to Jan for the first time. The irony of it was that she had instantly trusted Angie and not Sean, which had rankled since and made her aware of her own fallibility.

Last time, to Reg's indignation, Sean had warned Jan off buying a horse which she and Reg had liked the look of. He had been proved entirely right several months later.

Sean had also been responsible for introducing Jan to Margaret Berrington, the distinguished Anglo-Irish breeder from whom she'd bought the young star hurdler, Supercall. Thanks to him, she'd been able to do it under the noses of a dozen top trainers who probably would have paid a great deal more than she had for it. Now the horse was being talked of by scribes as a future Gold Cup prospect.

It was at Sean's small farm in County Wexford that she had arranged to spend a couple of days after the sales, viewing several proven horses which he thought might be suitable acquisitions for Gary West.

Sean returned with a tray and placed a fresh mug of tea in front of Jan. He slid onto a chair on the same side of the table so he could read the catalogue with her. 'Right,' he murmured. 'Let's have a look at what you've been up to.'

Jan showed him a list of orders and the approximate budget each owner had given her.

'Hell, Jan! You'll be up there bidding with the big boys. Some of them mightn't like it – they'll make you pay through the nose, if you're not careful.'

'They wouldn't do that.' Jan shook her head in disbelief.

'Most wouldn't, o'course. But there are some greedy people out there: you only need a couple trying to cause mischief and you could find yourself spending a lot more than you should.'

'OK. Thanks for the info, we'll have to see how it goes. But you'd bid for me, wouldn't you, if I asked you nicely?'

'Of course I would and I'd charge you a lot less than you'd save.'

'Who will they think you're buying for?'

'They won't have a clue; I've a dozen or so customers this time round. Some have plenty of money, some less.'

Jan considered what he was saying for a moment, before nodding. 'Thanks, Sean, I think we'd better do that.'

'Right, now. Let's have a look at what you've earmarked so I can put a red line through any duds you might have selected.'

🐎

The Band of Brothers had authorized her to spend up to £100,000 on a suitable youngster. She had explained to them at some length that if they wanted a future long-distance chaser, whatever they bought as a three- or four-year-old would take time to mature and would be unlikely to get on a racecourse for some time. If, on the other hand, they bought a smaller animal with a distinct amount of speed in its pedigree, they might have a chance of seeing their newly named 'nag' run in a bumper around Christmastime.

As she'd expected, they had opted for instant gratification, and she marked a horse in the catalogue that she thought would fit the bill. On the page, Lot 153 was a classically bred bay gelding, by Moscow Society out of a winning mare who was by the Derby winner, Teenoso, called Teenager; the breeder had decided, on the strength of its conformation, that it would be more suitable for jumping than flat racing.

Sean told her he had already seen the unbroken gelding and had found nothing to criticize. 'He's your type of animal; muscular, good bone not *too* heavy and he's a great mover. I would say he'd be just right for your pop-singer fellas.'

'Will you come with me and have another look?'

'No – don't be silly, not if I'm to bid for you. In fact, we've probably been sitting together too long as it is. If you want to see me again over the next two days, give me a buzz on my mobile and I'll meet you somewhere quiet.'

Jan agreed, but wondered if he wasn't being a little over-cautious with his cloak-and-dagger approach. But still, he had consistently marked her card accurately in the past, so she had no reason to doubt him now.

They parted unobtrusively in the tea room and, breaking her proposed itinerary, Jan made her way straight to the barn where the Moscow Society gelding was lodged.

All the walkways between the main buildings were filling up, and there was a distinct increase in tension as prospective purchasers began to focus on what they wanted to buy. Jan noticed how most people were non-committal as they requested the grooms to lead a horse from its stable. Apart from the concern that a rival buyer might note their enthusiasm, they didn't want the vendor to pick up on it either, in case they were encouraged to have the reserve price taken up a few bids higher.

On her way through the first barn Jan heard her name called by a soft, female voice. She spun round and recognized the spoon-faced girl who had been looking after the horse which she'd bought for Toby Waller the year before.

'How're you doing with the Gypsy King gelding?' the girl asked.

'Fine, thanks. The owner named him "Flamenco", I'm afraid.'

The girl nodded. 'I saw that in the racing calendar.'

'He's doing OK, but it takes time to prepare a big lad like him; he'll probably have his first run in November when the ground's a bit softer.'

'Best of luck,' the groom said with genuine goodwill. 'Would you like to have a peek at this fella?' She nodded over her shoulder at the stable door behind.

Jan glanced at her catalogue and smiled regretfully. 'No, sorry, not this time. He's not quite what I'm looking for.'

She walked away, thinking that the small stud which had consigned the horse probably only sent one or two to this sale, pinning all their financial hopes on them each year.

As she carried on through the barn, wondering where on earth Reg had got to, a couple of other breeders lurking around their animals' boxes flashed hopeful grins at her. But Jan, her confidence strengthened since her talk with Sean, didn't want to be deflected any longer from her current target.

She found the horse she was looking for in the charge of a middle-aged woman dressed in a tweed skirt and silk blouse, unlike most of the people around her.

The woman greeted Jan with a nod of recognition. 'Mrs Hardy, isn't it?' she asked.

The horse had been sent to the sales by a breeder called Alastair

Nichols from an Irish address, but from her voice Jan knew instantly she was dealing with an Englishwoman.

'Yes, that's right, though please call me Jan. You must be – ' she consulted the catalogue – 'Mrs Nichols?'

'Lady Nichols, actually, not that it matters. Alastair's my son. Did you want to have a look at the gelding?'

'Yes please.'

Lady Nichols took a lead rein from the hook beside the door, opened the stable and went in. A moment later she led out a bay gelding that exactly matched Sean's description and one of the most handsome and beautifully turned out horses Jan had ever seen at the sales.

'He's bonny!' she declared before she could stop herself.

The horse's handler looked pleased. 'Thank you,' she said. 'Preparing them for the sales is one of my favourite chores.'

Trying to curb her obvious appreciation, Jan asked the woman to hold the horse steady while she looked him in the eye, walked around him and felt each of his front legs. 'Would you mind giving him a trot outside?' she asked.

'Not at all.'

The woman led the gelding at a leisurely walk through the barn and Jan, knowing it was absurd, prayed that despite his attractive entry in the catalogue, not too many people would notice what a superb specimen he was.

The barn doors opened onto a quadrangle formed by adjacent buildings, on which a stretch of level cinders had been laid for vendors to trot their horses while the buyers inspected the quality of their gait.

She waited while Lady Nichols led the animal to the far end of the track and turned him around to face Jan. Lady Nichols paused before running back towards her, leading the horse in a brisk, ground-covering trot.

Jan squatted slightly so her eyes were almost level with the top of the animal's legs. She wanted to be sure that his legs weren't twisted and that he moved forward in a straight line without dishing his feet or turning his toes. She noted his chest was plenty broad enough for a jumper, his ears were pricked and his eyes alert in a way that suggested intelligence and good humour.

Though struggling not to display too much enthusiasm, she still couldn't resist asking Lady Nichols to trot the gelding once more. Finally Jan thanked her politely and made a cursory note in her catalogue before moving on, looking around as if one of the other horses being shown was also of interest to her.

Deep inside, she knew she'd just seen a horse she desperately wanted to buy, and she would have to do everything she could to persuade Darius, the only member of the band coming over for the sale, that he must be prepared to go all the way to get it.

🐎

With a sigh of relief, Jan found Reg soon afterwards and they spent the rest of the afternoon together, viewing horses, comparing notes and arguing the case for the horses they preferred.

A.D. O'Hagan's driver was waiting outside the main gate at seven p.m. and opened the rear door of the Mercedes. Jan followed Reg in and collapsed beside him on the soft upholstery.

She was utterly exhausted. She felt as if she had walked twenty miles back and forth between the stuffy barns. Her head was swimming with impressions of all the horses they had inspected so closely. She had met Sean again beside the lorry park at Billy's tea bar during the afternoon to run through her findings so far; although she still had a lot of horses to see, she felt they had whittled down her list to about twenty animals that she wanted to bid for – as far as her varying instructions allowed.

She also had a few calls on her mobile phone about minor dramas back at Edge Farm and a particularly weepy conversation with Megan, who had wanted to know why her mummy wasn't going to be back to see her jumping Monarch for the first time on Saturday. Tears welled up in Jan's eyes as she reassured Meg that Annabel would be just as good at plaiting and grooming as she would, and told her that Bel was going to make a video so Mummy could see how well Megan had done when she got home.

Right now, the last thing she felt like doing was entertaining a volatile rock singer, ten years her junior, in a Dublin restaurant. She knew it was too late to cancel, though; she should have done it the night before when she'd spoken to him on the telephone. She was mightily relieved he hadn't turned up at Tattersalls that afternoon demanding to be shown any likely purchases, before she'd had the chance to brief him without the distraction of a few hundred horses, all looking pretty much alike to an untrained eye.

Jan and Reg arrived back at the Shelbourne to find a message that Darius was expecting her at half-past eight in a well-known seafood restaurant, not far from the hotel.

Resigned, Jan went up with Reg and saw him to his room. Satisfied that he was happy and not too worn out, she gave herself a long soak in the bath to steam away the rigours of the day.

At least, she thought, *I've broken the back of the hard work.* She knew, though, that the next day and the sheer tension of bidding would take their toll on her, even with her father there as her ally. Despite her increased knowledge, she couldn't help feeling intimidated by the prospect of handling a budget ten times greater than she'd had on her previous visit to Fairyhouse the year before.

Reluctantly, she climbed out of the bath, determined to convince Darius that she'd found just the right horse for him and his band.

Contemplating while she briskly dried herself with an oversized, fluffy towel, she couldn't deny that so far she'd found the singer very good company and that it was flattering to be with a man whom half the girls in the country wanted to leap into bed with. But suddenly, without warning, Eddie Sullivan floated into the forefront of her mind. She stopped drying herself and gazed at her naked body in the steamy mirror.

For a few galling moments she thought of Eddie in Australia with the pregnant Louise and the tears rolled down her face. Quickly turning away, she locked her jaw tight and rubbed her eyes with the towel.

'I won't give in!' she muttered desperately, trying to rid herself of Eddie's image.

The hall porter couldn't have been more helpful when Jan asked him how to find the restaurant where Darius had arranged to meet her.

'It'll only take two minutes to walk, mind. 'Tis a grand place if you like a few oysters and a bit of lobster,' he added with approval. 'My cousin is maître d' there; you tell him I said he's to look after you.'

Jan tried to lighten up as she strolled along the broad pavements under a clear blue evening sky. Despite her thoughts of Eddie, the bath had done a great deal to revive her and there was a hint of a bounce in her stride. She was wearing a simple cotton dress which showed off her figure well and always made her feel confident. And she was looking forward to describing to Darius the gelding she had fallen in love with.

Turning a corner, she saw the restaurant and crossed the road. The hall porter at the Shelbourne had evidently already been in touch with his cousin, who greeted Jan effusively and showed her to a quiet corner of the busy room, which was decked out with fishing nets and lobster pots.

'Mrs Hardy, there's a message from your host,' the maître d' confided in a discreet voice. 'He's a little held up. He's very sorry about it but he'll be with you as soon as he's able. Now, I'm to ask you what'll you have to drink?'

When he had gone, Jan sat back in her chair and inspected her surroundings. She presumed that the flagstoned floor, open fire and rustic wooden furniture were meant to reflect the west of Ireland, source of seafood for the menu, but they also gave the place a relaxed and homely feeling.

Just as well, she thought, feeling rather peeved to find herself yet again waiting alone in a restaurant for one of her owners. *Why are they all such lousy time-keepers?* she wondered. She noted that the table was laid for three and wondered who else was going to join them.

Twenty minutes later Darius was being ushered obsequiously across the restaurant by the manager. As the other diners became aware of his presence, the volume of conversation dipped and several pairs of eye followed him to the table.

'Jan! How are you?' he said, beaming. 'Look, I'm really sorry to keep you hanging about on your own. I hope none of these waiters tried to molest you,' he added, turning to grin at the maître d'.

'Not yet,' Jan replied with a laugh, standing up to return his kiss. 'But it's early days, I've only been here twenty-five minutes.'

'God, I'm so sorry!' the singer said, and sat down opposite her.

He made no mention of the third place laid at the table and Jan wondered if it was simply an oversight by the restaurant staff.

It was her first tête-à-tête with Darius and she was surprised to find, in many ways, how normal he was. She gathered he had been a promising pupil called Darren Cooper at a Kent grammar school where, like thousands of teenage boys, he'd formed a band. It consisted of four individuals, including two musically trained brothers; they all understood that original harmonies and lyrics were paramount and they had the talent to convert them into their own unique sound.

It was when Darren started talking as himself that his real character shone through. Then the small gestures and verbal tics that seemed part of being a rock star faded away and Jan realized he was an intelligent, perceptive and vulnerable human being.

It also occurred to her, not for the first time, that successful people often seemed to have two entirely different personae, and only revealed as much of their private identity as they felt necessary.

She had seen it briefly in a film-star girlfriend of JCB's and more recently in Gary West – the private, thoughtful and rather sympathetic man one minute, the public, brash billionaire gambler the next.

After they had ordered their supper, Darius talked a little about the Band of Brothers' album which had been produced by her brother. It had been released in May to a great reception and was going to form the basis of a major tour the following autumn.

'What are your plans after that?' Jan asked.

'I'd much rather hear about your ambitions,' Darius answered, evidently bored with talking about himself.

'Are you really interested in racing?' she asked doubtfully.

'As it happens, I'm interested in almost everything – OK, not

170

train-spotting or Morris dancing – though, come to think of it,' he laughed, 'maybe that's part of our musical heritage too.'

Jan grinned. 'They do it outside the pub near us a couple of times a year. I confess it doesn't do a lot for me, but I know what you mean about being interested in everything. The trouble is I haven't got the time and, quite frankly, I'm probably too educated to get involved in the acts. Still, as my old man would say, "Jack of all Trades, master of None".'

'I understand that, but what I'm saying is that in any human activity – and that includes horse racing, even if the horses do most of the work – there is still a degree of art, skill, craft, guile, jealousy, ambition and dishonesty – especially in a field where huge lumps of dosh get shuffled around regularly.'

Jan grinned. 'I don't suppose there's much corruption in Morris dancing, though.'

Darius sucked his teeth. 'You never know. I bet it's competitive in its own way and riddled with petty jealousies. But to get back to horses.'

'My ambitions?' Jan repeated. 'I suppose they're the same as any National Hunt trainer's – to win the Grand National and the Cheltenham Gold Cup, and as many other big races as possible and hopefully to be champion trainer one day.'

'Which means doing what, in practical terms?'

'Sending out over a hundred winners a season, I guess. The current record for a jump trainer is well over that.'

'What size yard was that from?' Darius asked, evidently appreciating the significance of the numbers.

'About a hundred and fifty horses with probably at least another fifty or so being prepared in satellite yards.'

'So you haven't got much of a chance with just thirty or forty?'

'Nope,' Jan agreed. 'Still, if I can produce a strike rate that's better than the others, people will sit up and take notice, but quality is my main aim.'

'I know this may sound stupid, but what's a strike rate?'

'The percentage of winners you get in relation to the number of runners you send out. If I sent out a hundred runners in a season and scored thirty wins, obviously that's thirty per cent, which is high in this game.'

'And just about where you ended last season,' Darius added, to Jan's gratification.

'I think twenty-eight per cent in the end.'

'Think?' the singer asked with a grin and a lowered eyebrow.

Jan smiled. 'All right, "know". I try not to send out too many runners that I don't think have a reasonable chance. It can frustrate some owners, but in the end, I tell them, one winning run is worth ten losing ones.'

'Yeah, I can see that, but surely a lot of these guys just want to run a horse for the hell of it? They don't mind if it doesn't win as long as they can bring their mates along and swan around the parade ring before the race.'

'Occasionally that happens.'

'Well, rest assured, Jan. We'll only want you to send our nag out when you think it's got a bloody good chance of winning. Is that OK?'

'That's what *you* say, but what about the others?'

'I may only be the singer in our band, but I'm in charge of this project,' Darius said uncompromisingly.

They talked about racing and the gelding Jan hoped to buy the next day, as they ate their first two courses accompanied by a good bottle of Chablis. Jan found she was really enjoying the man's company, though not physically, despite the fact he was very attractive. As they were being served coffee, however, she became a little apprehensive.

Since she'd become a widow she had grown used to the almost inevitable rise of the male ego after a good meal and a few drinks, and she was aware that even the mildest of men could become surprisingly persistent if his blood was up. She prayed that after such an enjoyable evening she wouldn't end up having a tussle with her new junior owner.

After Darius had signed his credit-card receipt and a few auto-graphs, they walked from the restaurant into the still balmy air of Dublin.

'I think we're both walking the same way,' the singer said, looking at his watch, 'so I may as well give you a bit of company.'

'Thanks,' Jan said, already on her guard.

Darius talked about the unexpected pleasures of the city and its architecture as they strolled back to St Stephen's Green and continued up the steps, through the revolving doors into the lobby of the hotel.

Darius looked at her with a twinkle in his eye. 'Nightcap?'

Jan shook her head a little more briskly than she had meant to. 'No thanks,' she said, trying not to panic. 'I've got to be on my toes tomorrow, and so have you if we're to buy that lovely horse.'

'OK, I understand, but just come over and meet Becky, my girlfriend; she's over there waiting in the Shelbourne Bar.'

Jan winced guiltily. 'Why on earth didn't you bring her to dinner?'

Darius laughed. 'I was going to, but her plane was delayed – I'd been out to meet it; that's why I was late. So I left a message for her to come straight to the hotel; she won't have been here long.'

Extremely relieved, but wishing he had told her earlier, Jan continued walking through the lobby with Darius and was introduced to a slender blonde girl, whom she vaguely recognized.

It was only later, as she climbed into her big soft bed, that she remembered where she'd seen Becky – she was a singer-songwriter, a bit like Eva Cassidy, who had just broken into the charts.

Jan shook her head in amazement. When she'd first gone into the business of training racehorses it had never occurred to her that she would be entering a world of celebrity and glamour – not, she thought ruefully as she dropped off to sleep, that there was anything remotely glamorous about Frank Jellard or Bernie Sutcliffe.

🐎

At seven-thirty the next morning, on her way out to the sales with her father in the Mercedes, Jan reviewed the list of purchases she hoped to make over the next two days.

From the shortlist of twenty she and Reg had managed to isolate the day before, and the few more she planned to inspect today, she was confident that she had found enough animals to fill her orders, provided they didn't exceed her budget. But now the moment of truth was getting closer, she was extremely nervous.

She decided to ring Sean on his mobile and arranged to meet him briefly the moment she arrived at Tattersalls. As soon as she had finished the call, Toby Waller rang to say he had just landed at Dublin airport and would be at the sales in an hour or so. Jan thought to herself that, of all her clients, Toby was the one she would most like to have by her side. John Tanner had already arranged to meet her at eleven o'clock in the main bar before the lots she was hoping to buy for Gary West came up. Darius was due to arrive around lunchtime and meet JCB in the restaurant, where they were expecting her to join them.

Jan remembered the previous year, and how difficult it had been when she'd sat at the end of a large table of rich, noisy men presided over by A.D. O'Hagan, and how completely out of her depth and intimidated she'd felt.

At least, she thought, *that isn't going to happen this time.*

13

By the time Jan walked into the restaurant to meet Johnny Carlton-Brown, who was having lunch with Darius, she had looked at thirty more horses with her father, earmarked a few possibles and had successfully bid for two with Sean McDonagh acting as her agent: a workman-like gelding for Bernie for the equivalent of £15,000 and a lovely-looking, well-bred filly for Gary West for 90,000 Irish guineas. Toby Waller bid for himself on Jan's recommendation and bought a strapping black gelding for 35,000 guineas.

Jan was greatly relieved that John Tanner had brought two friends along; it meant he wasn't hanging onto her coat-tails as much as she'd feared and he seemed quite unconcerned when she informed him she was meeting Darius and JCB in the restaurant. No doubt, she thought, it would have been a different story if Annabel had been with her.

Reg had also been invited to join Carlton-Brown's table for lunch, but he was being 'nappy' and refusing to come.

'Jan, you go,' he said. 'I'll be much happier on my own, reading the paper with a bacon sandwich at Billy's.'

Jan really wished she could have done the same. As she wasn't feeling at all hungry, she couldn't relax over the meal; she didn't dare touch a drop of alcohol – she knew she would need to have all her wits about her for the afternoon session as there were three more horses going through the ring she wanted to have a crack at. JCB and Darius understood completely and were thoroughly enjoying the whole scene. Becky had been entrusted with Darius's card to go shopping in Dublin. Although Darius was new to the fringes of the racing world, he seemed quite at home.

Lot 153 was due in the ring at about two-forty. But the pop star had already been out to the barn as discreetly as he could to look at the horse for himself.

He agreed that, as far as he could tell, it looked a cracker, but he would rather rely on Jan's judgement.

In front of the octagonal sales building, two large turfed areas, tarmacked around the outer edge, were arranged in timber-railed circles where vendors could parade their wares before leading them into the sales arena. The space was brimming with men and women chattering intently, keeping a wary eye on one another, while they watched the thoroughbreds being led around.

Lady Nichols was leading her son's gelding, totally unconcerned about the spectators but preoccupied with the horse's state of mind. Jan could see she was talking to the animal to reassure it, to calm its fear of the unfamiliar crowds and the echoing drone of the auctioneer's voice coming through the loudspeakers.

There were a dozen or so people standing by the rails of the second ring, watching the animals closely.

'Do you see what I mean about the way he moves?' Jan said quietly, hardly moving her lips.

Darius nodded. 'Yeah, it's like his feet are hardly touching the ground.'

'Perfect, he's not short of bone either. Look at him, he's got good strong limbs, a good chest and a great big arse.'

'I can see most of it, but I'll take your word for the rest,' the singer said.

'The trouble is,' Jan went on, 'I think there's a lot of other people here who like him as well, which is hardly surprising. He's by a top-class sire and his mother was a winner several times.'

'Has she had other foals?'

'Yes, but none that have raced yet,' Jan said, consulting the entry. 'This chap was her second, the first was a filly and she was kept for breeding.'

'And he's four years old, right?'

'That's it.'

Darius straightened up and turned away from the ring. 'Oh well, let's go for it,' he said, his eyes sparkling with anticipation.

'Nobody's going to know it's you bidding, by the way. My man Sean McDonagh is going to do it from the other side of the gallery, but I'm going to give him his cue, so you'd better stick close by me.'

Ten minutes later Jan and her excited client were in place, sitting towards the rear of the raked seating in the timber-lined amphi-theatre.

Jan's heart started to beat faster as she opened her bag and pulled out a bright red silk scarf, which she began to wrap around her neck.

'What do you want that on for?' Darius asked. 'It's not exactly cold.'

'As long as I'm wearing it, Sean will go on bidding,' she answered in a conspiratorial whisper.

'So if I want you to stop, I just yank it off, right?'

'Just nudging me will do.'

Lot 153's aristocratic groom led her charge into the arena as if it was something she did every day. No doubt she could have got someone else to do it, but she patently didn't want anyone or anything to upset the young horse, which suggested to Jan that the animal had been thoughtfully handled for the first few years of its life and, she knew, that could be as important for horses as it was for children.

The thoroughbred strode out beautifully. Its preparation and impeccable turnout were obvious.

Jan was disheartened to see that the lots at this important stage of the sale were being auctioned by the most experienced member of the team – a wily man who knew how to squeeze every ounce out of his audience.

'Now,' he announced with satisfaction, 'Lot 153, by Moscow Society out of Teenager. An exceptional-looking animal, with unlimited potential, so – ' he paused and his eyes swept the theatre in an all-inclusive gaze – 'who'll put me in at fifty thousand?'

On the wall above the arch, opposite where the horses came in, the bid price of the current lot was shown on an electronic display board in Irish guineas and pounds sterling, as the sale was being conducted. A row of orange noughts awaited the first offer.

'All right, who'll give me forty thousand?' the eagle-eyed Irishman on the rostrum intoned. He nodded at the first response. 'Twenty thousand, I'll take; twenty-two; twenty-four; twenty-six thousand, twenty-eight, thirty thousand.'

There was a moment's pause after the first flurry of early bidders who had hoped to grab a bargain. Across the hall from Jan, above the auctioneer's left shoulder but well within sight of one of the red-uniformed women spotters, Sean had not moved a muscle.

The man on the rostrum continued to scrutinize his audience like a drill sergeant inspecting a bunch of sloppy new recruits. 'We've a long way to go here,' he admonished them. 'This is a serious horse, and we're looking for serious bids. Thank you, sir.' He nodded at someone up in the gallery behind Jan. 'Thirty-two thousand, thirty-four, thirty-six. Thirty-eight thousand guineas, I'm bid. He's going to sell for a lot more than this, so if you want him, you're going to have to be more serious.'

Jan felt a gentle prod in her side.

'When will your man start?' Darius whispered out of the side of his mouth, nodding approximately in Sean's direction.

Jan said nothing, but she lifted her hand a fraction of an inch from her thigh to indicate that he should be patient.

In the ring below them, Lady Nichols remained calm as she led the horse, who seemed quite unaware of the drama and tension surrounding his future.

Above the doors the display board showed orange figures: IRE Gns 38,000; £30,400.

Below it, Jan saw a man leaning against the railings lift his index finger.

'Forty thousand!' the auctioneer said a little more smugly. He leaned forward over the front of his podium and his piercing blue eyes searched out the next bid, until he saw it and his head jerked back. 'Forty-five,' he declared, and swung round to face the entrance. 'Fifty thousand.' He acknowledged this first benchmark with a momentary upward twitch of his lips.

The girl beside him, looking backwards, raised her hand. He glanced over his shoulder and acknowledged Sean McDonagh's first bid.

'Thank you, sir, fifty-five thousand; sixty; sixty-five, seventy.'

As the bidding increased, Jan snatched her breath at the speed and the mounting price. A round of applause from the spectators greeted the one-hundred-thousand-guinea bid, equivalent to eighty-five thousand pounds.

Jan gulped as it was nearing the limit she had agreed with the band, but she could clearly see from the manner in which the auctioneer's eyes were swinging from one corner of the room to another that there must still be at least four active bidders out there. She knew Sean was right to have started when he did, but she could detect dangerous energy which could force the pace and whip up the buyers to go higher than they had originally planned.

Jan deliberately untied the scarf around her neck and discreetly pulled it off.

Opposite them Sean immediately stopped bidding.

Darius turned to her and whispered hoarsely, 'Jan, what's going on?'

'It's OK. We just want to cool it for a bit.'

Jan felt a slight easing of tension, as if she had stepped out of a ring where she'd been taking part in a free-for-all. But, to her dismay, the removal of one bidder only seemed to encourage more into the pit.

The bidding passed one hundred and ten thousand guineas. The non-participating audience had long ceased to chatter and the whispers that had persisted throughout the early stages ceased; the energy coursing through the building seemed to grow and the man on the rostrum clutched the head of his wooden gavel, stabbing the air with the handle like a conductor working his orchestra up to a finale until, suddenly, the bids stopped flowing.

'One hundred and twenty thousand,' the auctioneer announced slowly. 'This horse still looks cheap to me.' He took a step back and straightened his shoulders, contriving to include more of his audience, before homing in on the well-known English trainer, still leaning with studied casualness on the railings by the entrance. 'It's with you, sir.'

Jan once again felt a gentle nudge in the ribs, though thankfully, in the pin-drop silence, no words accompanied it.

Slowly, as casually and unobtrusively as possible, she pulled the red scarf back around her neck and tied it in a loose knot beneath her chin.

A second later she saw Sean raise his hand.

The spotter caught it instantly and drew it to her boss's attention. He didn't bother to turn this time, but smiled knowingly, as if to say: *What did I tell you?*

'A hundred and twenty-five thousand guineas!' he declared.

He leaned forward and stared piercingly at the previous bidder down in the arch.

Without realizing it, Jan stopped breathing; she felt hot and clammy; a hundred and twenty-five thousand guineas was equivalent to the band's limit of a hundred thousand pounds. She gazed at the man in the gateway and tried to read his expression, watching his hands for any sign of movement.

The auctioneer was becoming impatient. 'Well? D'you want him . . . ?'

Jan's heart stopped. The man nodded and slowly raised his hand. As he did, Jan fumbled with her scarf and started to pull it off. Suddenly she felt Darius's hand on hers, holding it tight, preventing her from bringing it further. She glanced at him, alarmed, with her eyebrows raised in question.

With no more than a barely perceptible nod, he issued his instruction for her to go on bidding. But she didn't have the authority in writing from him or anyone else in the band to exceed their budget. If Sean got the gelding for her and they changed their minds, she wouldn't have a leg to stand on.

She looked at him and mouthed, 'Sure?'

Looking her straight in the eye, he nodded.

She sighed and left the scarf where it was. She loosened her grip and lowered her sweating hand.

All around them there had been an audible gasp and a rustle in the crowd as, this time, the man on the rostrum swivelled himself to look at Sean McDonagh.

'There you are, sir. A hundred and twenty-five thousand I'm bid. It's against you. You know you want him; and you know what you have to do.'

Sean stared back at him without blinking or moving until he screwed up his face into an expression of indecision, which suggested that he could be tempted, with great reluctance, to go on.

The auctioneer read his signal. 'Fill it up,' he offered.

Sean nodded.

Instantly the auctioneer swung back to address the man under the arch. 'A hundred and thirty thousand I'm bid. If you want this exceptional horse, who will thrive on those chalk downs of yours, you'll have to go again.'

Jan felt light-headed. She could hardly bring herself to look, but after what seemed like an eternity, though in reality it was less than fifteen seconds, she had heard nothing. She opened her eyes to see the trainer dismiss the offer with a rueful shake of his head.

'Are ye sure?' he was asked.

He shook it again.

'All right, is that it?' the auctioneer asked, looking around with disappointment. He sighed, reversed his gavel and banged it on the front of his rostrum. 'Sold to Sean McDonagh at one hundred and thirty thousand guineas.'

There was a round of applause and a murmur of approval and congratulations, which suggested the horse had still been cheap.

Jan, ghostly white, looked at Darius. 'I hope you're happy.'

He grinned back at her. 'Yeah, that was wicked!' He shook his head. 'It's terrible, isn't it, the way you want to go on and on.'

'Thank God we didn't have to, then – as it is, it's more than I was authorized to spend. To tell the truth, at one stage, I thought he was going to go for a lot more. I still think he's probably the best horse in the sale.'

'Don't you worry about the money – it's only one gig!' the singer chortled. 'Let's go and have another look at him.'

Jan shook her head. 'No not yet. Let him get back and settled in his box first.' She didn't want to tell the world that Sean McDonagh had been bidding on her behalf; there were a couple more lots where she might want to make use of him again.

🐎

On Saturday morning as Jan woke in her broad bed at the Shelbourne, she looked at the clock and realized she had slept solidly for ten hours. Which wasn't surprising. When she had eventually got back to her room the night before, she had been exhausted.

Darius and Johnny had gone home, taking Reg with them, but Tanner and Toby Waller as well, thank goodness, had stayed on in Dublin and had insisted on taking her out to dinner and to a bar afterwards.

The second day had been a disappointment for Jan. The prices had hardened to a point where she was being consistently outbid, and the good animals were going for more than her budgets. Although she had managed to buy one for A.D. and a chestnut gelding for Colonel Gilbert, there was nothing for JCB, much to his well-controlled disappointment; and she had found not a single thing suitable within Frank Jellard's price range either. In the end, she left the sale having made just five purchases, including Toby's.

It wasn't the end of the world – she'd told Frank – there were other sales, Doncaster in August, and at least she had made contact with a couple more breeders who had young stock at home.

Before leaving the sales complex the previous evening, Jan had made arrangements with Brennan's, her shipping agent, to have the new horses delivered back to Edge Farm. Toby and Tanner had checked out and flown to London early that morning. Over the next two days she was going to make her way down south, to visit Sean McDonagh for the first time on his home territory.

Sean had turned out to be exactly the ally she needed at the sales and she was positive she wouldn't have done so well without his knowledge and support. Undoubtedly, though, by the end of the week, people realized he had done a lot of the bidding on her behalf.

Jan was really looking forward to the extra few days in Ireland without the usual stresses and strains and decided that she would take up Siobhan O'Hagan's invitation to stay at Aigmont overnight. The horse she had found for A.D. had been a bargain by his standards and she was keen to tell him about it first hand.

Before she left her room, Jan rang the O'Hagans' house and was put through to Siobhan, who told her A.D. wasn't back, although he hoped to be that evening, and she reiterated her invitation to Jan to come and stay.

Once she had packed and checked out of the Shelbourne a porter piled her luggage into a small Ford Escort. Jan had hired the car because she didn't want to be too reliant on A.D.'s generosity. And, as she was driving on to Sean's farm afterwards, she didn't want A.D.'s chauffeur earwigging and reporting back to him on the studs and horses she had been to see for Gary West. She drove out of St Stephen's Green in good spirits just before noon, looking forward to the weekend ahead of her.

Aigmont, A.D.'s Georgian mansion, was more than fifty miles south of Dublin, on the western slopes of the Wicklow Mountains. The last time Jan had visited the house, she'd been driven there by Daragh on an autumn evening, when the short days following had revealed a romantic but leafless and misty landscape.

Now in June, with a bright sun lighting the lakes, the woods, the hills and the lush grass of southern Kildare and County Wicklow, she found the journey completely breathtaking.

Her map-reading proved surprisingly reliable and just after two o'clock she found herself gazing at the imposing pair of iron gates hung from massive stone piers, which marked the entrance to A.D.'s country estate.

She stopped the car, climbed out and was hunting around for a way to open the gates when she noticed a small intercom inserted in one of the pillars. She pressed the buzzer and waited a moment or two. When it was answered, she announced herself and there was a soft click as the gates swung quietly apart.

Jan clambered back in and drove through. Glancing in her rear-view mirror, she saw the gates close slowly behind her. She carried on up a long sweeping drive, which curved back and forth across the sloping parkland until, beyond a final stand of beeches, the elegant pillared front of the Palladian mansion came into view. Side-lit by the afternoon sun, with a thickly wooded hill rising behind, it looked extraordinarily beautiful, like a vision from a distant past.

Jan stopped the small car in front of the grand portico, let herself out and climbed the flight of shallow stone steps which led up to a pair of glazed double doors.

They were opened as she reached them, and she was greeted by Mario, the smoothly handsome Italian butler whom she had met the previous autumn.

'Welcome back to Aigmont, madam,' he said with a polite smile. 'If you give to me your key, I will deal with the car and your bags. Mrs O'Hagan is expecting you in the drawing room.'

'Thank you,' Jan said, gazing around the hall, which seemed even more magnificent than she remembered.

A massive Waterford crystal chandelier hung down from two storeys above. Last time, there had been logs blazing in the marble fireplace, where now there was an extravagant arrangement of purple irises in a Chinese vase.

Mario opened the door to her right and ushered her into a large, airy room, quietly furnished with a concert grand piano, original Georgian furniture and three large damask sofas. Siobhan was standing in front of the fireplace talking to a burly, red-faced man dressed in country walking garb.

'Jan,' she smiled. 'It's so lovely to see you; I hope you had a pleasant journey. This is Michael Wasilowski, my accompanist. He's about to venture ten miles along this route called the Wicklow Way,' she said, pointing at a map. 'I'm sure it's just an excuse for him to work up a thirst though, isn't it?' She laughed.

The man shook Jan's hand with an embarrassed grin. 'I don't need to walk to enjoy the Guinness,' he said with a faint Polish accent. 'I'm sorry to be so brief, but I must leave now or I'll never be back before nightfall.' He picked up the map and bowed slightly before he left the room.

'Now the unfortunate news is A.D. won't be back this evening. You know how he hates flying? Well, he's got held up with rather more meetings than he expected in Zurich, so I'm afraid he won't arrive back here until lunchtime tomorrow.'

Damn it, Jan thought as she tried not to let her disappointment show. After all, she swiftly reminded herself, A.D. is an important man. But she disliked being messed around. When she made an agreement, she stuck to it, come what may. Well now, no matter what the consequences, she had no intention of reneging on the arrangements she'd made with Sean McDonagh, who was expecting her for lunch at his farm down near Enniscorthy in County Wexford the next day.

'That's a pity,' she said. 'I'll have to be gone by then. I so wanted to tell him about the new horse I've just bought for him. Still, I can leave you all the details. I expect he'll let me know what he thinks.'

'I expect he will,' Siobhan agreed. 'Now what would you like to drink?'

❧

Suddenly another question entered Jan's head: how on earth would she spend the next twenty-four hours with Siobhan – a woman who made no bones about being bored by too much talk about horses and horse racing, and whose own profession provoked a similar reaction in Jan? But Mrs O'Hagan – she knew – was a skilled and tactful hostess.

After a light lunch which passed in a polite but friendly atmosphere, Siobhan left Jan in a small sitting room to watch the racing on television. That evening she had thoughtfully invited a small-time but voluble local trainer and his wife to join them and the pianist for dinner, which provided Jan with plenty of entertainment and a few new insights into the Irish jump racing scene.

❧

The following morning Jan set off immediately after breakfast and was sorry to be leaving so soon. She found that the journey along the empty roads took much less time than she'd anticipated, but knowing Sean's easygoing nature, she felt sure he wouldn't mind if she arrived earlier than originally planned.

She had marked the nearest village to Hilltower Farm and found it easily enough on the banks of the River Slaney. As Sean had suggested, she asked the first person she saw for directions to the place.

'You'll not find anyone there,' she was told by a tall, doleful man. 'They will be in church until half eleven.'

'Never mind. I'll go anyway and wait in my car, if you could give me directions how to find it, please.'

With the details echoing round her head, Jan drove west, up the side of the river valley with the bulk of Mount Leinster crouching in the sun ahead of her, and followed the deserted lanes between stock-filled pastures until a cluster of stone buildings matched the description she'd been given. A large horsebox was parked beside one of the barns, and a faded sign confirmed that she was at the gates of Hilltower Farm. She smiled and carried on up a rutted grassy track, which was in sharp contrast to Aigmont's approach. But the timber-railed fences surrounding a series of neat, weed-free paddocks were all in good condition. In most of the fields there were two or more horses of various ages. One glance at their rounded bodies and glossy coats told Jan they were well cared for and in obvious good health.

Reaching the buildings, she drove on through a gap between two low stone barns and into a courtyard, where she stopped and clambered out of the car. She stretched and stood for a few moments looking around, taking everything in. The house stood in front of her on higher ground. Behind it, a cluster of tall oak and ash trees housed a busy colony of crows, whose harsh calls were the only sound that broke the silence of the summer morning. Beyond the trees, on the next ridge, Jan could see the ruins of an ancient tower, which she presumed had given the farm its name.

A horse stamped its feet on a stone floor somewhere inside one of the barns, while an assortment of chickens scratched and pecked around the yard. The peeling, pale blue front door of the house was ajar, but there was no immediate sign of human life. Jan knew that Sean was married with children, but she had no idea of what age or how many. A weather-worn, seven-seater estate car parked in a corner suggested several. A new red plastic tractor was a sharp reminder to Jan of her own children and she realized how much she was missing them.

Jan thought that the man in the village was probably right about where the family would be and decided to fill the time by taking a closer look at the horses in the paddocks.

She made her way out between the old buildings, walked back

down the track and let herself through the first five-barred gate she came to.

Two mares, each with a foal about three or four months old, were grazing contentedly.

Jan made a clicking noise with her tongue. The foals skittered back to be closer to their mothers, who raised their heads on long, elegant necks to see what was going on.

Seeing an unfamiliar face and no bucket or head-collar, they turned and slowly walked away to resume their grazing elsewhere. Jan wandered on through several more paddocks, thoroughly enjoying, as always, the sight of such superb animals in natural surroundings, totally relaxed and unbothered.

She had often thought about the depth of the relationship between man and horse – how for millennia humans had relied on the horse for communication, transport, battle, entertainment and sport. Arabs had been riding their horses in races since before the time of Christ, while Romans and Byzantines raced them harnessed to chariots.

Mounted soldiers had been marauding through the ancient world since centuries BC, always achieving superiority over their unmounted adversaries – it was still less than a century since horses had last been engaged in front-line combat.

It wasn't surprising that for thousands of years there had been such competition to breed horses with a range of characteristics so diverse that they included the extraordinary biddability of the Andalusian, the endurance of the Arab, and the perfect conformation for speed found in the thoroughbred.

Standing in Sean's fields, watching his horses in such a peaceful setting, living in harmony with humanity, made Jan feel extremely privileged to be involved with such wonderful creatures and able to call them her friends.

A big smile spread across her face.

I just love 'em, she thought.

14

Jan was still leaning on one of the paddock gates surveying a pair of well-formed geldings, when the sounds of the countryside were disturbed by the noise of a large diesel engine making its way up the lane. A few moments later a big white Land Cruiser came into view and turned in through the gate at the bottom of the grassy track.

A saluting arm appeared from the driver's window. Jan acknowledged it and started to walk back towards the yard, arriving as the four-by-four pulled up. Sean clambered out, followed by a short, dark-haired woman, half a dozen years younger, and five children, whose ages probably ranged from four to fifteen.

Sean took her hand warmly. 'My, it's great to see you, Jan. I heard you were here already.'

'Good heavens! News travels fast round here,' Jan chuckled. 'I only spoke to one man in the village.'

'He told me when I dropped into the bar to collect my newspaper. Anyway, this is Teresa, my wife, and Mary, Sean Junior, Michael, Jessica and Liam. This is Mrs Hardy, who's from England and is a very important client.'

Jan shook hands with the shy young McDonaghs, and was instantly impressed by their good looks and quiet manners.

'Now, come on in,' Sean said briskly. 'We can have a drink and a bite to eat while we watch a few videos and look at the pedigrees of the nags I've arranged for you to see.'

'Will I be able to see some in the flesh today?'

'You will. There are two or three here already, which Teresa fetched in yesterday, and there are a couple not far away, back up by Tullow; we'll take a look at them later on. Tomorrow we'll drive over to Cashel to look at half a dozen more – if that's OK with you?' he added, as if he'd suddenly thought he might have mapped out too heavy a schedule.

'That's fine,' Jan said emphatically. 'I need to see as many as possible now I'm here. I wouldn't mind looking at a couple of bargains – if such a thing ever exists for an English trainer,' she added, teasingly. 'Something from a farmer's field that's well made, not broken and without a fancy pedigree or price tag would fit the bill nicely.'

Sean grinned, 'There's plenty of those if you know where to look. And they can be the most entertaining visits, I can tell you.'

After a sociable family lunch of cold meat and baked potatoes, Jan spent a tiring but ultimately satisfactory afternoon viewing horses and saw five she would gladly have taken home; two had huge potential and price tags to match, but were still within Gary West's budget. Sean tempered her enthusiasm when he told her that, in his opinion, they still had three of the best horses to see the following day, all in different yards.

'But, right now,' he said, looking at his watch, 'it's not seven yet. We've still time to go and have a look at a decent animal that'll not be a lot of money. If you'd like to do that?'

'Oh please.' Jan nodded, thinking of her order for Frank Jellard and how difficult it would be to fill. 'I've got an owner who wants a young horse so he can name it himself – something rather embarrassing I shouldn't wonder – but he doesn't want to spend much.'

'Right, let's get a move on.'

Sean drove as if he was in the Lombard rally along lanes that were narrow and often provided zero visibility.

'Do you always drive like this?' Jan asked. And soon found the only way she could bear the journey was to close her eyes, hang onto the door handle and keep talking. 'Is he expecting us?' she asked, greatly relieved when they turned off the road onto a faint pair of wheel tracks across a scrawny upland field.

'I told him we might come and look at the filly. But he's nearly always here anyway; he's not a very sociable fella.'

'Is this horse really worth looking at?' Jan asked doubtfully, with her eyes now open, gazing at the farmland they were crossing – all covered with docks and thistles.

'She certainly is, and she's not too badly bred in my view, though her sire's not proved to be fashionable and her dam never did more than the odd bit of point-to-pointing around here. But I did see the mare run once and she'd a bundle of talent, if only poor old Joe had the slightest idea how to train her. I told him, if he'd sent her off to a real trainer like Dermot O'Hare, she could have done great things for him. But there it is; he was always too damned mean. So, although there's not much in the dam's pedigree, she'd plenty about her; she just never had a realistic chance to prove it.'

As they rounded the shoulder of the hill, the farm came into view.

'That's the place,' Sean said with a chuckle.

Jan gasped in disbelief. It was one of the most dilapidated places she had ever seen. As they drover nearer, she could see chunks of abandoned farm machinery scattered randomly among the tumble-down barns with rolls of rusty barbed wire and twisted sheets of corrugated iron. A few plastic feed bags scuttled around in the hill-top breeze or flapped from power lines where they had caught. And large bales of discoloured, rotting hay were heaped in haphazard piles.

Anything less likely to inspire confidence than an animal reared in these surroundings, Jan found hard to imagine.

'Jesus!' she said. 'I hope the horse doesn't look as rough as this.'

'It'll not be in plaits, that's for sure, and I doubt it will ever have seen a dandy brush in its life. But you'll have to look through that and see the yoke underneath.'

Sean drove up to a sagging five-bar gate tied up with yards of orange baling twine. They stopped, climbed out and carefully untied a dozen or so knots to let themselves into the yard beyond, retying the gate behind them. The yard was edged on three sides by crumbling stone barns, roofed with twisted and battered corrugated iron. The only thing that moved was a dark brown head sticking out from a window in the makeshift timber frontage of one of the buildings.

'Hello! Joe?' Sean shouted into the dung-scented air.

'There's no need to wake the dead,' a voice growled behind them.

Jan spun round, startled by the abrupt greeting, and saw a small, wrinkled man, wearing a grimy tweed jacket tied with a double strand of orange twine and short rumpled wellies with inner-tube patches attempting to cover the holes. He glowered at them both from dark, hooded eyes as Sean introduced Jan.

Jan tried not to stare at the strange little figure as she stuck out her right hand.

'Sorry to disturb you, Joe, but Jan's a friend of mine. We've come to look at your filly. Jan's wanting a cheap horse.'

The man grunted. 'This filly'll be good, all right, but won't be cheap.'

Sean sighed loudly, 'OK, Joe, but we may as well have a look at her now we're here.'

The farmer hesitated for a moment with a show of reluctance before he walked across to the stable from where the little brown head was still poking out inquisitively. He pulled an old halter off a nail and let himself in. He came out a few seconds later with the rope lashed around the animal's head and stood her on the uneven and pot-holed surface of the yard.

The filly's mane was matted and almost down to her knees. There was a thick layer of mud on her back and her tail was so long it wrapped around her fetlocks as she walked.

Jan took a deep breath and stepped forward to take a closer look. One glance at the filly had told her it would be worth trying to negotiate with this truculent farmer.

In Jan's view, as the filly stood, everything about her looked right. She was broad and strong, with plenty of power in the rear, enough bone and moderately sloping, impact-absorbing shoulders. As Jan leaned down and felt each foreleg, looking for splints and any other sign of injury, the filly watched anxiously, her eyes as big as saucers. There was nothing amiss, so Jan continued looking at the animal from all quarters, trying to keep her expression as neutral as possible.

'What have you done with her?' she asked the farmer lightly.

'Did he not tell you?' Joe Corrigan glanced accusingly at Sean. 'She's only a three-year-old, so she's been in the field more or less since the day she was born.'

'What, even in winter?' Jan asked, taken aback.

'Of course not in winter, though she always spent her days out.'

'You haven't long-reined her or anything?'

'I've not had the time and I can't afford any help on this place now.' He looked around the desolate yard and fields beyond.

Jan believed him and felt a pang of guilt.

'I'd like to see her move. Have you got a level place where you could give her a trot for me?' she asked doubtfully.

'Follow me,' Corrigan ordered as he manoeuvred the filly through a narrow gap between the buildings in the far corner of the yard. Beyond was a small area of grass, comparatively free of weeds but untidily fenced with flapping white electric tape and twisted blue plastic posts, apparently placed at random.

Jan went and stood at the far end so the farmer could trot the filly in a straight line towards her.

A few moments later she was satisfied that the animal moved athletically.

'That'll do fine. Thanks,' she said.

Without a word, the farmer led the filly straight back to the yard and into her stable. He emerged a moment later and hung the halter back on the rusty nail.

Jan attempted a friendly smile. 'She looks a useful sort of filly, but she hasn't much of a pedigree, has she?'

'Who gives a damn about that?' the little man countered fiercely. 'It's the individual that matters, not the flaming grandparents.'

'She *is* nice-looking, I'll give you that,' Jan conceded. 'How much do you want for her.'

'I don't really want to sell her,' the man answered grumpily.

'Oh, I'm sorry we've wasted your time, then. We'd better get off home and out of your way.' Jan looked at Sean, who, with the faintest shadow of a smile, nodded his head.

'All right, Jan – sorry about that. Joe, you should have told me you'd changed your mind before.'

They turned and started walking towards the gate from the yard without a backward glance.

Sean had his hand on the latch when they heard the farmer's voice croak behind them.

'Hold on a minute!'

Jan looked over her shoulder.

Corrigan was standing in the middle of the yard, twisting his face this way and that, as if he was taking part in a gurning competition, while he tried to reconcile his strongly conflicting emotions.

Jan tried not to show any relief at his sudden change of heart. 'Why?' she asked.

'Maybe I *could* sell her to you – for the right money, mind,' he added, intensifying his stare.

Jan turned and, followed by Sean, walked slowly back into the yard.

'What do you call the right money?'

'Ten thousand.'

Ten thousand punts was equal to a little over eight and a half thousand pounds. Jan knew Corrigan would be extremely lucky to get that sort of price at auction, and he would know it, but in her view the filly was worth it.

'I'll give you six thousand,' she said, as a matter of course.

Corrigan filled his small chest with air. 'Don't waste my time!' he spat.

Jan shrugged. 'It's an offer, here and now, and it's better than her getting fast in that gate and being worth knacker price.'

'I'm not accepting it. Ten thousand, or she goes to the sales next year.'

Jan took a deep breath. The filly might be a good buy for Frank Jellard, *although God knows*, she thought, *he doesn't deserve a bargain*. But after all he had given her a budget of ten thousand pounds. And he would certainly be getting a nice horse and in her opinion really good value for money.

'OK,' she said, decisively. 'Done! Ten thousand punts.'

Corrigan winced violently. 'Sterling, not punts!'

'Oh no,' Sean said, joining in the negotiations for the first time. 'You can't do that. We have to deal in the existing currency.'

'Well, she's English, ain't she!' the farmer hissed.

'All right.' Jan held up a hand. 'Seven thousand pounds sterling.'

Corrigan stared back at her. 'Nine,' he muttered defiantly.

'Seven and a half, or I'm walking out and leaving her here,' Jan said with an air of finality.

For a moment, the farmer sucked air noisily through his tightened nostrils. 'You're a hard woman, Jan Hardy, to take advantage of a poor man.'

She flinched, but said nothing and relaxed her stance, as if she were preparing to walk away. *This is a tough business*, she thought.

'All right,' Corrigan muttered with a show of defeated pride. 'Seven and a half, sterling.'

Jan extended her hand to seal the deal. He shook it reluctantly.

'Well done, Joe, you won't regret it,' Sean said. 'You're lucky Mrs H has a kind heart. I'll be back with the money the day after tomorrow and we'll pick the filly up when she's passed the vet. Is that OK?'

Jan flew back from Dublin to Birmingham the next evening, exhausted but reasonably happy with what she'd achieved. She had filled most of her orders for young horses from the sales, although she had bought only one for A.D. and nothing for Johnny Carlton-Brown.

Even Tanner accepted that going to any sale determined to buy irrespective of the price was a recipe for disaster. But she had acquired three with impressive form for Gary West on her trip to Tipperary with Sean. Two of them, the Magic Maestro and Gylippus, she deemed would possibly turn out to be a couple of the best horses to leave Ireland that year. She'd really enjoyed her two days with Sean and his family and she could almost envy Teresa her uncomplicated life of rural domesticity with unlimited time to spend with her five wholesome children. Now Jan was itching to see her own two.

Registering the fact that she now had committed herself to some very valuable horses that would arrive at Edge Farm during the week, she was suddenly feeling exposed. It dawned on her she would be responsible for a considerable number of expensive animals, far more than she had ever handled before. She was still extremely worried about the risk involved in laying out all the money needed to build the all-weather gallop, as well as taking on three new members of staff, and with the risk of West's company, which was the official owner of the horses, welshing on her. 'I could lose the whole bloody lot,' she moaned.

She guessed that Eddie would have told her to stop being so bloody ridiculous and reminded her that West was reputed to be worth several hundred million pounds. *Maybe he's right*, she conceded, she didn't find it hard to trust Gary West himself, but John Tanner was far too slippery for her liking. Suddenly, though, an idea occurred to her that would set her mind at rest to some degree.

She needed to talk to a lawyer and considered going to see Mr Russell of Morris, Jones & Co, the solicitors in Broadway whom she had used before, but she was concerned they might not be tough enough. After much deliberation she decided to consult Toby Waller, her favourite owner and one of the few experienced businessmen she knew to whom she would have entrusted her life.

Jan arrived home just after midnight to find Megan was still waiting up with Fran. The little girl rushed to greet her and bounced up and down with her arms outstretched until Jan scooped her up and hugged her tightly.

'Mummy, Mummy! Monarch was absolutely brilliant at the show! I won three things.'

'I know, Meg. You told me on the phone, remember?'

'No, Mummy, I didn't. I only told you about two; I forgot the handy pony I did on him.'

'Wonderful,' Jan said, kissing the blonde crown of her exuberant daughter's head. 'I told you he'd be good and win you lots of rosettes.'

'Thank you for getting him for me, Mummy,' Megan blurted earnestly, remembering that Jan had told her never to forget a 'thank you'.

'It's Colonel Gilbert you should be thanking.'

'I did, I did. He was there. He said he was really pleased with the way I rode Monarch. And he said you went to Ireland to get him another horse.'

Jan laughed at the way Meg's words tumbled out, barely keeping up with her thoughts. 'I did; I found a lovely chestnut three-year-old for him.'

'A boy or a girl?'

'A boy, sort of,' Jan said. She had yet to get round to explaining to Megan why most male horses were gelded. 'But come on, my girl, it's way past your bedtime. Let's go up and you can tell me again just how wonderful darling Monarch is.'

Four days after Jan's return from Ireland, Brennan's had already delivered her purchases from Tattersalls and Sean arrived in his own lorry with the four she had bought with him.

It was his first visit to Jan's establishment, and she was proud to show him round her freshly painted yard, introducing him to the staff on the way. He scrutinized everything, though she noticed he only offered his opinion when she asked for it. He was greatly impressed by Gerry's new row of stables and its central archway, topped by a weathervane in the shape of a rearing horse, which had been specially wrought by Jan's farrier as a present. Above all, he approved of the way the horses in the yard looked so obviously well cared for.

'Keeping horses happy and relaxed is half the battle,' he said with a thoughtful nod. 'It doesn't matter how fit and talented they are, if they're not content they won't perform for you.'

Although it wasn't a scientific theory, she was pleased to know he completely understood her philosophy.

That evening Jan and Annabel decided to take Sean for supper at the Fox & Pheasant in Stanfield with Dec and Con. The Irish boys laughed at his alarmed reaction to the barmaid's appearance, with her spiky, jet-black hair, gothic pallor and jagged eye make-up. Jan chuckled too and told Sean she couldn't imagine any of his angelic children taking that route. He soon recovered, however, when they were joined by a loud but more or less normal Shirley McGregor. Jan had been persuaded by Annabel not to read too much into Shirley's antics with Eddie and she had to admit that the vet was good company as well as being good at her job.

Fortunately, it seemed that Shirley was perceptive enough not to flirt too outrageously with the good-looking Irishman. Since Jan had spent time in his family environment with his shy, devoted wife, she was certain Sean didn't fit the racing stereotype of the philandering male.

Jan wasn't at all surprised to find that he was liked by everyone he met at Edge and she hoped the visit would help to cement a long and fruitful friendship.

Sean climbed into his lorry on the Friday morning and a warm glow of affection and gratitude towards him filled Jan as she watched him set off for Fishguard and the ferry home.

The first of the new horses' owners came that afternoon. Darius had rung just before lunch to say that he and two other members of the band would drop in on their way to a recording studio in Shropshire. When they arrived, Jan went out to greet them as they piled out of a blacked-out, chauffeur-driven people carrier like a gang of excited teenagers.

'Hi, Jan!' Darius called with a smile that acknowledged the rapport they'd established at the sales. 'How's our new baby?' He gave Jan a kiss, while the girls in the yard looked on in envy and disbelief.

'He's travelled well, which is a start.' Jan smiled.

'Where is he, then?'

'He's in one of the stables over there. We haven't labelled them yet, so why don't you see if you can recognize him?'

Jan knew it wasn't a fair test for an amateur, but she had got the impression that now Darius was committed he really wanted to learn and a close inspection of the new horses and the differences between them wouldn't do him any harm.

The other two musicians laughed. 'He won't have a bloody clue – I bet they all look the same to him.'

'No.' Darius held up a hand in protest. 'I know I looked at a hell of a lot of horses last week, but I reckon I can identify him.'

Taking the challenge seriously, he marched off across the yard, watched adoringly by the girls. Jan's other tenants, who were already back in their stables, had typed labels by their doors with their name, breeding, date of birth and owner clearly displayed. Darius ignored these and carried on looking in each of the unmarked boxes.

'Nope,' he said at the first. 'Too small.' He moved on to the next. 'Too ginger.' And the next, 'Too big. No, two white socks. Ah, this could be him.' He spun round for a reaction from Jan.

She was non-committal. 'Well he's the right colour.'

'And he's a "he". Definitely a possible, but we'll look at a few more first. No, not this one; too dark; another ginger one.'

'For God's sake.' Jan laughed. 'Chestnut, not ginger!'

Darius nodded. 'I've noticed everyone likes to be conventional in the racing world, and since I started reading the racing pages I've realized nearly all the hacks use the same jargon and clichés – as if there's a little rule you have to follow. Anyway, let's have a look in here,' he said, reaching one of the end boxes. He poked his head over the door. 'Aha!' He turned round with a look of triumph on his face. 'This is him, this is our boy! I recognize that twiddly bit on his forehead.'

'Bravo!' Jan nodded with a pleased smile. 'It's called a whorl. They have them on their bodies as well; they're like human fingerprints and no two horses have them in exactly the same place.'

Jan opened the stable door and got Roz to lead out the new acquisition for his owners to have a proper look.

The horse looked almost as good as he had when Jan had first seen him with Lady Nichols, despite his long journey to Edge Farm.

'What d'you think, guys?' Darius asked his colleagues anxiously.

Micky, the band's drummer, shrugged. 'Well, it's an 'orse; it looks nice and shiny, but how do we know it can run fast?'

Darius nodded at Jan. 'Because she says so.'

'But – over a hundred grand?'

'There were worse-looking ones making a lot more, I can tell you.'

'Ah well, JCB says we can write it off against tax, so – what the 'ell!' Micky grinned.

Jan chuckled. 'That's all very well, but it also means when he wins, the taxman will want you to pay him a percentage.'

'I could handle that,' the other laughed. 'Anyway what are we going to call him?'

'You can call him anything you like, so long as it isn't already registered or hasn't been used recently and it's not obscene or more than eighteen letters. People often try to come up with something that ties in with the mothers' and fathers' names.'

'And this one,' Darius said, 'is by Moscow Society out of Teenager.'

'There you are,' Jan said. 'You could have some fun with that.'

Before they left, Jan asked the group if they would like a drink, praying that they wouldn't ask for some exotic cocktail. To her relief, all they wanted was a mug of builder's tea.

An hour later Jan was still trying to get the female workforce back down to earth when she answered the phone and heard A.D. on the line.

'How's Galway Fox looking for tomorrow?' he asked without preamble. He and Jan had spoken several times since her Irish trip to discuss the horse she had bought for him at Tattersalls.

'Fine, I think.'

A.D. quickly picked up the hint of doubt in her voice. 'What's wrong with him?'

'You know what it's like; sometimes for no particular reason you get a gut feeling they're just not firing on all cylinders.'

'There's always a reason,' A.D. said dryly. 'D'you still want to run him?'

'We'll see. He may be fine tomorrow,' Jan answered.

'So be it. I'll be there for lunch, if you'd care to join me.'

'Thanks, but he runs at two-fifteen, so I won't have a lot of time.'

'Quite so. I'll see you there.'

Jan said goodbye and put the phone down. She couldn't identify exactly what it was she sensed in A.D.'s voice that made her feel they'd moved a little further apart than they had been previously. Of course, in any relationship there was an ebb and flow of goodwill and quite possibly he was preoccupied with some other business problem. She would have a proper chance to gauge how things were when she saw him the next day; she just hoped to goodness she was making the right decision in running the Galway Fox.

The following afternoon from A.D.'s box at Sandown, Jan watched the horse canter down towards the railway line for the ten-furlong start. Her impression that the Galway Fox was being moody about something was confirmed. She could tell from the uncharacteristic way he was poking his nose in the air and making it difficult for his jockey to keep him going in a straight line. To her frustration, she hadn't been able to identify the cause of the problem at home, although she was convinced it was nothing physical.

After the horse had run at Newbury, it had been Jan's idea to help him in this more demanding race by booking a seven-pound-claiming apprentice jockey who she had judged was competent enough and considered very promising by most observers.

'That boy's not coping too well,' A.D. remarked quietly.

Jan took it as an admonishment. 'It's not his fault, A.D. – Lester Piggott would have trouble with that horse, the mood he's in today.'

'I'm really sorry you haven't been able to get to the bottom of his problem though.'

The implied criticism hung in the air. Jan turned away, gritting her teeth in her effort not to rise to the bait. She could only pray that once the horse had been put in the stalls he would settle and race more sensibly.

Once the fifteen runners had sprung away from the start, it was obvious that Galway Fox had no intention of behaving. As the track turned slightly right-handed just before the seven-furlong marker, he cocked his jaw to the left and cut sharply across the field. As a result he carried several runners wide and continued the frenzied fight with his jockey, losing a good ten lengths in the process. By the time the runners had reached the straight, A.D.'s horse was trailing the field.

Jan took a quick glance at the owner. The only visible reaction in his face was a slight hardening of the muscle at the back of his lower jaw. She knew he was thinking she shouldn't have run the horse – especially not ridden by a still wet-behind-the-ears jockey. When she turned her attention back to the track, it seemed the Galway Fox had a sudden change of heart. Though still hanging violently to the left, he managed to quicken and passed half the field like a rocket, looking as though he could easily have caught the leaders if he'd been in a better frame of mind.

Jan was relieved when he crossed the line a close-up sixth, but it didn't stop A.D. glancing at her with one eyebrow faintly raised. She was poised to go down and meet her runner as he made his way from the track and to quiz the jockey about the horse's strange behaviour when A.D. interrupted.

'When that horse is right, he should win a decent race,' he remarked dryly. 'After you've done with him, would you come back up here? I'd like a word.'

Jan looked straight back at him, determined not to be cowed by the strength of his personality. She nodded curtly. 'Right. I'll see you in a minute.'

Pushing her way through the crowds towards the paddock, she tried to hold back the tears of frustration pricking her eyes. The horse hadn't done that badly; horses had off days, for God's sake, she told herself; and she still believed that even an experienced jockey would have had problems with it today. But there was something in A.D.'s manner, as there had been on the phone the day before, that hinted at a rift between them.

She found Joe Paley leading the horse in, with the sour-faced young jockey still perched on its back as it jogged sideways up the walkway towards the unsaddling enclosure.

'He's a right bastard, this 'oss,' the rider muttered.

'You've seen him run before,' Jan said brusquely, resenting his attitude. 'He's not always like that.'

'Yeah, well, I did my best, Mrs Hardy.'

'It's OK; I know you did. I'm not blaming you. What d'you think his problem is?'

'Teeth, more'n likely.'

Jan shook her head. 'I checked them yesterday; there's no sign of sores or anything.'

'Well, his mouth's sore now.' The jockey indicated a rawness in the corner of the animal's mouth where it had been fighting the bit.

'Anyway, apart from that, how was he going?'

'It was a bit difficult to tell, really.' The jockey shrugged before unshipping his feet from the irons and slipping to the ground. 'But he's got some speed if you could only get him to stop pissing about.'

While he was unbuckling the saddle, Jan prised open the horse's mouth and looked carefully at the ridge of gum between its front and back teeth, where the bit lay. She could find nothing untoward.

Jan let herself back into A.D.'s box, braced for whatever was coming next.

The Irishman was talking quietly on his mobile. The only other person left in the box was a waitress scuttling about clearing the used crockery from the table.

A.D. ended his conversation and turned to Jan. 'Ah,' he said, 'thank you for coming back. Look, I want to know a bit more about Gary West. How many horses do you have for him now?'

'I've got four so far. He'll almost certainly want more, though.'

'Are they all paid for?'

Jan looked at him in a way that conveyed it was none of his business. 'Yes,' she answered. 'I wouldn't have got them otherwise.'

'Have we paid you for the one you bought for me?'

'Of course.'

'Good.' A.D. nodded. 'Listen, I don't want you to take this out of context or misunderstand my motives for saying it, but Gary West does not have the best name in the financial markets.'

'How do you mean?'

A.D. waggled his left hand vaguely at chest height. 'Let's just say that people wouldn't take his guarantee – or his word – as copper-bottomed.'

'Is that so? Well, I speak as I find, and he's done nothing so far other than what he's promised. I admit I don't much like his sidekick, Tanner, but when I met Gary myself I found him totally straight . . . and very charming,' she added pointedly.

'Charming – there's a word,' A.D. said with quiet disparagement, but showing no desire to expand.

At least, Jan thought, *I know what I'm dealing with now. A.D.'s miffed because he feels he's not the number one in the yard any more. It's as simple as that.*

'All right,' she said. 'What do you think I should do?'

'How do you mean?' A.D. asked.

'It seems you're telling me I can't trust the man; do you think I should tell him to take his horses away?'

'No, no. I'm not saying that.'

'What are you saying, then?'

'Just be careful.'

'In what way?' Jan pressed.

'Look, I know it's none of my business – I just happen to be another owner in your yard, but I do feel I have a certain position, inasmuch as I was prepared to back you from scratch when you were still struggling to train a few point-to-pointers.'

Jan saw that, for once, she had him slightly on the back foot. 'Of course, I realize that, A.D. That's why I'm asking what *you* think I should do.'

'I would suggest that you safeguard your position as regards the training fees by making a proviso in your agreement that, in the event of . . .' He stopped for a moment and looked at her. 'Who owns the horses?'

'A company called Harlequin Holdings Ltd.'

'An English company?'

'Registered in Jersey.'

'It doesn't really matter. What you must do is ask Mr West personally to guarantee any training fees and give you the right to sell any of his horses at public auction to pay those fees if they're more than two months overdue.'

'Surely that would be a bit unusual, wouldn't it?' Jan countered, although she had been thinking along those lines herself.

'Not really. I don't doubt there are a few big yards that apply the same principle to owners already. You're running a business, after all, not a charity, and you must protect yourself.'

'I doubt whether he'll sign it,' Jan said simply. 'And John Tanner will resent it very strongly.'

'It sounds to me as if you shouldn't be too worried about what *he* thinks; just make it very clear to Mr West that's the way you want to do it. If you tell him as firmly as you're talking to me now, I'd be very surprised if he doesn't agree. Then at least you won't be looking over your shoulder all the time, worried in case you get knocked for several thousand in training fees with no way of recovering them.'

'He might just get the hump and take his horses away.'

'And I'm suggesting that's a risk you must take because I would not be amused if you were to ring me up one day and tell me you'd gone bust.'

Jan looked back at him and knew it was more than a suggestion. She also knew A.D. was right and realized she owed him the greater loyalty.

'OK, thanks for the advice.' She nodded. 'I'll see to it.'

15

Toby Waller telephoned Jan at eight o'clock on Sunday morning to check that a meeting they had arranged with Harold Powell at Stonewall Farm, her former home in Wales, was still on.

'He hasn't told me any different,' Jan said, 'so we'd better make sure we're not late. I do know he's playing hard to get and won't need much of an excuse to shoot off.'

'He'd better not. I won't be too chuffed if we drive all the way there and he doesn't show up.'

'I'll ring him anyway,' Jan said, 'just to make sure.'

'Fine. Unless I hear from you otherwise, I'll pick you up at midday.'

A few minutes before twelve, with his usual punctuality, Toby cruised effortlessly up the hill to Jan's yard in his Range Rover. He stepped down from the vehicle, wearing light maroon chinos and a pink open-necked shirt.

Jan looked up from the recently planted pyracantha that she was attempting to train along wires at the back of the new stable block. Annabel was up a ladder, making a few adjustments to one of the gargantuan hanging baskets that had been placed on either side of Gerry's new arched entrance.

'Good heavens! He looks like a stick of candyfloss,' Jan exclaimed with mock surprise as she walked round the corner. 'If I didn't know Toby was a respectable merchant banker, from the way he's dressed I'd have said he was a hairdresser or an interior designer.'

'Or possibly an MP,' Annabel giggled. 'Actually, I think conservative men seem to work off the last of their adolescent rebellion by wearing outrageous colours at the weekend.'

Toby was walking briskly across the gravelled area towards them. He hadn't heard what they'd said, though he guessed it was about him. 'You two never stop, do you?' he grinned. 'Giggling like a couple of schoolgirls. Look at you now, beautifying the place as if it were a doll's house, instead of giving those horses a bit of useful work.'

'Those horses have had plenty of work, don't you worry about that,' Jan said, stuffing her secateurs into the pocket of the smock she was wearing. 'Anyway, I like it looking pretty, so why shouldn't we add a bit of a woman's touch if we feel like it?'

'I agree there's nothing like a woman's touch,' Toby admitted, with a grin spreading over his chubby red cheeks, making him look almost attractive, Jan thought. 'But I'm afraid we'd better shoot off and deal with a seamier side of life. We don't want Mr H. Powell to get off the leash before we arrive.'

Jan pulled the smock over her head and attempted to smooth down her tousled hair. 'I've got everything here,' she said, gathering up the folder she'd left on her wheelbarrow. 'I'll just nip up and put a bit of make-up on, then I'm ready. Bel, are you sure you'll be OK with the kids?'

'Of course! I'm looking forward to it. Roz is coming up shortly to give me a hand.'

🐎

'Where's Bel taking Megan and Matty?' Toby asked once Jan was strapped into the passenger seat and the Range Rover was coasting down the drive.

'A local farm park; it has all manner of old-fashioned goats and cattle, spotty pigs and loads of whatnot. Matty absolutely adores the pigs for some reason.'

'He probably appreciates the value of a good crispy chunk of crackling,' Toby laughed. 'Anyway, tell me what happened yesterday.'

'You mean with Foxy at Sandown?'

'Yes. I watched the race on the telly. He looked like he'd been on marijuana.'

'Well, he was extremely moody in the paddock before the race, but I didn't know what the hell his problem was. After the race the jockey said he thought it might be teeth, but I'd already checked them and so had the vet, but we couldn't see any sign of soreness. Anyway, my dad came up earlier on this morning and had a look at him for me – needless to say, he found the very first signs of a wolf tooth coming through. It hadn't broken the skin or anything, but it was obviously quite painful.'

'Is that a big problem?'

'Not really. Hopefully we can just pull it out when it gets a bit bigger or, at least, Shirley can.'

'If she's strong enough. Still, that should make A.D. a bit happier,' Toby observed.

Jan glanced at him. 'Is it that obvious he's got the hump?'

Toby chuckled. 'Only if you know what to look for.'

'Actually I think he's not too happy about Gary West's position in the yard, though I don't know why he should worry; he knows damned well I won't kowtow to any particular owner. I really do try my best to treat them all the same.'

'Jan, I know that, but nevertheless he did offer to move you into a far bigger, posher yard, so I can understand him feeling a bit brassed off. However – ' Toby held up a hand with a laugh to stop Jan trying to defend herself – 'we won't go into it any further for the time being. Let's concentrate on the matter in hand,' he went on, becoming serious. 'What do *you* think the present state of play is with Harold Powell and the farm?'

'It's really kind of you to bother with all this, Toby, but are you really sure you want to get involved? I mean, it's a lot of hassle for you with no return.'

'Who says there's no return? You can't always measure things in money, you know.' He smiled. 'So please just tell me the latest.'

'Basically, the council has given Harold outline planning permission to develop the house and the buildings.'

'Develop them how exactly?'

'He wants to divide the place up into small units – Eddie called them yuppie hutches – six of them, I believe. It means splitting the house in two and both the barns. Harold also wanted to put mobile holiday homes in the lower field, but they turned that down.'

'Thank goodness. What's he done so far?'

'Not a lot, actually. As you know, thanks to that ridiculous cock-up by his office, he bought the farm without any access from the road. Technically, the only way he can get to it is across the hill at the back – and he can only do that on a tractor, so in reality he can't get any vehicles up the road without our permission. We allowed him to send some builders up to put the roof right because Olwen said it depressed her seeing it falling apart in front of her eyes. But since then we've said he can't use the track and there's very little he can do about it.'

Toby nodded. 'Yes, that's pretty much what I gathered from my lawyers. It's no wonder he agreed to meet us; he must be getting rather desperate by now. What do you really want to do about the situation?'

'To tell you the truth – nothing. Not yet, anyway. The whole problem's his own doing; he's put me through hell, the bastard! I had to scrimp and scrape and was really worried when I was trying to buy Edge Farm and turn it into a training yard, and he still had horses with me, for God's sake! So I'm afraid my feelings towards Mr H.P. are rather less than benevolent.'

'I can understand that, but you might make quite a bit of money here. He's got planning permission but he doesn't need to act on it for five years if he doesn't want to. He can just sit it out, hoping that Olwen will die and he can buy the bungalow. Whereas, if you take the farm back off him for what he paid you in the first place, with the planning permission for those six units it will be worth at least twice as much. He can't realistically sell it to anyone else until he's sorted out the access problem, so he's stuck between a rock and a hard place.'

Jan nodded slowly. 'I can see that and I could certainly use the money. As it is, I've had to get a bank loan to pay for the new stables and the all-weather gallop we're putting in.'

'Because Gary West insisted?' Toby asked.

'Yes. Toby,' Jan said, jumping off at a tangent as she remembered what A.D. had told her the day before. 'Do you think I'm mad to take him seriously? A.D. says he's got quite a dodgy reputation in the financial markets, whatever they are.'

'I told you that when you asked me about him in the first place. He's really an unknown quantity; but having said that, I would have thought spending a million or so on bloodstock was a pretty insignificant commitment for him. I feel sure you haven't got too much to worry about.'

'I did want to ask you another favour. Could your lawyers draw up an agreement so he personally guarantees me for the training fees and, if they don't get paid, I can sell some of the horses to recover them?'

Toby glanced at her. 'Sounds a bit heavy. I can't imagine Tanner liking that.'

'Maybe not, but it's up to Gary in the end.'

Toby took a deep breath. 'Ah well, if he refuses and takes the horses away, at least you'll know where you stand.'

'But, Toby, I really can't afford to lose them now I've committed all that money to gearing myself up.'

'There'll always be plenty of others who want you to train their horses, I'm sure.'

'That's what you say, but it's not easy. Some people are still very reluctant to have a woman trainer.'

'So, if we can persuade Harold to sell the farm back to you and then pass it on for a fat profit, you won't be so exposed. I guess we'd better go down that route, don't you?'

❧

Harold Powell was standing beside a new Jaguar in the middle of the extremely dilapidated old farmyard, where Jan had previously trained a few point-to-pointers that the local farmers and people like Harold had sent her. It was the first time she had been right up to the farm since she'd left, and the sight of the cobbled surface, the old moss-covered stone of the barns and house which had been her home for eight hard but mostly happy years reached in and grabbed her soul for a moment.

As Jan and Toby climbed down from the Range Rover, Harold stepped forward and shook Toby's hand with an overstated grip but made no attempt to shake hers.

Harold had lost a considerable amount of face and – more painfully – money as a result of trying to swindle Jan, and she knew it must be a source of great irritation to him that, before her first flush of success as a public trainer, he had owned the best and most successful horse in her yard. Nevertheless, this morning, meeting him for the first time in over a year, Jan thought he looked as affluent as ever and wrapped in his usual smug self-confidence.

Harold had been a successful estate agent and auctioneer in the small Marches town of Hay-on-Wye for over twenty years. He was generally popular and had close connections with a number of the larger farming families in the area. He was a high-profile supporter of local charities and sports clubs and also, Jan had been told privately, a bigwig in the local lodge.

Jan knew his charm was entirely assumed, but standing at six foot, with thick dark hair and blue eyes which could twinkle to order, he was always dressed in expensive country suits, and he was an impressive man in the context of a small market town.

But Jan was also conscious of how far *she* had moved on in the last year. She thought Harold shrank into insignificance beside people like A.D. O'Hagan, Johnny Carlton-Brown and Gary West.

'So, Mr Powell,' Toby said with studied formality, 'where have we got to and where do you think we should go?'

Harold Powell looked at him with supercilious vagueness. 'I don't know where you've got to, but I have outline planning permission for six houses here,' he said in his soft Herefordshire burr.

'So I hear. Thought I haven't seen the official permission yet, but I imagine it's subject to satisfactory routes of access?'

'Of course it is, but there's no rush.'

'Then why did you agree to see us?'

Harold shrugged his shoulders with a grin. 'Why not? Maybe you . . . she wants to sell me that little strip of land down by her mother-in-law's bungalow.'

'Do you want to buy it?' Toby asked.

'Maybe.'

'What are you offering?' Jan joined in the conversation for the first time.

'It's about a third of an acre; as a piece of ground up here it's worth about eight hundred quid. But I'll give you five grand for it.'

Jan smiled. 'Oh, come on, Harold! That's a bit bloody cheeky – offering me that piffling amount of money. Do you seriously think I don't know how much it's worth to you?'

'Well, what would you think that's likely to be?'

'Fifty grand. At least.'

'Now who's being impertinent!'

'Harold, the planning consent's worth next to nothing without access and you know it. And you won't even be able to sell the farm without it. It really is such a shame we never had any roadside fields on the farm, apart from the one where John built his mother's bungalow. But there it is.'

'There's no way I'm paying you fifty grand; that's bloody blackmail.'

Toby cleared his throat to calm the conversation. 'It may just be a matter of market forces. But I have another idea: if you don't want to buy the bit of land, are you prepared to sell the farm buildings, or the whole farm for that matter, back to Mrs Hardy?'

'What? And have her develop it when I've done all the graft? Don't make me laugh.'

'I wasn't trying to, though I dare say she might find it worth her while to sell the buildings including the bit of ground you've just refused to buy from her.'

'I haven't refused to buy it. I just won't pay fifty grand.'

Toby dismissed this point. 'The result is the same. Would you like to sell the buildings?'

'Nope,' Harold said firmly.

'Don't you even want to hear what we would offer?'

'We?'

'I'm acting as adviser to Mrs Hardy.'

'Maybe you are, but I still don't want to hear what you're offering because I'm not selling it to her or to you or to anyone else, for that matter. I might even live in the place myself.'

'Oh? And how would you get here?'

'I could put a track in over the hill.'

'That's about three miles.' Toby laughed. 'And you'd still need permission from the council, the graziers and the farms you'd have to cross.'

'Maybe people round here aren't so bloody money-grabbing as her.' Harold's eyes blazed.

'Money-grabbing?' Toby said quietly. 'That's an odd choice of words from you in the circumstances. However, we didn't come here for a slanging match. You have a problem, we don't. We've suggested two ways of resolving it. You've made your position clear, so I think we'd better leave it there. And, by the way, we have to inform you that we will not be granting further permission for you or any of your employees or agents to cross Mrs Hardy's land at the bottom of the drive. And just in case you're thinking you might be able to persuade Mrs Olwen Hardy, she's in full agreement, so from now on the track will be permanently closed. If you come round to recognizing the commercial imperatives of the situation, please contact my lawyers; you know who they are, I expect?'

'I'm not effing contacting anybody,' Harold growled thunderously. He spun round on the heel of a well-polished brogue, let himself into his Jaguar and slammed the door.

Jan and Toby stood back as he revved the engine fiercely, spun the car round and skidded out of the yard.

During the quiet fortnight that followed her visit to Stonewall with Toby, Jan pushed Harold Powell to the back of her mind and submerged her gloom over Eddie by putting all her energy into positioning the new gallop and the upgrading of some of the original stables. She was also making plans to have a tarmacked walkway for the horses laid in a circle around the house, so she could inspect the string before they headed up to the gallops.

With the help of Toby's lawyers, she had drawn up an agreement between herself and Gary West along the lines A.D. had suggested. She had sent it express to Gary's office ten days ago. Now she was beginning to wonder why she had heard nothing since.

It was a fine Friday evening, and with only one horse scheduled to run the next day on the continuing firm ground, Jan had given the children their bath and left them playing upstairs while she and Annabel sat outside in the evening sun. Gerry had built a solidly railed deck in front of the French windows that led from the drawing room, and it had become one of Jan's favourite places in the warm sunset. She and Annabel sat quietly drinking spritzers, listening to the peaceful sounds drifting up on the still air from the valley below.

The phone was still on the floor. Jan had placed it there after making calls to the owners about the handful of entries she'd made for early next week. She had just finished her drink and was thinking about getting Matty ready for bed when the phone chirruped. She lifted the receiver.

'Hello. Edge Farm Stables,' she answered cheerfully.

'Hi, Jan!' It was Eddie.

There was faint echo on the line and, although it was the first time Jan had heard his voice for months, the two syllables were as familiar as if he'd spoken them that morning. She sighed, closed her eyes and clenched her teeth before she answered. 'Eddie? Where are you?'

Annabel drew in a sharp breath and leaned across to put a hand on her friend's arm.

'Still in Oz, I'm afraid,' Eddie answered.

Jan said nothing. There was an awkward pause.

'I just wondered how things were going?' he went on.

'Fine, thanks,' Jan replied, regretting at once the sarcastic note in her voice. 'I've got ten new horses in the yard,' she said more mildly, 'and a big new owner. He's an Aussie, as it happens.'

'Is that Gary West?'

'Yes, it is!' Jan blurted. 'How the hell did you know?'

'Didn't he say? It was me who told him about you. I said if he was going to have jumpers in England, he should have them with you.'

Jan was flabbergasted. Gary had never mentioned that Eddie had recommended her and it had never occurred to her that there might be a connection between them.

'Well, he never mentioned it,' Jan mumbled. 'How on earth did you two meet?'

'I know this is a big place, but the Aussie racing world's quite small,' Eddie replied. 'I'm glad he's got in touch with you, though. He has an awful lot of money and a bit of a reputation with the ladies, still you can look after yourself, can't you? At least, I hope you can.'

'I thought he only went for film stars,' Jan retorted.

'Usually.' Eddie laughed. 'But he might try to make an exception in your case.'

'Just let him,' Jan said with deliberate ambiguity. 'Anyway, how are you getting on?'

Even over a distance of twelve thousand miles, she could hear him take in a deep breath. 'I'm staying here, Jan; for the time being I have to.'

'When are you coming back?'

There was another ominous pause.

'I really don't know.' Eddie sighed. 'Not until after the baby's born, at least.'

'When's it due?' Jan asked before she could stop herself.

'End of January, early Feb.'

Jan looked across the valley. The hills on the far side seemed to quiver and dissolve. *Why?* she thought. *Why the hell are you telling me this and why on earth did I ask?*

She tried to pull herself together and focus more positively. 'Eddie, why have you phoned?' she asked brusquely.

'I . . . I just wanted to know how you were getting on, and how everyone's doing at Edge.'

'Everyone's fine,' Jan said through tight lips. 'Thank you for calling. And thank you for sending Gary West to us. I'm going to have to put in an all-weather gallop and six new stables, so I hope he's worth it.'

'It wouldn't be like you to do anything you didn't agree with,' Eddie said. 'Look, Jan, I really do hope it all works out OK.'

'I'll let you know.'

'Please do, Jan.'

'OK, fine. I expect I will. 'Bye, Eddie.'

''Bye, Jan.'

She put the phone down with her lip quivering and her eyes full of tears. She couldn't meet Annabel's look for a moment.

'I'm so sorry,' Annabel said sympathetically. 'That didn't sound as if it went too well.'

'The dopey wazzock still doesn't know what he wants – at least, I don't think he does, he's so bloody full of "doing the right thing".' Jan scratched quote marks in the air. 'Why can't he stand back for a moment and see where he's going?' She shook her head. 'January!' she moaned. 'Does he really think I'm going to sit around on the off-chance he might be back in five or six months' time?'

They heard the noisy blast of an engine as Gerry's old pick-up came into sight, trundling up the track, piled high with materials for the stable repairs, which he'd moved on to since completing the new phase.

'There's one guy who'll be extremely happy not to see Eddie for a very long time,' Annabel observed with a chuckle.

Jan let out a long sigh. 'God! I know I shouldn't let myself get so wound up. If only it hadn't all been going so well when Eddie upped sticks and left.'

'You know, Tony Robertson's still dead keen to take you out; you should let him – even if you tell him you don't know whether it'll go anywhere, he'd still like it. As a matter of fact, I think you would too. At least you know he's not a lecher, and it's not as if it's embarrassing to be seen out with him.'

'I know you're right; he's such a nice, normal guy. There was a time when I could almost see myself being with him long term,' Jan confessed.

'Your mother would be so pleased.'

Jan thought of Mary's anxious little face. 'Bel, please don't, I wouldn't want to get her hopes up.' She smiled faintly with a shake of her head, grateful for her friend's bolstering. As she leaned over the side of her chair to replace the phone, it chirruped again.

'Hello, Edge Farm Stables,' Jan answered, less brightly and rather more cautiously.

'Hello, Jan.' John Tanner's nasal voice was in sharp contrast to Eddie's more mellifluous tones. 'I've got this agreement of yours and we're not having it. You don't ask people like Gary West for personal guarantees.'

Jan's hackles were already up. 'I do,' she retorted, 'when the client is an anonymous company called Harlequin Holdings. Training horses is a business just like any other, and I shouldn't have to tell someone with your experience that a large part of running a business is steering clear of risk, which is why I need a personal guarantee.'

'Well, you're not getting mine, and I've never known Mr West give one either.'

'That's up to you,' Jan said.

'Up to us?' Tanner echoed in fake bewilderment.

'Yes, up to you. I'm really sorry, Mr Tanner, but if you and Mr West want me to train your horses and you're not prepared to give me the security I need from this agreement, you can tell me where you want me to send the horses and I'll make the necessary arrangements to have them delivered there.'

16

Over the next few days Jan wouldn't admit, not even to Annabel, how worried she was that she'd thrown down the gauntlet to John Tanner. Her final words to him as she'd ended their telephone conversation echoed in her head, and each time the thought recurred that he might move Gary West's horses from her yard she was engulfed by a wave of fearful nausea.

Nevertheless, between bouts of remorse for taking such a substantial risk when she had a family to rear, she reminded herself that with people like Tanner you had to make a stand and mark your territory.

By the Thursday afternoon following their conversation, she had still heard nothing from Tanner or his boss. Her mood was vacillating between the optimistic view that six days' silence was a good sign and then certainty that it was not.

When Tony Robertson phoned in the early evening, after one of those days when nothing seemed to go right, Jan was floundering in the depths of pessimism.

'Are you all right?' he asked, detecting her mood.

'I'm fine.' Jan sighed, straightening her back as she looked out of the kitchen window at the sunny scene outside, where Roz and the two Irish lads were larking about as they left the yard to walk down to the village. She tried to brush aside the fatalistic gloom that had settled on her. 'Just not much of a day really,' she said.

'It can't be much fun, with everywhere being so dry.'

'No, it isn't,' Jan agreed. She was coming to the conclusion that whatever it was that enabled some trainers to produce horses that could deal with the firm going which had persisted on all English racecourses for the past few weeks she didn't have it. Or, at least, she wasn't as prepared to take the risk of damaging them as some others might be.

'Look,' the doctor ventured, 'I know it may not be what you want at this precise moment, but it might make a change – you never know.'

'What are you talking about?' Jan asked, puzzled.

'Sorry, I'm skirting around – fear of rejection, I suppose. I was wondering if you'd like to consider the possibility of coming out with me one evening. I thought, perhaps Saturday week – which would give you a chance to sort out a babysitter?'

'Saturday week?' Jan repeated vaguely, trying to focus on the straightforward, unthreatening offer, while some instinct at the back of her mind was suggesting that a bit of 'straightforward and unthreatening' was just what she needed right now. 'Yes, why not?' she said, nodding to herself. 'That'd be nice.'

'Great!' the doctor enthused, surprised at his success, before quickly reining himself back. 'But absolutely no pressure, OK? A nice dinner at L'Escargot, and back early, if that suits you?'

'Yes, whatever. Thanks, Tony. I'll probably need a bit of cheering up by then.'

'See you then, Saturday, about seven?'

'All right. Thanks, Tony. 'Bye.'

Jan replaced the receiver. She wanted to make a note of the date and was rummaging for her diary among the papers piled high on the dresser when the phone rang again. She picked it up absent-mindedly.

'Jan? This is Gary West.'

She froze for a moment.

'Hi, Gary,' she croaked with unconvincing lightness when she had regained control of her muscles.

'Look, Jan, about this supplementary agreement you've asked me to sign.'

'It's not supplementary, Gary. At the moment we don't have

any formal agreement between us at all, and I feel it's right for both of us to know exactly where we stand, considering the number of horses involved and their value.'

Jan heard him sigh. 'You should have told me your terms at the outset. I have to tell you it's a bloody long time since I've given anyone a personal guarantee on a business deal, let alone a leisure activity.'

'But this *is* business to me, Gary. I know you're keeping the horses for your personal enjoyment and, with a bit of luck, they will be profitable, but I'm sure you're not so naive as to think that's likely with every horse.'

'No, of course I'm not, and I admire your frankness,' Gary responded with a deep chuckle, whilst changing tack. 'All right; I really do appreciate where you're coming from and that's fair enough. So consider it done. The documents will be returned to you by courier tomorrow. And the best of luck. I'm hoping to be over soon to check my new boys out. It looks like you've bought an interesting bunch. John will be in touch with you about a name for the youngster.'

'Great!' Jan said. The single word was charged with all the relief she felt at his complete understanding of her predicament.

She dropped the handset and clasped her hands over her face for several seconds before doing a couple of joyful twirls around the kitchen.

'What are you doing, Mummy?' a small, puzzled voice asked from the doorway. 'You look very happy.'

Jan turned to see Megan gazing at her in amazement.

'I am, quite.' Jan giggled. 'I've been a bit worried for the last week or so because I'd done something that might have been a bit rash.'

'What? Were you going to send Monarch back to Colonel Gilbert's?'

'No, nothing like that. I told a man who'd asked me to buy a lot of horses for him to guarantee that he would pay me to train them because I've had to spend such a lot of money building new stables and everything,' Jan tried to explain. 'And I could have lost an awful lot of money if it went wrong. Anyway, he's agreed now and it's all fine.'

'But, Mummy, you're always worrying about money, and our teacher says money's not as important as loving your family or being kind to starving people.'

'Maybe she hasn't got two children to bring up on her own,' Jan answered more sharply than she had meant to.

'I know she hasn't got any,' Megan confirmed.

'Still, I'm sure she's right in many ways, and there are lots more important things than money, but if you told all the starving people in the world it wasn't important, I don't think they'd agree with you.'

'Oh look,' Megan interjected excitedly. 'Bel's here.'

Jan followed her daughter's gaze through the window and saw Annabel walking towards them from the new parking area that had recently been laid, nearer the house.

Megan ran to the back door and squeaked an excited welcome. In the last few months it seemed to Jan that the little girl had adopted Annabel as a surrogate aunt, following her around like a goose and hanging onto every word she said.

There was a rather sheepish expression on Bel's face as she entered the house.

'What are you going to tell me?' Jan asked. 'You're taking the day off tomorrow to go gallivanting with your lord?'

'No, I always give you at least two days' notice,' Annabel protested. 'I wanted to talk to you about my holidays. I'm hoping you'll let me take the whole of August off to go and stay at JCB's house in Provence.'

'What on earth are you going to do there for a month?'

'Not a lot. Read, water-ski, eat too much and sleep.'

'And Lamberhurst, will he be there?'

'Some of the time, I expect. I think he part owns it.'

'But why do you have to take a whole month?'

'Well, there's not a lot going on here and I feel like a good long break – obviously I'm going to miss you and the horses, but a month goes by pretty quickly, then I'll come back all refreshed and ready to get stuck in.'

Jan had already discussed with Annabel her plan to take a couple of weeks off in August, but somehow a whole month seemed a chasm in time to be without her.

'Is he getting a bit enthusiastic, then, his lordship?'

'Patrick doesn't really do "enthusiasm",' Annabel said with a grin, 'but let's say more than mildly interested.'

'What about you?'

Annabel shrugged. 'I like the laid-back approach, so I'm rather impressed by the way he's biding his time.'

Jan shook her head. 'It's not for me – all that iron-willed self-control. But I know what you mean. Just you make sure he knows that Edge Farm comes first, though.'

Annabel nodded briefly as if she was about to add something, but evidently changed her mind. 'Anyway, you look cheerful.'

'I am. Gary West just phoned. He's going to sign the guarantee.'

Annabel raised an eyebrow. 'That's excellent – slightly surprising, but very good news.'

'Why do you think it's surprising?'

'He doesn't strike me as someone who likes to be told what to do.'

'I wasn't telling him what to do – it was up to him. If he didn't want to sign, he could have taken the horses away.'

Annabel chuckled. 'OK, if you want to put it like that. Did you mention Eddie?'

Jan shook her head vigorously. 'God, no. There wasn't time and, anyway, I'd rather let him raise the subject if he wants to. The main thing is everything's agreed. I'm just so bloody relieved. I was worried sick, but had no idea until now how much it was getting me down. Still, at least I'll be feeling more positive when A.D. arrives.'

'You never told me he was coming.'

'I'm sorry; I meant to. Actually, I don't think I've seen you since Jimmy O'Driscoll phoned to say they would be arriving on Saturday morning.'

'Well, the best of luck.'

'Thanks and, Bel, that's fine about France by the way, if you really can bear to be away from us for so long.'

If A.D. was impressed by the collection of horses Jan had put together for Gary West, he was damned if he was going to show it. He was, however, generous in his appreciation of the one she had bought for him.

Discussing the strapping Roselier gelding Jan had bought for him at Fairyhouse, which was still at Aigmont, he nodded with approval. 'He's every bit as good as you described him. Very well done. We'll send him over here with the others next month.'

He walked on to look at the horse in the next stable. 'That's a good sort,' he remarked and leaned down to read its breeding on the card by the door. He made a face. 'Not much background to it, though.'

'She was quite cheap.' Jan shrugged. 'I got her for an owner who doesn't like spending his money.'

'Mr Jellard's lucky he had you to buy her for him,' A.D. said. 'Where did you find her?'

'On a little farm in Kilkenny.'

A.D. raised an eyebrow. 'You're getting to know your way around. But you really don't want to waste too much valuable time buying this type of animal. It seems your new client Gary West has given you a pretty free hand,' he went on quickly, giving Jan the impression he hadn't really wanted to refer to the Australian tycoon. 'That's his way, I believe – to start with.'

Jan refused to rise to the bait. 'Oh, by the way, thanks for your advice the other day. He's agreed to be personally responsible for all the training fees,' she delighted in saying.

A.D. turned to her sharply. 'In writing?'

'Yes. All the documents came back yesterday. Signed, sealed and delivered by courier.'

A.D. was already moving on and had reached the horse Jan had bought for Darius and his band. 'Teenage Red? Is this the Moscow Society you bought for those pop singers?'

'That's the one,' Jan said joining him at the stable door to admire the bay gelding.

A.D. was nodding his head. 'I wouldn't have minded this one myself. It wasn't too much money either.'

'Aren't you happy with the one I got for you, then?' Jan asked mischievously.

A.D. was aware she was pricking his bubble. He turned to her with a wry smile. 'Mrs Hardy, you know damned well I'd own every single horse in your yard, if you weren't so stubborn.'

🐎

On the first day of August the sun's persistence was still making life difficult for the few horses Ian had kept in training. She was back from Worcester unloading another unsuccessful runner when Annabel tore into the yard, the back of her BMW piled high with suitcases.

She leapt out of the car, looking as if she had stepped from the pages of a *Vogue* travel feature. 'Hi,' she said, clearly showing her excitement at the thought of a month in the south of France. 'What happened?' She nodded at the horse Roz was leading down the ramp.

Jan's mouth drooped. 'Usual story; he didn't like the fast ground. Even though they've watered the course, it's still too firm for him. Finbar had to pull him up. Frankly, if it wasn't for certain owners insisting on them running, I think I'd keep them all at home until the ground's had a really good soaking.'

'Then you won't be missing me at all.' Annabel laughed.

'Bel, don't be ridiculous. Of course I will miss you and you know it. I really do wish you weren't going – at least, not for so long. Are you sure they'll let you take that lot on the plane?' Jan nodded with a grin at the back of Annabel's car.

'It's JCB's own jet and he said I could bring as much as I wanted.'

'I wonder if he knew what he was letting himself in for? Anyway, how many bikinis take up that much room?'

'An awful lot.' Annabel laughed as she turned to greet Megan and Matty, who had just run down from the house. She bent down to lift up the skinny child and give her a hug. 'You'll look after Mummy while I'm away, won't you, Meg?'

'And me!' Matty chimed in.

'Course we will, but she still needs to talk to you about grown-up stuff,' the little girl said anxiously.

'Don't worry, Meg. I expect I'll be ringing every day to find out how things are.'

'You'd better,' Jan demanded.

Megan and Matty held Jan's hands tightly as they stood and watched the BMW disappear, taking Annabel off to another world – a world Jan knew she would never be part of, nor did she want to be, for that matter. She squeezed her children's hands in return. 'It'll be funny without Bel for a whole month,' she said.

'Do you think she'll *ever* come back?' Megan asked doubtfully.

'I'm sure she will.'

'But what if that man really wants to marry her?'

'I don't expect she wants to marry him, though. Anyway, if she did, she'd always want to work here, so she'd have to tell him they'd need to live nearby.'

Later, Jan tried to forget the temporary loss of Annabel and was throwing herself into the enjoyable task of bathing her two children, when she glanced out of the window and saw an unexpected car trundling up the track.

After a moment, she recognized the small Rover and realized with a shock that she had completely forgotten about dinner with Tony Robertson that evening. She'd just been going to write the date in her diary when Gary West had rung to agree terms and it hadn't crossed her mind since.

She was overcome with remorse at her absent-mindedness; of course, she hadn't even arranged a babysitter.

While Tony parked with his usual care, Jan hurried along the landing to her bedroom. She grabbed the phone and quickly dialled her mother. By the time the doctor knocked on the door, she had arranged to drop the children off to spend the night at their grandparents', which happened to be on the way to the restaurant.

🐎

'How did it go then?' Mary Pritchard asked, looking anxiously into her daughter's face.

As Jan arrived at the old cottage to pick up the children the next morning, her mother had suggested she might as well stay for lunch and watch Reg giving Mattie another lesson on Rocket.

'How did what go?' Jan asked airily, sitting down at the kitchen table while her mother filled the teapot on the range.

'You know – your meal with the doctor?'

'Dinner was fantastic, actually,' Jan said. 'I had this really lovely roast duck and a delicious sticky toffee pudding.'

'I didn't mean the food, dear. I meant with him.'

Jan sighed. 'I'm not really sure, Mum. I did enjoy myself, but I don't know if it was just because it's flattering to have someone show an interest in me when I'm feeling a bit lonely.'

'Why are you lonely? We're only twenty minutes away and you've got all those people in the yard to talk to.'

'It's just that Bel's gone off for a month, and for goodness sake, Mum – we don't need to pretend – you know I miss Eddie.'

Mary placed the teapot and cups on the table before lowering herself arthritically onto a chair opposite her daughter. 'But he's not coming back, is he?' she said, looking steadily into Jan's eyes. 'He's made his bed and he's got to lie on it.'

'It can just as easily be the woman who makes the bed, Mum. Maybe she just wanted him to stay and tricked him into it.'

'I wouldn't know about that, dear. I like Eddie, of course; he's a very charming person, but you can never really trust a charmer, can you?'

'I'm not sure how much truth's in those old sayings. Anyway, Eddie was more than just a charmer, Mum. He really cared what happened to me and put a lot of effort into helping me sort out Edge.'

'I know he did, but Tony – he's here, now. He's got no other commitments; he must like you a lot and you like being with him. And at least he's got a good, steady job in a worthwhile career.'

'The life of a country doctor, you can't beat it,' Jan said with a hint of irony. 'I expect I could handle it if I had to, but please don't keep pushing me, Mum, or you'll just put me off for good.'

Mary resisted the urge to talk about Tony again. To change the subject, while they were eating the roast lamb which she had insisted on cooking even though the temperature outside was in the eighties, she wanted to know everything about Annabel's trip to France with Johnny Carlton-Brown and Lord Lamberhurst. It emerged that she was almost as pessimistic as Megan about Annabel returning to Edge.

'When she's Lady Lamberhurst she's not going to want to come and muck out horses and such like, is she?'

'Well, I really don't think she and Patrick will marry,' Jan answered patiently. 'I'm sure he's not her type, even if he's trying hard to pretend he is because he fancies her so much. Anyway, Bel isn't suddenly going to change if she happens to become a viscountess. She'd still be the same person.'

'You might like to think that, but she'd be a proper lady then.'

'As far as I'm concerned, she's a proper lady now.'

'Well, you mark my words; if she marries that chap, and she must be thinking about it at her age, she won't be hanging around your yard any more. He wouldn't allow it.'

Mary was also keen to hear about Darius and his band. Since she'd heard that they were going to have a horse with Jan, she seemed to have done a crash course on the history of the band.

'What's it going to be like if they come round to the stables smoking all those drugs?' she asked.

'As far as I know, all they've smoked so far are cigarettes, anyway they're not allowed to smoke anywhere near the yard. But they're really nice guys. In fact, they've asked me to one of their concerts next weekend at the NEC in Birmingham and they're sending me a pass. I said I couldn't stand for hours with the crowds, so they said they'd put a commode at the side of the stage.' Jan burst out laughing at the image.

Mary shook her head in amazement that her daughter should be keeping company with such celebrities – notorious or otherwise.

'Don't just write off that doctor, will you, Jan, even if he seems much more ordinary than your new-found friend or that Gary West with all his film stars I've seen in the papers?'

'Please, Mum, you know I won't. I really like Tony and I know he's a good bloke, but that isn't always enough to make you want to spend the rest of your life with someone.'

'I wish I'd had all that choice when I was a girl,' Mary said wistfully.

'Why? You ended up with Dad and who could have been better for you than him?'

Mary looked away thoughtfully.

🐎

The last guitar chords and the massive wall of sound created by the Band of Brothers' synthesizer died away as their final song was eclipsed by an unbelievable uproar of whistling, screaming and stamping under the vaulted roof of the Birmingham Arena. Jan put her hands over her ears – she believed she'd never heard such an incredibly loud noise in her entire life.

Backstage, a few yards away from where the band had played, strutting, leaping, thrusting, howling and murmuring tenderly into their mikes, Jan's ears were ringing. But despite the discomfort, she had loved the sheer exhilaration the band projected. And between the mega-volume numbers there had been quieter, beautiful songs she could really enjoy. She'd been fascinated to see the different personae that the boys adopted on stage and just how big and important they were to their fans.

She was still shaking her head, trying to get her hearing back, when she felt a pair of hands on her shoulders. Looking up, she found her brother staring at her thoughtfully.

'OK?' Ben asked, with a doubtful smile.

Jan nodded. 'Too bloody loud, but absolutely fantastic. I've heard their music before, of course, but I hadn't realized just how good they are.'

'They're one of the best live bands around at the moment,' Ben said simply. 'Now, you can either hang around and come to the party or . . .'

'No, thanks,' Jan laughed. 'I don't think it'll be my sort of do.'

'Then I'll take you home.'

'Don't you want to stay?'

'To tell you the truth, I like to chill a little after a gig. It'll only take me a couple of hours to drive to Edge and back, and by then I'll probably feel in the mood.'

Jan didn't get a chance to say goodbye to the band, who had been whisked away in a darkened limousine from behind the Arena before any of the fans could mob them. In any case, she guessed they'd be so hyped up after the performance that it would be a while before they made much sense.

In the quiet comfort of Ben's recently acquired Jaguar, Jan leaned back and seriously hoped her ears would clear before too long.

'Music?' Ben asked as they cruised out of Birmingham towards the M5.

'Do you mind if we don't?' Jan asked. 'No reflection on your band.'

'I often like a bit of silence too, you know. When you live with rock all day, every day, it can be a hell of a relief to hear nothing. Sometimes I might play a bit of classical stuff.'

'It's really strange you being so musical when I can hardly sing a note – and yet we must have the same genes.'

'You ought to know – being involved in all that thoroughbred breeding – genes can be very unreliable. I expect you could put an Oaks winner to a Derby winner and still get a dud.'

Jan nodded. 'You're right; that's what makes the whole business so absorbing – there are so many unknowns. The Glorious Uncertainty, they call it.'

'And that's just the owners.' Ben laughed. 'Talking of uncertainties, have you heard from Annabel since she went off with my boss and Patrick?'

'She sends us postcards with naked girls on to tease the lads in the yard, and she did ring me to catch up with the news when she'd been gone a week.'

'Did she sound OK?'

'Why are you so interested?'

'I like her – even if she did turn me down – and although Patrick's all right to deal with if you're a man, I'm not sure I'd want him to end up with anyone I care about.'

'I think she likes him because he's not always all over her. Anyway, she's big enough and old enough to look after herself now – in fact, I'd say she was a pretty good judge of character.'

'Mmm,' Ben mused, without taking the discussion further. 'Talking of unknown quantities, what news of your Gary West?'

'I haven't seen him since that first meeting we had at Crockford's. I've bought him four good horses. I'm supposed to get a couple more, preferably already in training, but nothing much has come up so far. I may have to wait until the September sale at Doncaster or Tatt's autumn one.'

'Still, that's good. It looks as if you're going to have a reasonably full yard, doesn't it?'

'I guess so.' Jan shrugged. 'Barring disasters.'

🐎

Three weeks into August, Jan was feeling rather isolated with no one to confide in. Following his recent display of touchiness, A.D. had hardly contacted her since his last visit. She knew it wasn't unreasonable, given that none of his horses was doing anything important and it would be a couple of months before Jan sent any of them to race. But she had become used to speaking to him on the phone two, three or even more times a week and now she found his silence disconcerting.

Gary West hadn't been in touch either after bowing to her request for a personal guarantee, although she'd had a brief letter from John Tanner asking her to check if Weatherbys would allow his choice of name for the young horse, and confirming that they definitely wanted her to buy two more quality horses for Harlequin Holdings.

At least the horses coming back in from their summer holidays, which they'd spent either at Edge Farm or away on their owners' land, were showing no signs of illness or damage after the long, dry summer. Tom and Darren, the two boys who had been coming up to work at Jan's during the weekends and in the school holidays since they were twelve, were now experienced and big enough to ride out. Nothing pleased them more than the chance to get up on Jan's well-built horses to exercise them, and she was hopeful that one or both of them might be good enough to ride in races some day.

But with Annabel away and the two cocky Irish lads back home, the yard was noticeably quieter and the heady days of late spring, when a steady flow of winners had climaxed with Russian Eagle's triumph in the Irish National, seemed a long time ago.

At times like this Jan had the impression that the only successful animal in the yard was Monarch. Megan was winning increasingly challenging competitions with him, which caused the Colonel to talk about entering them at Peterborough and the Horse of the Year Show.

It was so quiet one Friday evening that even the sight of Bernie Sutcliffe's iridescent motor turning into the gate at the bottom of the drive had a cheering effect on Jan. And by the time Bernie had clambered out and picked his way gingerly across the yard to her office, with a contented smile on his face, she was genuinely pleased to see him.

'Jan, how are you?' he asked as his small tobacco-hued eyes darted around.

'Looking for Annabel, by any chance?' she asked.

Bernie's head jerked round on his scrawny neck to face her with an embarrassed look.

'I was wondering . . .' he murmured.

'She's gone to France. In fact she's been there since the beginning of August.'

'She's not left the yard, though?' Bernie asked sharply, not attempting to hide his consternation.

'Not as far as I know. Look, here's a card we got from her a couple of days ago,' Jan said with a smile, taking it from the wall and handing it to Bernie. Addressed to Dec and Con, it showed a group of semi-naked girls on a St Tropez beach.

'Blimey! She's over there is she?' Bernie gasped. Jan guessed he was imagining Annabel lying on a sun-soaked beach in a brief bikini. 'She'll never come back.' He shook his head.

'I'm sure she will; she reckons she'll be back in ten days.'

'Oh good! I was thinking, Jan,' Bernie went on in his thin, Black Country voice, 'I really like the look of the horse you bought for me, and I wouldn't mind a couple more – not too much money, mind. My mum's getting really keen, though; she says she likes to read my name in the papers when I've got one running, and she watches them on the TV all the time. I've even had to pay for that Sky channel that shows the racing every day.'

This was the first time Jan had heard of someone buying race-horses so their mother could watch them on television, although she had heard a few stranger reasons. 'If it makes her happy, then why not? How much do you want to spend?'

'Not more than eight or ten grand apiece.'

Jan immediately thought of A.D. telling her not to waste her time with lowly horses. She smiled at Bernie. 'That's not a lot these days, but I'll try my best to find something – maybe from Ireland; I've got a really good contact over there.'

Bernie looked doubtful. 'Are you sure? You know what them paddies are like.'

Jan bridled. 'No, I really don't, Bernie, and I can tell you my friend in Ireland is one of the most honest men I've ever met.'

'All right, all right. There's no need to get your knickers in a twist.'

'I'm sorry,' Jan said. 'But there's no need for you to be insulting either. You must learn to trust me – I wasn't born yesterday, you know.'

Bernie smiled awkwardly as a prelude to an attempt at gallantry. 'I know, but you still look young and very innocent sometimes.'

'Only sometimes?'

'Not like that slapper I saw your new Aussie owner with in the *News of the World*.' Bernie chuckled. 'I hope you haven't been having trouble with him.'

'What sort of trouble?'

'Any sort; I should think a bloke like Gary West's up to all sorts of tricks.'

'I don't normally discuss one owner's business with another, but I will say he's been totally above board with me. So far he's done everything I've asked him to. Although I've only met him once, he behaved perfectly – he could give a few Englishmen I know a lesson or two, I can tell you.'

'I'd like to meet him, then,' Bernie said. 'Now what I really want to do is have a look at the horses I've already got here, while you tell me what you think they should do this season.'

❦

A little to her surprise, Jan really enjoyed the next hour she spent with Bernie Sutcliffe. She was impressed by how much his knowledge of racing had improved since he'd first arrived at Edge Farm two years before, when he'd asked Jan to find him a point-to-pointer to impress his then girlfriend.

When he had finally seen enough and drunk a mug of tea with Jan in the office, he seemed to be happy with his new purchase, and well pleased that his two chasers, Dingle Bay and Arctic Hay, had already started their road work – although Jan had told him not to expect to see them on a racecourse until the ground had had enough rain to make it safe.

'They may not run until October or even November,' she'd told him, and for the first time he appeared to take the news without any of the impatience he had previously shown.

'I wouldn't mind if you bought something that could run a bit sooner, though,' he added as he firmed up his order. 'Preferably a young hurdler with a bit of potential.'

Jan waved at his departing Bentley, feeling pleased that, despite the unpromising start to their relationship, she and Bernie had now almost become friends.

She couldn't say the same about Frank Jellard when he turned up twenty minutes later, just as she was thinking about putting the children to bed.

Jellard was a big man, built like a breeze-block outhouse and with as little visual appeal. Jan had always found his character impenetrable. He seemed to be one of those people for whom anything that involved human interaction produced conflict. He rubbed everyone up the wrong way, as if there were something in his psyche, some deeply scarring childhood experience, which wouldn't allow him to conduct any transaction without creating a scene in which he would be seen to be superior, or to have performed better, or in some way to have outmanoeuvred the other person. It must, Jan thought, have made a very unsatisfying existence and at times she almost felt sorry for him.

From her kitchen window, she watched while he parked his car erratically, as always, and at an angle probably designed to cause maximum inconvenience, she thought. He walked into the yard with an arrogant stride as if he partly owned the place, reflecting his frequent implications to Jan that, in view of his substantial contribution to her income, he did.

Now he was out of sight, Jan thought she would leave him alone for a while. He couldn't get up to any harm while Roz and Joe Paley were still there, finishing evening stables. But, as expected, he soon re-emerged and was making his way up to the house in his usual truculent manner. He hammered on the door and let himself in before she'd answered.

'Hello, Frank,' Jan said, walking into the back hall. 'I was wondering when you'd appear.'

'I've just been in the yard; those horses of mine look bloody terrible – they're as fat as butter and look like bloody carthorses. I knew I should have had them back at my place for the summer, where I could keep an eye on them.'

Jan opened her mouth to speak, thought better of it and snapped it shut. She took a deep breath and shut her eyes tightly for a moment before she turned back towards the kitchen with Jellard in tow.

'I mean it, Jan. It's not good enough.'

Jan knew from bitter experience that if the horses hadn't been too fat, they would have been too thin.

She remembered the last few years of continuous aggravation and abuse she'd put up with from Frank Jellard, and the difficulty she'd had getting his less than classy horses to win an occasional race – for little or no thanks and constant quibbling about his bills.

She turned and faced him.

'If you really feel like that, Frank, I'm sure you'd be happier if your horses were trained somewhere else. I work my arse off trying to do the right thing, to keep everyone happy and to be fair.'

Jellard stopped in his tracks.

'What are you talking about?'

Jan was thinking of Bernie's new order for two more horses, and Gary West's willingness to understand her position.

'Frank, if you feel we haven't done a good enough job for you, then you should move on.'

Jellard looked dumbfounded. 'Move my horses? Where? There isn't another proper yard near me.'

'That's tough. Look, you're the one who's complaining, and not for the first time may I add, so I think we'd both be much happier if you took them elsewhere.'

'What? All of them?'

Jan shrugged to underline her indifference. 'Of course. There'd be no point leaving just one of them here.'

'What about the new filly you bought for me in Ireland? I don't think I want her. I showed her details to a friend of mine, and he said her breeding's lousy and she'd never make a useful brood mare, which is what I told you I wanted in the first place.'

'If you're not happy, I'll buy her back from you,' Jan said lightly. 'And if you want a yard near here, try Virginia Gilbert. She's only just up the road and her set-up's better equipped than mine.' Jan paused. 'Though, come to think of it, she probably wouldn't take you on either.'

'What do you mean – wouldn't take me on?'

'Have you ever met Virginia? No? I didn't think so, Well, she's what you might call a bit of a snob.'

'If she thinks I'm not good enough to keep my horses with her, she's got another bloody think coming,' Jellard said, his face reddening and his eyes blazing wildly.

This is going to be really interesting. Jan smiled to herself. *Virginia's welcome to him.*

17

Frank Jellard was probably under the impression that he was demonstrating his strength by insisting Jan reimbursed him for the filly she had bought in Kilkenny, but, in fact, he was doing exactly as she had hoped.

Half an hour after giving Frank the cheque, she rang Bernie. He had already seen the filly in the yard at the weekend and been impressed with her quality. He'd be delighted to take her on, he told Jan, particularly when she told him Jellard hadn't yet registered a name.

So it was with only a mild pang of regret that Jan watched two of Virginia Gilbert's staff load Jellard's other horses onto their lorry. Virginia had phoned earlier, but had pointedly failed to ask Jan anything about them or the owner she was taking on.

It was the first time Jan had told an owner point-blank to remove his horses from her yard; and, satisfying as it was in this particular instance, she couldn't help feeling that it was not a habit to get into, especially as she had done such a lot of hard work schooling them and had even managed to get a few modest wins from some.

Tony Robertson arrived just as the lorry was turning to leave. He couldn't have pitched up at a better time and Jan was very relieved to see him.

He climbed out of his car and walked across to join her. 'What's Virginia been doing here?'

'She didn't come herself.' Jan frowned. 'In fact, she hasn't been here since I moved into the place. Her driver and a lad were picking up Frank Jellard's horses.'

The doctor spun round and looked at her anxiously, trying to assess how much of a blow it had been.

'It's OK,' she grimaced, touched by his concern. 'I asked him to shift them, but not before I'd persuaded him to sell me back that lovely filly I found in Ireland.'

'Jan, why on earth did you do that? And to let them go to Virginia, for heaven's sake?'

'Because I've had more than enough of him and his bullying. Anyway, encouraging him to send them to her appealed to my bizarre sense of humour.'

'But, Jan, I really don't think you should be telling people to take their horses away just because you don't like them. You have to be totally professional about this.'

Jan looked at him, feeling a little guilty as he voiced her own doubts.

'I know you're right to a certain extent,' she said. 'And don't think I haven't told myself that, but every time he came here he complained, whatever I did, he'd find fault. That's the kind of man he is.' She smiled grimly. 'I'm happy to walk in it; I'm happy to work in it; but I'm not going to eat too much of it.'

Tony nodded. 'I do know what you mean, Jan. I've got patients like that, but unfortunately it's rather more difficult for me to pack them off to another practice if they don't want to go. Anyway, let's forget about Frank Jellard. Are you and the kids ready?'

Jan smiled. 'They certainly are.'

Megan and Matthew had been yattering all day about the trip they were going on. Tony had promised them a picnic on board a luxurious boat which one of his patients had lent him for the evening.

'And you?' he asked.

'Yup, I'm shipshape,' she said, turning back to the house to call the children, who came running down the track so fast that they arrived breathless and excited beside his car. Jan's heart leapt as Tony wrapped his arms around them and gave them both a warm hug.

'OK, all aboard!' He grinned, opening the back door for them.

An hour later, as they left the mooring in Worcester and chugged gently downstream on the broad, lazy Severn, where willows swept the river's edge and swans glided effortlessly, with the sun blazing in a final flourish above the hills in the west, Jan couldn't deny that the worries of the world seemed to be ebbing away from her.

She had always found it easy to talk to Tony and he understood a lot about her job – he was a horseman himself and his late wife had been a successful eventer until her tragic accident. He had sometimes claimed that running a medical practice was similar to looking after a yard full of thoroughbreds with all their foibles.

With the children, he seemed to understand instinctively what they liked and would respond to, despite having none of his own. And they chattered happily as Mattie trailed a fishing line over the back of the boat and Megan tried to identify the birds she could see through a pair of Jan's old binoculars.

While the children were eating the baguettes Tony had made with their favourite fillings, he and Jan shared a bottle of champagne with a delicious lobster salad. For a while, she could sense how it might be if they were a family. Her mother would be delighted, she thought to herself as she watched Tony at the back of the boat, retying the spinner on the end of Matthew's line, his tanned good looks profiled against the water as he focused on the job.

He glanced up and saw her watching. Then he smiled at her more confidently.

Jan lowered her eyes, and her thoughts turned to Eddie; now she found to her relief that the hurt wasn't quite so bad as it had been.

Later that night, after Jan had put the children to bed, she took a last look around the yard, checking the horses. As she popped her head over each stable door to look at a sleepy inmate, she wondered why she had sent Tony home so soon after he'd brought them back, when he obviously wanted to stay for a while. After all, it had been a wonderful evening, they'd all agreed.

She cast her mind back to a radio programme she'd heard while cleaning tack earlier that afternoon, which had been about the psychology of relationships. It suggested there were three phases of attraction between a man and a woman – love, lust, and lastly the desire for companionship, which had the greatest long-term value.

Now, reflecting on her evening with Tony, she had to accept that, although he scored strongly on the last point, on the other two he scarcely registered, and she couldn't help thinking that, for her, it would be essential to go through those stages to validate the third.

The following Thursday, 3 September, Jan felt very emotional as she took Matty to school for the first time. The little boy had been looking forward with feverish excitement to this milestone in his short life. Jan guessed he thought he would at last be on a par with his elder sister. She had tried to prepare him for the disillusionment that being in the reception class four years below Megan would bring, but he wouldn't hear of it. He was convinced he would be reading the same books and bringing home elaborate paintings like Megan's within a matter of days.

Jan knew who he had inherited his self-confidence from and she was reluctant to do anything that might repress it.

She watched him hare across the playground with his new rucksack flapping on his back. He had reached the door and was about to rush in when he turned, just once, to see if his mother was still there, and waved goodbye.

Jan drove home through the warmth of the late summer with tears running slowly down her cheeks. She recognized that Matty's going to school represented a milestone in her own life too unless, one day, she was persuaded to have another child herself.

For the time being she knew it was out of the question and she had to accept that now she had carved out such a demanding career for herself it simply left no time or space for more children.

Her mind leapt off at a tangent for a moment and she found herself wondering if Eddie Sullivan would enjoy being a father when his child in Australia was born. She forced the image from her mind, helped by the sudden sight of a familiar BMW convertible approaching the bottom of her drive from the opposite direction.

Jan slowed and with an exaggerated gesture from the driver's window of her Shogun, waved Annabel in through the gate ahead of her. Her face beaming, she followed the BMW up the drive, thrilled that her friend was back and impatient to see her. When Annabel leapt from the car Jan thought for a moment she was looking at a stranger – a tall, golden woman who radiated femininity, health and confidence in her physical beauty.

Annabel was wearing flared cotton jeans with a short embroidered top, which revealed a firm, tanned midriff. Her hair looked longer and bleached like golden honey as it fell in rippling waves to her shoulders. Her flawless lips were spread in a broad smile and her blue eyes sparkled with pleasure at seeing Jan again.

'Hi, how *are* you?' she called and held out her arms before wrapping them around Jan.

'Cor, Bel, you look fantastic – and you smell a million dollars!' Jan laughed as they released each other from a long, warm embrace.

'Patrick did go rather overboard on the duty-free and I couldn't resist a little splash on the drive down,' Annabel admitted with a grin. 'But how have you been?'

'Great, I can't wait to hear what you've been up to, though. I just need to take a quick look at a couple of horses Shirley's coming to examine this morning, then we'll go up to the house for a proper gossip. Is that OK?'

'Fine, I'll tag along – I'm longing to see Eagle again. How's he looking?'

Jan laughed. 'Same as usual at this time of year, more like a Ploughman's horse than a racer, but we're getting stuck into his road work. The only problem at the moment is the ground's so firm everywhere. Thank God the new all-weather should be finished by the end of next week.'

'So that's all gone ahead then?'

Jan nodded. 'I'm afraid so, but Gary West agreed that I needed the extra security his personal guarantee would provide so, as far as I'm concerned and despite what anyone else says about him, he couldn't have been straighter.'

Annabel shrugged. 'Well, I couldn't possibly judge – not from just one evening.'

'Well, I really do feel I'm getting better at recognizing bullshit. I made eye-contact with him at several crucial moments that night

and I saw no signs of it. OK, I admit he knows how to charm the
birds out of the trees, and he could probably sell fridges to eskimos,
but I feel inclined to trust him.'

'I hope you're right.'

Jan grunted. 'Well, I'm committed now and I'm in deep shit if it
goes wrong,' she said, waving a hand at the new stable block and
the digger which was putting the finishing touches to the walkway
around the house. 'I've already spent more than seventy thousand
of the bank's money this summer.'

They walked into the old barn, where Russian Eagle occupied
one of the original stables. The horse already had his big, friendly
head over the door and nickered in recognition as soon as Annabel
started cooing her usual endearments.

'Hel*loo*, Eagle, my big beautiful baby. Goodness, you're *so* fat!
Has everyone been spoiling you while I've been away, or did you
eat more 'cos you missed me?'

'Yuk.' Jan chuckled. 'That's enough of that. I've already had
Frank Jellard up here behaving like something wrongly wired
because he thought his horses were too fat.'

'How did you placate him?'

'Easy. I told him to "naff off" and take them to Virginia's.'

'Jan! You *didn't*! My God, you *did*!' she exclaimed, seeing her
friend's mischievous grin.

'Well, actually, I told him Virginia wouldn't have him in her
yard, so he decided for himself.'

'But what about that lovely filly you bought from the farmer in
Ireland?'

Jan explained that it now belonged to Bernie Sutcliffe and was
still on the premises. Then they checked the horses Jan had arranged
for the vet to see – one with an inexplicable bump on its shin, the
other, she suspected, with a mild bout of colic. Jan told Roz to
make sure she came and found her the moment Shirley arrived.
Satisfied, she grabbed her friend's arm and led her up to the house,
where she spooned some of Annabel's favourite Colombian coffee
into a tall cafetière and placed it on the big pine table.

'So – ' Jan gazed eagerly at her assistant – 'how did it all go?'

Annabel gave a slightly embarrassed smile. 'It wasn't what I was expecting, but I really enjoyed myself. I did all sorts of things I hadn't even dreamed of.'

'Like what?'

'Like swimming in lakes up in the mountains, going to an alfresco opera in Nice; the trotting races in Cagnes, which are a bit hairy; having dinner with Prince Albert; sleeping under the stars on Cap Ferrat; watching a bull fight at Saintes-Maries-de-la-Mer, which I can't say I enjoyed.' Annabel shrugged. 'The whole month seemed to whiz by in a sort of blur.'

'How much of a blur was Lord Lamberhurst?'

'A bit fuzzy round the edges, I suppose,' Annabel said. 'But he and Johnny are like a pair of naughty schoolboys when they're on holiday – they keep trying to outdo one another.'

'What I want to know,' Jan said sternly, 'is whether or not you and Patrick are now a permanent item.'

Annabel didn't answer at once. 'Yes,' she said eventually. 'I suppose we are. He was great . . . and pretty good . . . you know. He seemed to want to make sure I was enjoying myself all the time. Frankly there were times when I just wanted to spend a day in a hammock reading a book, but it hardly ever happened. We were always gadding off to the next thing.'

'But . . . ?' Jan queried.

'Oh, I don't know. He's great to be with and all that, and I'm looking forward to seeing him again, but I don't feel I'm going to miss him too much, not at the moment, anyway.'

'That's just the way you are because you're so independent, and there's so much warmth for you back here, I suppose,' Jan said thoughtfully. 'I must admit, though, if I'm honest I still miss Eddie badly.'

'Have you heard from him again?'

'No, not a bloody word.'

'Oh, Jan, I'm so sorry.'

'I suppose it's not the end of the world,' Jan said. 'And, to tell you the truth, Tony's taken me out a few times, and the kids too. It's been really great. We had a beautiful evening on a boat last weekend – Matty fishing, champagne and lobster for me. But when he dropped us back here I still sent him straight home.' Jan shook her head. 'The poor sod. Of course, my mum's even more keen on him now she's heard the news.'

'Haven't you been to bed with him yet?'

'Oh God, no,' Jan declared.

They sat in silence for a moment, until suddenly Annabel jumped up from the table. 'I've brought back a few prezzies for you and the kids, and the rest of the gang. I'll just pop and get them from the car. By the way,' she went on, looking out of the window, 'this walkway's going to be handy.'

'I'm not so sure now.' Jan laughed. 'I've only just realized that while I can see out, all the staff can see in.'

'Oh, you're right, but it's not as though you'll be wearing a gossamer-thin nightie or anything. Though it does rather make it seem like the house is an island surrounded by a moat. Perhaps we should have a drawbridge and only let in nice people,' Annabel giggled.

'At least our visitors can now drive right up if they want to. Not everyone's as fit and lithe as you.'

After Shirley McGregor had been and dealt with her patients, the staff crowded round Jan's table for a celebration lunch to welcome Annabel back. They were delighted with the presents she'd brought home for them – Joe Paley, especially, with a pair of buckskin chaps made for the cowboys of the Camargue.

Afterwards Annabel went back to her cottage to unpack and volunteered to drive on to the school to collect Megan and Matthew.

Jan knew they would be thrilled to see Annabel and particularly her presents. They arrived back, strapped into the rear seats of the cabriolet, with huge grins on their faces and their hair on end. They raced into the house, yelling at the tops of their voices about the gifts they'd been given.

By late afternoon the following day it was almost as if Annabel had never been away as Jan joined her overseeing the evening feeds.

'Doesn't it seem a bit strange doing this, dealing with sweaty horses and lippy lads, after all that glamour in the south of France?'

'I suppose it does a little, but lovely too,' Annabel said. 'I'm really pleased I had such a long break; the real bonus is it's let me see just how much I love this life.'

'So you're not thinking of moving on just yet?'

'No, Jan, of course not. Not at all. Why?'

'It was the first thing Bernie asked when I said you'd gone to St Tropez for a month. "She'll never come back," ' Jan said, imitating Bernie's nasal twang.

'Well, I certainly didn't come back to see him.'

'Oh, he's OK,' Jan said in his defence. 'And don't worry, I'm sure he won't try it on with you again. He's much better behaved now and he seems to have learnt a lot about owning horses in the last couple of years. Do you know, he suspects he was manipulated by you and Eddie into selling Russian Eagle, but he said he hasn't complained because it was entirely his own decision and he simply made the wrong one?'

'But he'll have loads more wins with Dingle Bay, won't he?'

Jan nodded. 'I hope so, though the horse probably needs a really long trip and heavy ground.'

'I was listening to the lunchtime forecast,' Annabel said. 'It sounds as if this dry spell is going to break soon.'

'Not before time,' Jan sighed. 'It's not much fun going eight weeks without a winner. We all need a carrot and even ghastly Virginia's had a couple of successes.'

'She's probably knackered the horses doing it, though,' Annabel remarked.

'I hope not,' Jan said with genuine concern, 'but I'll be very surprised if she manages to get any of Frank Jellard's to win.'

🐎

The rain finally arrived during the second week of September in a massive downpour, drenching the sun-baked pastures, which absorbed it like a sponge.

Jan was extremely grateful that the all-weather gallop had been laid in time, as the rain helped to settle the new surface. Most of the horses were still at the walking and trotting stage of their programme, but it was a great relief to know she had somewhere safe to exercise those that were ready for some faster work. All the horses had visibly improved in physique, apart from the youngsters who had recently been broken in. There was no great hurry with them, anyway, as she didn't plan to run them in bumpers until after Christmas, apart from Toby's new big black gelding from Fairyhouse, now named Nero's Friend, which was well advanced and already muscling up.

The week had started badly for Jan with the opening of the Sharps' trial for fraud at Bristol Crown Court, although she didn't go. The prosecution had warned her that they might have to call her to give evidence, but not during the first week, and she didn't want to prolong the inevitable strain by spending any more time there than she had to.

At the same time, with half a dozen horses nearly ready to run and only waiting for some give in the ground, she was preoccupied with placing them in the right races. The change in the weather would inevitably produce a great surge in the number of runners at all the National Hunt meetings, which were still relatively scarce at this stage of the season.

However, there was more scope on the flat at this time of year, and she judged Mr Gaylord, one of the dual-purpose horses she had bought in Ireland for Gary West, to be firing at full throttle. Although she had originally picked him to go hurdling, she thought it wouldn't do him any harm to have a couple of spins on the flat and she'd found a suitable race for him at Warwick that weekend.

Over the last couple of months sending out runners had become a rare and distant prospect, but now it was as though everyone in the yard had suddenly woken up and there was a renewed sense of purpose about the place. Jan was conscious that the long lazy summer had left her staff less sharp and less focused than in the spring, when they'd been turning out winners. In her frustration, she found herself being irritable, even with Roz, who at her best was the most dedicated groom a trainer could have asked for. However, they understood the demands of the job and took it in their stride.

But when Mr Gaylord finished his race at Warwick halfway down the field, Jan's heart sank to her knees and she felt she could only blame herself.

Not surprisingly, Gary West hadn't turned up to see the horse run. Nor had John Tanner – luckily, in the circumstances – but he rang her as she was driving home.

'Great start,' he grunted sarcastically. 'Mr West won't be too impressed – not with something that just cost him eighty grand. What on earth d'you want to run the horse on the flat for, anyway?'

'I told you yesterday, Mr Tanner. I thought it would be useful to see how he went before we ran him over hurdles. You knew I wasn't expecting him to win today.'

'But you told us you only sent out horses when you thought they had a fair chance of winning.'

'I do usually, but I had nothing to judge him against. He's worked really well at home; it's possible he needed this run to get back into the swing of things after the change of scenery.'

Jan hated having to produce reasons for the horse's poor per-formance out of a hat, but she accepted that owners deserved an explanation and some reassurance in return for their training fees. When the horse had come back in after the race, she'd found nothing untoward, but she had already phoned Shirley to ask for his blood to be re-tested. 'I'm sure he'll do his stuff sooner or later,' she told Tanner, 'although I don't think we should run him again until I've been over him with a fine-tooth comb.'

Back home and alone in the house apart from the children, who were already upstairs in bed, Jan wished she could have sat down and talked it through with Annabel, but she had gone out with some old friends who had driven to Gloucestershire especially to see her. Nevertheless, when Tony Robertson rang to commiserate she was grateful, but when he asked if he could pop round she put him off, saying she had a lot of owners to ring.

As if to prove to herself that she hadn't been prevaricating, she sat down and phoned every one of her owners to tell them how their horses were and to let them know her plans.

Feeling rather virtuous and thinking she'd done enough, she was tidying away the last few things in the kitchen before an early night, when Toby Waller rang.

'How's my new baby?' His warm baritone voice reflected the affection he had for his new young horse, Nero's Friend.

'As big and strong as ever.'

'Great, I'm looking forward to seeing him. I'm arranging to come down next Saturday; there's a group of five guys I know who want to form a syndicate and buy a horse for you to train. I wanted to introduce you to a couple of them, if you're going to be there.'

'I'll be here. We're not having any runners – the nearest meeting's at Market Rasen.'

'That's good. I think they could be useful owners.' He paused before he went on. 'I'm afraid the other news I've got for you may not be so good.'

Jan detected an edge to his voice that put her instantly on a state of alert. 'What's that?'

She heard Toby sigh, as if he was reluctant to tell her. 'There are very strong rumours going around about Gary West.'

'Aren't there always?' Jan tried to fend off what was coming.

'Yes, I know, but these are far more serious.'

Jan closed her eyes and felt sick. 'What's happened now?'

'It's not directly his doing, but in the past four or five years he's known to have built up a major stake in a huge American energy company – a spin-off from one of the biggest oil traders who've broadened their field into gas and hydro-electricity, as well as wind power and dams in India, wave projects in the Gulf of Mexico and God knows what else. Posidian have seen the most incredible growth in the value of their shares over the last five years, but it's beginning to look as if there's been some massive fraud, with artificially inflated profits and dubious accounting. The whole thing's a massive house of cards.'

'Is it going to collapse?' Jan asked, wondering what overall difference that would make.

'Maybe not for a while; it's all inside rumour at this stage, but if they go do down, I suspect they'll take Gary's whole operation with them. I have to say this is only my view because I have privileged information on some mind-boggling borrowing he's done to fund his position. But I am certain if the company does go Gary isn't going to have time even to *think* about racehorses.'

'Oh no! I was planning to buy him more at the Doncaster Sales next week. There are a couple of real prospects coming up.'

'If I were you, I'd bide my time until I knew which way things were going.'

'But then I'll be two short for what I was planning.'

'If he's going to be in a sticky position about paying, that may turn out not to be such a bad thing.'

18

On Saturday morning the persistent rain, which had lasted almost a fortnight, ceased, and by eight o'clock a strong autumn sun was already casting its beams over the top of the ridge behind Edge Farm, helping a little to lift Jan's spirits as she led out her second lot. She was riding Bernie's new filly, alongside half a dozen others who were starting to do light canters. Beside her Annabel was on her old favourite, Russian Eagle.

'At least he's a bit slimmer now,' she said, looking down at her horse as they pulled out into the long field and made their way to the bottom of the new woodchip gallop.

'He'll always look a bit chunky with such a round barrelled ribcage,' Jan said. 'He's that type of horse. I only hope he doesn't take as long to peak as he did last year.'

Annabel nodded. 'It would be great if we could give him a couple of runs before Christmas.'

'Have you discussed it with your co-owner?' Jan looked at her friend, wondering if A.D. had been talking to Annabel but not to her.

'No, I'd have told you if I had.'

'I haven't heard a squeak from him for well over two weeks now,' Jan admitted.

'Does that worry you?'

'A bit. I was sure he would ring after the court case when those bloody Sharps suddenly decided to plead guilty.'

'That was a fantastic turn-up, wasn't it?' Annabel grinned.

For the last few days the papers had been full of the story. In the second week of their trial, Angie Sharp, her parents and Jan's former jockey, Billy Hanks, had unexpectedly changed their plea to 'Guilty' to the string of fraud charges against them. They admitted they had been fixing races by bribing jockeys to lose and they were prepared to take the consequences. Or so it seemed.

'I still feel there's more to it than meets the eye, but I'm relieved all the same,' Jan said, raising an eyebrow. 'I was dreading having to appear in court and give evidence with that lot sitting in the dock, glaring at me. But I wish I knew what really caused them to change their minds.'

'I dare say it will come out sooner or later. But I know what you mean about A.D. I'm amazed he hasn't rung. Still, there's probably a good reason for it. Do you know where he is? Perhaps he's away.'

'But that wouldn't make any difference; it hasn't in the past. What worries me is that he's been distinctly cool ever since Gary West's horses arrived, although he was really helpful at first with advice and everything. In fact, it was his idea to tie Gary down with a personal guarantee.'

'Perhaps he was hoping it would annoy Gary enough to make him change his mind about having horses with you.'

Jan turned to Annabel sharply with a quizzical look. 'What? Do you really think so? I never even thought of that.'

'But it was you who managed to talk Gary into it, so what the hell?'

Jan let out a long breath and glanced over her shoulder to make sure the other riders weren't near enough to hear. 'I just hope it all works out OK, after what Toby told me last week.'

'You mean about Gary West's company being in trouble?'

'How on earth did you hear that? Toby said it was his personal view, from private information which most people wouldn't know.'

'I guessed something was up when you cancelled your trip to Doncaster Sales. Then Toby told me about Gary's problems when he came out to dinner with me and Patrick last night.'

'Good God! Did he tell Patrick as well?'

'No, of course not; Patrick had gone for a pee and we were alone. He assumed you'd told me already. Why didn't you, by the way? You can't keep on trying to handle everything on your own, you know. What do you think I'm here for, for heaven's sake?'

Jan accepted the rebuke. She'd longed to discuss her worries, but hadn't been able to unburden herself even to Annabel, mainly because she didn't want to admit that her judgement about doing business with Gary West might have been wrong. 'I should have done, I suppose. I'm just praying Toby's got it wrong and it'll turn out OK in the long run, but I'm not very hopeful.'

'I hope you don't mind me asking,' Annabel said pointedly, 'but what have they been like with money so far?'

'They paid for the first four horses I bought, of course, no trouble – they'd lodged funds in my client account before I started bidding. But nothing extra was transferred before the sales this week, which is obviously why I didn't go.'

'And the training fees?'

'John Tanner sent me a cheque in late August which cleared the account up to the end of July. I reminded him I liked to have any training fees settled within twenty-one days, but I still haven't had anything for August yet. I know a lot of big companies drag their heels, but small ones like us can't afford for them to do that.'

'Oh dear,' Annabel said. 'Still, maybe you shouldn't worry too much. Let's see how things go over the next week or so.'

'That's all very well, but the trouble is, with the investment I've had to make to accommodate the new horses and put in the all-weather, I can't afford John Tanner to be playing bloody games with me.'

'Assuming it's Tanner's decision and it is a game.'

'I think it must be. I can't see Gary messing us about like that. Anyway, that's just between you and me. OK?' They had reached the start of the gallop, which stretched from the flat ground at the bottom of the farm by the road right up to the point just below the ridge where Jan's land ended.

Jan stood up in her irons and turned to beckon the rest of the string past her so she could watch them as they set off up the new strip. When the last of them had gone by, she and Annabel set off at a steady hack.

It was a good long haul up a gradually increasing slope and both horses were ready to pull up once they reached the top.

Annabel leaned forward and patted her horse's neck. 'Well done, boy! And you're not blowing too much either.'

Jan put her head forward and down one side to listen. 'Oh, that's good! At least something's going right,' she said with a grin.

Toby Waller was already waiting in the yard when Jan arrived back with the string just after nine-thirty. He was gazing over the stable door at his new horse. Standing beside him were two men who at first glance seemed in complete contrast to one another.

Jan nodded and called out a greeting. In the few moments it took her to ride across the yard and jump down, she observed that one of the new visitors was short and stocky – no more than five foot four, with a thick brush of jet black hair and obvious Chinese features, while the other was about six foot three, with a broad, russet face and an unruly haystack of fine blond hair streaked with silver.

The Chinese man could have been anywhere between twenty-five and forty, while the other man looked a well-preserved sixty or so. They must be members of the syndicate Toby had told her about.

Before she introduced herself, she unsaddled her horse and sponged it down, scraping off the excess water, as she always did when she had ridden out on a muggy day. Toby stood with his two companions, waiting until she was finished.

Eventually straightening her back with a twinge of pain, Jan asked Annabel to check on the rest of the horses while she dealt with her visitors. Still holding her horse's head, she strolled towards them.

'Sorry about that, but if I walk away from the regular chores it sets a bad example to the others. I won't be a minute, I'll just put this lady away first.' She led the filly away and put her into the stable next to Nero's Friend.

'Is that the horse you bought for Frank Jellard?' Toby called, following behind.

Jan nodded. 'He said she wasn't well enough bred, so Bernie's got her now.'

'Lucky chap – she looks really nice.'

'She is,' Jan said, closing the door. 'Anyway, I take it you've had a good look at your new "baby"?' Jan grinned at Nero's stable.

'He's looking excellent,' Toby said smugly. 'How's his work going?'

'We've just started doing a little bit of work with him and it's very encouraging.'

'Encouraging?' Toby echoed with a quizzical look. 'That's not a word I like. It's one of those catch-all terms that means "nothing's actually gone wrong yet".'

Jan laughed. 'Well, I was using it in its true sense – I wouldn't bullshit you.'

'You wouldn't bullshit anyone, Jan, we all know that. I'd like you to meet a couple of friends of mine who've decided they have a certain amount of expendable income and they'd like you to help them expend it with a little panache.'

'I don't know about panache,' Jan grinned, 'but if they want to spend it buying racehorses, I'm here to help.'

'This is Bobby Ng.' Toby pronounced the name 'urng', and gestured towards the Chinese man, who held out a small hand and took hers in a strong grasp. He released her hand with a smile on his face and when he spoke his accent was much more reminiscent of New York than Hong Kong.

'Pleased to meet you, Mrs Hardy,' he said with a slight bow. 'I've heard a lot about you and I was very impressed with Russian Eagle's win in Ireland last spring.'

'Thank you. You're very kind,' Jan said, warmed by the compliment. 'Have you followed National Hunt racing long?' she asked doubtfully, given that in Hong Kong and the United States almost all racing was on the flat.

'For the last five years really, since I've been in England,' Bobby said. 'There's more unpredictability about jumping, which in my book makes it a better gambling sport with much better odds.'

'In his job, Bobby tries to deal in certainties at very short odds,' Toby said dryly, 'so racing's a sort of escapism for him.'

'What's your job?' Jan was intrigued.

'It's another form of gambling really and there are *no* certainties in it either,' Bobby said. 'I'm an FX dealer in the same bank as Toby.'

Jan looked blank. 'What's FX?'

'Foreign exchange,' he answered simply. 'I buy and sell large parcels of currencies for commercial operations, other banks, speculators – whoever thinks they're going to need the stuff.'

'And this is Sandy Wilson.' Toby turned to the taller man. 'Until a month ago Detective Chief Superintendent Wilson of the Fraud Squad at the Met, I might add.'

Jan shook his hand. Once again, she was struck by the confident grip and the focused blue eyes, which seemed to be reading her mind already.

'Hello, Jan. I'm very pleased to meet you.' He spoke for the first time in a deep, ragged voice with a strong London accent. 'Like Bobby I've been a fan of yours since you hit the headlines last year.'

'Oh?' Jan replied modestly before she could think of anything better.

'Yeah, and I was really sorry to see you get robbed by those Sharps.'

'You followed the trial, did you?' Jan asked cautiously.

'I did, and I can tell you the only reason they pleaded guilty was to stop a whole pile more stuff being laid on 'em. There'd certainly have been some heavy plea bargaining. I bloody hope they get a good long stretch when they're sentenced next week.'

'I was so relieved.' Jan sighed. 'I was dreading being cross-examined. I was really hurt by what happened; I genuinely thought Angie was a good friend of mine – I was so gullible.'

'Don't blame yourself, Jan. Most animals have parasites looking for a free ride at one time or another and almost all con artists pretend to be nice people. They have to, otherwise they wouldn't get close enough to take advantage of their victim,' Sandy Wilson observed. 'Anyway, if we decide to do business, and if you're ever in that kind of trouble again, you come and see me first, all right?'

Jan nodded. The man's manner and his obvious knowledge of the seamier side of civilization inspired great confidence. Now she really hoped that they would be doing business together.

'Thanks,' she said, before turning to Toby. 'Anyway, how do you know the chief superintendent? Has he felt your collar?'

'I never let him catch me.' Toby grinned. 'No,' he went on quickly, to make it clear he was joking, 'he's sometimes cajoled me into appearing as an expert witness when the Crown Prosecution Service hasn't been up to scratch.'

'And a very good expert he is too,' the ex-policeman confirmed, grinning.

'I bet,' Jan said. 'Now let me show you round the yard before we go up to the house and talk about what sort of horse you think you want.'

Bobby laughed. 'We *know* what we want, don't we, Sandy? A fast one. We want to win the Gold Cup.'

Jan raised an eyebrow. 'You and about ten thousand others,' she teased.

As Toby and his friends climbed into his Range Rover to drive to the afternoon's flat meeting at Ascot, Jan was delighted they had expressed their preference for National Hunt racing so firmly and was confident that she would soon have another horse in her yard. She smiled to herself and felt touched at the efforts Toby made to promote her as a trainer. Although in the last two years Jan had won several races with the horses he owned, he was by no means in profit, but he fully appreciated that wasn't the point.

It was evident that he had also made this clear to the syndicate, who were nonetheless aware that there was always a chance, albeit a faint one, that they just might end up with a wonder horse which would be a massive money spinner.

She had agreed with Bobby and Sandy, who were speaking for the other members, that she would look for something with a bit of experience at the next big sale and ask around the breeders in Ireland through Sean McDonagh.

Thinking that these were the sort of people it could be really enjoyable to train for, she turned and walked slowly up to the house feeling more content.

Megan was jumping up and down impatiently in the kitchen.

'Mummy, Mummy! When are we going?'

'Right now, Meg. Your class is at twelve. Have you groomed Monarch and picked his feet out?'

'Yes, I've been grooming him for ages and I've oiled his hooves.'

'Did you clean his tack properly last night?'

'Of course.'

'Well done. I'm just going to change, so make sure you've put your jacket, hairnet and Pony Club tie in the Shogun, then go and get Monarch out; Roz will help you. She's coming with us – she wants to see how you get on, and her little brother's going to be there too.'

As Jan watched Megan jog down the path, she was overjoyed that, without any runners to deal with, she could spend the rest of the day with her children. They were taking Monarch to a hunter trial ten miles to the south in Cotswold Hunt country. Although their strongest hope for Monarch was in show-jumping, rather than cross-country, Jan didn't think it would do the talented pony any harm to be taken round a course of twenty comparatively small and friendly rustic fences. Megan was quivering with excitement at the prospect. Even though the highest obstacle was only three feet, it would be the first 'proper' hunter trial she had ever entered.

Jan pulled off her boots and went upstairs to swap her jodhpurs for a pair of jeans. She was feeling very much brighter than she had been recently. Her horses had worked well that morning and she felt they were really beginning to come together. She thought two of Gary West's, in particular, would be ready to run shortly, and she'd spent ages poring over the conditions of entry for suitable races. She was even more determined, especially after John Tanner's snide reaction to their last runner, to bring back a winner for them.

She was also gearing up for the inevitable confrontation with Tanner over the late payments of her training fees or, better still, with Gary West himself. After all, she told herself, she had been able to face up to him over the guarantee and she felt confident that, once she had explained it was vital that her invoices were paid promptly to enable her to run the yard efficiently and pay her suppliers, he would understand and take action.

Digging Matty out of his room, where he was watching a video, Jan made her way back down to the yard, ready and willing to devote the rest of the day to her children and especially encouraging Megan's undoubted talents.

🐎

The event was being held in a broad piece of parkland that rose gently from the meadows beside the Windrush. The morning sun had delivered a warm September day, which, after the recent rain, had produced perfect going on the old sheep-grazed turf that made up most of the course. As Jan had guessed earlier, there was a large turnout for the four classes which the trials had been divided into. Megan's was the youngest and the most subscribed. An hour before the class was due to start, Jan turned the Shogun through a gate onto an expanse of concrete between a collection of old stone barns and steel-framed buildings, where a hand-written sign indicated where cars with trailers and horseboxes should park.

'Right, we haven't got much time. The first thing to do is to walk the course,' she said as she climbed out with Megan, Matty and Roz. 'Monarch should be all right in the trailer until we get back. I'll get someone to keep an eye on him.'

Eventually, they set off with a steady stream of other young competitors, most being vociferously briefed by their mothers. Occasionally, a wail of dismay at the angle of a fence would drift across the rolling pasture, to be cut short by the impatient command of an over-eager tutor.

Megan was completely unfazed by the fences. She looked at them matter-of-factly and asked her mother the best approach to take, particularly at the difficult water jump, which crossed a brook as it bounced and gurgled its way down to the tranquil river at the bottom of the valley.

Jan was more impressed by her daughter's unruffled determination than she allowed herself to show and she was pleased to recognize a lot of herself in this skinny, feisty little creature. Matthew tagged along behind, muttering his own views on the easiness of each fence, until Megan exploded.

'Shut up, Matty! If you were doing it on Rocket, you'd be really scared and you'd probably fall off at every single one.'

'I expect Jamie will,' Roz said of her younger brother with a chuckle.

'No, he won't,' Megan retorted defiantly. 'He's really good – much better than Matty and he'll probably beat me and Monarch anyway.'

Let's hope not, Jan thought, pleased, however, to get a glimpse of the more generous side of Megan's nature.

Roz and Jan stood side by side at a point in the centre of the course where they could see most of the fences, until the route took a long sweeping loop through the woodland surrounding the park.

Jan felt herself tense up as Megan was released from the starting box and headed for the first simple fence. Monarch quickly gathered up his neat little feet and leapt it with a foot to spare. Jan could almost feel her daughter's exhilaration and relief that they were on their way.

As Megan and the colonel's pony galloped on strongly over the course with relentless sureness, the commentator's voice echoed from a PA system around the ground.

'Megan Hardy and Monarch are going well, and clear across the water that's been causing the most trouble.'

Jan watched through her binoculars as pony and rider flew without a moment's hesitation over a small wooden gate before disappearing into the dark oak woods beyond.

'My God!' she murmured to Roz as she lowered her glasses. 'Watching your own flesh and blood go round is far worse than doing it yourself – even worse than watching your horse go round Aintree.'

'I know what you mean,' Roz replied. 'Look, Jamie's just started.'

Her nine-year-old brother, who had been in a saddle regularly since the age of three, was already a natural, and as bold as brass out hunting. He had started well on the course, but the water caught him just as Megan reappeared in the open.

'Megan Hardy and Monarch clear through the woodland fences

and the timed section. They're still going very nicely by the look of things.'

Jan's heart thumped as she glued her eyes back to the binoculars and focused on her daughter. Megan was covering the ground at a comfortable pace with her pony still happily on the bridle. She was checking carefully that they got the right stride at each of the last four fences, before crouching down like a jockey and galloping on with a flourish to the finish.

Jan found her legs were weak and trembling as she walked back towards the barns where the trailers were parked; her chest was bursting with pride at her daughter's and Monarch's performance. She had watched Megan win competitions in the show-jumping ring, but after a long and varied course like this, the tension and the relief which followed were much greater.

By the time she was near the roped-off area where the children clambered off their mounts at the end of the course, Jan was running, anxious to reassure herself that Megan really was all right and still in one piece.

'Well done, Meggy,' she called as she drew near. She wanted to sweep the little girl up into her arms and kiss her, but she knew it was important not to overdo the praise and restricted herself to a quick hug before turning to check the pony.

Shortly after, Jamie Stoddard finished. 'I went clear, too,' he gasped. 'Except the water.'

'Well done, Jamie! That was brilliant,' said Roz, hugging her little brother with more abandon than Jan had greeted her daughter with. Proudly, she walked him and his pony back towards the field beyond the barns where her mother's lorry was parked.

Jan, Megan and Matty led Monarch slowly back to their trailer, where Jan made sure Meg gave the pony a small drink of warm water from the old milk churn they always brought with them, while she sponged the sweat from his coat.

Megan was full of excitement and couldn't stop chattering, reliving every fence, the doubts she'd had on the way round and how she'd overcome them.

'Well, you've gone clear; we've just got to hope you did the best ride through the timed section.'

'We went really calmly and Monarch was *so* good,' the excited little girl continued, still talking nineteen to the dozen after they had put Monarch back in the trailer half an hour later.

They were just coming round the side of one of the big steel Dutch barns when they saw Roz burst out, running.

Jan stood and stared at her head girl.

Roz spotted her and turned, not slowing until she reached her. Her face was bright red, she was breathing heavily and there were tears in her eyes.

Jan instinctively wrapped her arms around her.

'For heaven's sake, what's the matter, Roz? What on earth's happened? Is Jamie all right?'

'Yes, yes,' Roz gasped. 'He's fine. He went off to check the scoreboard and I said I'd finish the pony and put it back on the lorry. I was just getting down when I bumped straight into that bloody vet!'

'Which vet?' Jan asked, puzzled. 'D'you mean Shirley?'

'No, of course not! She wouldn't try and rape me!'

'No, of course, you're not a man,' Jan couldn't help answering with brusque dryness, thinking of Shirley and Eddie. She turned to her children, standing wide-eyed behind her. 'Megan, you take Matty and go off to the scoreboard, check to see if they've put your time up. I'll be along in a minute.'

The desire to know how well she'd done overcame the conflicting urge in Megan to hear what had happened to Roz, and she jogged off, towing Matthew along behind her.

'It was that ghastly bastard, McNeill,' Roz hissed when the children were out of hearing.

'Bloody heck!' Jan exclaimed. 'What the hell's he been up to now?'

'He was drunk, absolutely plastered. He must have been in the hospitality tent all day. His breath stank of wine. He said some crap about how much he'd always liked me, which is complete balls because he's never even noticed me before. He couldn't even remember where I work.'

Jan guessed from Roz's indignation that she was beginning to recover her composure and was mightily relieved that nothing too serious seemed to have occurred.

'What happened after that?' she asked.

'He grabbed my wrists and started pulling me towards the hay bales at the end of the barn. I was too shocked to do anything at first. I suppose I thought there'd be someone around who would see him and make him stop, but he just kept dragging me and when we got to the bales he pushed me against them with his front – it was horrible! He was all excited and – you know, it was so obvious, I just couldn't believe it – I'd never seen him like that before – he's always been so pompous.'

As she spoke, Jan's thoughts were yanked back to the time when the vet, in similar circumstances, had astonished her in a barn at Edge Farm by throwing his drunken body at her. He'd only scrambled off when she had aimed a vicious, well-directed knee at his genitals.

'You know, that's almost exactly what he did to me. The man's a complete animal,' she gasped. 'He should be bloody prosecuted. How did you escape?'

'I was really lucky; he slipped and lost his balance for a moment. As he let go of me, I was able to get away and I just ran – until I saw you. Some other people were passing the end of the barn and I just prayed he wouldn't chase after me.'

'I can't see him anywhere now, so it looks like he's incapacitated. It serves the pig right. Poor you,' Jan said with compassion. 'Thank God he didn't get any further. I wonder what he's doing here anyway?'

'He's one of the official vets! I noticed his name in the programme when we were walking the course with Meg.'

'But that's terrible! You mustn't let him get away with it, Roz. You should make an official complaint against him to someone now – tell the police, even.'

'No,' Roz shook her head vehemently. 'No, I don't want all that hassle. I couldn't prove it anyway; no one saw us, so it would be my word against his. But don't you worry, I'll make damned sure he regrets it; I'll find a way, if it's the last thing I do!'

From the determination glowing in Roz's eyes, Jan didn't doubt her for one minute.

19

After three weeks of unpredictable, blustery weather, October began under a calm and sunny sky. The oaks standing guard on the margins of the undulating parkland that encompassed Chepstow racecourse were still green and in leaf. Their branches barely moved in the light breeze of the summer's reprise, while the same gently drying wind rippled the dark grass of the turf, over which close to a hundred horses were due to run on the first Saturday of the month. Jan Hardy had brought three of these from Edge Farm, with Roz and Joe to help out.

Once they'd reached the course, she told them to take their horses to the stables they'd been allocated in the security area. Annabel had already arrived in her BMW and the two women set off to walk the beautiful course above the steep slopes of the lower Wye valley.

Jan was anxious to see for herself if Captain Freckle, the clerk of the course, had spoken the truth the previous morning when he'd told her the going was *good – good to soft* in places. She was beginning to learn that some clerks were rather economical with the truth and told trainers what they wanted to hear instead of what they would find.

'He was right,' she said after they had walked almost two miles around the chase track, poking a thin walking stick into suspect sections of the course. 'If I'd found any really heavy ground, I'd have told him what I thought of him, loaded my horses and gone home – and put in a bill for my diesel.'

Annabel chuckled. 'Knowing you, you'd have got away with it.'

'What d'you mean – got away with it? If I know the horses I've

262

entered just won't act in certain conditions, what's the point of me traipsing them a hundred miles or so just because the racecourse hopes when I get there I'll overlook the fact they've misled me – purely to make sure they've got a full card? Last summer there was one clerk telling us there was a bit of give in the ground and when we got there it was like the sodding road. Well, that just won't do.'

'All right, all right, Jan,' Annabel said soothingly. 'At least the going should suit ours today.'

Jan nodded and they turned to make their way back towards the stables. 'Don't, for God's sake, quote me, but the way Gylippus has been working, I'm *really* hopeful. He's got loads of speed and feels a hundred per cent on the gallops. I think he could be our first winner for Gary West.'

Annabel nodded. 'At what distance did he win on the flat?'

'A mile and four, so I'm pretty sure he'll get the extra half-mile, particularly now he's older, and it is a hurdle today so they will be going that bit steadier.'

'But why did the yard sell him?'

Jan shrugged. 'I suppose in that sort of set-up, amongst all the high-class stock, he looked a bit common.'

'What?! By Petoski and with Northern Dancer in his dam's line?' Annabel asked doubtfully.

'No, what I mean is the sort of horse we like looks too heavy in a flat yard. Apparently they hadn't run him this year because there was a bit of a question mark over his wind. But I haven't seen any sign of the problem so far. And from the way he's developing he should make a smashing chaser, especially if he can get longer trips.'

When they arrived at the racecourse stables the four-year-old gelding was looking proudly over the box door. The dark, almost black-coffee bay, with a pair of white spats on his forelegs, pricked his ears as if in polite interest when Jan and Annabel approached.

'I don't know how you can call him common looking,' Annabel said. 'I think he's one of the handsomest boys in our yard.'

'What – even more than Russian Eagle?' Jan laughed.

'Russian Eagle doesn't aspire to beauty,' Annabel said with exaggerated dignity.

Jan slipped a hand under the horse's rug and was reassured to find his coat dry and not too warm. He had travelled well and was show-ing no signs of stress on his first visit to a racecourse for over a year.

'There's a good boy, Gilly,' Jan murmured. 'I know you're not going to let me down.'

In the next stable, Bernie Sutcliffe's eleven-year-old chaser Dingle Bay also had his head over the door and was watching everything intently. As usual, he was completely relaxed. To Jan, he epitomized an old-fashioned English steeplechaser. She stroked his muzzle and tweaked his lower lip.

'Well, boy,' she said, 'you've got some pretty strong opposition today, but if you watch your fences, you could do all right.'

'Who's riding him?' Annabel asked.

'Finbar can't because unfortunately Virginia's got a runner in the same race. And Murty's in Ireland, so I've booked a good young claimer called Luke Lacy. He only claims the minimum now, but that'll still be a big help over three and a half miles.'

Her assistant nodded. 'I've seen him ride. He's good. Is Finny riding the other two?'

'Yes. He's looking forward to it. He loved the feel Gylippus gave him when he worked on Thursday morning, and he's already seen Murty win on Supercall.'

Supercall, two doors beyond Dingle Bay, was another of Jan's stars – the tall, rangy gelding she'd bought in Ireland for Johnny Carlton-Brown the previous season. The horse had won nearly twenty-five thousand pounds since he'd spent his novice-chasing year in her care, and she was hopeful that he would double that during the current season. He would be running in stronger com-pany, but the prizes in the feature chases were considerably greater.

Jan left the stables feeling more optimistic than she had for months. And she was convinced that all three horses had a good chance of winning. Of course, she was aware that, in racing, particularly National Hunt, there were unpredictable factors, but the two chasers were ideal jumpers, and the young hurdler had taken to his job with real enthusiasm as he flew over the obstacles, gaining lengths in the air.

The feature race, with Dingle Bay competing, was a three-and-a-half-mile chase; which had a twenty-thousand-pound purse, making Chepstow the day's principal jump meeting in the country. As a result, four of the races were to be shown on terrestrial television, encouraging all three of Jan's owners to announce that they were coming, although John Tanner would be representing Gary West.

Tanner was the first to arrive, parking his red Porsche prominently in the owners' car park. Wearing a long brown leather coat with a navy, wide-brimmed fedora, he bustled up to Jan as she stood chatting outside the weighing room. Without waiting to shake her hand or offer any other kind of greeting, he leaned down with an exaggerated stoop and whispered in her ear.

'Gary's expecting a bloody result today,' he said hoarsely.

'If you want a private conversation, Mr Tanner, let's go somewhere a little less crowded.' Jan tried to admonish him with a withering look.

She walked off briskly towards a deserted spot near the empty pre-parade ring, where she waited, fuming.

'I spoke to Mr West this morning, on the way here,' Jan said as he caught up with her. 'I told him I thought Gylippus had a really good chance and I still think so, but there's no way in the world I can guarantee he'll win. I'm glad to say that your boss fully understands and is aware of that.' She fixed her eye firmly on him. 'So, Mr Tanner, I already know what he's expecting. All right?'

If he had any further plans to reassert his authority over his boss's trainer, they were suddenly interrupted by the swelling sound of a helicopter, which had swept in over the trees at the top of the Wye gorge and was now dropping towards an area of level ground in the centre of the course, opposite the main stand.

Jan glanced at Tanner. 'I'd like to talk to you later about the running of your horse, and several financial matters, but you'll have to excuse me for now. That's one of my owners and he'll be keen to know how his horse travelled.'

Jan stalked off before Tanner could object. She was grateful Johnny Carlton-Brown had turned up at that moment, providing her with an escape route; she was worried that if she'd been obliged to talk to the obnoxious Mr Tanner any longer she might not have been able to resist a powerful urge to clout him.

She marched round to the front of the grandstand, collecting Annabel on the way, and leaned on the rails so they could watch Johnny and Patrick Lamberhurst as they stepped down from the helicopter.

Jan glanced at Annabel. 'I see he's brought your boyfriend.'

'Yeah, Patrick said he might come along; I think he wants to see me working.' Annabel laughed.

'We'd better not disappoint him then,' Jan answered with a grin as the two men spotted them and veered in their direction.

'Hi, Jan,' Johnny called over the throbbing hiss of the aircraft, which was already revving up to take off again.

When he finally reached her, Jan was amused to see he was wearing a traditional Donegal tweed suit. He leaned over the fence and lightly brushed his lips over each of her cheeks. Out of the corner of her eye, Jan saw Patrick kiss Annabel warmly on the mouth like an established lover. She was rather surprised by the sight and, in a curious way, a little jealous; she was accustomed to being Annabel's closest friend, but she still knew very little about Patrick Lamberhurst and Annabel had seemed reluctant to talk about him much since she had returned from her holiday in the south of France.

Jan knew Bel had been seeing his lordship every other weekend or so and sometimes in the week too, when he'd been up to Stanfield and stayed at her cottage. She hadn't asked Jan to join them on the grounds, she'd said, that it would come into the same category as introducing him to her parents.

'Jan,' Annabel was saying now, 'you've met Patrick before, haven't you?'

'Of course, at Ben's party,' Jan said with a grin and was conscious of his pale blue eyes surveying her, with how much real interest it was impossible to say. 'I hope you've brought a little luck for JCB's horse with you.'

'So do I,' Lord Lamberhurst said in his languid, craggy voice. 'I've got five grand on him.'

'I'll make sure the horse knows before he starts,' she said

brusquely. And regretted the lapse at once when she saw from Annabel's face that she had picked up the negative vibes. 'I can tell you, since you're already committed, that he has got a pretty good chance.'

'What's the exact distance?' Johnny asked.

'Two miles, three and a half furlongs,' Jan told him.

'I see the race is worth fifteen grand, added to the stakes,' Lamberhurst remarked to Carlton-Brown. 'No need for you to have a bet.'

'The paper says his probable starting price is eight to one, though; that's quite tempting,' Johnny interjected.

'Unless you're addicted,' Jan said, 'I'd settle for pocketing the prize money, if I were you.'

'Very wise,' JCB confirmed with a teasing grin. 'And, Patrick, next time don't tell the trainer how much you've put on the horse or even that you've backed it at all. It's possible she might transfer the pressure that puts her under to the horse while she's saddling it.'

'Well, yes,' Lamberhurst said, 'that was rather what I was hoping.'

Does Annabel really like this plonker? Jan said to herself as the men left to walk along the rail to a gate that would let them through to the enclosure. 'I hope your lover's not going to blame you if he loses all that money,' she said to Annabel.

'I'm sure he won't,' Bel assured her, 'but I'm really sorry he told you. Anyway, with a bit of luck and some praying, let's hope . . .'

'Look, Bel, whether he bets five pounds or five thousand, it won't make Supercall run a yard faster.'

🐎

Johnny had already organized lunch in a hospitality suite and when he heard that Jan had two other owners at the meeting – Tanner and Bernie Sutcliffe – he generously invited them to join him.

John Tanner readily accepted, although he was unable to disguise his petulance at having been so comprehensively outclassed by JCB in his helicopter.

Bernie, on the other hand, was totally unimpressed by the

chopper and the vintage champagne, and apparently thought it quite proper that as the most longstanding owner in Jan's yard he should be included in the party.

They sat down for lunch at one o'clock, but just three-quarters of an hour later Jan and Annabel had to leave to attend to their duties. They collected the tack from their jockey in the weighing room, before making their way to the saddling boxes to meet Roz and Supercall, who was due to make his seasonal debut in the two-thirty.

'How's he been?' Jan asked.

'He's a bit full of himself. He knows he's back on a racecourse, all right.'

Looking at the well-presented horse, Jan smiled. 'Good,' she said, nodding. 'Right, boy. Let's get your kit on.'

Roz stood in front of Supercall, holding the reins tight, while Jan saddled him. The horse jittered and jigged in anticipation of what was to come, as if he were hyping himself up like an athlete. Jan felt her confidence grow; in her experience, he tended to go out and give of his best when he behaved like this before a race.

When Jan had finished titivating her horse, they all set off towards the parade ring. Johnny Carlton-Brown and Lord Lamberhurst were waiting by the entrance and walked in with them. Roz led Supercall round, while the owner stood in the middle, looking on with a smile of approval.

When Finbar Howlett joined them, wearing Johnny's pink and gold hooped colours, his eyes were fixed on the animal he would soon be piloting round the course.

'The ground's a little sticky on the inside at the far end of the course, so keep off the rail there,' Jan told him. 'Otherwise ride a normal race. Have him midfield along the back, when you've swung round into the home straight move up a bit handier. Make sure you're in the first three at the second last, then hopefully you can take it up and use his speed after the last.'

Without looking at her, Finbar nodded, indicating that he would have suggested the same strategy himself.

They all trooped back up to watch the race from JCB's box, where Patrick Lamberhurst insisted everyone should have a drink before the race started. Jan did wonder if he was as nonchalant about his five-thousand-pound wager as Annabel had suggested.

The two-and-a-half-mile chase start was at the entrance to the home straight, with the fifth of the sixteen fences almost in front of the stands. Peering through her binoculars at the horse as he circled behind the tape, waiting for the starter to call them in, Jan felt he should have been first or second favourite on the strength of his glorious physique alone. But he was in far better company than he'd met in his career to date and, although his price had come in to five to one during the morning, he was still third in the betting.

The starter pressed the handle firmly to release the tape which let the horses go. Finbar had easily settled his horse in fifth place by the time they reached the second fence. Supercall took the open ditch a whole stride too soon, but cleared it with such dexterity that Finbar had to ease him back on the flat to stop him getting too near the front. Even the commentator mentioned the magnificent leap Supercall put in over the fence in front of the stands, before the tightly packed field ran downhill towards a sharp left-handed bend, which was followed by a steep uphill rise and a slightly gentler turn coming up to the sixth.

Along the undulations on the far side of the course Jan watched the horse continue to jump flawlessly, while two of those behind him fell.

'That Irish boy's giving him a super ride,' Johnny said beside her. 'I'm glad you were able to get him.'

Jan nodded. 'He really likes riding for us. I think it's only because he's a good, straight kid that he's still at Virginia's.'

The field was swinging round the long, smooth curve at the far end of the track and Jan watched Finbar taking his horse to the outside to give himself a clear view of the fences up the home straight. He flew the open ditch for the second time and landed in third place, still on the bridle as far as Jan could see. At the next Supercall landed in second place, and Jan wondered if Finbar was planning to take up the running. In the circumstances, there was no reason why he shouldn't. The horse didn't mind being in front and at present his only rival appeared to have shot his bolt.

At the second last, just a length behind the leader, Supercall stood off to put in a massive leap. Even if Finbar had seen the horse in front stumble and come down right across their path, it would have been too late for him to do anything about it.

As Supercall jumped the fence with a foot to spare, he saw his stricken rival and, fearful of landing on it, he twisted violently in the air, met the ground all wrong and crashed heavily onto his left shoulder, projecting his jockey like a cannonball halfway across the course.

Along with half the spectators, Jan let out a loud gasp, though it was nothing to the howl of anguish from Lord Lamberhurst, who just a few supremely optimistic moments before had abandoned his dignity enough to yell his encouragement like any other punter in the stands.

'Fucking hell!' his lordship spluttered as he saw his chance of an easy, tax-free forty thousand pounds disintegrate in front of his eyes and as the faulty jumping of the horse in front denied him his success.

Lowering her glasses for a moment, Jan saw Annabel's quick look of consternation at Lamberhurst's bloodless face.

Feeling uneasy, Jan quickly turned her attention back to the track and the plight of her horse, which was already on its feet and trotting brightly back towards the stables.

'He looks all right, but I must go down and check him,' Jan said hurriedly.

JCB, crestfallen but philosophical, turned to her with sympathetic eyes. 'We were robbed, I'm afraid. Our horse was definitely going to win. He ran and jumped perfectly as far as I could tell.'

'He did; we've got nothing to worry about there.'

'I see Finbar's up and walking straight. That's good. Let me know how our fellow is, won't you?'

'Of course,' Jan called, hurrying towards the door, Bel following.

Annabel almost had to run to keep up with her boss.

'Bloody hell!' she said, much more affected than usual. 'I've never seen a horse that was so obviously going to win brought down at the last like that.'

'Nor have I, at least not often,' Jan agreed. 'Nor has the handi-capper, I expect. I'm sorry Patrick lost his money.'

'So was he by the look of it,' Annabel said, showing her surprise at his reaction. 'Maybe it was because he was so close to winning. I suppose he thought he had it in the bag two from home – I certainly did.'

'Maybe,' Jan said thoughtfully. 'Is he really interested in horses, do you think, or is it just the gambling and glitz?'

'I wouldn't call Chepstow on a Saturday in autumn particularly glitzy,' Annabel replied. 'But, to be honest, I don't think he's a great animal lover, if that's what you mean.'

'Isn't that a bit of a problem for you two?'

'Not really – not so far.' Annabel sounded a little resentful of Jan's implied criticism. 'I don't think two people have got to be absolutely identical to get on or spark off each other.'

'No, but surely it helps if they have a few fundamental principles in common,' Jan said more softly.

She had slowed her pace as they neared the stables and met Roz leading their riderless horse as she was just about to turn into the yard.

'Hold on, Roz,' she called. 'Let's have a look at him.'

She quickly and expertly ran her hands up and down each of his limbs, checking carefully for cuts or signs of swelling. When she straightened herself, she put her head on one side with a satisfied smile. 'He's fine – nothing obvious. Give him a good wash down and hose his legs off before you put him away. Now, let's see how Joe's getting on with Gilly.'

'Do you have to call him that?' Annabel laughed. 'It makes him sound like a pet.'

Jan laughed too. 'His real name's such a gobful, but I know what you mean. All right, Gylippus,' she went on with exaggerated diction, as they looked into the big gelding's box, 'how are you feeling?'

'He's pretty good, Mrs H,' Joe Paley answered from the depths of the stable. 'I've just been giving him a final polish.'

Jan opened the door with her foot and waited while the lad clipped on the lead rein and led the horse out. She nodded her head with approval. 'Well done. He looks as shiny as Bernie's patent leather shoes.'

They all burst out laughing, remembering the first time Bernie Sutcliffe had turned up at Edge Farm and picked his way fastidiously across the yard, stepping over a pile of fresh horse muck in a pair of shoes so lustrous Jan could almost see her reflection in them. It hadn't gone unnoticed that he'd never worn them to Edge Farm since.

As Joe led Gylippus towards the saddling boxes, Jan noticed the horse caught several people's eye as he passed.

Harlequin Holdings' name on the card wouldn't mean much to the racegoers and the colours would be unfamiliar. Jan felt relieved the racing press had also failed to pick up on the fact that she'd been building a private string of horses for Gary West. But, no doubt, once several different horses had appeared under the company's name, they would start to scrutinize it. For now, at least she was only under pressure from John Tanner and that was unpleasant enough.

Jan stood in the paddock. Alongside her, Tanner oozed self-importance. As Joe proudly led the horse round the ring, Jan was alert enough to observe several people hanging over the rails take one look at her horse then glance down at their race cards to find out who this magnificent animal belonged to and, above all, who trained it.

The short synopsis of the horse's form printed below its name would have told them that it hadn't raced for 392 days, that it had won in Ireland on the flat at a distance of one mile four furlongs; this was its debut over hurdles and, in the form writer's opinion, there was too much of a question mark over its ability to inspire much confidence.

But Jan and Finbar, on the evidence of the work they'd done at home, held a different view.

Annabel nudged Jan gently in the ribs to get her attention while John Tanner was looking the other way.

'Patrick wants to know if he should back him,' she said from the side of her mouth.

'Well,' Jan answered, 'do you think he should?'

'Frankly, knowing you think the horse can do the trip, and looking at what he's up against today, I'd say yes.'

'So say it.'

'Is that what *you* really think? I mean, he'll probably have an absolute monster of a bet to make up for losing on Supercall so I daren't get it wrong.'

'Oh no, Bel, leave me out of it!' Jan chided her. 'You can use your own judgement.'

'Hell!' Annabel made a face. 'I wanted to have someone else to blame if he loses.'

'I know you do. And I would normally say blame me, but if the horse wins, and Patrick starts thinking I'm in the habit of tipping winners, he'll be on the phone the whole bloody time – that's why I never get involved and tell owners, or anyone else for that matter, how to bet.'

Annabel took a deep breath. 'Right, that's it, if it loses and he makes a scene, I'll just tell him to naff off and do it somewhere else.'

Jan grinned as she watched her friend leave the parade ring. As far as she was concerned, on her admittedly scanty acquaintance with Lord Lamberhurst, she was pretty sure that the sooner he moved on the better.

As long as it doesn't leave her feeling like I did over Eddie Ruddy Sullivan, she thought bitterly, before Tanner interrupted her thoughts with a demand to know what her tactics for the race were going to be.

'You can listen to what I tell Finbar,' she said, feeling even less charitably disposed towards him than usual, since he'd twice blocked her attempts to discuss the £8,000 due in training fees and had offered no explanation or apology for not making the funds available for the remaining two horses they'd ordered.

But she was determined that, win or lose, she would tackle him again about the money as soon as this race was over.

In the meantime, when he gathered that Lamberhurst was going to have a bet on Gylippus, he badgered her to know if he should do the same. Jan refused to be definite.

'The horse looks well,' she said. 'And I'm confident he will get the trip on this ground or I wouldn't have brought him here.'

'What about the little paddy? Is he OK?'

'If you mean Finbar,' Jan said coldly, 'he's fine. He landed well and there isn't a mark on him.'

'That's good, but is this horse fast enough?'

'His flat win confirms he's got the speed and his jumping's great. But whether or not he's faster than the other fifteen runners, I couldn't really tell you.'

The bookies, it seemed, had yet to be convinced and some were offering Gylippus at odds as long as sixteen to one. Tanner couldn't resist a price as generous as that, and as soon as Finbar, in Gary West's colours of orange cross belts on a purple body, was mounted, he barged his way from the paddock to the bookies in the club enclosure.

🐎

Jan didn't want to impose Tanner on Johnny Carlton-Brown and took him up to watch the race from the owners' and trainers' stand instead. Once they had found a good vantage point, Tanner leaned down with a conspiratorial smile.

'I've got a grand on him. The bookie knocked the odds right down from sixteens to eights as soon as I went in,' he chortled.

And you've got a good chance of winning, too, you jammy bastard! Jan thought. Still, at least there'd be no excuse for him not to pay her what she was owed.

🐎

Jan gave Finbar similar riding instructions for the hurdle race as she had for the chase.

In a hurdle race, the obstacles were much smaller and easier to jump than in a steeplechase, which made a horse's speed more important. Nevertheless, if an animal knocked the jumps or checked his stride, it slowed him down compared to those who took them cleanly.

In the two-mile novice hurdle race for four-year-olds, Jan's horse was moving as easily as if he were on the long grass gallop on top of the ridge behind Edge Farm. He was, quite literally, taking the hurdles in his stride, bouncing over them like a gazelle.

As they raced down the far side, Jan could see that Finbar had the horse well in control, halfway down the field and moving sweetly without any fuss while the two favourites Boxed and Coxed at the front, exhausting themselves with youthful exuberance.

Once again Jan was feeling very grateful to whatever power had sent Finbar her way – until she suddenly remembered it was Eddie who had met him in the pub and brought him to the yard. She smiled to herself. Eddie might be hopeless at looking after his own affairs, but he did have his uses.

The Irishman was once again taking his mount a little to the outside of the long left-handed bend that would bring them back into the home straight. By the time they reached the next hurdle he had Gylippus lying in fourth place. They jumped the last alongside the favourite, and two strides after landing Finbar asked his horse to stretch.

Gylippus's response was breathtaking, so much so that Jan couldn't help thinking that Finbar had rather overdone it as it could affect the horse's rating.

Even the beastly John Tanner, who knew very little about racing, knew enough to be impressed by what he had just seen.

'Cor, bloody hell! Wheelspin! Come on, my son!' he bellowed and turned to Jan with a broad grin on his narrow face. 'Bloody hell, Jan, he's going to win!'

Jan couldn't speak during the short time it took Gylippus to cover the last two furlongs.

She could scarcely breathe as the horse, whom she had picked and meticulously trained to peak fitness, gained ten lengths on his nearest rival and thundered across the line to a huge cheer. The crowd hadn't backed him, but they obviously knew a rising star when they saw one.

The handsome gelding, with suspected wind trouble, who had never raced more than a mile and a half and whom Jan had bought from a major flat yard as a comparative bargain at sixty thousand pounds, had totally vindicated her judgement and, she thought wryly, Gary West's judgement of her as trainer.

Glancing sideways, she saw John Tanner beaming with reflected glory as the surrogate owner.

'I'd better get hold of that bleeding bookie before he scarpers,' he declared.

'Don't worry about it,' Jan told him. 'He's not going to run away with your sixteen grand; he's probably laid most of it off anyway, just in case.'

But Tanner wasn't going to be made to look a fool. 'Well I'm bloody well going to get it right now. I'll see you in the bar for a few bottles of bubbly later – right?'

'Sorry, I've got another horse to saddle,' Jan said, trying to suggest with her expression how disappointed she was not to be sharing in Tanner's celebration.

'Well, I'll see you after that, then?'

Jan nodded and watched him stride away to secure his winnings. She was no prima donna, she thought, but a few words of thanks or congratulations from the owner's representative, who had just won most people's annual salary tax free, would not have gone amiss.

Shaking her head in disgust, she dismissed Tanner's behaviour and hurried off to meet her triumphant horse and jockey.

As Joe led them in triumphantly, Finbar was beaming like the morning sun, acknowledging the applause with a touch of his cap. Gylippus was as fresh as paint, not too hot, not blowing hard. Jan wondered what the people who had sold him to her would be thinking and if they'd watched the race he had just won with such spectacular ease.

As they entered the enclosure, the jockey leaned down towards Jan.

'That was superb!' he said. 'He *really* delivered when I asked him.'

Jan smiled up at him. 'We saw.'

'His jumping's something else, too. Y'know, this could be a Champion Hurdler one day!' he said.

'We'll talk about it later,' Jan replied, to warn him that there were people close enough to hear everything that was being said.

But she didn't blame the Irish jockey for being excited.

She was already convinced that Gylippus was one of the best things to have happened to her since she'd been granted her licence and, if she handled him right, she was sure he would deliver the next big break in her career.

20

Jan gazed proudly at her new star as she waited in the winners' enclosure for the presentation, her whole body tingling with pleasure at the way the horse finished and what that promised for the future.

But the moment was tarnished by the knowledge that Gylippus belonged to owners who either couldn't or wouldn't pay their bills. She could live with Tanner's failure to acknowledge her achievement in finding the horse and training it to win, but she couldn't keep on doing the job for nothing.

The woman making the presentation had stepped onto a temporary dais with the managing director of the racecourse, who was looking around trying to identify the winner's connections.

Jan suddenly realized that Tanner might be unaware he would be presented with a trophy, or, in his haste to collect his winnings, had forgotten.

Serve him right, Jan said to herself as the course commentator's voice boomed through the PA system, 'We'd like to welcome Mr John Tanner of Harlequin Holdings Ltd, the owners of this very impressive winner, to the rostrum.'

Moments later John Tanner shouldered his way through the crowd that had gathered around the entrance of the unsaddling enclosure and strutted towards the dignitaries with his long leather coat flapping in the breeze.

Immediately after the presentation, as Joe took the horse back to the stables, John Tanner vanished. He was already striding away from the ring when Jan spotted him and almost had to break into a jog to catch up.

'Hang on, Mr Tanner, I need a word with you,' she called.

He glanced at her angrily. 'Not now. I'm in a hurry. I've got to get back to London.'

Jan ignored his dismissal and with an extra spurt managed to plant herself squarely in front of him. 'Mr Tanner, before you go anywhere I am going to talk to you. Your horse has just won a really good race and you've won a very substantial bet,' Jan continued quietly, but with an icy edge to her voice. 'You've obviously been paid out and I haven't had any training fees for your horses since the beginning of August. The bill stands at nearly eight thousand pounds, which may not be a lot to you, Mr Tanner, but it's absolutely vital to me.'

Tanner glanced rapidly from side to side to see if anyone else was listening. 'Do you mind not discussing this sort of thing in public?' he said huskily. 'You know perfectly well the horses are the property of a company that belongs to Mr West.'

'That's fine. I'd be delighted to discuss it somewhere more private. Where do you suggest?'

For a moment, Tanner looked like a rat in a trap until his natural resilience came to the rescue. 'Look, shut it, Jan! I can't do anything about it.'

'But you've just won sixteen grand!' she spluttered in disbelief. 'You could quite easily give me eight, which would bring the position up to date.'

'What I've won is mine, anyway it's not me that owes you.'

'I see, so when everything's hunky-dory you're an equal owner and I take my instructions from you, but when the shit hits the fan you're nothing to do with it, is that right?'

'What are you talking about – "shit hits the fan"?'

'I'm talking about Posidian about to go bust for billions of dollars, which will include your governor's colossal shareholding and the extra money he borrowed to get it.'

Tanner, who had started to move away, stopped dead in his tracks. 'What do you know about Posidian?'

'It's been in the papers.'

'It's got absolutely nothing to do with us,' Tanner said harshly, recovering himself. 'It's total bollocks! You've got to understand, there's always rumours about us – we're very big players.'

'Is that so?' Jan said, now walking fast to keep up with Tanner, who had brushed past her and was heading for the car park. 'Well, if you're so big and your business isn't in trouble, why the hell aren't you paying me?'

Tanner stopped abruptly and glared at her. 'Look, I can't do nothing about it,' he hissed. 'Now piss off and let me get out of here.'

Jan watched him go with anger seething through her. She had disliked him at first sight, now his manner and actions confirmed her judgement and at this present moment she loathed him.

On the other hand, she trusted Gary West completely.

She would simply have to deal with him in future and ignore 'the pig'. She shook her head in frustration that her magnificent win should have been so spoilt by the horse's owner.

After they'd dealt with their runners and seen them off in the lorry, Annabel and Jan were told that their other owners had already left. They had an early evening appointment with an American management company which apparently did not understand the sanctity of a Saturday afternoon's racing.

As Annabel drove home from Chepstow, she insisted that Jan should join her for dinner with Patrick and Johnny at the Manoir du Chèvre d'Or, which they were going on to after their meeting. Bel persuaded Jan that, by any standards, her three horses had run well. Supercall would certainly have won if he hadn't been brought down, Gylippus had been spectacular and Bernie's horse, Dingle Bay, had finished a very creditable second in the big chase. She felt a minor celebration was justified and Jan would be mean-spirited to refuse.

Sipping a glass of white wine in front of the vast fireplace in the hotel's hall, Jan found it hard to relax, despite her friend's encouragement.

'Look, Jan, I know it's making life really difficult for you not getting any money from Tanner, but I'm sure you will sooner or later – at least you've got that personal guarantee from Gary West.'

'That doesn't look as if it's worth the paper it's written on. I haven't been able to get hold of him for weeks. I've left dozens of messages in his office. Besides, it's knowing what bloody good horses we bought that hurts and seeing them win without him even acknowledging it, let alone paying, that really rankles. But listen.' Jan glanced up at her friend's anxious face. 'I'm OK now. I really am trying to look on the positive side. And what that horse did today makes me think it could be the most exciting I've ever trained.'

'How about Magic Maestro? He hasn't been beaten on the gallops.'

Jan nodded. 'Until I've seen him on the track, I really couldn't say. He's obviously got tons of talent, but Gylippus has an incredibly strong finish and that's always going to give him a massive advantage, especially on courses like Cheltenham, where they need that extra bit of class.'

'Now what are you two women gossiping about?' Patrick Lamberhurst asked, advancing with Johnny Carlton-Brown to join them by the fire.

'Not gossip,' Annabel said firmly. 'Shop. She's worried about Gary West.'

Jan shot her a warning glance as there was no reason for other owners to know about that sort of problem.

'I'm not surprised,' Johnny said. 'I would think he's spread very thinly these days. Did you know – ' he turned to Patrick – 'he's even taken a stake in a couple of American record companies and I would guess he knows diddly squat about the business.'

'Good heavens. Perhaps he wants to launch one of his starlets with a singing career and thinks that would make it easier.'

'If the rumours are to be believed, Gary West has stakes in so many different businesses he can't possibly know what they're all up to; I'm afraid he must be one of life's supreme jugglers. How do you two find him to deal with?'

'We've only met him once,' Jan said cautiously. 'And he was

totally charming, if that's anything to go by. He's certainly very attractive, and I'm sure he knows all the right buttons to push with a woman.'

'An enviable skill,' Lamberhurst observed sardonically. 'But would you trust him?'

'As a matter of fact, I did, and I probably still do, if only he'd talk to me. I'm fairly certain he's not interested in ripping me off for a few quid – not after he's just bought four hundred thousand pounds' worth of horses – it seems pointless.'

'I would think he's got plenty of other things on his mind at the moment,' JCB said. 'Still, he must be very pleased with the way that horse won today.'

'I've no idea. He hasn't been in touch for ages and his gofer couldn't wait to get home with his loot.'

'Tanner had a punt, did he?'

'Yes, he had a grand on – at sixteen to one.'

'Ah.' Lamberhurst pulled a face, as if there was a nasty smell under his nose. 'That must be what dropped the odds just before I got my money on. Still,' he added smugly, 'I did manage to get five on.'

Jan was amazed she hadn't already heard that story, but judging by Annabel's expression, she hadn't either.

'Well done,' Jan said unenthusiastically, reluctant to be overly impressed by this spectacular win.

'Thank you. You'll note that, following Johnny's request, I didn't tell you before the race so as not to put you under any pressure.'

'That was very considerate of you. I'm really glad you were able to recover your losses after Supercall's fall in the first.'

'Personally,' JCB said, 'I won nothing and I lost nothing, though I'm delighted my horse ran so well. By the way, I wanted to ask you about the other one you got from the Sharps that you were thinking of selling – King's Archer, wasn't it?'

'What about him?'

'Would you be kind enough to give me first refusal after his next run?'

'That may not be until Cheltenham at the end of the month, but fine,' Jan agreed with a smile, thinking that Johnny deserved it.

'It would be nice if you could salvage something from all that unpleasantness the Sharps caused. You must have been delighted when they got sent down for five years.'

'Yes I was, but extra pleased to see Billy Hanks get his come-uppance for taking advantage of me when I trusted him completely.'

'How long had you known him?'

'Since he was born. I gave him all his best rides in point-to-points. I had complete faith in him – until it was obvious he was pulling half my runners. I just couldn't believe he was capable of doing such a thing.'

'Do you think you'll be able to get hold of Finbar Howlett as your stable jockey?'

'I really do hope so.'

'How would you get him from Virginia?'

'Don't worry, if I just let him go on riding her horses, sooner or later he'll leave of his own accord.'

The following day, after a traditional Sunday lunch with Mary and Reg at their cottage in Riscombe, Mary agreed to look after Megan and Mattie while Reg and Jan went over to the next village for a drink at the White Horse.

On the way to the pub, Reg told Jan of his worries concerning Mary.

'The old girl's not so good,' he said. Jan was immediately concerned as she knew it was his policy to understate any medical problem. 'She's not just arthritic, her kidney's playing up too. I took her to the doctor and he wants her to go in for tests at Cheltenham General, but she won't do it – she says she'd sooner not know if something's wrong.'

'She seemed fine today,' Jan said, not expecting to talk Reg out of his pessimism. 'She's pleased as punch how well her geese are coming on and how many orders she's got for them for Christmas.'

'Hmm,' Reg grunted. 'She is now, but when the time comes she'll get upset. Allus when she kills the first few they dies pretty easy, but the others they're much harder, and even when I do it, it takes a bit of strength.'

Jan took her eyes off the road for a moment and glanced at him. He was a wise old bird, she thought, and he was right – her mother had always found it hard to deal with the paradox of loving the birds while she reared them and then having to kill them. It was easier with stock that was sent away to the abattoir.

'I'll come over and help,' Jan volunteered. A rush of affection overwhelmed her for her quiet, stoical parents, who would rather not bother other people with their troubles.

'She would like that,' Reg agreed. 'If you have the time.'

'I'll make time,' Jan said sincerely.

The pub was heaving when they arrived. But Jan and Reg were still greeted warmly, and she didn't mind admitting that she felt more comfortable here than she had in the rarefied surroundings of the Manoir du Chèvre d'Or.

Like the regulars in the Fox at Stanfield, most of the locals in the White Horse had been following Jan's fortunes closely since she'd come back home and set up her yard in Gloucestershire. Many of them had also known Billy Hanks since he was born and were as incensed as she was by the double-dealing he had done with the Sharps. So their good wishes were as much to do with Billy's three-year jail sentence as Gylippus's magnificent run at Chepstow.

Bernie Sutcliffe had suddenly turned up out of the blue. He had driven down when they told him back at the yard he would probably find her in the White Horse. He was full of goodwill after Dingle Bay's brave run. His horse had been well written up on one of the racing pages that morning, and for the first time he had been mentioned as the owner.

He had managed to get Jan to himself for a few minutes and was talking about future plans for his horses. They were standing a little apart from the main bar in a quiet corner when Bernie suddenly stiffened and Jan saw a look of burning hatred in his eyes.

'Don't look now,' he said through clenched teeth, 'but that *bas*tard McNeill's just come in.'

Jan resisted the urge to turn, though she desperately wanted to, as she immediately thought of Roz Stoddard, who was sitting at the far end of the bar.

'My God!' Bernie went on, in a guttural undertone, 'he looks bloody pissed – he must be completely mad.'

Jan had to see. She swung round and watched the vet shove his way through the customers towards the bar. Others were watching his progress in astonishment; his drinking bouts and the dreadful behaviour they seemed to evoke were few and far between, and he was generally held in some esteem, if not warmth, by his clients.

The level of conversation dropped several decibels as he reached the bar and the landlord's voice could be clearly heard across the room.

'I'm sorry, Mr McNeill, if I was to serve you now, I'd probably lose my licence.'

'Who the hell . . .' McNeill started to protest, when he was interrupted.

With grim fascination, Jan watched as Roz approached and tapped the vet on the shoulder.

'Hey, you!' she said, her voice husky with anger, 'I've got something for you.'

The vet turned to confront her. Across the bar, Jan could almost feel the heat of his rage. His face was glowing a purplish red and his eyes were bloodshot and blazing as he opened his mouth, but before he could say a single word the contents of a pint glass full of the best local bitter had drenched the whole of his head and run down the front of his shirt and jacket.

Jan stared, mesmerized and surprised by just how much liquid there was in a pint when it was spread about.

For a fraction of a second McNeill looked dumbfounded, as if he couldn't work out what had happened or why beer was dribbling off his nose. Stunned silence in the pub awaited his reaction – all of a sudden the vet did exactly the opposite to what Jan had been expecting. He blinked, put a hand to his face and rubbed some of the liquid from his cheek. He put a finger in his mouth to taste it while he glared at Roz, then, without a word, he pushed her to one side and walked slowly towards the door and let himself out.

The heavy ledge-and-brace door clunked shut behind him. A few seconds later everyone burst out laughing at the bizarre and unexpected exhibition, but Jan noticed Roz staring after the vet, until she suddenly rushed out after him.

'Bloody 'ell!' Bernie laughed. 'I did enjoy that!'

Jan thought of the abuse she herself had suffered from McNeill, and looked at Bernie with a smile. 'Not as much as I did.'

During the week following James McNeill's soaking Jan began to feel a growing optimism about her prospects. Although she was a long way down the trainers' table, with only eight winners to her name that season, her strike rate was high and so far she'd only sent out a few of the good horses in her yard. The four horses she'd bought for Gary West all looked fairly impressive, with Gylippus only the second of them to run so far.

A.D. O'Hagan's, though, had yet to win a race between them. Along with the youngster Jan had bought at Fairyhouse, four of her former charges had arrived back from Aigmout at the end of August, which was several weeks later than she had asked. So it was inevitable they were less fit than the others, which had done nothing to heal the minor rift in her relationship with their owner. Nevertheless, A.D. had been careful not to criticize her; he had owned horses long enough to know that patience was an important attribute in an owner. And she had recently been able to tell him that one of his better horses, Tom's Touch, had been quicker to come to hand than the rest and would be entered for several races in the not too distant future.

The feeling in the yard, and particularly on the gallops, was that all the horses were working exceptionally well. When Finbar managed to get away from Virginia's clutches, he was really keen to school and ride fast work for Jan; and the champion jockey, Murty McGrath, had also found time to come down twice when Jan had asked him. On both occasions he had gone away impressed with what he'd seen.

With a lot of support from Annabel, Fran her nanny and the rest of the team in the yard, Jan had been able to accept that Eddie Sullivan, with whom until a few months ago she'd imagined spending the rest of her life, was now considered officially an 'also ran' as far as any long-term relationship was concerned. Since then Tony Robertson had got into the habit of dropping in for supper with her and whoever else was around, and he had taken her out on several occasions since the river trip. He was considerate and unobtrusive, fitting into her life easily and without awkwardness, and she had begun to look forward to his visits for the reassurance and stability they gave her.

The only dark cloud on the immediate horizon was her relationship with Gary West and his obnoxious sidekick. Two weeks into October, and she still hadn't been paid for August, let alone September. She had received a brief fax from Gary, thanking her for the win on Gylippus, but it made no reference to the money he owed.

She could scarcely believe he didn't know what immense pressure this put her under – or perhaps, having been born with a silver spoon in his mouth before he'd turned it into a platinum ladle, he had never known what it was like to be on a financial knife edge. When Cellarman, another West horse, won comfortably first time out on a wet Friday at Huntingdon, Tanner hadn't been to watch, so Jan rang him on the way home.

The receptionist at his London office said he was engaged.

'I'll hang on,' Jan said.

After a few minutes of expensive mobile call time, Tanner's voice fuzzed over the phone.

'Well done, Jan; nice win.'

'Never mind well done,' Jan snapped. 'What about my money?'

'What? Haven't you had it yet? I'm sorry, Gary told me he'd put it through. Don't worry about it, Jan. It'll happen soon.'

Jan tried to identify how sincere he was from the tone of his voice. He hadn't used this apologetic manner before and she found it impossible to judge whether she should believe him or not.

'All right, I'll give it a few more days, but then I'm going to have to do something more positive.'

'I've just told you, Jan; it's being paid, if you haven't had it already, which I find hard to believe.'

'If I'd had it, I wouldn't be telling you I hadn't, would I? Anyway, like I say, I'll give it a couple of days—'

'You do that,' Tanner said.

'By the way, can you tell me why I can never get hold of Mr West?'

'He's a very busy man, Jan, you know that – he runs a massive operation, and – not trying to put you down or anything – he's got much bigger things on his mind at the moment than a few spaggy horses.'

🐎

Jan arrived back at Edge during evening stables. Several of the staff came up to the house afterwards for a cup of tea, as they often did if they weren't going straight to the pub.

The two Irish lads appeared with Roz. Dec plonked himself down at the kitchen table and put a copy of the local paper in front of Jan.

'Did you see what happened to Roz's friend?' he asked with a grin.

Jan glanced down at the headline.

LOCAL VET ARRESTED THREE TIMES OVER LIMIT

She picked up the paper and read aloud the report of James McNeill's arrest for drink-driving, not far from his home near Broadway.

'That was the evening we saw him in the pub, wasn't it?' she asked Roz. 'I'm amazed he got that far. Oh look!' she went on. 'It quotes the landlord at the White Horse saying he had refused to serve him and that was followed by an "incident".' Jan laughed and looked at Roz, who turned away, her face crimson.

'My God! You shopped him, Roz, didn't you? *You* must have phoned the police – I saw you going out after him.'

'Well – after what he'd done to me *and* you – I thought . . . you know.'

'Don't apologize. It serves the pig right,' Jan said. 'Well done, you; he'll probably be banned for at least two years. That'll cost him a bloody fortune in drivers!'

'If anyone's stupid enough to allow him to look at their animals after this,' Roz added. 'If you've got an expensive racehorse with problems, the last thing you want is some drunken skunk messing about with it.'

Jan smiled to herself at the justice and comeuppance that McNeill had received. Later, when Roz and the staff had gone home and she was on her own with the children, she left them upstairs while she made some telephone calls.

First she tried Toby Waller.

'Hi, Jan,' he answered, as exuberant as always. 'What are our chances with Gale Bird at Bangor tomorrow?'

'That depends on the going, though if it rains any more tonight, I won't be so hopeful.'

'That's a shame. I'll give you a ring in the morning to find out what you think. Now, what about a horse for my syndicate friends? I saw Bobby Ng today and he says they haven't heard anything from you yet.'

'No, I know they haven't. Because the kind of horse they want isn't easy to find, it doesn't just walk into the yard. But I've got my ear to the ground and there are a few sales coming up. I'm just going to ring my man in Ireland and see if he's got anything suitable.'

Sean McDonagh sounded pleased to hear from Jan when she called him later.

'I meant to ring to say well done with Cellarman. I knew you'd have him winning soon and – did I tell you? – they're hopping mad down at the stud for letting Gylippus go. Accusations flying around all over the place.'

Jan smiled. 'I'm not surprised. I know I was taking a bit of a punt when I bought him, but I really do think he's the best hurdler I've ever had. Pity about the owners though.'

'Problems?'

'You could say,' Jan answered, not offering any more details. 'I used something similar for a syndicate that's come to me. I think they could be a good crowd to work with – they were introduced by Toby Waller, an old owner of mine.'

'How much will they spend?'

'Up to a hundred, I would think. There are five of them and they'll put in around twenty thousand each.'

'Wouldn't they rather spread their risk and have two or three cheaper ones?'

'No, not this lot. They're punters.'

'I'll see what I can do.'

On a blustery Wednesday in the middle of October, and for the first time that season, Jan was running one of A.D.'s horses. His secretary rang at eight while she was cooking breakfast for her staff.

Jan assumed Miss Bennett had another name, but she'd never heard it used. She had never seen the woman smile either, or heard her laugh, during the brief conversations they'd had. This call was no exception.

'Mr O'Hagan has asked me to ring and confirm that Tom's Touch is still running at Wetherby today.'

'He's already left.'

'He hopes there won't be any problems, and would like to know how you assess the horse's chances.'

This was A.D.'s indirect way of asking if she thought he should back it.

'Tell him I wouldn't have sent the horse all the way to Yorkshire if I didn't think he had a strong chance. As far as I can see, he's only got one horse to beat.'

'Thank you, Mrs Hardy.'

When Miss Bennett had rung off, Jan replaced the handset thoughtfully. It was unlike A.D. not to make that sort of call himself, but she guessed he was too busy and hoped that his secretary's icy manner didn't reflect her boss's frame of mind.

Nevertheless, it was an enormous relief to her five hours later when the horse fought his way to the winning post and reached it a head in front of his nearest rival.

When a huge bunch of extravagant flowers arrived the next morning from a florist's in Broadway, Jan knew her relationship with A.D., after months of tension, was at last almost back to where it had been the day Russian Eagle had won the Irish National.

🐎

A month before, Colonel Gilbert had asked Jan if she and Megan would like to be his guests one Saturday evening at the Horse of the Year Show, which was being held in London at the Wembley Arena. He said he thought it would encourage Megan in her show-jumping if she saw what there was to aim for.

Megan had been looking forward to it wildly, but the whole event only became real for her when the colonel's silver Daimler glided up the hill and stopped outside Edge Farm to collect them and take them up to London.

Beneath the high, vaulting roof of the arena, they had a wonderful view from the seats Colonel Gilbert had earlier arranged for them. Jan was fully prepared to sit back and enjoy herself, and her pleasure was enhanced by Megan's rapt expression throughout the event. Afterwards the colonel took them to the restaurant for dinner and pointed out anyone of interest in the equestrian world who was there. He introduced Jan to several riders who were top names in their field, and she found that a surprising number of people in this other branch of equestrian sport seemed to know who she was. Colonel Gilbert introduced Megan as a future show-jumper with a confidence Jan hoped wouldn't go to her daughter's head.

'One of these days, Megan,' he said as the little girl concentrated on munching her way through a large, succulent hamburger, 'you'll be riding here – maybe on Monarch. Do you know, there was a time when Britain reigned supreme in show-jumping, sadly when I was a much younger man. It was before your time, of course, Jan, but I'm sure you've heard of the great British team at the 1952 Olympics – the same year poor old Chris Chataway fell in the five thousand metres, but that's by the by. Colonel Harry Llewellyn, on a great horse named Foxhunter, beat Chile and the USA to win gold with the rest of the team. What a day that was!' Colonel Gilbert leaned back in his chair, savouring a moment of nostalgic glory, until he leaned forward and looked at Megan with bright sparkling eyes. 'What do you think? Could you tackle those fences the other youngsters were jumping?'

'Oh yes! I'd love to do it, but I wouldn't have gone the way they all went – I would have cut across and saved a lot of time.'

Jan and the colonel laughed at the small girl's avid competitiveness.'The only trouble is,' Megan went on, 'I don't like jumping indoors. But I really enjoyed that hunter trial Monarch and I did.'

The colonel nodded. 'That can be fun, too. And if you think you can get to grips with the dressage, I've no objection to steering you towards eventing, where you do cross-country, dressage *and* show-jumping. The problem there is that you need a real all-rounder for that.'

'Monarch can do dressage,' Megan protested. 'I've tried. I can get him to cross his legs and everything.'

Colonel Gilbert laughed. 'I don't think you'll be needing to do half-passes at this stage, but maybe I should arrange a few lessons for you if your mother doesn't mind.' He looked at Jan.

She shook her head. 'Of course I wouldn't. That would be really kind of you. I'll just have to accept that I won't have my daughter race-riding for me for some time.'

'Oh, Mum.' Megan stared at her wide-eyed. 'I do want to be a jockey too, you know.'

'OK, OK,' Jan said with a gentle smile. 'It'll all come to you if you're patient, which you're not always, are you? That's why I'm wondering if you'll manage the dressage. It's about teaching a horse obedience, and showing how supple and fit he is, but it takes an awful lot of time and practice.'

'Mummy, I can do it; I know I can with Monarch.'

Colonel Gilbert nodded. 'There's no reason why not, but let's see how we get on with the rest of the winter show-jumping first, Meg. Then we'll decide what to do next year. Is that OK?'

Megan looked at him with her big blue eyes, which she was already learning to use. 'Can I really still ride Monarch?'

'Yes, of course. That's the whole idea. And I'm very pleased with what you've done with him so far – very pleased indeed.'

🐎

The visit to the Horse of the Year Show and the chance to think about Megan's future had been a welcome interlude in what seemed like endless hassles in Jan's roller-coaster career, but she was quickly brought down to earth first thing Sunday morning when her mother-in-law rang.

Olwen Hardy didn't phone her very often and when she did it wasn't to pass the time of day.

'What is it?' Jan asked, trying not to sound too impatient.

'That Harold Powell's still got builders up at the house.'

'But, Olwen, we arranged to block off the entrance by your bungalow. Has that been done?'

'Oh yes, I made sure of that. He must be bringing men in across the hill.'

'What? But that's miles round!' Jan exclaimed as she tried to picture how on earth builders would get their trucks to Stonewall Farm without going up the old drive.

'Whether 'tis or not, they're coming.'

'What sort of work are they doing?'

'Just cleaning up like; they've took down the old iron Dutch barn and scraped up all the cobbles off the yard.'

'So they're not doing any actual building?'

'Not yet they're not.'

'Harold must have got some cowboys in to do a bit of the preparation. I bet he won't get any proper builders there. I shouldn't worry about it too much.'

'But I don't like it, Jan. I don't like it at all.'

Jan sighed. 'Olwen, it doesn't really matter. He'll still never be able to sell the place without a proper road.'

'Well, you'll just have to do something about it, Jan. You sold the farm, and I said then you should never have done it.'

Jan put the phone down, thinking uncharitable thoughts about her mother-in-law. She didn't need the extra aggravation of dealing with Harold Powell right now. She had more than enough on her plate trying to run a busy yard, and deal with the problems of her biggest owner.

21

Finbar Howlett, always self-effacing and mild-mannered on the ground, wore a thunderous face as he drove his horse over the last fence at Ludlow.

His mount was twenty-five lengths short of the leader, with the gap likely to widen on the run-in. Blue Boar, the horse leading the field, was trained by Jan for a restaurateur in Bath. Finbar had ridden work on Blue several times and had been looking forward to riding him in his first race of the season. But he had been claimed by Virginia to flog round on an old animal who had lost whatever interest it once had in racing a long time ago.

Finbar's scowl was offset by the jubilation on the faces of Ray Bellamy, who owned the Blue Boar, and Jan, who had been looking forward to seeing the burly horse perform as she knew one day it would. Ray had been patient and had never expected miracles from a horse which Jan had bought on his behalf for just seven thousand pounds the year before. He'd believed her when she'd said it would be difficult to find a race with suitable conditions, but in the end she had and his trust in her had been vindicated.

In the unsaddling enclosure, Ray Bellamy, who was a large man, turned to Jan with a hint of a tear in his eye. 'D'you know, Jan, I've been wanting to see that happen with a horse of my own ever since I was a lad. I can't tell you how good it feels.'

Jan smiled as she looked at his big Roman nose and wondered how many other owners looked so like their horses. 'I know. I remember training my first winner under rules, a hunter chase on this very course three years ago and it still feels like yesterday. But I can tell you what the icing on the cake is for me – beating the ghastly Virginia Gilbert – she knew bloody well I wanted Finbar to ride your horse. Still, Luke Lacy handled him well enough, and he didn't even need the allowance he was receiving.'

'I see you've got one of A.D. O'Hagan's in the last. What are your chances with him?'

Jan shrugged. 'Hard to say. As it's his first time out, I think he'll need a bit of waking up, but he might be OK – we'll have to see. Now we'd better look after this chap and get him washed off.'

Jan finished helping Emma hose down the Blue Boar's hefty legs, and made sure he was comfortably bandaged before he was put back in a stable. As she was leaving the security block, she heard a familiar but unexpected voice behind her.

'Well done, Jan! I never thought we'd get beaten by that huge great thing of yours. He looks more like a carthorse than a racer.'

Jan didn't answer immediately, but turned slightly to face Virginia's long, arrogant features. 'Thanks, *and* you had the better jockey too.'

'I wish you'd leave Finbar alone. You know he's got to stay with me for the rest of the season,' her rival hissed.

'Virginia, you don't own every minute of his day, and if he was getting enough good rides at your place, I don't suppose he'd be round at my place so much.'

Jan felt she had said enough for now. She had no intention of getting into a slanging match, especially not here in public and on a racecourse; she focused her eyes on a point some way over Virginia's left shoulder and started to walk on.

'By the way,' Virginia said as she passed her, 'I don't know if you're interested, but I've heard that your dashing boyfriend Eddie Sullivan is living with a pregnant girl in Sydney, in a massive house overlooking the harbour in Vaucluse. Apparently, he's very busy out there and it's unlikely he'll ever come back.'

Jan's step faltered; she closed her eyes and swore inwardly at her rival for finding her rawest nerve so easily.

'Thank you for the information, but I did know,' she said quickly.

'He rang to tell me.' She walked on before Virginia could see the tears filling the corners of her eyes.

🐎

Spurred on by Virginia's bitchiness, Jan was even more determined to book Finbar Howlett as often as possible. At the next Cheltenham meeting she asked him to ride two horses – Gary West's Magic Maestro and her own King's Archer, which she judged were both a hundred per cent fit, despite the fact that they were running for the first time in six months.

Finbar had called round to Edge Farm two nights before the race and had stayed for supper with Annabel and Jan.

'D'you know something?' he said, taking a gulp of fizzy water. 'I was brought up never to tell a lie, and that sort of included what you might call lies of omission, like not telling someone something you know they'd want to know. But there it is, I've not said a word to Virginia about my rides for you at Cheltenham and I don't feel at all guilty about it.'

'Just as well,' Jan remarked dryly, 'because she'd do anything she could to mess me about, even run a couple of no-hopers just to claim you. We'll have to keep our fingers crossed she doesn't try to pull a fast one when the final declarations are made tomorrow morning. She'll never forgive me for getting Miller's Lodge, will she?'

'And thank God you didn't get bogged down in a quagmire of Catholic guilt, Finnie,' Annabel chuckled. 'Anyway, you've been in this business long enough to know that an awful lot of it exists purely on bullshit, surely.'

'I don't think you're right, actually. Why should it?' Finbar asked.

'It's OK for you,' Jan chipped in. 'You've got bags of talent, people can sense you wouldn't dream of stopping a horse to order, but you've got to realize there's quite a few not-so-honest people out there, also trainers who string their owners along with all sorts of excuses and promises – "He'll need a few runs before we know where to place him. He's gone off the boil. He'll need a little time to grow into himself" – I admit a lot of that may be true, but some people will say just about anything to make sure the punters leave the horse where it is so they can collect the fees.' Jan leaned back in her chair. 'Declan told me about one trainer he knew, who had a horse that died. The owner hardly ever came to the yard, so the trainer thought he'd just carry on drawing the fees. Apparently he did it for six months without registering the animal's death at Weatherbys, which he's supposed to do; he probably got a few quid from the knacker for the carcass as well. Anyway, the owner phoned up out of the blue and said he was in the area, so he was coming to see his horse.' Jan paused for dramatic effect.

'The trainer didn't think the owner would recognize his horse, but didn't want to take the chance. He thought he couldn't simply say it had died that morning, so he looked up the dead animal's passport to check its markings and found it had a long, thin white blaze the whole way down its face. There wasn't another horse in the yard with markings anything like that, so he found one that came closest in size and colour, and had one of the lads paint it with white emulsion.

'Well, the owner came and the trainer took him into the horse's stable without turning the light on to show him the horse, which was well rugged up. He told him his horse had a touch of flu, but they hoped he'd be better soon and would be able to run in a couple of weeks when he was fit again.

'Well, apparently the owner bought all this bullshit and went away satisfied. Then the trainer rang him a couple of days later to say that, unfortunately, the horse had got worse and died. A forged vet's certificate was produced. And that was that,' Jan concluded with a cynical laugh.

Finbar was shaking his head. 'How come I've never met any of these people then?'

'Like Jan said, Finnie.' Annabel smiled. 'Everyone knows it would be a waste of time trying to involve you in any scams – and that's why we like using you, isn't it, Jan? We're feeling a bit vulnerable after what happened with our last jockey.'

'What Billy Hanks did, you mean?'

Jan nodded. 'And I'd known the little squirt all his life.'

The Magic Maestro was well fancied against tough opposition to win his chase at Cheltenham – a useful indicator to his chances in the following spring's Cathcart – and Finbar proved the pundits right when he drove his horse up the hill with his characteristic determination to a narrow victory. On her way down to the winner's slot, Jan was showered with congratulations from her peers and her growing band of fans.

Half an hour later, King's Archer almost followed suit, beaten only by a short head.

There had been no sign, however, of the Magic Maestro's owner, or of John Tanner. Jan tried not to let the worry spoil her day though, and was delighted that Johnny Carlton-Brown had taken a box especially to watch King's Archer and agreed to buy him at Jan's asking price as soon as the horse crossed the line.

Patrick Lamberhurst, with one arm around Annabel's waist, looked on with approval. 'So, Johnny, you must be one of Jan's biggest owners now.' He turned to Jan. 'Just remind me – what horses has he got with you?' he asked.

Jan really wanted to like Patrick as he was her best friend's lover, but she just wished he wasn't so damned snotty and aloof when he was talking to her. She couldn't show her disapproval but, not for the first time, she asked herself why Annabel put up with his nonsense. In the meantime, to show willing, she reeled off the names of JCB's horses. 'He's got Supercall, Miller's Lodge and August Moon. Then there's the gelding we bought after Fairyhouse – what have you called it, Johnny? – Rohan Raider – and now King's Archer. Five in all. If you get one more, you'll outvote A.D.'

Carlton-Brown smiled. 'I'll think about it. Have you,' he went on tentatively, 'heard anything from Gary West recently?'

Jan shook her head sharply. She wouldn't have minded talking to JCB about the problems she was having with this particular owner and the state of uncertainty it had left her in, but she couldn't possibly with the large crowd that had gathered in his box. 'I'm sorry,' she said, 'I've got to get off and deal with my horse. Do you want to come along now he's almost yours?'

JCB nodded happily before they rushed down the stairs and out to the walkway from the course, where Declan was leading King's Archer in.

🐎

Jan woke from a short night of troubled sleep. She should have been brimming with pride and optimism after the way her horses had run the day before, but she was desperately worried that the situation with Gary West was getting more out of control.

Getting out of bed and walking to the window, she drew back the curtains on the pre-dawn darkness and looked across at the dark outline of the hills to the west. When she saw a pair of headlights turn in at the bottom of the track, she prayed it was Annabel, arriving as she sometimes did.

She watched as the vehicle crept up to the parking area, then carried on up to the house. She hurried downstairs to turn on the outside light and open the back door just as Annabel reached it.

'Hi, Jan! I'm glad you're up. I was worried about you when I left last night. I'm sorry, I would have stayed, but Patrick wanted to get back.'

'I'm sure he did,' Jan said, more sourly than she'd meant to. 'But I'm so glad you're here, I've had an awful night. I've been awake for most of it, worrying about what I'm going to do about Gary bloody West.'

'Tanner hasn't rung then – even after the Magic Maestro's performance yesterday?'

'No! I'm afraid not. I've not heard a single word for nearly three weeks now! It's getting ridiculous. Last time I told him I was going to take things further if no money turned up and he told me categorically it was on its way.'

'What happens when you phone him to say the horses are running?'

'I don't know why I bother,' Jan said. 'I'm never put through to him directly, I just leave a message with someone in his office. I'm sure he's told them not to put me onto him under any circumstances. I've left loads of messages about the money too.'

'What sort of messages?'

'Pretty angry ones, I can tell you.' Jan grinned for a moment. 'And last night at about one in the morning, I was feeling so desperate I tried a number I'd been given for Gary West – a mobile, I think. Of course, I only got an answering service, but I let him know it was vital I talk to him.'

'Poor Jan, I don't blame you.'

'Actually I have done it before,' Jan admitted, 'though so far I've never heard back.' She shrugged hopelessly. 'I really am at the end of my tether, Bel. It's spoiling any success we have and it's making my finances so damned tight all the time.'

'At least you're getting the money for King's Archer and you know there are several other owners who'd help you out.'

'Maybe there are, but there's no way I'm going cap in hand to Toby or JCB, and certainly not A.D., just because I made a serious error of judgement.'

'But didn't Toby reassure you when we first met Gary that he was sound and likely to be good for the money?'

'Well, yes, he did, and so did A.D. But that's not the point.'

'No,' Annabel agreed. 'You'd rather die than admit you'd over-faced yourself, wouldn't you?'

Jan bit her lip and nodded.

'What about asking your solicitor?'

'No way,' Jan said. 'There's no point going after some tinpot company like Harlequin Holdings – and unfortunately they're the legal owners of the horses. As far as I can see, the only thing I can do is call on Gary's personal guarantee, or use the clause in our training agreement that would allow me to sell one of his horses to recover the debt.'

'But you'd still be left with the others, which have to be fed. They are meant to be producing income!'

'Thank God I'm only owed for training four, and not the six he was originally planning on.'

'Yes, that's rather ironic, but I suppose you really needed all six to help pay for all the work you've had done.'

'It's a complete bloody nightmare, Bel.'

'Look, Jan, the others'll be here soon. Let's ride out and when we've done second lot we'll have to talk to Toby or someone.'

300

Jan sighed. 'I suppose you're right. I just wish Eddie were here, though.'

'Jan, now you're just feeling sorry for yourself! What on earth could Eddie have done?'

🐎

Jan came back into the house just after eight, having ridden out with first lot. The children were having breakfast with Fran when the telephone started to ring. She sighed before answering it.

'Jan? Gary West.'

Relief flooded through her; there was a strength in his voice that was instantly reassuring, as if, now he was back in circulation, everything was going to be all right.

And yet, Jan quickly reminded herself, she had been trying to contact this man for several weeks and had drawn a blank. She'd left innumerable messages either hinting at or, more recently, spelling out the dire position he'd put her in.

'Hello, Gary,' she answered guardedly. 'You got my messages, then?'

'Yes, I did – several, and I'm very concerned. I can't talk for long; there's a lot going on here, but I authorized a payment to you last month. I don't know why you didn't get it: I'm looking into that myself, but I wanted you to know the money will be with you today. Just sign for it and we'll sort out the rest later.'

'Sign for it?' Jan queried.

'Yes, that's right,' Gary said with a hint of impatience. 'And we'll talk again soon. I may be in the UK after Christmas, but keep up the good work and, by the way, that was a brilliant result yesterday. Thank you.'

'Thanks . . .' Jan started to say.

'I'm sorry, Jan, I've got to go.'

The line from Australia, or wherever Gary West was, went dead, and Jan was left feeling bemused and bulldozed by the force of his personality, even over a long-distance phone line.

The others were starting to come in, expecting their daily fry-up. Jan carried on cooking, but all the time Gary's few words were reverberating in her head as she tried hard to stop herself from getting too excited.

❧

Halfway through the morning, Jan was working at her desk with her diary and the racing calendar, absorbed in the arduous task of deciding which horses to run where over the coming weeks. Without allowing herself to be distracted, she was aware there was the roar of a motorcycle coming up the drive. She wondered vaguely who it could be. Not a lad or an owner, as far as she knew.

She carried on working until she heard the hard footsteps echo under the arch and across the yard, followed by a brief conversation as Roz directed the caller to Jan's office. A few moments later a tall, slim figure, clad entirely in black leather and a large black helmet stood in the doorway, blocking out the daylight.

'Mrs Jan Hardy?' The muffled voice behind the darkened visor gave the words a sinister edge.

Suddenly Jan felt alarmed and started to wonder who else was outside in the yard. 'Yes, that's me,' she answered croakily.

The man stepped into the room and Jan saw he was carrying a small rigid briefcase. 'Do you have any identification?' he asked.

'Why? What do you mean?'

'I mean a driving licence or a credit card. I've got an important package here for you.' The shiny black helmet inclined towards the case he was carrying. 'And I've instructions to give it to Mrs Jan Hardy only.'

'Who's it from?'

'I don't know. The receipt you have to sign may say; it's in an envelope in the case.'

Jan briefly considered her options, then reached down for her handbag, which was beside the desk; taking out her driving licence, she handed it over to the messenger.

He lifted his visor, to reveal a small boyish mouth and emerald green eyes, which seemed incongruous under the black paraphernalia. 'OK,' he nodded, and his unmuffled voice sounded almost adolescent. 'Shall I put it here?' he pointed at the desk.

'Sure.'

He put the case down, unlocked it with a key from one of his zippered pockets and clicked open both the catches. He lifted the lid and revealed eight neat bundles of fifty-pound notes. 'That should be eight thousand pounds. Please check it and sign the receipt in the envelope.'

Jan picked up the envelope with her name on it. She opened it and pulled out a single sheet of paper, on which were typed the words: *Received from Harlequin Holdings Ltd, in respect of fees for horses in training at Edge Farm Stables, £8,000 on account of invoices rendered to date.* Her name was typed below.

Jan looked at it and sighed. By the end of the month, in two days' time, Gary West would owe her a little under £12,000 for his four horses' fees over three months.

She glanced up at the skinny biker. 'That's it, is it?'

'That's all I've got for you,' he answered, uninterested.

'Fine. I'll check it then.'

Cautiously she lifted out and quickly counted the eight bundles with twenty notes in each, carefully placing them back where they'd been. 'Is the case mine?' she asked.

'Oh, yes. We always leave the case.'

'Right.' She picked up a biro from her desk and read the brief receipt once more. 'Is there a copy of this?'

'Not that I was given.'

'Hmm,' Jan grunted. 'I don't suppose it makes any difference to me, as long as I've got the money.' She put her signature at the bottom of the piece of paper and handed it back to the courier.

'Thanks, Mrs Hardy. Er, can you tell me the best way to get to Cheltenham from here?'

Amused, Jan told him, and watched him stride from her office. When he'd gone, she took one more look at the £8,000, then closed the lid and locked the case before putting it into the bottom drawer of her filing cabinet. She didn't have a safe in the yard or the house; she had no reason to, not many of her clients paid in cash. She wouldn't have it for long, anyway, she thought; the money would have to go straight into her bank account.

And then she could start worrying about when she was going to get the next £4,000 Gary West owed her.

Jan told no one about the money, except Annabel, when the rest of her staff were having their lunch down at the pub.

'Frankly,' she said, while they drank coffee in the office, 'I'm even more certain I'm going to get tucked up than I was before. You'd have thought that when he eventually made up his mind to pay me, he'd have paid up to date, unless he's under extreme pressure. All along everyone's told us that a few thousand, even a million, would be small beer to him.'

'I can't really see what's going on,' Annabel mused. 'But I suppose paying you a bit is what people do when they're trying to keep everyone off their back: they don't want anyone rocking the boat.'

'Whatever, we'll just have to brace ourselves for more trouble. But at least I know where I am now,' Jan added.

'And at least you've got eight thousand quid, which is better than nothing. And you get your share of any prize money. So you'd better keep those nags winning.'

Jan was being honest when she told Annabel she was relieved to know what she was dealing with, instead of hanging on to the improbable hope that Gary West and John Tanner were genuine. She felt more resolute than she had for months when she woke next morning with three horses to take to the races. The only new event to blight her day was an early phone call from her mother-in-law.

When Jan heard it was Olwen, she prepared herself for the usual litany of complaints about Harold.

'Jan? Is that you?' The old woman's voice sounded faint and crackly.

'Yes, Olwen. Are you all right?'

'No. I'm not. I don't know what the trouble is, but I've been sick, vomiting like – and the other end.'

'Poor you – it must be something you ate,' Jan said practically, but rather unsympathetically, though it was the first time her mother-in-law had ever phoned to complain about her own health.

'I've ate nothing unusual.'

'But you can't tell these days, can you, with food coming in from all round the world while our farmers are struggling to make a living?'

'I know it weren't anything like that,' Olwen insisted.

'Have you phoned the doctor?'

'I rang the surgery in Hay; they wants me to go in.'

'Then you must tell them you can't. You're not well enough.'

'I could get a taxi, I suppose.'

'Well, it's up to you, but it's not as if you've taken up a lot of their time over the years. I'm sure they won't mind a home visit, especially at your age.'

'All right.' The old woman sounded doubtful and uncertain of herself for once. 'Jan, can you come over?' she asked quietly.

'You mean with the children?'

'Bring them if you want, you'll have to be careful, though, they may catch something. But I really wanted you to come over soon. There's no one else in the family now.'

Jan was astonished and unexpectedly moved by Olwen's admission at last that she was actually a member of the family. 'Of course I'll come, but I'm afraid I just can't do it before Sunday. I've got runners today and tomorrow. Will you be all right until then?'

There was a moment's silence before the old woman spoke. 'I suppose I'll have to be, won't I,' she croaked, with a hint of her old fractiousness.

Over the next two days Jan sent out five runners without a result. There were no disasters, no fallers and none of them disgraced themselves, but the failure affected Jan more keenly after the recent successes she'd been having. And now she had the long-drawn-out struggle with Gary West on her hands, she was relying on success in the field to sustain her operation until it was finally sorted out.

Realistically, Jan didn't think she would go bust, but even the possibility, when she had her young, vulnerable children to keep, was terrifying. So it was in a sober, rather pessimistic mood that she set out to drive back to Wales with the children. With Patrick away and no other invitation in the offing, Annabel had suggested she should accompany them.

Jan put her off. 'The mood I'm in, you wouldn't enjoy it and, anyway, Olwen's got a bug of some sort and I don't think she'd want anyone else there.'

The dreary weather in the Welsh hills didn't do anything to cheer Jan. The clouds seemed to crouch a few feet above the hills and were already shrouding the tops of the Black Mountains. From this endless grey expanse, a fine drizzle fell and turned the view into a blur.

Jan was reminded of the eight winters she'd spent there, the long dark nights and short damp days in the valleys. Now she felt none of the nostalgia for her former life with John that had sometimes afflicted her when she returned. Jan wished she could turn round and didn't have to carry on to Olwen's. She had already decided to keep the visit as brief as she possibly could without upsetting her mother-in-law.

The Shogun dropped gently down the switchback road on the empty hillside towards Olwen's bungalow. Jan could see evidence of the work Harold Powell's men had been doing in the old farmyard and the heavy fence that had been erected across the bottom of the drive beside Olwen's garden.

Jan drew up outside and turned to the children, who were strapped in their seats in the back.

'Granny's not feeling too well, so don't go asking her for things or be disappointed if she hasn't got presents for you. All right?'

Megan and Matthew both nodded gloomily as Jan got out of the car.

'I'll just make sure she's up first. You two stay here and don't scrap.'

They shook their heads solemnly.

Jan walked up the short path to the front door and rapped gently on it with her gloved knuckles.

When there was no reply, she knocked again a little louder, and stood shifting from one cold foot to another beneath the small porch, now clad in a tangle of naked brown rose briars, like a crown of thorns.

After a while, with no hint of movement inside, she hammered on the door. 'Olwen! Hello! Are you all right? It's Jan!'

There was still no response. Jan wondered if the old woman was bed-bound and simply couldn't get up. She tried the handle of the door; it was locked. Olwen might have gone out, she thought, or perhaps she'd been taken to church by a neighbour, but it was unlikely, and there would have been a note on the door to say so.

The windows on the front of the bungalow belonged to Olwen's bedroom and small sitting room. In both, the heavily lined chintz curtains were drawn together. Jan turned and saw the children staring at her from the back of the Shogun. 'Granny can't hear,' she called. 'I'll just go and see if I can get in at the back.'

Jan walked round the side, through the neat little garden where Olwen grew flowers in the summer. Behind the back door a couple of tea towels flapped on a washing line, probably getting damper by the minute, Jan thought.

She tried to open the door. It was locked also; she shaded her eyes to look in through the window to a small kitchen.

There was no light on, but everything looked neat and normal.

'Olwen,' Jan called again as she rapped on one of the panels of reeded glass set in the flimsy door.

When it was obvious that she wasn't going to get a response, Jan looked around for the least disruptive way to break in.

Using a stone from a small rockery which John had made for his mother ten years before, she broke one of the glass panels in the door, knocked out the protruding shards and reached through to release the catch.

She walked in, carefully stepping over the glass splinters, and stood for a moment to listen for any reaction.

The only sounds she heard were the harsh calls from a colony of rooks in a tall ash tree beside the farmyard.

'Olwen?' Jan called softly as she walked cautiously through the tiny dining room, which was empty and unprepared for any meal, through the hall into the small front parlour, where Olwen usually gave the children the toys she had bought for them. She gazed into the gloom of the heavily curtained room.

In an upright winged armchair, which was Olwen's favourite, the old woman was sitting, quite still. Her head was resting on her right shoulder, with her mouth slightly ajar. Both her eyes were wide open.

22

Olwen was dead.

Jan was sure of it. She felt deeply shocked and a cold shiver ran through her body.

She gazed at the pasty, pale grey features of the old woman with whom she'd often battled during the past ten years; who never yielded an inch of the emotional territory which she had so jealously guarded.

For a few moments Jan felt weak; still holding the door handle, she felt for the doorframe with her other hand to steady herself. She took in more detail as her eyes adapted to the gloom, and her nostrils sensed the faint whiff of death, making her wonder how long Olwen had been there.

She was suddenly conscious that she hadn't phoned back to find out how Olwen was feeling since the old woman had rung two days before. In the meagre hearth on the other side of the room were the remains of a frugal fire – the few small logs Olwen would have treated herself to when the wind was getting up on the hills – and on an oak table beside her stood her favourite Queen Elizabeth II Coronation mug.

Jan turned away into the hall and walked back to the kitchen, revived by the cold fresh air that was blowing in through the open door. She took a few deep breaths while she considered what to do next.

She dreaded going anywhere near the wrinkled remains of the bitter old person Olwen had become, until she suddenly remembered her mother-in-law's words in their last conversation: *There's no one else in the family now*. Jan knew it was her duty to deal with Olwen's death no matter what.

Summoning up all her courage, she walked back into the sitting room and switched on the light. A forty-watt bulb glowed bleakly under a parchment lampshade and accentuated the furrows on Olwen's face. Trying to ignore the smell, she walked a few paces towards the silent, immobile corpse and gingerly reached out to touch the grey-brown, corrugated skin of one hand, which still seemed to be clutching the arm of the chair.

It was completely cold.

Wincing as she tried to overcome her natural revulsion, Jan took a step nearer. She put her fingers up to Olwen's eyes and clumsily pulled the lids down over their staring emptiness.

Jan stopped and told herself there was nothing more she could do. Turning, she walked swiftly through the house and went out, pulling the door to behind her.

While Jan had been inside the clouds had descended from the hills and were swirling around the tops of the trees by the farm-house. Now it looked bleaker and more menacing to her than it ever had.

She took the mobile phone from her pocket to dial the emergency services and stared in frustration when she saw she had no signal.

Reluctantly, she went back inside to the passage by the front door, where Olwen had kept the old black telephone with a circular dial which she'd had up at the farm for thirty years or more.

Slowly Jan dialled 999. When she was connected to the operator, she explained that she had found her mother-in-law dead in her chair. She gave detailed directions to the remote bungalow and was assured that an ambulance and the police would be on their way soon.

Jan put the receiver down and picked it up immediately before dialling Annabel's cottage in Stanfield. She gritted her teeth while she listened to it ring until, just as she was about to give up, Annabel answered breathlessly.

'Bel, are you doing anything important?'

'Not really.'

'Thank God for that! Can you do me a big favour?'

Jan told her as calmly as she could what had happened.

'Oh, Jan, how ghastly! Are you all right?'

'Just about, but I've got the kids with me . . .'

'I'll come over and pick them up right away,' Annabel offered.

'Thanks, you're a star! That was just what I was going to ask. I haven't told them yet; they're still in the car.'

'I'll be as quick as I can, but it'll take an hour or so.'

'I know. They'll just have to stay where they are while I deal with the police and anyone else who turns up.'

'Don't worry, I'm on my way.'

Jan put the phone down, relieved to have a friend so reliable and willing to help. She hoped she would have done the same in similar circumstances.

Now, gritting her teeth, she went outside and walked round to the Shogun, where two anxious little faces gazed back.

She opened the rear door and leaned in.

'I'm afraid I've got some very bad news for you. Granny has died.'

Megan's eyes opened wide. 'Has she?' she asked excitedly. 'Can I see her?'

'No, you certainly cannot. And that's not a very nice way to react when your grandmother's just died.'

'But, Mummy, she was very old and you won't be too sad, will you? You didn't like her very much, did you?'

'Does that mean she won't give us any more toys?' Matthew asked.

'Don't be silly, of course she won't, Matty. And Megan, please try and behave with a bit of kindness when someone in your family dies.'

'Sorry, Mummy. Would you like me to pray for her?'

'That's a very good idea,' Jan answered. 'I've phoned Annabel and asked her to come over and take you out while I deal with everything.'

'What do you have to do?' Megan asked, intrigued. 'Can I see?'

'No, you can't,' Jan said more sharply. 'You're both just going to have to sit here and wait.'

'But, Mum,' Megan wailed, 'we're really bored and Matty keeps hitting me.'

'Well, he's half your size – you'll just have to tell him a story or something.'

The little girl thought about it for a moment. 'All right – I'll tell him a really scary story about how Granny died.'

'Megan, stop it right now.' Jan shook her head wearily, not wanting a fight with her strong-minded daughter. 'Please don't upset Matty. I've got enough to deal with at the moment and I don't want to referee your squabbles. Would you like a drink? I may be able to find something in the kitchen.'

The distant wail of a siren drifted from the hilltop and through the mist before the police car came into view descending into the valley.

It was followed soon after by an ambulance and for a while Olwen's small home became a centre of activity, with more visitors assembled there than ever before. The ambulancemen and the police had completed most of the obligatory investigations for the death of an elderly woman in such circumstances, but Annabel still hadn't arrived from Stanfield.

Jan went back into the house and rang Annabel's mobile, but she was answered by a messaging service and guessed there was no signal. Accepting she would just have to wait a while longer, she went and sat in the car with the children until Olwen's emaciated corpse, zipped in a dark-coloured body-bag, was carried on a stretcher to the ambulance out in the lane.

'Ooh, here's Annabel!' Megan cried out suddenly.

Jan looked to where the grubby finger was pointing and saw the shiny black Beemer speeding down the hill.

Annabel screeched to a halt outside the bungalow just as the ambulance was drawing away to take Olwen's body to the hospital in Brecon.

Annabel stood with her arm around her friend's shoulder as they watched the vehicle wind its way back up the hill. 'Poor you,' she said. 'It must have been awful finding her.'

Jan nodded. 'It was the most awful thing I have ever seen. She was all cold and grey; she'd been dead at least a day and a half the paramedic thought.'

'Was it that obvious?'

Jan wrinkled her nose. ''Fraid so. Bel, thanks so much for coming. If you could take the kids into Hay and give them something to eat, that would be great. I'll finish off here – I think the police want to interview me before they leave.'

Jan arranged to meet Annabel and the children in a cafe in the small border town over the hills which Jan had always considered the nearest outpost of civilization. As she watched the BMW tracking the ambulance back up to the shrouded ridge, the police sergeant who had driven over from Hay-on-Wye came out and asked if he could have a chat. Jan followed him back inside.

Sitting at the round oak table in the tiny dining room, Jan told him how she had arrived at the bungalow and only decided to break in after she had looked round and waited several minutes for a reply. She explained that she had found Olwen in exactly the same position as they had when they arrived, and had only touched her once, to close her eyes.

'The paramedics couldn't identify the cause of death,' the policeman said quietly, looking into her eyes. 'I'm afraid that means there'll have to be a post-mortem.'

'Does that mean you suspect foul play?'

'Not necessarily, though of course we can't rule it out.'

'My mother-in-law rang me on Friday and told me she had a gippy tummy. She said she was being sick and . . . you know.'

'Did she know what had caused it?'

'No, she didn't,' Jan admitted.

'That's probably what we need to find out, then. Can you tell me when you were last here, before today that is?'

'Some time ago, I'm afraid,' Jan confessed, her sense of guilt growing at her neglect of Olwen. While she'd been waiting for Annabel, she'd had time to reflect on the events of the last few days and had convinced herself that if she had driven over on Friday when Olwen had phoned, she could probably have staved off what had happened by getting her into hospital. 'I used to live in the farm up there with my husband; sadly he died three years ago.'

'Yes,' the policeman nodded. 'I remember – they thought it might be the sheep dip.'

'It was never confirmed. But after that I didn't want to stay. So I sold up and left Olwen here alone, it was what she wanted. I run a busy racing yard over in Gloucestershire and it was hard to find enough time to get down here and see her as much as I should.'

'I see. How did you get on with the old lady?'

Jan took a deep breath. 'Not brilliantly, if I'm honest. She thought I'd taken her son away from her when we married. She felt John should have been caring solely for her after her husband died.'

'Yes, well, that wouldn't be an unusual scenario up here in the hills, it's tradition. That's the way these folk do things. Look after the old 'uns.'

'I do know that,' Jan said wryly. 'Actually, I think I was just beginning to get on a bit better with her; at least she admitted I was part of the family . . .' Jan's voice trailed off as it occurred to her that Olwen had only said this primarily as a reason for her to come and visit.

'I'll just take a few details, if I may,' the policeman went on. 'I'll probably need to contact you again, and I'm afraid any arrangements for burial will have to wait until after the post-mortem. Did the deceased have any other living relatives?'

'No, I don't think so. There may be one or two distant cousins over near Lampeter, where she came from, but none that I know of.'

🐎

The police contacted an emergency glazier to come out and fix the back door. Then they packed up their equipment and left.

Jan filled in the time as she waited for the repair man by sweeping up the broken glass and tidying the sitting room. She found some extra keys that fitted the doors, and looked through the few items of post that had been dropped through the letter box the day before, corroborating the senior ambulanceman's view that Olwen had died sometime on Friday.

Once the door had been repaired, Jan had paid the glazier and set off to join Annabel and the children. Driving over the misty hills, where even the sheep looked dispirited, Jan thought about Olwen's life, the frustration of it and the emptiness she must have endured, especially after her only son had died.

Jan guessed that the only thing she had lived for in recent years was her two grandchildren, Megan and Matthew. She resented sharing them, especially with Jan's parents, whom she hadn't wanted to see after her daughter-in-law had moved away.

It was hard to imagine that Olwen had died anything other than sad.

Since Mr Carey from the big house had died, the landlord of the Fox & Pheasant had taken on the job of organizing the village bonfire on Guy Fawkes Night. Jan went down with the children and most of the troop from her yard to watch fireworks, drink mulled wine and sample the hot dogs.

The display was held, as it had been for years, in the park at Stanfield Court in front of the house. It was a community occasion which Jan always liked, and she was hoping it would help her to stop brooding about Olwen's death.

Apart from Annabel, none of the staff at Edge had known Olwen, so for them life had gone on unaltered. Local people and friends had made polite comments, but they really didn't expect the death of a distant mother-in-law to affect Jan too much.

Toby Waller, practical as ever, had driven up to join them and arrived as the fireworks ended. In the pub afterwards, while the children watched *The Lion King* at home with Fran, he commiserated with Jan, before reminding her that it would make resolving the position with Harold Powell a lot easier and, in the long run, more profitable.

'Thanks,' Jan said mournfully. 'But I really don't feel I should be thinking about that sort of thing when the poor woman's only been dead a few days.'

'No, of course not, I fully understand, and actually, though she was a tricky old thing, I could see the last time I was there she was really quite fond of you and absolutely adored her grandchildren.'

'Of course, I always knew she loved the kids, but do you actually think she was fond of me?' Jan asked doubtfully.

'Yes I do, but people like her find it hard to show their affection. They almost see it as a sign of weakness. There's still a strange belief among some country people that saying "sorry" somehow weakens you in other people's eyes.'

'I know what you mean,' Jan said, 'although it seems to me that it's a bigger sign of strength to admit your dues and to own up to the mistakes you've made.'

'Anyway, it must have been a dreadful shock finding her the way you did and quite exhausting trying to sort out your own emotions. Presumably you'll have to organize the funeral as well.'

Jan grimaced. 'Yes, but it'll be very small. I don't have the address of a single relation on her side, nor has her solicitor.'

'You've spoken to him, have you?'

'Yes. He said she didn't leave a will – she didn't have much to leave anyway, but what there is is all mine and the children's.'

'Obviously it'll take a bit of time to sort out the probate and Harold, so you won't be able to count on any money from the sale of the bungalow for quite a while. What are your finances like at the moment?'

Jan was tempted to pour out all the troubles she was having with Gary West to Toby, but resisted. Instead, she shrugged a shoulder. 'Things are still a bit tight, though selling King's Archer helped.'

'Johnny Carlton-Brown must be one of your biggest players now. Not a bad thing, I suppose, though I suspect A.D. isn't the easiest of owners.'

'And that Tanner's a complete bloody nightmare,' Jan blurted out.

Toby frowned. 'When is Gary West coming over?' he continued, trying to get to the bottom of things.

Jan didn't answer for a moment. 'I don't know. He doesn't ring very often.'

'Well, I hope I didn't alarm you too much the other week when I told you about his exposure through Posidian. Since then, Posidian seem to be hanging on in there somehow; they've booted half a dozen scapegoats off the board to convince the financial watchdogs they're cleaning up their act, and so many influential people have too much to lose to let them go under. Basically, what I'm saying is that the rats are hanging on still, hoping the ship won't sink.'

'Well, I hope they're right,' Jan said fervently, thinking of the courier with the eight thousand pounds and West's outstanding debts, which were continuing to rise at a serious rate of knots.

A week after she had found Olwen, Jan was doing her best to make sure the routines at Edge Farm carried on as usual, but the repercussions of the old woman's death were still making themselves felt. The coroner hadn't yet released Olwen's body and a detective from the police station in Brecon telephoned to ask if he could come and do a further interview with Jan at her house.

She saw the cautious young Welshman in her office. He perched awkwardly on one of the rickety bentwood visitors' chairs opposite her desk.

'The first thing we have to tell you,' he said without preamble, 'is that your late mother-in-law died from poisoning.'

Jan went limp. She had dismissed the talk of foul play by the policeman who had come to the bungalow as no more than routine procedure. It hadn't remotely occurred to her that Olwen's death might have been caused deliberately. 'Are you saying she was murdered?' Jan asked hoarsely.

'No. We're saying she died from ingesting strychnine. We've carried out forensic investigations to establish the source and found it in the water supply, which comes from a reservoir up at the farm that's spring-fed. The current owner's been having work done there, tidying up and all that. Well, two empty containers of the stuff have come to light.'

Jan nodded. 'They'd have been left by the rat catcher my late husband had round six or seven years ago. Are you actually saying the well was contaminated?'

'It looks like it.'

'What? Deliberately?'

The detective's face was deadpan. 'Can you tell me, is there anyone you can think of who might have wanted to see Mrs Hardy dead?'

Jan tried to absorb the horror of what he was saying. For a moment she was silent, unable to bring herself to say what was ringing in her head.

'What about the new owner of the farm?' the policeman prompted. 'Mrrr . . . ?' He hesitated and checked his notebook. 'Mr Harold Powell? We know he's had a building project blocked by old Mrs Hardy's actions regarding a right of way.'

Jan nodded as he put her thought into words. 'Well, I know he was bloody annoyed about that, but . . . to go that far? I can hardly believe it.'

'You had dealings yourself with Mr Powell before, didn't you, and since he's bought the property from you?'

'Yes, I had to threaten to take him to court over the unethical way he sold the farm to himself.'

The policeman had been writing down her answers in a small black notebook. He continued for a few moments more until, abruptly, he flipped it shut and snapped an elastic band around it. 'Thank you, Mrs Hardy,' he said, getting up. 'That'll be all for now. I'll give you a ring if I need to see you again.'

Jan felt she had been left in a state of limbo. 'Is that it?'

'Yes. Thanks for your help, I'll see myself out.'

'There's just one thing,' Jan called after him as he started to open the office door. 'Am I allowed to bury my mother-in-law yet?'

'Oh yes. Ring the coroner's office and they'll release the body for you. And I'm sorry to have brought you such unpleasant news.'

For the next few days Jan was relieved to have plenty of work to do as it helped to take her mind off the idea that Olwen had been deliberately poisoned, maybe by Harold Powell.

She had found two potential horses for Toby's syndicate, one in Ireland and another at the horses in training sale at Doncaster. Sandy Wilson, the retired detective, was bringing Bill Luard, another member of the group, to meet Jan at the sale.

Trojan Banquet, a dark brown seven-year-old gelding, had an impressive track record as a hurdler and seemed ideal to go novice chasing. The animal had caught Jan's eye in a way that was reassuring, he looked totally honest with an agreeable manner.

Sandy inspected the animal with a puzzled look on his face, as a groom trotted it on the rubber matting laid for the purpose.

'I could spot a recidivist villain at a hundred paces, just from the way he walked, but there's no way I could tell whether that horse can run fast.' He shook his head with a smile. 'So it's down to you, Jan.'

'You can tell from the slope of his shoulder and the length of his stride when he trots that he can cover the ground and he's completely sound,' Jan murmured to him in a voice too low for the handler to hear. 'All his other bits are in the right place for a jumper and the form book tells us he knows how to use them. Besides, didn't you look at the video I sent you?'

'Yes, of course I did, and he looked terrific over hurdles, but we want him to go chasing. Do you think he can jump that high?'

Jan laughed at the innocent remark. 'He'll love the job,' she confirmed.

'Let's go for him, then,' Sandy said gleefully.

An hour later they had acquired Trojan Banquet for seventy thousand guineas, and Jan arranged for him to be transported to Edge Farm. To celebrate the purchase and to mark the start of their new relationship as owner and trainer, Sandy and Bill bought Jan lunch in the restaurant behind the sale ring.

Bill had also been a colleague of Sandy's in the Met, but neither of them specified in what capacity. Jan noted that although he was a much quieter character, Sandy treated him with considerable respect.

'I see your family's been the victim of a bit of villainy,' Sandy remarked casually once they had ordered their food.

'You mean my mother-in-law?' Jan asked, wondering how he knew.

Sandy nodded. 'I read it in the *Telegraph* on the train this morning. Didn't you see it?'

'No,' Jan said, amazed that no one else had told her about it until now.

'It mentioned your connection with Olwen Hardy. Of course, they didn't say there was any villainy, just that the old lady had died from strychnine poisoning through a contaminated well. But wells don't get contaminated with that amount of stuff unless someone's decided to put it there.'

'The police have already told me that,' Jan admitted. 'A young bloke came from Brecon to ask me if I knew of anyone who disliked her enough to do it.'

'And do you?' the ex-policeman asked.

'Yes, I'm afraid so.' Jan nodded. 'But they'd already sussed that anyway.'

'Will they nail them for it?'

'I bloody well hope so, but I think it'll be hard to prove this chap's done it deliberately. And there's no way I want to be a witness or anything.'

'If you can be of any help, by law it's your duty to testify. And just remember, he could do it again if he gets away this time.'

🐎

The first day of the Cheltenham November meeting was on Friday the thirteenth. It seemed an inauspicious day for sending horses to the races, but Jan reckoned everyone was in the same boat. The cross-country race was being run over a track especially laid in the middle of the course. Last year, for the first time, Jan had run Lady Fairford's horse, Young Willie, in the race; this time she was running Arrow Star for Penny Price, one of her first and delightful but least well-off owners. Penny had bred and foaled her horse at home in west Herefordshire and had taken a second job at nights just to pay the training fees. Jan knew she would be delighted if the precious animal completed the race in one piece, and ecstatic if it came in the first three or four. It mattered so much to Jan that this dedicated woman wasn't disappointed.

Jan had taken on Arrow Star in the first place because he was just the type of animal she liked and not dissimilar to Russian Eagle. He wasn't the slimmest or most streamlined horse in the parade ring, but Jan knew he would gallop relentlessly round the three-mile seven-furlong track with the loops and sharp turns that made up the unusual course. She thought he would comfortably take the banks, ditches and high laurel hedges in his long stride. And, above all, he had the best jockey to do it with.

Virginia had gleefully rung Jan the previous evening, specially to tell her that if she was expecting Finbar to ride in the cross-country race, she could forget it as she had a strong contender of her own and it was definitely running. Jan was devastated; Finbar had previously assured her that Virginia's runner had suffered a setback, so Jan hadn't bothered to look elsewhere for a pilot.

Annoyed and in a last-minute panic, she rang Murty McGrath's agent on the off-chance that he might be available; she was amazed to find his intended mount had been withdrawn and he hadn't yet taken another ride. The agent came back to Jan within minutes to tell her the champion would be delighted to ride her horse.

Jan hadn't been expecting Murty to be overjoyed at his first sight of Arrow Star, but the Irishman was broadminded and experienced enough to know that good horses come in all shapes and sizes.

'He's a bit of a hippo,' he said to Jan, out of Penny's hearing. 'How's his jumping?'

'Brilliant, totally genuine; you won't have a problem there, and he'll get you out of trouble if he has to. Just keep up with the pace; he won't run out of puff; but he could get beaten on the run-in if there's anything with a bit of toe, but he'll be in with a chance and he'll give you every last drop.'

'The owner seems very genuine,' he murmured to Jan; a moment later he turned to Penny. 'We'll be doing our very best for you, miss.'

🐎

Jan drove the lorry home, content that Arrow Star had come third. Penny Price had been overwhelmed at seeing her horse in the frame at Cheltenham, albeit in the knowledge that this strange race was about the only one in which he would have had the slightest chance at such a premier course.

Jan turned to Connor, who was sitting next to her.

'You should have seen Penny's face when she met Arrow and Murty coming back into the winner's enclosure.'

'I did,' the Irish lad grinned. 'When she led them to their slot she'd a smile on her face like a nun going to heaven.'

'That's the best thing about this game,' Jan said. 'When you see the owners really proud and happy and you know you've made it happen.'

'I'd agree,' the Irishman said. 'My dad had a winner once at Galway; he didn't stop talkin' about it for the next two years.'

Jan's pleasure at the day's achievement was bluntly curtailed by a second visit to the yard from the policeman who had come to see her at the beginning of the week.

'I thought you should know,' he said, once they were alone and ensconced in her office, 'we've charged a man called Dai Meredith in connection with your late mother-in-law's demise. His finger-prints were as clear as crystal on one of the containers we took away.'

'What have you charged him with?'

'Manslaughter at this stage, but we're hoping to be able to include the man who told him to dump the stuff in the well.'

'You mean Harold Powell?'

'You don't sound very surprised.'

'Well, I'm not. I've already told you, he was annoyed about not being able to get on with his development.'

'The difficulty we're going to have is proving he did it on purpose, in which case he'd be looking at a murder charge. That's why we need to know if he ever said or implied anything to you that might have indicated his intentions.'

Jan looked back at the man candidly. 'I really wish I could help you there. He did look at me fairly murderously a couple of times when I had my set-to with him over the sale of the farm, and that's because he knew, in the end, whatever happened with the bungalow was my decision, not my mother-in-law's. Frankly, I wouldn't lose any sleep if he got sent down for murder.'

23

Jan drove over the top of Llanbedr Hill and began to drop down into the valley beyond, heading towards the simple white Norman church, which stood within a ring of ancient yews; it seemed no time at all since she had made that same journey with the children to their father's funeral. But in fact it was just two months short of three years since John had been buried there, the first event in a chain that had moved her from Wales back to Gloucestershire and spurred her on to become a full-time professional trainer.

On that occasion, Jan remembered, Olwen had gazed at her with obvious disapproval when she had failed to wear the usual black widow's weeds. She was now wearing the same green suit for John's mother's service as she had for his. Megan and Matthew, conscious of where they were going, sat neatly dressed and quiet in the back of the car.

For John's funeral, cars had lined the narrow lane down to the church for several hundred yards. Now just half a dozen vehicles, including the hearse with Olwen's coffin, were parked by the lychgate.

The contrast to her husband's funeral was even more marked inside; where it had been full to capacity and overflowing into the churchyard for his, no more than a dozen people had come to witness the burial of his mother. As the vicar intoned the words of the brief ritual and spoke genuinely about Olwen's commitment to the Church in Wales, and her exemplary attendance at his church, Jan wondered how much genuine affection there was in the hearts of those few who had come.

She had often noticed how older people in the hills would use a funeral as an impromptu social gathering which required no invitation. But these people, she concluded, were here out of regard for the woman Olwen had been. She recognized all but two of them, and she wondered if they were distant relations from the far side of the Cambrians.

The small gathering clustered around the earth-walled pit beside the headstone marking the grave of Olwen's husband. Despite herself, Jan felt tears welling up in her eyes, while her children looked on, fascinated but unmoved, as the coffin was lowered slowly into the ground.

Jan had organized the customary wake in the village hall, a small, forlorn building clad in pale grey corrugated iron a hundred yards from the church. The small band of mourners walked silently down the lane and trooped into the damp room for the traditional tea and sandwiches, very similar to those Olwen had prepared for John's funeral. Jan shook hands with everyone and discovered that the strangers were indeed two of Olwen's few remaining cousins who had not seen her for fifteen years.

When Jan had thanked the vicar and everyone else had left, she walked back to the church with the children, where they stood for a few moments holding hands beside her late husband's grave. She remembered tenderly his huge strength and simple honesty. How different he was from Eddie, Tony Robertson, or owners like A.D. and Johnny Carlton-Brown. She reflected how dramatically her life had changed since his death left her to fend for herself and the children.

She wondered if John Hardy would have approved of what she had achieved, with all the single-mindedness and thrusting determination it required.

Probably not, she thought, as the tears rolled down her face.

🐎

The drive back from Wales to the lowlands of Herefordshire and the Severn plain helped to bring Jan back to the present, gradually easing the pain of Olwen's death and her own past life, yet marking the day as another staging post.

Her mother-in-law's death was brought back into sharp focus

during the evening, as Jan settled down to watch the regional news. Suddenly Harold Powell's photograph appeared on the screen with a story about his arrest in connection with the late Olwen Hardy, whose funeral had taken place that day.

Jan let out a huge sigh of relief that the media hadn't found out about the funeral sooner and marred it with their presence. It also seemed that they had either ignored her connection with Olwen, or didn't consider her sufficiently newsworthy.

But the news that Harold had been arrested and would presumably be charged for his part in Olwen's death left her with an even stronger feeling of revenge.

Annabel was adamant that Jan should come to her dinner party and suggested Jan brought Tony Robertson along with her – to make the numbers even.

Jan sensed an underlying motive in the arrangement, but decided it could be rather amusing to go along with it anyway. Tony had been particularly thoughtful in the three weeks since Olwen's funeral. He seemed instinctively to understand how the events had sucked Jan back into her past and her former, very different existence with John Hardy on the remote Welsh hill farm.

By Saturday evening, when the dinner was due to take place at Glebe Cottage, the only obvious but unpredicted cause for celebration was Flamenco's first win for Toby Waller.

Jan had bought the horse for Toby at the Derby Sale in Fairyhouse the previous year, but he had taken a disappointing length of time to settle into a satisfactory training routine. On his first outing over hurdles he'd fallen at the last, still travelling well; the next time he hit the top of an early flight so hard he was pulled up. But with Finbar on board in a Novice Hurdle at Chepstow that afternoon, he'd jumped fluently and come home an easy winner.

Tony Robertson was so delighted when Jan asked him to accompany her that she wondered if she'd been a little rash. They arrived together, and Jan noticed immediately the table in Annabel's dining room was set for eight.

When the other guests arrived, Jan realized Annabel hadn't needed Tony to make up numbers; it was obvious that she'd been short of female companions and had made up the imbalance by asking her regular standbys, Lucy and Victoria Thorndyke, the stunning blonde twins in their early twenties whose father had a large estate near Chipping Camden.

The men in the party included Johnny Carlton-Brown, Toby Waller, still ecstatic about Flamenco's win and, predictably, Patrick Lamberhurst.

Annabel made everyone a dry martini as soon as they arrived to get them relaxed and chatting. The Thorndyke girls were always a challenge, mercilessly fascinating to Johnny and Toby with their identical looks. And as Annabel had hoped, they kept the conversation from centring on horses and racing. Jan found Tony's presence reassured her and she felt at ease in this gathering in a way she couldn't possibly have been three or four years before.

After a delicious dinner and some exceptional wines Patrick had brought along, Annabel tapped her empty glass with a spoon until the room was quiet. 'One of the reasons I asked you here tonight and,' she turned to Jan, 'the reason I insisted that you should come, Jan, even after such a long day at the races, is that Patrick and I have an important announcement to make.'

Jan guessed at once what was coming and her heart sank as Patrick got to his feet and took over, confirming her fears.

'Annabel, risk-taker that she is, has agreed to have a crack at being Lady Lamberhurst.'

Jan stared at Annabel, unable to understand why on earth she wanted to marry a man who could describe their forthcoming union in such a flippant way. But Annabel looked more radiant and happy than she ever had, and Jan knew her friend wasn't a fool and that she was usually a very good judge of character.

Perhaps Patrick had got it right when he described Annabel as a risk-taker, who baulked at picking the obvious quiet and more thoughtful type of man she would have been expected to marry.

Not wishing to show any doubts, Jan smiled and lifted her glass with the rest of the party, murmuring, 'Annabel and Patrick.'

She walked round the table to give Annabel a quick kiss. 'Congratulations, Bel.'

'What about me?' Patrick protested pathetically.

'Just wait your turn,' Annabel said, and Jan was relieved to see that her friend had no compunction about putting her self-centred future spouse in his place. She wondered how long he would accept it because when he stopped accommodating her, Jan thought, there was bound to be trouble.

Johnny Carlton-Brown phoned the next morning and asked Jan if he could buy her dinner at L'Escargot that evening.

'Only if I'm back home by ten at the latest. I've got an early start and a busy week.'

'That's fine.' Johnny laughed. 'We're both in the same boat. I'm flying to LA at seven.'

Jan assumed they would be dining with others, but as he drove her to the restaurant in a new Aston Martin, he said there were just the two of them. Jan didn't ask why, but he made it clear as soon as they sat down at the table.

'What do you think about Patrick and Annabel?'

Jan shrugged. She didn't want to say anything derogatory about Lamberhurst, who, she believed, was an old friend of Johnny's as well as his business partner.

'Well, I'm not sure they're ideally suited,' she answered guardedly.

'Are you saying that because you're worried you'll lose her from the yard?'

'No, of course not, though I really wouldn't want her to leave. In fact, I'd be far more worried from that point of view if they *were* better suited because there'd be a greater chance of the wedding actually going ahead.'

Johnny leaned forward a little and Jan was struck by the obvious passion in his eyes.

'Do you mean, you think she'll find out it's a non-starter before it happens?' he asked eagerly.

'I guess so. For a start, I think even if Patrick says he doesn't mind Bel working with me now, sooner or later he's going to get peed off not having her to himself twenty-four seven; and I certainly don't think he'd like her being answerable to anyone else – especially not someone with my humble background.'

Johnny leaned back. 'You think he's an arrogant, chauvinistic snob, then?'

Jan chuckled. 'In a nutshell. Sorry,' she added hastily. 'He's a friend of yours, isn't he?'

'Yes, but I don't expect people to think my friends are without blemish; that would imply that I think I'm perfect – and I'm far from it. Still, you're right about Patrick, though – at least, up to a point. There *is* a very perceptive, sensitive and self-critical side to him as well, but he just doesn't seem to have the willpower to correct his flaws.'

A waiter hovered and Johnny turned for a moment to order the wine.

'But in principle I agree with you,' he went on when they were alone again. 'I feel Patrick and Annabel aren't at all well matched either.'

'Please tell me how you see it,' Jan asked, intrigued by the most perceptive conversation she'd ever had with this private man.

'Patrick can be very charming and thoughtful in a completely superficial way; sometimes he can be entertaining and witty, though I accept that you may not think so. But he's essentially very selfish; he's simply not interested in other people – not for themselves, anyway. He would see Annabel as an enviable social accessory and a desirable outlet for his own physical urges.'

'That's a bit strong isn't it,' Jan observed, 'considering he's your friend?'

Johnny shrugged his shoulders. 'I've told you. I take the view that practically every member of the human race is flawed to a greater or lesser extent. I certainly am, I expect you are too. Well, so are my friends. We gain nothing if we delude ourselves that we only have saints for intimate companions.'

The waiter returned with the wine they had chosen and the menus. Jan and Johnny selected quickly, both really anxious to get back to their conversation. As soon as the waiter had disappeared, Jan went on eagerly. 'OK then – how would you sum up Annabel?'

'Annabel, curiously, is one of those extremely rare individuals who are almost unflawed. I don't think there's an ounce of malice in her. She views everyone with the same quiet, unthreatening friendliness. I do think she's been really wounded at some point in her life, though, perhaps not all that long ago; if she does have a minor fault, it would be that she's a little too defensive. But that apart, she's very good company, she's got a great sense of humour and she is, in my view, staggeringly beautiful.'

Jan was astounded by this litany of Annabel's virtues. She couldn't disagree with anything Johnny had said about her friend, but it brought home to her the surprising fact that there was nothing about Annabel to which she had ever objected in the five years they had known each other. It also threw a new and revealing light on Johnny Carlton-Brown and his attitude towards Bel.

'Good heavens,' Jan said, looking him straight in the eye, 'you really fancy her, don't you?'

'Of course,' he answered simply. 'But please don't tell her.'

'She certainly hasn't got a clue that you do – at least she's never mentioned it and normally she would.'

'I haven't given her any reason to suspect how I feel, though I will – if the right moment ever arises. In the meantime, I'm trusting you not to tell a soul.'

'I understand,' Jan said, although she didn't completely. 'But why are you telling me this now?'

'I wanted to be sure that you weren't any happier than I am about this engagement – for your own perfectly valid reasons. Without asking you to compromise your relationship with Bel, I thought if you heard my views about Patrick and her, you might try really discreetly to persuade her not to do something she could regret.'

'I was going to try,' Jan admitted frankly. 'Though it would have to be discreet. Bel may be all the things you said, but she's totally independent. We have never argued, but she always manages to let me know if she disagrees with me.'

'I never suggested she was a pushover.'

'In a way, I think Patrick's attraction for her is partly about her reluctance to do what she knows her family would like and expect,' Jan continued, 'him not being military or a banker or something like that.'

'On the other hand, I imagine her father wouldn't object to his daughter marrying a member of the House of Lords.'

'And Bel would enjoy the irony. But,' Jan went on, 'she does have a minor flaw, although you might say it's not her fault – she doesn't like her father at all.'

'I've never met him, so I don't have a particular view on that. She's never mentioned anything to me.'

'She wouldn't say anything unpleasant; I've just picked up on a few comments, that's all.'

Johnny shifted in his chair and seemed to flex his shoulders inside his linen jacket. The gesture marked a change of identity, from the close friend talking of intimate, personal things, to JCB, the big-time record company boss, talking to a business associate.

'Well, thanks for listening to my views, which I'm sure will go no further. Now, let's talk horses.'

Ten days before Christmas Mary Pritchard began preparing the geese she had reared over the previous ten months. Two dozen of them had to be killed, plucked and dressed. Mary had produced her Christmas geese for thirty years or more, and it had become an unshakeable tradition in her life. She had a roster of regular customers who had bought them from her every year and she had no intention of letting them down.

Jan, remembering the promise to her father, drove over one afternoon as there were no runners and no emergencies to be dealt with at Edge Farm. She had picked up the children from school so they could help out and extend their understanding of country life, and, if the rain held off, Matthew could have a riding lesson on Rocket as a reward.

Jan had vivid childhood memories of plucking the geese with her mother and nothing had changed since. They sat together in the old dairy with the first four birds lying on the table between them.

'Did you . . .?' Jan started to ask.

Mary shook her head remorsefully. 'No. I couldn't. Your dad neckholed them, and they'll get harder as they knows.'

'Oh well, best get at it. It wouldn't do your customers any harm to see what goes on to produce and dress a bird like this – some of those poor townie kids have no idea how milk gets into a bottle even!'

'I don't know as you're right,' Mary replied. 'Seeing this might put 'em off for good.'

They settled quickly into the routine of manual plucking. Jan didn't bother any more to suggest that Mary should send her birds off to the butcher, who had a machine to do the job, as it would eat up most of her profit, and besides it was part of the tradition to do it herself. The whole point of the geese was that they gave Mary her only independent source of income. Her 'goose money' was sacrosanct, ring-fenced to pay for special household items and her few personal indulgences.

As they worked, they talked and Jan soon saw that Mary wasn't going to waste this opportunity to share a few intimate secrets.

But Jan quickly took the initiative.

'Dad told me about your kidney problems.'

'Oh, well he shouldn't have; it's not important.'

'Mum, kidneys are very important especially when they go wrong. Is there much pain?'

Mary's jaw clenched as she tugged at a fistful of feathers beneath her bird's wing.

'Mum?' Jan pressed. 'It's just daft to pretend things aren't there, you know.'

Mary nodded reluctantly. 'It can hurt a bit.'

'Just a bit?' Jan asked doubtfully.

'Like hell sometimes,' Mary admitted with a sigh.

'Why on earth don't you go and see the specialist at the hospital like your doctor said, then?'

Mary grimaced and shook her head. 'Once you gets into one of them places you've a job to get out. When they've got you, they keep finding other things wrong with you and they don't want to let you go.'

'Mum, that's ridiculous. You've got to let me take you,' Jan said firmly, wondering how on earth she was going to find time. 'What's the point of putting up with all that pain if you don't have to? It doesn't help anyone and it'll worry Dad to death.'

Mary knew her daughter too well to continue fighting. 'Maybe after Christmas,' she conceded.

'And don't think I'll forget,' Jan promised.

'But tell me,' Mary went on, deftly moving back to her own agenda. 'How's it going up at the yard? Dad says you've had a bit of a sticky time of it.'

'Well, it's all relative, I suppose. We're getting a few winners, but not so many in proportion to the number we're running.'

'He says you've got some bloke not paying his bills.'

Jan nodded. 'It is causing me a few nightmares at the moment, but I'm sure it'll be all right in the end because I can sell the horses to recover the debt. It's just trying to juggle all the finances in the meantime that's the problem, and I hate being in to the bank for so much.'

'Can't you sell that bungalow old Mrs Hardy used to live in? Wouldn't that help?'

'Toby Waller – you know, the owner – he says I should wait and see what happens to Harold Powell, then maybe we can buy the whole place back and sell it off for development.'

'Do you want to get involved in that sort of thing, though, with even more risk? You're a farm girl.'

'Mum, if the opportunity to make a really good profit and build up a bit of capital is there, I can't turn it down. I'm a single mum with two young kids, remember, and I need some security behind me to make the best of it.'

'Don't you think I know that? But the way I see it is you've got someone offering you that on a plate already and you won't take it.'

'If you're meaning Tony Robertson, he hasn't asked me to marry him or anything and, frankly, I'm not sure he needs the hassle of being involved with two children and a racing stables. Besides, Mum, although I'm really fond of him, I've told you before I don't think I love him and I wouldn't want to compromise. You know what I'm like, it's all or nothing.'

'It seems to me that life's full of so-called compromises.'

Jan looked up from a goose almost denuded of its feathers. 'You don't need to tell *me* that, Mum, after what I've been through over the last three years.'

Mary looked back at her with unexpected intensity. 'Well, just don't keep telling yourself that Eddie Sullivan's coming back, Jan. If he hasn't by now, I doubt if he'll be coming at all and I don't want you getting hurt any more.'

❧

Mary's words were still echoing in Jan's head as she drove herself to Newbury the following morning. She and Annabel had been discussing plans for Russian Eagle, who was now ready to run once they'd decided on the right race for him, which had reminded Jan of Eddie.

But as she approached the Berkshire track, on her own as Annabel had taken a runner to Bangor-on-Dee, her thoughts couldn't dwell on Eddie for long as she had two runners to saddle, both with a reasonable chance.

Gylippus and the Magic Maestro were well fancied. Finbar Howlett was riding them both, as well as one of Virginia's – the only good horse she had in her yard, in Jan's opinion.

The lorry had already arrived two hours earlier with Joe and Emma, who informed her the horses had travelled well – always the first hurdle to cross in a day's racing. Jan made sure that they were both turned out to perfection, and watched with pleasure the pride that her team took in maintaining Edge Farm's growing reputation for the way they presented themselves and their runners.

❧

There was a big cheesy grin all over Finbar Howlett's shy, altar-boy face as a television commentator interviewed him on air straight after the race he'd just won on Gary West's gelding, Gylippus.

'I think that's the first treble you've ridden, Finbar, here or in Ireland – is that right?'

'It is,' the jockey agreed.

'How does it feel?'

334

Finbar looked at the man as if he were mentally deficient. 'It feels bloody marvellous. I was very lucky to get the rides from Mrs Hardy, as well as the horse from my own stable.'

'And what about the Magic Maestro? Do you know Jan Hardy's plans for him?'

Jan, watching on the monitor in the weighing room, laughed. 'Not unless he's a bloody mind reader.'

'I don't really know,' the jockey was saying, 'but he was just a novice last season so he's still eligible for the Cathcart at the Cheltenham Festival. He goes well up to two and half miles, and if I were her, I'd be aiming at that. He's absolutely the right sort of horse for it.'

'Thank you for that, Finnie, and very well done.'

Reviewing the day's performances as she drove home, Jan felt inclined to commend Finbar for his perceptiveness, if not for expressing it publicly. She had already earmarked the Magic Maestro as her first Festival runner. Now for the first time in months she was feeling more in control of her destiny. When she rang Tanner to tell him about Gary West's two winners, she also took the opportunity to inform him that if they didn't get their outstanding account sorted, she was going to start selling the horses to recover the debt, which was in line with the agreement he had with her, she reminded him.

'You do that,' Tanner almost snarled, 'and you'll find yourself in big trouble. You have a good look at that agreement of yours and you'll see you can only sell them if the debt to you exceeds the value of any one horse. And you've got a while to wait before it gets that high.'

Jan felt her guts seized in an icy grip. She had a horrible feeling he was right, and that would inevitably leave this dreadful tension hanging over her for much longer.

'I can tell you this, Mr Tanner, I'm not at all amused by achieving the success I have with your horses for little thanks and no reward.'

'I presume Weatherbys are sending direct your share of the prize money?' Tanner said.

'You know perfectly well that that's the icing on the cake for a trainer, and it doesn't come within a mile of covering what you owe me.'

'Well, there it is. Sorry I can't help further, but I've got other fish to fry.'

The line went dead before Jan could tell him exactly what she thought. And she had to spend the rest of the journey, which should have been pleasurable after the day's success, trying to curb the fury burning inside her.

24

It is traditional that no racing takes place anywhere in Britain in the last few days leading up to Christmas. This gave everyone at Edge Farm a chance to take a quick breather and prepare for the important and manically organized racing on Boxing Day.

On the 23rd December Major and Mrs Halstead took advantage of the lull to hold a party to celebrate their daughter's engagement to Lord Lamberhurst.

At noon, after most of the chores in the yard had been done, Annabel walked into the office and perched her small behind on the edge of Jan's desk. She took a brush from her capacious leather shoulder bag and started to draw it through her hair and examine the extremities for split ends.

'Is it OK if I go to Mum and Dad's now?' she asked. 'I really ought to help them out a bit.'

'Of course – I thought you said you weren't coming in today, anyway.'

'I wasn't going to, but Mum seems to have everything well under control and I wanted to know how Tom's Touch felt this morning.'

Jan nodded. 'He looked pretty good, didn't he?'

'Yeah, I suppose so – though I did feel there was something not quite—' She shrugged. 'I don't know, maybe I was imagining it. Anyway, there's not a lot more we can do between now and Boxing Day.'

'Exactly, so you go home and enjoy yourself.'

'Right.' Annabel nodded warily.

'What?' Jan exclaimed. 'Aren't you looking forward to it?'

'Yes, of course, to the wedding whenever that is, but somehow, when you announce you're getting married it starts a chain reaction which seems to go completely out of your control, and you just have to let yourself get carried along on a wave of activity and planning that you couldn't stop if you wanted to.'

'Bel, you don't want to call it off, do you?'

'No, of course I don't; it's just that I would like to have a bit more control. And, by the way – ' Annabel stopped brushing her hair and looked directly at Jan – 'I do know that you wouldn't mind too much if I did.'

Jan sighed. This wasn't a conversation she wanted to have, especially not now. She shrugged. 'Bel, all I want is for you to be happy. I sometimes find it rather hard to believe Patrick will achieve that for you. To be frank, since you've brought the subject up, I really don't understand what you see in him.'

It was Annabel's turn to feign indifference. 'I wouldn't expect you to because you didn't spend your teenage years with a father trying to brainwash you into thinking that unless a man had been commissioned in the Household Cavalry, lived on a large estate with a bloody good shoot, two Labradors and a few good hunters, he wasn't worth considering.'

'Patrick Lamberhurst isn't exactly a penniless yobbo, Bel.'

'No, but he's the sort of man Dad just wouldn't understand, doing things he can't envisage any of his friends doing. And, as it happens, although Patrick may not be superficially charming, there is a romantic streak in him, I promise you.'

'Well, I'll have to take that on trust,' Jan said, asking herself why on earth she was criticizing her closest friend's fiancé on the day they were celebrating their engagement. She couldn't deny, though, that one of her strongest objections to the marriage was a fear of losing her assistant. With all the other troubles she'd been having, although she would never have admitted it to a soul, not even to her father, she really did not want to face the future without Annabel's support. 'I'm sorry, Bel. I really shouldn't have said that. I know you wouldn't want to make a mistake about something as serious as this; there are obviously other sides to Patrick and at least he's bloody good-looking so you won't have to leave the bedroom light off.'

'That's not funny,' Annabel came back sharply. 'I know plenty of "good-looking" men who do nothing for me. I like the fact that he's so elusive, though I know that wouldn't suit you. I mean, you could hardly call Eddie Sullivan subtle, could you?'

Jan held up a hand in surrender. 'Bel, please, I've said I'm sorry. What more do you want? Anyway, I feel I'm over Eddie now, even though what actually happened wasn't what he wanted. But I'm sure he'll make a go of it in Oz being the kind of man he is. I'm fully resigned now to the fact that he won't be back.' She sighed and thought of the dependable Tony Robertson.

'Jan, and I think you should also have enough faith in me to know that, even when I marry Patrick, I'm not going to leave you in the lurch.' Annabel gave her friend a black look which made her feel even worse for having criticized Patrick.

Jan drove to Annabel's party in her large four-wheel drive with six other members of her staff packed inside, while the rest travelled with Roz in her mother's Land Rover.

When they arrived, Jan was astonished at the large number of people who had made the effort to come to the Halsteads' beautiful Georgian mansion, which was in a remote north-west corner of Herefordshire. She guessed that well over two hundred people filled the hall and reception rooms.

Johnny Carlton-Brown, dressed with customary quirkiness in an aubergine velvet jacket, caught Jan's eye and gave a faint shrug of resignation as he made his way across the drawing room towards her.

'This is what you might call an eclectic gathering,' he remarked, 'demonstrative of Annabel's own lack of pretension and her father's excess of it, I should say.'

'Bel insisted that everyone from the yard should come. Of course, her father was dead against it, but the fact is the yard's been her life for the last three years and there was no way she was going to leave out the people she spends the best part of her life with.'

'Quite. I do wonder how clearly Patrick appreciates that fact. By the way, it's evident that you didn't make any serious headway with what we discussed over dinner.'

'No, I did try, all I've done is criticize Patrick so far, which seems to have had an adverse effect and made her even keener. I really do hope she'll suss him out before it's too late.'

Carlton-Brown nodded gloomily. 'Anyway, I suppose I'd better shake myself and look as if I'm enjoying this. I think I'll go and tease Annabel's father about his future son-in-law.'

Although Annabel had invited Jan to her parents' house several times before, it had never seemed convenient, so this was the first time she had been there. Seeing the whole set-up, and meeting some of the people Annabel had grown up with, brought home to Jan the huge difference in their backgrounds. She smiled and couldn't imagine, for instance, Annabel and her mother chatting as they plucked and drew home-reared geese over the pantry table, though she concluded it might have been a valuable experience for them both.

Annabel's parents had been to Edge Farm a few times and Jan had tried really hard to please them, but she found they were too reserved and uncommunicative to make much progress. Here, on their own territory, they were obviously relishing this highfalutin' party.

Mrs Halstead spotted Jan and made a beeline for her. She was almost as tall as Annabel, though slightly fleshier. She had her daughter's looks, but with less striking eyes and a weaker chin. Jan guessed she had never been quite as stunning as Bel.

'Jan, how lovely you could come!' she gushed. 'I'm *so* glad you managed to get here at last. I was talking to a very old friend of mine the other day who has a horse with you – Lady Fairford. She was telling me how it's all going terribly well for you now.'

'We've had a few ups and downs, it goes with the territory, but I'm afraid we haven't done much good with Lady Fairford's horse.'

'Young Willie, isn't it? Yes, I remember. She says he's really a bit too old now.'

'I'm hopeful we might get another couple of runs out of him, though.'

'It really is time Simon and I had a horse with you. The trouble is he's not all that keen, as you probably gathered from Bel.' Mrs Halstead's laugh was an unexpected titter. 'Of course, I don't suppose she'll be able to help you for much longer once she and Patrick are married.'

Jan looked at her sharply. 'Really. I don't think she has any plans to move on just yet. In fact, I think she's rather keen to stay on.'

'But I can't imagine he'll want her tied to a racing stables. Working in the yard and all that.'

'I'm sure she'll make up her own mind when the time comes.'

There was a hint of bleak frustration in Mrs Halstead's eyes. 'Well, I really do hope she doesn't dilly-dally and makes the right decision. It would be a great shame to jeopardize a marriage like this.'

Jan couldn't have agreed less. 'Mrs Halstead, I'm positive Bel will do the right thing,' she said non-committally. She glanced over the woman's shoulder as she was speaking and saw that Tony Robertson had just walked into the room and was looking around, presumably for her.

'Excuse me,' Jan said to her hostess as she waved to Tony. 'I've just spotted someone who won't know anyone else here, I think he's looking for me.'

As Tony reached them, he kissed Jan warmly on both cheeks before she introduced him to Mrs Halstead, who shook his hand, smiled vaguely and moved away.

Jan guessed Tony being there had something to do with Annabel. 'I didn't know Bel had invited you,' she said.

'She rang me at the last minute,' Tony replied, 'and said she'd meant to get you to ask me. Anyway, it's great to see they're really going ahead with it.'

'Do you really think so?' Jan questioned. 'I'm not at all sure it's a good match.'

'I know what you mean: Annabel's an angel and Lamberhurst's a bit of a shit. But lovely women often go for shits,' he added thoughtfully.

'I just hope it's not too late to talk her out of it,' Jan murmured under her breath. 'Now, Tony, you must let me introduce you to some of these other people; you don't want me to monopolize you all evening, do you?'

'I wouldn't mind.' The doctor smiled warmly.

'Ah, there's Colonel Gilbert; do you know him?' Jan asked.

Tony shook his head; Jan quickly caught the colonel's eye and a moment later was explaining to him who Tony was, and telling the doctor how much Colonel Gilbert had done for Megan by lending her such a smart pony as Monarch. Jan judged they had enough in common for her to leave them on their own, so she went through to the next room to find Penny Price, who had also been invited.

Jan found her shuffling her feet in a corner, looking abandoned and uneasy. Penny and her family lived a few miles away in Kington, and her mother had at one time been Mrs Halstead's cleaner. She was more than pleased to relive Arrow Star's run at Cheltenham with Jan and, for her part, Jan felt happier discussing horses with a genuine, knowledgeable owner than with any of the other guests at the party.

An hour or so later Jan felt she'd spoken to all the people she should and began looking around with a view to gathering up the members of her staff who had travelled with her. She was just wondering what had happened to Tony Robertson when he appeared looking slightly flushed and with an odd, benign smile on his face.

'Jan,' he said, and she realized at once that he'd been overdoing the freely flowing champagne. 'I want to ask you a really big favour.'

Jan looked at him as if he were a naughty child. 'Tony? What have you been up to? I've never seen you plastered before.'

'I do seem to have had rather a lot. That's why I was going to ask you if you could drive me home, please, Jan.'

'But I came here in the Shogun with six passengers. Who's going to get them back?'

'I know, I know. Emma says she hasn't had a drink – she doesn't like it – and she's quite happy to drive your car home.'

'I see.' Jan couldn't help grinning. 'You have been busy, haven't you? OK, Emma's driven it before and one thing's for certain – you can't possibly drive, the state you're in.'

❧

As Jan and Tony cruised along the dark, empty but narrow roads of west Herefordshire, they chatted warmly about the party, the horses and her plans for Christmas. Then suddenly he asked, 'Don't you think we should have a bit of supper?'

'Actually I had plenty of nibbles at the party,' Jan answered, thinking she would rather just get home.

'I didn't and I'm absolutely ravenous. I know there's a really good pub in about four miles. Would you mind if we stopped there for a quick bite?'

Jan was becoming suspicious. 'Tony, you seem to have sobered up pretty quickly. I think you've been pretending to be more drunk than you are, just to con me into driving. Is that the case?'

He laughed. 'A really well-meant subterfuge, I promise. I didn't want to pass up the chance of having you all to myself for a bit.'

Jan smiled. She didn't know Tony had it in him to pull off a performance like that. 'OK,' she said, 'but not for long, mind.'

When they reached the pub in the tiny hamlet of Ullingswick, Jan guessed Tony had been doing his homework. It was an enchanting little place, candlelit, with log fires and the aroma of good country cooking.

Once they had ordered and were settled at a small round table close to the fire with a bottle of wine between them, Tony reached out his hand and covered Jan's with a squeeze.

'Sorry to get you here under false pretences.'

Jan smiled, her eyes shining with good humour. 'I don't mind really; it's lovely here, and Fran's at home with the children. I'd better not have any wine, though.'

'One glass,' Tony insisted. 'I'd like to make a toast after all the excitement with Bel and Patrick. To Tony and Jan.'

Jan accepted the glass he had filled and lifted it halfway to her lips. 'But, Tony, we aren't a couple.'

'Aren't we?' he asked, head on one side. 'Don't you think we should be, Jan? We always seem to enjoy our time together. I want to be with you and the kids more than anything else in my life.'

'Are you about to ask what I think you are?'

Tony nodded slowly. 'Will you marry me, Jan? Please?'

Jan felt a lump in her throat and couldn't answer; she quickly looked away at the flames flickering over the apple logs in the fire; moments later she turned back to see his eyes filled with love and wanting.

'Oh, Tony,' she said softly, 'you've been so patient. I know there are lots of reasons why I should say "yes". You'd be a brilliant help with Matthew and Megan, and a tremendous support in my work. But, but . . . I just don't know; I guess I'm still not quite ready to make that total commitment. You'll have to give me a little more time.'

'But you're not saying "no"?' He looked eagerly into her eyes.

'No, Tony, I'm not.' She smiled tenderly. 'I promise you I'll think about it.'

🐎

Reg and Mary had come to Edge Farm for Christmas dinner with Jan and the children.

Although she'd considered asking others to join them, the extra work involved would have been too much of a burden as Jan had to get up early the following morning for a busy day's racing. Now she was glad that they weren't a large party, although she felt guilty about not asking Tony. He'd told her that he was going to see some friends in Oxford, so she suggested he dropped in for a drink on his way back during the evening.

He arrived while Jan's parents were still there and, as usual, focused his charm on Mary. Jan smiled at his tactics as he tried discreetly to find out whether or not she had told her mother about his proposal – which of course she hadn't.

Jan decided to take advantage of the situation and persuaded Tony to discuss her mother's renal problems with her. After a while he had convinced Mary she should go into hospital for the treatment her GP had recommended.

They ate Christmas cake and played the usual board games amidst a lot of laughter and when Tony left at the same time as her parents, Jan found she was grateful for the contribution he'd made to their day.

She watched thoughtfully from the kitchen window as the headlights of his car disappeared down the drive and turned north towards Broadway.

Jan let Megan stay up and watch *The Sound of Music* for the third time, while Matthew built a complicated Lego set his grand-parents had given him. With the children fully occupied, Jan began to tidy up. She wanted an early night herself, so she would be feeling extra fit to take a runner to the Boxing Day meeting at Kempton Park for the first time. A daunting experience.

It was going to be an important day for her, with Tom's Touch due to compete in a race a good step up from his previous encounters, but, in her view, capable of making a good impression. A.D. had already told her that he couldn't come over because of other commitments in Ireland. However, he said, he was delighted she thought the horse worth entering and would be watching on television.

As she finished washing up and was putting away the fine old canteen of silver cutlery that John had left her, Jan assessed the past year at Edge and decided that it had been rather patchy. But now, here was Tony Robertson, kind, good-looking, quietly amusing, and ready to throw everything he had at her feet. She nodded to herself. It might have been a tough year, but there had been some good and in fact even some great moments in it.

🐎

She put the children to bed tired and content. She read each of them a different story before she settled down herself, wrapped in her own soft duvet. Within minutes she had lost touch with the waking world, only to have her slumber shattered by the ear-piercing squeal of the telephone.

She stumbled around in the dark, still half asleep, until she found it.

'Hello,' she murmured.

'Hi, Jan. Happy Christmas!'

'Oh my God!' Jan jerked and sat bolt upright, fully awake. 'Eddie, is that you?'

'Yes, of course. How are you? I couldn't let Christmas go by without speaking to you, could I, even though it's already Boxing Day over here.'

'You always were late with everything.'

'Not true. Anyway – how's it all going?'

'Not bad,' Jan answered, while all the things she really wanted to say charged through her mind.

'I've been seeing a few good results coming through from Edge. Is Harlequin Holdings one of Gary West's?'

'That's right.'

'You've done really well for him – I expect he's delighted, though things seem to have gone rather sour for him out here.'

Jan closed her eyes. 'Please don't talk about it, Eddie, not tonight, I've had terrible problems with him.'

'Oh God! I'm really sorry, Jan. I felt really awful it was me that sent him to you!'

'For goodness sake, I'm not going to blame you. I thought it was manna from heaven when he first turned up. Anyway, they say his major problem might be solved soon.'

'Good, I hope so. But how are you, Jan?'

'I'm absolutely fine, thanks,' she answered breezily. 'I've been having a great time. Bel's getting married, by the way – to Patrick Lamberhurst.'

'Good God!' Eddie bellowed down the phone. 'Why on earth does she want to marry a prize shit like him?'

'That's what we're all wondering.' Jan laughed. 'I'm still keeping my fingers crossed she has a change of mind.'

'I should bloody hope so. Anyway, give her a big kiss from me and my love to everyone else.'

'Eddie, do you know if you're coming back?'

'Jan, don't ask me, not yet. Right now, I'm doing what I have to.'

'But are you happy?'

'You ought to know by now that I make it my business to be happy wherever I am.'

Jan choked back all the questions that seemed to follow on from there. 'Well, I'm glad to hear it,' she said.

'Oh, come on, Jan. You know I didn't want this to happen. But I can't put the clock back. It's happened and there it is.'

'OK, Mr Fantastic,' she said sarcastically. 'Thanks for calling. 'Byeee.'

She heard his answering 'Goodbye' as she put the phone back, knowing there was no way she could have kept the conversation going any longer without breaking down and making a complete fool of herself.

She lay back on her pillows, but this time she didn't sleep. For what seemed like an eternity she tossed and turned, as images of Eddie and Tony flashed through her mind, taunting her with the dilemma they posed.

Jan knew, even over the phone, that the slight change of inflection in A.D.'s voice signalled a major mood swing.

Almost from the moment Tom's Touch had set off at the start of his two-mile race at the busy Kempton meeting, she had regretted her decision to run him. It wasn't only that he was outclassed – on a good day she was sure he could have been more competitive – but there'd been something in his eye when they saddled him that had told her he just wasn't right.

She hoped the blood sample which Shirley would take and test in two days' time would pinpoint the problem, but she knew with this particular horse it was just as likely to be a psychological blockage that had put him off his racing.

She tried to explain this to A.D. afterwards.

'What d'you mean – a psychological block?' he asked. 'Are you telling me we should call in some equine shrink to have a little chat with him and find out if his mother deprived him of love when he was a foal?'

'No, of course I don't,' Jan answered, choosing to take A.D.'s words literally. 'I mean that sometimes, for no apparent physical reason, he just doesn't feel like racing. Of course, I could be wrong; that's why I'm getting Shirley to blood-test him as well to see if there's an underlying reason.'

'Well, I have to tell you, I'm really disappointed, Jan. Apart from that lucky win with Wexford Lad at Cheltenham, your yard has barely produced a result for me in eight months. And when I'm spending over a thousand quid a week with you, that's just not good enough. It's not as if your whole yard's out of form. You've been winning some decent races for your new Australian owner, who, I understand, doesn't even have the courtesy to pay you; and it's not as if the horses I've sent you aren't talented animals. We know that because you and other trainers have already won races with most of them in the past.'

'A.D., you know perfectly well that there's no pattern to these things. I can assure you I'd far rather be winning races for you than for Gary West, and I'm willing to admit that situation's turned into an entire nightmare. I'm doing everything I possibly can to get the best out of every horse in the yard, whether it's yours, West's, Penny Price's or whoever's.'

'Listen, Jan, I hear what you say, but I think we need a bit of a talk. You've Galway Fox entered for a two-mile hurdle at Ayr on January the second. I'll come over on the ferry to Stranraer and watch the race, then we can have dinner at the Turnberry Hotel; if the weather's nice, I can play a round on the Ailsa course the next morning.'

Jan put the phone down, conscious that A.D. telling her about his golfing plans was his way of making it clear she wouldn't be his only reason for making the trip across the Irish Sea.

🐎

Objectively, Jan could understand A.D.'s frustration, and she couldn't deny that until now he had been a model owner. She attributed his current attitude to the fact that he was seeing a pattern emerge which didn't make sense to him and he wanted to know what was going on.

In the week between Tom's Touch's failure at Kempton and

Jan's trip to Scotland's premier course with the Galway Fox, she sent out half a dozen runners with depressing results. On New Year's Eve, two days before she was due to travel up to Ayr with the horse, she had to ask Annabel to saddle their runners, while she drove her mother to the hospital in Cheltenham.

Tony Robertson had not only persuaded Mary to go, but had also, with her own doctor's consent, made sure she was seen as soon as possible.

Sitting beside Mary's bed before she went for a whole-body scan, Jan didn't resent for a moment the time she was devoting to her mother. It was, she felt, her chance to pay back all the years of care she had received at Mary's hands as a small and at times very wilful child.

'You don't have to stay, Jan,' the old woman said faintly, almost shaking with nerves at what lay ahead. 'You must have plenty of other things to do.'

Jan shook her head. 'Nothing as important as this, Mum.'

Mary gazed at her daughter with a mixture of worry and affection. 'It was your Tony that talked me into coming here.'

'Mum, I already know that, but he's not *my* Tony.'

'He's such a good man, Jan,' Mary went on, as if she hadn't heard Jan's denial. 'Well, don't leave him waiting in the wings for too long, my girl.'

Jan sighed. She didn't want to argue about it, not now; as it was, she was still questioning herself and she was no nearer giving Tony a definite answer to the question he had put to her before Christmas.

'The main thing is, Mum, now that you are here you've got to concentrate on getting better. They may keep you in for a few days and start the treatment straight away, so you must prepare yourself for that. OK?'

An hour or so later Jan drove away from the hospital, enveloped in an overpowering gloom that she could not disperse. Her mother was bravely facing up to the prospect of regular sessions on the dialysis machine to take some of the pressure off the one normal kidney that still functioned. Jan could sense Mary was dreading it, but knew her mother was determined not to make a fuss.

Hospitals always had a dispiriting effect on Jan and, given her concerns for her mother, the flat patch in her horses' performance, Gary West's evasiveness and A.D.'s cynicism, she felt she wouldn't be doing Tony Robertson any favours by saying 'yes' to him at this precise moment.

The following morning Jan set off to Ayr with a runner for the first time. Having learnt from her trip to Perth, she and Roz left early, allowing the whole day for the journey. Now she was glad that she had turned down everyone's invitation to welcome in the New Year. Roz had not shown the same restraint, however, and spent most of the journey slumped beside Jan in the cab of the lorry, her face a pale eau de Nil, while she slept solidly and groaned intermittently. But by the time they arrived at the racecourse stables some eight hours later, Roz had revived and started to earn her keep. A few other southern runners had already arrived. Their handlers greeted Jan and Roz warmly, making the unfamiliar surroundings of the Scottish track feel more normal.

About an hour later, when Jan was satisfied that the horse was settled and well wrapped up against the sharp, cold night, she and Roz went off to find the B and B where they were both staying. A.D. had invited Jan to be his guest in the much more luxurious surroundings of the hotel, but in view of the planned in-depth discussion she had decided to remain independent.

By the next morning the clear, star-filled night sky had been exchanged for a thick, dank mist which the local forecast gloomily predicted would lift perhaps just a hundred feet off the ground. Jan prayed that the racing would go ahead after enduring such a long journey and she judged that it probably would from the number of runners from the Scottish stables which began to appear, whose trainers understood the weather conditions in this area far better than she did.

The Galway Fox was having his first run since Jan's father had investigated and diagnosed a wolf tooth following the horse's erratic behaviour on the flat at Sandown. Since Shirley McGregor had extracted it, the horse had shown absolutely no sign of discomfort. But today he was going back over hurdles.

He had raced over them before and had jumped fluently, so once she'd seen the declared runners, Jan was quietly confident that he would put up a good performance and hoped his bit of speed would give him an extra edge over the opposition at Ayr, especially with the champion Murty McGrath on board.

Jan detected only a slight curtailment in the warmth of A.D.'s greeting when he arrived at the course an hour before the Galway Fox was due to run. And he was well up to date with the state of his horse's teeth and its fitness.

'So, Jan,' he said, 'do we feel we might be in for a bit of a result this afternoon?'

'I hope so. It was quite a slog coming up here.'

'But lovely once you arrive, don't you think?'

'It's beautiful,' Jan agreed, 'and the track is in good order, especially given the weather conditions over the last few days. Are you going to play golf tomorrow?'

'I hope so. Jimmy O'Driscoll's come over to join me for a game.'

'Is that one of the special duties of a racing manager?' Jan asked cheekily.

A.D. grinned. 'Provided he loses.'

Three furlongs from home, Jan knew that having Murty on board had given the Galway Fox a huge advantage. The canny Irish jockey had risked hugging the rail on the inside in fifth place as they came round the final, long, left-handed bend. He didn't move on his mount until they were well into the straight with just two flights left to jump, and lost little ground pulling over towards the stands side, where his horse could see a bit of daylight and stride out on the better going. But when he asked him for more, the Fox was immediately ready to deliver. They flew the last and continued to pull away on the run-in.

Jan glanced at A.D. as the horse crossed the line six lengths clear, still full of running.

The set position of his jaw and a barely perceptible nod told her the Irish tycoon was happy again and back on side.

He turned to face her with a slight smile. 'You've not lost your touch, girl. We can thank God for that!'

🐎

Dinner at the Turnberry Hotel was discreetly impressive. A.D. was well known there, whether by reputation or from previous visits Jan couldn't tell, but the Galway Fox's win was acknowledged by several people including the enthusiastic staff, who also recognized her as the trainer.

To Jan's relief, Jimmy O'Driscoll didn't join them, although she'd seen him at the racecourse, where he had grudgingly offered his bilious congratulations.

A.D., mellowed by his success, was now prepared to take a more lenient line than Jan guessed he'd originally planned. Nevertheless he wanted to go through the progress of every horse he owned in her yard, including the youngster who was yet to appear publicly and run in his first bumper.

'The thing is, Jan, I carry no passengers in my business, and I don't intend to carry them in my sport either. I don't expect my horses necessarily to make an operating profit, but I do expect most of them to make some contribution, however small, and, if they're not up to it, they don't get second chances – at least, not in my colours.'

'I hear what you're saying and that's fair enough, but like I've said before, I think every one you've got with me has a good chance of winning before the season's out. Some of them will take a bit of time to come to hand and it would be folly to rush them, but you have enough experience of this game to know that already.'

'Agreed. I accept that it would be most unusual to hold a full house as it were, but I can tell you you've got a reprieve for the moment. I was very pleased indeed with the way the Fox won today.'

25

For the next three weeks following Jan's success at Ayr the skies over the southern half of England seemed to dissolve. The few breaks in the clouds when the sun made a brief appearance didn't last long enough to dry the sodden ground into anything like a workable surface.

Jan had managed to keep most of her horses to their training schedule with the help of her new all-weather gallop, unlike the year before when the ground had remained frozen solid for almost as long. But with no regular racing to release the tension, she felt the frustration and stress levels in the yard increasing day by day.

At last the rain eased and a warm westerly blew long and hard enough to dry the ground. The going at Kempton Park on the last Saturday in January had been officially declared good to soft, as Jan set off with Annabel driving her to the Surrey course. The syndicate's Trojan Banquet was having its first run.

'I'm really looking forward to seeing your chief superintendent,' Annabel remarked as they sped east along the M4.

'Haven't you met him yet?'

'No, he's only been to the yard when I've been away.'

'They're a really good bunch: in a lot of ways more manageable than a single owner because they've all got different views, or no views at all, so it's easier, they said, just to let me decide what's going to happen.'

'Actually, I've heard it's not like that with all syndicates, especially if they've got an egotistical manager.'

'We'd better steer clear of them, then,' Jan chuckled.

'I'm so glad to see you in a half-decent mood again,' Annabel observed.

'That's not very fair,' Jan protested. 'You can't expect me to be full of the joys of spring when it's been pissing down with rain for the last three weeks and my biggest owner owes me nearly five months' training fees.'

'Maybe you'll be able to sell one of the horses soon now the debt's so high.'

'That is exactly what I've been thinking, and it just so happens that JCB's been making noises about getting another one.'

'Has he really?' Annabel said, pleased but a little surprised. 'I got the impression from Patrick that Johnny's interest was cooling a bit.'

Jan was puzzled. 'No, I don't think so – at least, not from the way he's been talking to me.'

'I'm afraid Patrick and I have had a bit of an antler clash. The trouble is he's beginning to give me stick for always working on Saturdays. He says we can never go away for a weekend.'

'What have you said to him about it?' Jan asked warily.

'I told him tough luck. "What do you expect me to do? Put a note on the horse's door saying 'See you Monday'?" Anyway, he knew I wasn't going to give up racing.'

'How did he take it?'

Annabel laughed. 'You could say he was a bit miffed, but he didn't throw any more toys out of his pram and eventually he backed down. He finally went on to say that people in racing are all totally boring because they never talk about anything else. So I told him at least we have something interesting and worthwhile to discuss.'

'Oh dear. Is that why we haven't seen much of him at the races?'

'There hasn't been a lot, but, basically, yes. He's coming today, though.'

'I'm looking forward to seeing him,' Jan said unconvincingly.

All of Sandy Wilson's syndicate came to watch Trojan Banquet run at the London course. They had booked a large hospitality box for the occasion and a no-expenses-spared lunch for their partners and friends. Jan and Annabel were treated like royalty; JCB had brought Patrick along to watch Miller's Lodge run in the big two-and-a-half-mile handicap chase, and they were both invited to join the party.

Shortly after she had arrived, Sandy Wilson touched Jan on the arm. 'A word in your shell-like,' he murmured, leading her away from the other guests. 'Have you gleaned any more about your old friend Harold Powell?'

Jan tensed, just at the sound of his name. 'I haven't heard a word from the police since well before Christmas.'

'My former colleagues in Powys seem to have given up the ghost, I'm afraid. They were advised by the CPS to drop the charges.'

Jan stared at him. 'Why? They've got a motive – sort of – and they've got a method.'

'Sadly, they don't have enough proof. I'm sorry, but it looks like you'll have to put your mother-in-law's death down as a tragic accident. If it's any consolation, they tell me it hasn't done Powell's standing in the community much good, so you'll have to settle for that for the time being.'

Jan wanted to ask him for more details, but now there were a number of people in the box whom she knew she should talk to. 'Can we discuss it some other time – I'll get all the details then?'

'Of course you can. Whenever.' The big man smiled and left Jan to the other members of the syndicate, who were anxious to hear her views on their horse's chances.

Miller's Lodge was running in the race before Trojan Banquet, so Jan and Annabel had to disappear soon after lunch to saddle him.

Patrick followed JCB down to the pre-parade ring and hovered there until he caught Jan's eye.

'OK, Jan,' he half whispered conspiratorially. 'JCB tells me this horse is a bit of a star. Will he be on form today?'

'Patrick, you know I won't give tips.'

'Yes, I understand that, but I'm practically part of the firm now and Bel's far too cautious to commit herself.'

'I can assure you it's not because she's too cautious; like me, she knows that tipping horses from the yard nearly always leads to trouble sooner or later.'

'So you do think it's worth tipping then?' he declared triumphantly.

Jan gave him a withering glare. 'I didn't say that. Use your own judgement. What I suggest you do is look at him in the paddock next to all the other runners and see if you think he's the best horse. What I can tell you is that his jumping's sound and when he's on song he's got a real turn of foot in a finish.'

Lamberhurst grinned. 'Well, that's good enough for me.'

Jan watched, shaking her head, as he strode off to find a bookie who would take whatever monstrous bet he was planning. As it happened, if she had thought Miller had no chance, she would have told him, but she was fairly sanguine about his prospects in this competitive field.

From the syndicate's box, Jan watched Miller's Lodge finish a creditable third. As previously arranged, Annabel dashed off to deal with their runner and bring him back to his slot in the unsaddling enclosure.

Anxiously, Jan glanced around to see if there was any sign of Annabel's fiancé, but he wasn't to be seen. *Too bad*, she thought, *if Patrick has 'lumped' on like he did at Chepstow and once or twice since, according to Annabel. I only told him what he could already have read in the morning papers, had he bothered to look.* And the horse had gone off third favourite.

Johnny had watched the race standing beside his trainer, and expressed himself well satisfied with the result.

'We should get a win out of him soon, all being well,' Jan said.

He glanced at her with an amused look in his violet eyes. 'Spare me the mushroom compost,' he said.

'But, Johnny, we will find a race for him,' Jan said more vehemently.

'If we do, we do. I pay you to train my horses; when I want a glimpse into the future, I'll consult a gypsy with a crystal ball.'

'That's fine by me.' Jan grinned. 'By the way, are you still interested in one of these West horses if it suddenly becomes available?'

'Yes, please. I'd be especially interested in Gylippus.'

Jan sighed. 'He's one of the most valuable, I'm afraid, so I may not be able to sell him first; it'll probably have to be one of the youngsters that hasn't run yet.'

Johnny looked at her quizzically. 'That seems a very odd arrangement.'

'I know, but that's the way it is,' she said apologetically. 'Anyway, I will have to do it soon.'

'Sooner than you think,' a voice growled behind her. She spun round and found Sandy Wilson standing right behind her.

'Sorry to eavesdrop,' he said, without a hint of apology in his voice. 'I've been doing it for so long I really can't help it. But I'm afraid I've got some bad news for you regarding your Mr West.' He glanced at Johnny Carlton-Brown. 'Do you mind if he hears? Still, it doesn't really matter. It'll be all over the papers by tomorrow anyway.'

Jan registered her resignation with a shrug. 'Go on. Tell me the worst.'

'The Serious Fraud Squad carried out a series of raids on the premises owned by West's British companies last night. John Tanner's been arrested and he'll be charged within the next couple of days. There's been some massive insurance and VAT swindle going on. Apparently, they've been trying to dig themselves out of the poo over Posidian, but now it's buried them. The FBI want Tanner extradited to the States, and no one can contact your man, Gary West. So, if he owes you money, you may have left it too late.'

'How come you know all this? I thought you were retired.'

'I am, but I was asked back to advise on some aspects of West's activities which I'd already started to investigate.'

Jan stared at him as she finally confronted the scenario which for some time her guts had been telling her was inevitable. 'But I thought they had a massive chunk of shares in Posidian and it was going to survive.'

Sandy Wilson shook his head. 'Oh no. They're in big trouble all right. There are half a dozen different agencies in the States after their blood and a lot of important people are going to lose an awful lot of money.'

'But I've got an agreement with Gary West that I can sell his horses to cover my training debts.'

'That won't be worth the paper it's written on if he and his operations are declared bankrupt. You'll just have to join the queue for your money with the rest – and I can tell you now, there won't be any.'

'When do you think this will all happen?'

'It could take a week before all the assets are frozen, at least.'

Jan stared at him bleakly, reluctant to believe what he was saying. 'But that could cost me everything.'

'Then you'd better see what you can do before it's all grabbed.'

Jan found herself trembling with fear at the prospect of Gary West's debacle and what it could do to her and she was struggling to focus on the next race, which Trojan Banquet was running in and the syndicate hoped to see win.

She left the box and met Annabel in the weighing room. It was only her own preoccupations which stopped her noticing that Annabel's face was like thunder.

'The bastard,' Bel hissed.

Jan glanced at her in surprise. 'Have you heard about Gary West, then?'

Annabel looked at her quizzically. 'What are you talking about?'

'What are *you* talking about? Who's a bastard?'

'Patrick – Lord bloody Lamberhurst!'

Jan tried to make the jump from her own crisis to Annabel's, in the faint hope that maybe the position there was looking a little healthier.

'What's happened?'

'He's absolutely fuming; he lost two grand on Miller and he says it's your fault – and mine. He says I should have told him there was a chance the horse might get beaten. I ask you! For God's sake! Where's he been all his life if he thinks any yard can guarantee its runners are going to win?'

Lamberhurst's behaviour didn't surprise Jan, but she felt extremely sorry for her friend. 'What did you tell him?'

'I told him to bloody well grow up and that he shouldn't gamble if he wasn't man enough to take the losses. Then he turned really nasty and told me he was sick of me spending my whole time shovelling shit, especially when I couldn't even tell him which of our horses was going to win.'

Jan's hackles rose at this direct challenge to Annabel's position in her yard. 'The stupid bastard!'

Annabel nodded. 'I said – in that case forget the wedding plans. I'd rather shovel shit than marry it!'

Even in her present state of anxiety, Jan laughed. 'Brilliant. And, Bel, I can tell you, with everything that's going on, I really don't want to lose you just at the moment.'

'Don't worry,' Annabel said grimly. 'I can assure you I'm not going anywhere. Now, tell me, what the hell's happened to Gary West?'

Jan and Annabel felt they had to stay to celebrate with the syndicate when Trojan Banquet won for them first time out, but using the excuse they must get back to Edge to put the precious animal to bed, they slipped away from Kempton soon after the lorry left with the horses on board.

They were both just coming to terms with Annabel's abrupt ending of her relationship with Patrick, and were relieved to talk about something else as they faced up to the new crisis at Edge.

'Somehow, I've got to get hold of Gary and tell him what will happen to us. If necessary, I'll have to beg him to agree to me selling all the horses to our existing owners.'

'Jan, you've got to be awfully careful. You don't want to do anything illegal or that'll get you into even more trouble. Why don't you ring Toby and ask him to come over? I'm pretty sure he's staying with George Gilbert this weekend.'

'Fine, as long as Virginia doesn't get to hear that the shit's hit the fan.'

'If you're talking about Patrick, I wish he would hit the fan.'

Annabel grimaced then tittered. 'But, seriously, Toby wouldn't dream of discussing your business with Virginia. You know that.'

Toby was as loyal as the women had predicted and immediately dropped whatever plans he had and promised to be at Edge Farm after evening stables.

The children were fed and playing in the drawing room as Jan, Annabel and Toby sat down round the kitchen table and tried to draw up a plan to deal with the crisis.

'Frankly,' Toby said when Jan had related the information she'd received from Sandy Wilson, 'I honestly don't see what we can do. I know you've been trying to get hold of Gary for weeks and have been fobbed off by everyone you speak to, which is not unusual in these circumstances. So, as I understand things, you can't sell the horses without his agreement other than to cover his debt to you. By law, if he goes under, it will be up to the receiver to sell his assets and that'll almost certainly mean selling the horses at public auction to avoid accusations of insider dealing.'

'So I could lose them all just when I'm beginning to get somewhere with them?' Jan asked shakily.

'Yes, as well as the money you're already owed.'

'Oh, my God, I just don't think I can swallow all that at the moment, Toby.'

'You mustn't panic, Jan. It won't be easy, I can see that. But there are several people around who'd be prepared to help out. After all, we should be able to sort out something with Olwen's bungalow in the next few months.'

'But what about now? I really don't want to go round with a begging bowl and I certainly can't borrow any more from the bank – they've already got a charge on this house.'

'Well, it's up to you, Jan. You may lose a bit of independence if A.D. gets involved, but at least your children's future will be more secure.'

'Actually, I'm not so bloody sure it would be. A.D.'s a business-man first and foremost – a fair-weather friend possibly.'

'Jan,' Annabel cut in, 'that's not fair, and you know it. As far as

I can tell, A.D.'s always told you exactly where he stands and has never suggested that he was doing you any favours.'

'I'm sorry,' Jan conceded. 'You're right and that's precisely why I don't want to do a deal with him like the one he put to us last summer. But how about this? Suppose I got a message to Gary that, if I sold his horses for him, after I'd taken out what he owes me I'd get the balance to him – he might go for that, particularly if he's up against it everywhere else.'

Toby shook his head doubtfully. 'Quite frankly, West's difficulties are so profound, a few hundred grand is barely going to touch the sides, and if you're not extremely careful, you'd almost certainly be perceived as having helped to defraud the other creditors.'

By the time Toby and Annabel had left, Jan felt no less fearful for her future than she had when Sandy first broke the news to her at Kempton. Reports of the raids, which had been carried out discreetly, were beginning to surface on the late-night news bulletins that interrupted the music Jan listened to on the radio as she tried to go to sleep.

But her mind was in complete turmoil and sleep was impossible. After an hour she leapt out of bed and switched on the overhead light before frantically rummaging through her wardrobe.

It had suddenly just come back to her. It was during the first and only time she had met Gary West, when he had taken her and Annabel to dinner after their foray in Crockford's, and he had become expansive. 'I'm going to give you something I never normally give to women,' he had said, taking an old cloakroom ticket from his jacket and scrawling two numbers on it. 'I can be pretty hard to get hold of at times; there are lot of people in my organization whose day is devoted to diverting callers away from me, and I have to say they're very good at it, but just in case you ever need to contact me urgently about anything, you can always reach me on my mobile or this private fax number.'

Up to now, Jan had completely forgotten about the incident and the slip of paper. Now she tried desperately to remember which handbag she had been carrying that night when, as she vividly recalled, she and Annabel had been dressed up to the nines. She had borrowed a dress of Annabel's and had taken the only evening bag she possessed.

Not used since, it was tucked at the back of a shelf. She pulled it out triumphantly and tipped it upside down over her dressing table. A clatter of odd items, make-up, a small pen and an invitation to a dance at Cheltenham from the year before tumbled out, and, fluttering behind them, Gary West's discarded cloakroom ticket.

She grabbed it, as if it was a lifebelt and she was in the middle of the ocean, and checked the numbers were still readable. At first her heart fell with a thud. The mobile phone number was the one she had originally rung, back in October, which had produced the courier and eight thousand pounds. But since then she had dialled that number probably two dozen times and it had never been answered.

But the fax number was completely new to her.

Carrying it carefully, as if it were a piece of fragile china, she went down to the kitchen, where her fax machine stood on a small cabinet.

On the table, still cluttered with the mugs and glasses she and the others had used during their council of war, she wrote the fax number in her address book beneath all the other contact numbers for Gary West she had accumulated. Taking a sheet of headed paper from the desk under the window, she sat down and wrote:

Dear Gary,

    I've just heard that John Tanner's been arrested and that all your offices in London and the US have been closed pending investigation by the Fraud Squad and the FBI.

    I really don't know what's going on and I don't want to know, but I have bought and successfully trained a lot of horses for you in good faith. I am the sole owner of a very small business, which is my only source of income, and as you are already aware I am a widow with two young children to bring up. I have borrowed a lot of money to improve my yard as you stipulated in order to take on your horses. Now, through your actions, all this is likely to be destroyed and I am in great danger of losing everything I own, including our home.

Please let me know immediately what you can do to help me avoid this complete disaster.
     Yours faithfully,
          Jan Hardy

Jan read and re-read the letter, tweaking it here and there until she felt it was as effective as it could be in appealing to West's conscience and the sense of fairness she hoped he possessed.

She inserted the sheet of paper into the machine and dialled.

She waited a few moments before she heard the hiss and whistles of the receiving machine. With a faint heart but slightly more hope that she might be getting somewhere, she pressed the start button and watched the equipment suck in her letter.

At last, after the gut-wrenching fluctuations of the day, Jan felt she had done all she could for the time being, so went back upstairs and climbed wearily into bed and this time she quickly fell asleep.

Jan was on tenterhooks for the whole of Sunday, although she'd tried to carry on with family life as if nothing unusual had happened. By the evening, when she still hadn't heard from Gary West, she had to convince herself that it was unrealistic to have expected a response over the weekend.

Jan and Declan set off early on Monday morning to take Holy Mist to Fontwell. She had left strict instructions that any calls from West should be forwarded immediately to her mobile phone. Holy Mist, the youngster she'd bought for Gary in June, was due to run in his first bumper, which she hope he might win – at least she would get her percentage. The irony that it was one of his horses hadn't escaped her.

Jan was going all-out to increase her tally of winners and she didn't care where she went to do it. She was making the long and tedious journey to the small Sussex course on a damp Monday morning at Finbar Howlett's suggestion. The horse was fresh and had worked so well on the gallops that Finbar felt he could win a small race first time out.

Despite the fact Jan kept telling herself she could handle the

West crisis if the rest of her life went on normally, she was now under so much pressure that she couldn't stop shaking as she adjusted her runner's bridle.

Waiting to watch the race on her own in the stands, she caught her breath with frustration. She sniffed back the tears that were welling up in her eyes and looked around to make sure no one had noticed, then quickly turned her attention back to the track.

Holy Mist, a beautifully dappled grey which had inspired the rather unimaginative name John Tanner had chosen for him, was skipping round the track and still well on the bridle with just two furlongs to run. Jan silently nodded her approval as she saw Finbar lengthen his rein a little. The gelding, free at last, lengthened his stride and slipped the field with one other horse, right behind Finbar's left shoulder.

The two leaders quickly opened up a gap of fifteen lengths from the rest of the field; but twenty yards from the finish Jan saw her jockey take a quick look over his right shoulder and drop his hands.

The second horse seized the opportunity and surged past on the far side. Despite Finbar's desperate efforts to pick his horse up and fight back, it was too late.

All the tension that had wound Jan up like a coiled spring since Sandy Wilson had dropped his bombshell exploded in a rush of anger as she ran down to the track to meet the horse.

'What the bloody hell was all that about?' she shouted at Finbar, oblivious to the other jockeys coming in from the track.

'I'm sorry, Mrs H. I thought it was in the bag and I didn't want to flog the horse. I never saw that other fella come through. He caught me napping.'

'Have I ever, ever told you to drop your hands on the run-in? My horses are always ridden out to the line. You do realize we are both going to be up in front of the stewards now, don't you? They certainly won't let that go; and you'll have to do a bloody sight better job convincing them than you have me, you stupid pillock.'

As Jan walked behind the horse into the unsaddling enclosure, she became aware that a lot of people were looking at her, mildly shocked by her outburst. Taking a deep breath to get a better grip on herself, she looked up at Finbar. 'We'll talk about this later,' she said through clenched teeth, 'but God help you if I find out you've been up to any monkey business, you'll live to regret it.'

Finbar, who had been staring at her in amazement since the start of her tirade, jumped down. 'Mrs Hardy,' he said, 'if you really do think I did that deliberately so as not to win the race, I'd prefer never to ride for you again.'

He whipped off his tack and marched to the weighing room, leaving Jan gazing after him remorsefully. She hadn't really believed he'd done it on purpose, but with all the extra stress she was under and the memory of Billy Hanks's disloyalty, it wasn't surprising that she had got a little wound up, she thought.

Jan took another deep breath. By now a small crowd had gathered around the enclosure and she glanced around with what she hoped was a cheerful smile. But inside she felt saddened by what she'd just said to Finbar.

When the stewards saw Finbar, they accepted his explanation, but suspended him for two days and advised him that it was his duty to always ride a horse out to the end of the race to avoid what had happened that afternoon.

Outside Jan touched the jockey on the arm as he walked away.

'Finbar, have you got a ride in the last?'

'Yes,' he answered guardedly.

'I'm sorry for what I said. I owe you a drink. Will you let me get you one afterwards?'

He looked at her steadily with his bright blue eyes and sighed. 'Mrs Hardy, I've heard you've a few problems not of your own making. Maybe that's put you under a bit of pressure and what I did today would have got me mad if I'd been in your position.' He nodded. 'Sure, I'll have a drink with you.'

'I'll see you in the owners' and trainers' then, after the last.'

Somewhat to Jan's surprise, Finbar won the last race. After he had weighed in, the owners of the horse wanted him to join them for an in-depth confab while Jan lingered a little impatiently, anxious to be on her way home. But when he eventually walked over to join her, looking all scrubbed and innocent, she gave him a big smile.

'Well done, Finbar! You didn't drop your hands that time and look what happened.'

'All right, all right, Mrs H. We've done that already.'

'Something tells me you won't be doing it again for a while. Anyway, what would you like?'

'I'll have a Coke, please,' Finbar said coyly.

Jan had completely forgotten that he never touched alcohol, but despite that, twenty minutes in the bar put their relationship back to where it had been previously, and Jan watched gratefully as he left to get his canvas holdall before driving home with another jockey.

She was just about to go and look for Declan and check over the horse when her mobile rang. She dived into the big leather bag dangling from her shoulder and scrabbled in it to find the bleeping phone.

'Hello?'

'Jan?' It was her assistant.

'Oh, hello, Bel. I was hoping it might be Gary West.'

'He's just rung. I told him to try you at the races, but he wouldn't; he's calling again tonight.'

'What did he say?'

'Only what I've told you.'

'Didn't he say anything about what he intended to do, or if I can sell the horses?'

'No, Jan. He just said he would ring you at nine o'clock our time.'

'Did he get my fax?'

'I've already said he didn't say a word other than what I've told you,' Annabel answered wearily. 'Jan, please calm down. Just wait until he rings you later.'

'It's all right for you, Bel. You have no idea how stressful this all is with the kids and everything.'

'Jan, I've every idea; I've been living with it for the last four months, remember. Anyway, what happened in the stewards' room?'

'Finbar told them he hadn't seen that other horse and thought there was no need to ride the horse harder to win the race.'

'Did they believe him?'

'Yes, they did, actually.'

'Did you?'

'Yes,' Jan grunted. 'But I was so bloody angry when he came off the course.'

'Oh dear,' Annabel said quietly.

'It's OK. I apologized after and bought him a Coke.'

'Good. Do you want me around when Gary West phones?'

'Please, Bel, that would be really great.'

Jan spent the next five hours in a semi-state of limbo, in which nothing was tangible and life had been virtually suspended. Waiting with her in the house, Annabel tried to drag her back to the real world.

'Jan, even if Gary won't help out, it's not the end of the world. You can't just throw everything else away; you'll have to be strong,' Annabel insisted.

'But this whole fiasco could set me right back if he doesn't. I'll have to change my plans, retrench and go cap in hand to the bank, asking for them to spread my repayments over God knows how long. I *never* wanted to be in this situation in the first place. If it was only me, it wouldn't matter so much, but you've absolutely no idea what it feels like to have two defenceless human beings so utterly dependent on you.'

'I can imagine. Besides, I've already told you, I'm quite happy to lend you the money, interest free, no strings attached and no partnership.'

'There's no way I'd let you do that. Suppose I didn't make it and I couldn't pay you back either. It doesn't bear thinking about.'

Annabel raised an eyebrow and stood up. 'I'll make some more tea,' she said flatly. As she walked across to the Aga, the phone rang. Jan glanced at the clock; it was exactly nine o'clock. She grabbed the receiver and gasped into it, 'Hello?'

'Jan. This is Gary West.'

'Thank God!' Jan couldn't help exclaiming.

'I don't know about that, but I got your fax. Of course I knew you would be in the mire as a result of my problems. I can't tell you how sorry I am. The situation I've found myself in now wasn't even on the horizon when I first asked you to get those horses for me. Jan, I hope you believe that. You've bought some excellent animals, and I wish I'd been able to enjoy the success we've had with them. And now I really do hope you'll be able to go on winning with them – if you can persuade some of your existing owners to buy them, that is, but they'll have to make up their minds pretty quickly.'

Jan clutched the phone fiercely as relief tingled through her like bubbles in a glass of champagne. She grinned at Annabel, who was staring at her, eager for enlightenment.

'I'm fairly sure I can,' Jan murmured.

'I've sent you by express mail my signed consent to sell all the horses owned by Harlequin Holdings at a valuation put on them by one of the reputable bloodstock agents. I'm authorizing you to hold the money in an escrow account for me, having deducted all training and racing fees and all other expenses to date. I'll let you know what to do with the balance in due course. By the way, I should also inform you that John Tanner is no longer a director of Harlequin Holdings and has no authority whatsoever in its affairs. Do you understand?'

'Yes,' Jan said. 'But is there any chance that what you're asking me to do is illegal? Will it get me into any bother with the law?'

'No, provided you do it within the next eight or nine days. It should take them at least that long to discover that Harlequin Holdings has any connection with me, which they might not. But if they do, I'm afraid things will be out of my hands, and you may be asked to pass the proceeds of the sale of the horses on to a receiver. I'd be grateful if you could resist these requests as long as possible. You shouldn't have any trouble hanging onto the funds that relate to your debt directly. The receiver should accept them as legitimate payable expenses.'

Jan's head was swimming as she tried to absorb the ramifications of what he was saying. 'You do promise me I'm completely in the clear?'

'Ask a UK lawyer to confirm it if you're in any doubt, but if you want to recover your money do it soon. Right, I've got to go, Jan. I'm really sorry our relationship has turned out the way it has, but we all have to take risks in life, and I'm afraid I've always taken the view that the bigger the risk, the bigger the reward.' Jan could almost see him shrug his shoulders philosophically.

'Thank you, Gary,' she said in a small voice, overawed by the scale of his downfall. 'Goodbye.'

'' 'Bye, Jan, take care of yourself and good luck.'

Jan stared at the phone before she put it down on the table.

'Well?' Annabel asked.

'That's it. He says I can sell the horses.'

'Fantastic! How are you going to do it?'

Jan took a deep breath. 'It'll have to be A.D. first.'

'Why? Johnny's definitely interested. I think Patrick was bullshitting when he said he wasn't.'

'I know A.D. will want Gylippus.' Jan shrugged. 'And I've got to do the whole deal as quickly as possible, before they make Harlequin Holdings bankrupt.'

She picked up the phone and dialled A.D.'s mobile number.

26

Less than twenty-four hours after Jan had spoken to Gary West on the phone, she was being driven by Annabel to Birmingham Airport to catch a Dublin flight.

A.D. was too busy to travel over from Ireland. 'If you want to do this, you'll have to see me here at Aigmont,' he had told her.

Jan had all the paperwork relating to the Harlequin Holdings bloodstock neatly stowed in a small briefcase. She and Annabel had discussed every permutation of the deal until their heads were spinning, but in the end they decided it was a question of whether or not A.D. would feel like playing ball and they had no way of telling whether he would or not.

'For God's sake, Jan,' Annabel reproached her, 'stop fretting about it. If he doesn't, we'll just have to think of something else. Now calm down and relax, or he'll take one look at you and decide you're too damned neurotic to be training any of his horses.'

Jan gave a faint smile. 'I suppose you're right. But I must admit, right now even a dozy slob like Eddie would be useful. He never got flustered by anything.'

'That's because he doesn't give a damn about anything.'

'That's not true, actually.'

'It's best left, Jan, but I think you're lucky to have someone like Tony sticking around.'

'I know I am,' Jan continued thoughtfully. 'I'm bloody positive Eddie's never coming back anyway. I could tell from the tone of his voice when he rang at Christmas, it was as if he was settled there and just needed to check up on his past.' Jan shrugged. 'And now

Tony's pressing me for an answer.' She turned and grinned at Annabel. 'Is that reasonable? I've only had a month.'

'Well, you need to tell him one way or the other,' Annabel chided her. 'Actually, I think he'd be very good for you. He'd be able to calm you down especially at times like this; he understands the business and the highs and lows of dealing with competition horses.'

'I know. I'm not being exactly fair and I am coming round to the idea. I'd just like to get this West business all done and dusted before I make a final decision about something so vitally important. I don't intend to say "yes", then blow him out a month later, like some people,' she added, squinting at Annabel scornfully.

Annabel glanced at her, open-eyed. 'Don't tell me you were upset about that,' she chastised Jan. 'I know perfectly well you didn't like Patrick.'

Jan coughed before continuing. 'Have you heard from him since Kempton?'

'No, not a squeak.'

'What about JCB?'

Annabel gaped at her friend questioningly. 'No, why should I? Or did you think Patrick would use him to try and talk me back into the marriage?'

'No, not really; I just wondered.'

'Johnny'll be sorry not to get Gylippus if A.D. does take all West's horses.'

'I know that, but I also know what A.D.'s like. He's not going to have any if he thinks a cherry picker's been there first.'

🐎

Daragh, as arranged, met Jan at the airport in one of A.D. O'Hagan's big Mercs and, with his usual patter, sped her round the edge of Dublin on a swishing wet motorway to the Naas Road, only stopping to pay the toll before heading on down to Aigmont, nestling on the lower slopes of the Wicklow Mountains.

A.D. and his wife were both still up when Jan arrived just after midnight. There had been a dinner party, they said, but the other guests had already left.

Jenny Pitman

'I told Daragh to make good time,' A.D. said, glancing at his watch approvingly. 'Now, can I offer you a glass of something as a nightcap?'

As they settled down in front of the glimmering fire in the luxurious drawing room, Siobhan asked about the children.

'Megan's been doing wonderfully well with Monarch,' Jan told her proudly. 'She's already been entered for Peterborough and she's really keen to take him to as many Pony Club events as she can this summer.'

Siobhan nodded. 'And how is she getting on at school?'

'Oh, fine. She's taken up the recorder and at the moment she loves it. And seems to have a natural talent, though I don't know where she gets it from.'

'I feel music is one of the best things a young mind can have – discipline, achievement and, above all, beauty, all wrapped in one.'

Jan nodded, although she hadn't seen it in those terms before.

'It was Virginia Gilbert's father who lent Megan the pony, wasn't it?' A.D. asked. 'There's a nice irony to that.'

'Not so much as there is in the fact that he's still got his best horse with me and not her.'

'He's no fool, then.' A.D. grinned in a way Jan found reassuring, particularly in view of the proposition she was about to put to him.

'Now,' A.D. said, rising to his feet, 'we'll talk about these horses in the morning, but I'm afraid it will have to be rather early; I've another important meeting here at nine o'clock sharp.'

Jan gulped. It seemed unreasonable to ask her over to discuss a deal so critical to her in a few snatched minutes after breakfast.

'There'll be coffee in my office at seven. I'll see you then. Mario's taken your things up to your room. I hope you sleep well.' He gave an ambiguous shake of his head and, taking his wife by the hand, walked from the room.

Siobhan looked back over her shoulder. 'Goodnight, Jan. Maybe I'll see you in the morning.'

Jan set the alarm clock beside her bed to go off at six, and fell asleep slightly more confident that she was at least halfway to transferring ownership of Gary West's four good horses.

When she woke in the dark, grateful for a night of deep untroubled slumber, albeit a short one, she washed and dressed quickly before picking up her leather briefcase and feeling her way quietly down the broad stairs to the library, which she knew A.D. called his office.

She switched on the light. In front of a heavily curtained tall bay window was a large mahogany coffee table placed between two easy chairs.

Taking her time, Jan laid out a display with the details of each horse she wanted A.D. to buy, which included a photograph and a neat printout of its form to date, its breeding and a record of the price paid at each change of ownership.

She had also brought along videos of Gylippus, Magic Maestro and Holy Mist in action.

She was just about satisfied when A.D.'s Italian butler walked silently into the room, barely showing any surprise at her being there. He was carrying a tray with a pot of steaming coffee and a plate of warm croissants. Seeing Jan's display on the table, he did a U-turn and placed the tray on the desk. 'Good morning, madam. Mr O'Hagan will be down very shortly – at seven.'

'Thank you.' Jan smiled and watched the servant glide from the room like a swan on a lake. She was impressed by the way A.D. ran his household and, as far she knew, all his business operations were the same. She had found that whatever target he set his sights on had to be achieved to the highest possible standard. There was, she supposed, something intimidating about such efficiency, but from where she stood in relation to him as an owner, it made dealing with him far easier than other more casual owners, who tended to have selective memories when it came to their horses.

As the large ormolu-cased clock on the mantelpiece struck seven, Jan heard the sharp click of A.D.'s metal-capped heels on the marble floor in the hallway.

He breezed in, looking as if he'd just returned from a week in a health spa.

'Good morning, Mrs Hardy. You beat me to it; still, the starter's not even lifted his flag yet.' He pressed on as though he was admonishing her for cheating.

'As there isn't too much time, I wanted to get everything ready that I thought you'd like to see.'

A.D. glanced at her neat display. 'Good thinking.' He nodded his approval. 'Coffee? Croissant?'

'Just coffee for me, please.'

'Ah, watching the carbohydrates, eh? Very wise. But these are my only indulgence,' A.D. said, as he helped himself to one of the flaky pastries and filled two cups with black coffee and hot milk. 'Right, let's get down to work,' he went on, glancing at his watch in what Jan guessed was probably a reflex action.

'OK,' she said tentatively. 'Gary West has given me authority to sell all the horses he has in our yard. I'm entitled to take what he owes me in training fees, racing expenses, vets' bills and so on.'

'Do you have that authority in writing?'

'It's on its way. I should have it by tomorrow.'

'Fine, but anything we agree today is subject to me seeing that authority. Is that all right?'

'Of course.' Jan nodded in agreement.

'As I understand it,' A.D. continued, 'all West's American and UK operations are under investigation, and his Australian business is already on the skids. So I don't really see how, if the vehicle which owns his horses goes bust, you'll be able to keep your money, but still that's your business not mine, so the best of luck to you.' A.D. leaned forward to inspect the documents Jan had laid out. 'Right, what have we got here?'

Starting with the best, Gylippus, Jan ran through the career and characteristics of each horse in turn. When she had finished, she didn't doubt that A.D. had absorbed every skerrick of information she'd given him.

He smiled. 'You did a grand job for the Aussie, I'll give you that. There are undoubtedly three very nice horses here. I'm not so sure about the bay four-year-old. I never really liked his sire, but otherwise that's a pretty good hand.'

'You'd have to take the lot though, A.D.'

'Well, maybe, perhaps you could sell any dross for me. Now – money. I'll tell you what I'm prepared to pay for each individual.'

'But I've got the BBA coming to the yard today – Annabel's dealing with them. They're going to do the valuations and that will be the price Gary West authorizes me to sell them for to avoid any comeback.'

'I completely understand what he's doing and why, but I'm not in the charity business – at least, not as far as the Aussie's blood-stock's concerned. Here's what I'll do – I'll write my offer for each horse on your list, and I'll pay that price, or the valuation price, whichever is the lower. That's fair enough, don't you think?'

Jan had been dreading the haggling. Normally she'd expect it, but in this case her hands were completely tied by West's stipulations and the possibility that she might in some way be held to account if she was deemed to have undersold the horses to an insider for less than their true market price.

She gritted her teeth. 'OK, fine,' she said. 'But A.D., please don't play games over this. We just don't have time.'

A.D. threw her a fixed gaze but said nothing. Holding the sheet of paper with the list of horses' names, he got up and walked over to sit behind his expansive mahogany desk; he picked up a pen and beside each name he wrote a figure. He folded the paper in half and handed it back to Jan.

'And please remember this, young lady: the only games I play are golf and poker.'

🐎

At nine o'clock precisely A.D. straightened his tie and went into his next meeting. He'd told Jan he was leaving the house straight afterwards and would not be able to see her again today.

Jan didn't really mind as they had achieved all they could for the time being, though she had booked a late-afternoon home flight. To change it would mean wasting enough money to offend her sense of frugality, but it also meant having to 'kill' half the day, and she hated wasting time almost as much as wasting money. She rang Sean McDonagh, who, despite the short notice, said he was completely free and would be delighted to pick her up and run her into

Dublin, and he could try to arrange for her to look at a couple of horses on the way. They spent a useful day together, meeting new breeders and inspecting several young horses that would be coming up for sale later in the year.

Feeling more hopeful of a satisfactory deal with A.D. and Gary West, Jan sat in the departure lounge at Dublin airport with her mood more relaxed than it had been for a long time. When Tony Robertson unexpectedly rang her mobile and asked her if she would like to meet in Birmingham and go out for dinner, she accepted with pleasure, sensing it would be just the right ending to the day.

Tony was waiting for her in the arrivals hall with a beaming smile on his face and a single long-stemmed red rose in his hand. When she saw him, Jan wondered what it was that still stopped her from giving him the answer he so desperately sought.

He hugged her warm-heartedly before kissing her lightly on both cheeks and fleetingly on the lips, then quickly picked up her case and led her to the car park.

Driving at a crawl through the rush hour traffic on the M42, he wanted to hear everything that had happened during her twenty-four hours in Ireland. She was rather surprised by how much he seemed to know regarding the places she'd visited. He was also aware of the significance if A.D. bought Gary West's horses and recognized what a huge load it would be off her mind once a deal was completed.

They stopped for an early supper in a cosy Italian restaurant near Evesham and Jan rang home to talk to the children. Megan, as usual, was bursting with exciting news of – what seemed to her – earth-shattering events in her life, and even Matty allowed himself to sound enthusiastic at hearing his mother's voice. She told them to behave, that she would be back later and would see them in the morning.

Tony sat opposite her at the small table, gazing at her as she checked her mobile phone was switched off before dropping it in her bag.

'So have you had a chance to think about the proposal I put to you before Christmas?'

'Of course I have, Tony. I've thought of little else until recently. And I want you to know how pleased I was to see you at the airport with that great big grin on your face and such a beautiful rose!' Jan chuckled and shook her head. 'You silly old thing. That was so romantic – you've been really good to me and I don't really deserve it.'

He leaned forward a little. 'But you do, Jan, and more. You've been so brave this past year when things have been going so dreadfully wrong. Of course, you've got Annabel to back you up, but in the end, as far as I can see, everything rests entirely on your shoulders. I really don't know how you do it.'

Jan shrugged. 'I do quite like a challenge sometimes,' she said with a mischievous grin.

'Well, that's good news, so what do you think about the one I've put to you?'

'Tony, I have to be honest and tell you exactly what I feel, funnily enough I only said this to Bel yesterday while we were driving to the airport. As soon as I've got this awful Gary West business sorted I'm hoping I can clear my head and take a completely balanced view of my life.' She gave him a quick smile, to encourage him. 'I wouldn't want to say "yes" unless it was for the right reason and I had given the decision a hundred per cent. I hope you don't mind too much, but I would like to leave my answer until then. Tony, I need to be sure for everyone's sake.'

He leaned back in his chair and Jan tried to gauge his reaction. He seemed only mildly put out, she thought, and was probably confident that she'd come round to the idea in time.

Maybe he's right, she thought. *I could certainly do a hell of a lot worse.*

🐎

Jan's relaxed mood persisted as they drove home. As they reached the outskirts of Broadway, Tony turned slightly and gave her hand a gentle squeeze.

'A quick nightcap at my place?' he asked.

'Why not?' She smiled.

Jan had paid a brief visit to Tony's Cotswold stone cottage once before with the children, when they'd been on their way to a show with Monarch. She had deliberately avoided going there on her own since, aware of the potential consequence.

It was an exceptionally pretty house, spotless inside and decorated in a typical country style. He had often told Jan about his fondness for paintings, so she took her time and inspected them properly.

Tony knelt down in front of the hearth and put a match to a pile of kindling and dry ash logs, which were blazing within minutes.

'Right,' he said, getting to his feet. 'Drink?'

'That would be great. What are you having?'

'Nothing, since I've got to drive you home.'

'Very wise,' Jan said reflectively. The thought had just flitted through her mind that maybe he wouldn't need to drive her home tonight.

'I'll have a glass of wine, please. Just a small one,' she added hesitantly, having suddenly decided that she couldn't handle staying here too long after all.

As Jan slowly sipped the merlot, Tony sat opposite with his coffee and considered how perfect this would be on a permanent basis. They chatted with an unhurried familiarity about the more personal things in their lives.

When her glass was empty, Jan abruptly declined another and quickly got to her feet. 'Tony, I really ought to be going, but thanks for picking me up and for such a lovely meal,' she said.

'I'm just glad you enjoyed it,' the doctor agreed, getting up briskly. Nothing in his manner suggested he was annoyed at her decision to leave. 'I'll have you home in less than fifteen minutes,' he continued lightly.

At first Jan didn't resist when he put his arms around her and squeezed her a little tighter than he had ever done before. And when he kissed her, she felt herself respond, just for a split second, before gently easing herself away.

'Tony, I promise I'll give you my answer soon,' she said quietly.

The day after Jan's meeting with A.D. in Ireland, the two documents critical to the deal arrived at Edge Farm.

Gary West's hand-signed authority, as an executive director of Harlequin Holdings registered in the Crown Dependency of Jersey, had been delivered by courier around mid-morning, followed shortly afterwards by a fax from the British Bloodstock Agency, which had viewed the horses for the official valuation.

Jan eagerly tore it off the machine and placed it on her desk alongside A.D.'s list. Annabel leaned over her shoulder, keen to read them with her. Before either had spoken a word, Jan let out a long exhalation in relief.

She leaned back in her chair, looked up at Bel and shrugged. 'Well, it looks as if he took a bit of notice when I warned him not to play games.'

Annabel picked up the lists for a closer look. 'Jan, correct me if I'm wrong, but unless I've misread it, A.D.'s valuations are higher than the agent's on all bar the young four-year-old.'

'And that's only a couple of grand different.' Jan exclaimed. 'If necessary, I'll find someone else to take the bay. As I know he's a lot better than A.D. thinks – he's only a baby and just a bit backward. Right then, we're in business. Assuming our friend Gary hasn't given me a load of bull about the legality of this document, I get my money and A.D. gets to own four more good horses in our yard. Of course, that'll mean he's got ten here, which will put him in a more dominant position than I really wanted, but I think I can trust him not to abuse the situation.'

'It certainly looks like it to me,' her assistant agreed. 'And Gary West gets a clear conscience, at least as far as his treatment of you is concerned.'

'I should think he's got far too much on his plate to care about that at this moment in time.'

'That's exactly why you should appreciate the fact that he took the trouble to do all that he has for you.'

'I know you're right,' Jan conceded, 'but in the final analysis it won't be any skin off his nose if the authorities never actually connect him with Harlequin Holdings and they might not because even the racing papers haven't realized there's a connection between Gary West and the horses owned by the company.'

It was just after nine in the morning, ten days after A.D. had agreed to purchase all the horses and had completed the transfer of the money into Jan's client account, when she spotted Tanner's red Porsche creeping up her long drive. She wondered why the receivers hadn't grabbed that too.

She walked back to her office in the yard and waited for him to appear. As he stood in the doorway, there was undoubtedly a chastened air about him and a fawning civility which Jan didn't recognize and didn't believe or trust for one minute.

'Good morning, Jan. I'm sorry I didn't phone you beforehand but I guessed you'd be here.'

'Was it you who called then put the phone down as soon as I answered it – about an hour ago?'

Tanner looked offended and sat down on one of the rickety chairs opposite Jan's desk. 'No, of course not. I just wanted to tell you how thrilled I am the situation's been resolved and you've got all the money we owed you. I told Gary he had to do it, in all fairness. And, er, I've come to pick up the balance. You can make out the cheque to me if you want,' he said, giving her a smarmy grin.

Jan stared at him blankly.

'If you're so delighted I've been paid, why didn't you pass on the money you were supposed to last October – instead of Gary having to send it here by courier?'

'Well, I never hung onto it if that's what you think. I never had it in the first place.'

'Yes you bloody did,' Jan growled. 'I always felt Gary was an honourable bloke, but you . . .' Her lip curled disdainfully. 'You're just a bloody parasite. Gary's a gambler who's played a massive game and he's lost; but he didn't cheat.'

Tanner's face was white and small bubbles of saliva appeared at the corners of his mouth. 'Look, Jan, I really don't know what you're talking about. Anyway, I brought Gary here in the first place, and don't you forget it; I was a partner in those horses . . .'

'Not when it came to paying for their keep it seems, if you recall our conversation at Chepstow,' Jan interjected.

'Look, I've got fuck all left. I'm out on bail; and those bastards are trying to accuse me of scams I haven't done; they've even took my passport away. I'm like a bloody prisoner in my own home. I've had a hell of a job giving them the slip this morning.'

'I notice you've still got your sixty-grand car.'

'That's because it belongs to my wife, not me or any of the companies.'

'Since when, I wonder?' Jan continued full steam ahead. 'Anyway, I'm not giving you any money so you may as well take a running jump. My arrangements are with Mr West. So piss off!' She flipped her hand at him.

Tanner stood up slowly, his face purple with rage and his eyes bulging. 'You effing bitch!' he hissed, full of venom. 'When I've supported you, and made bloody sure you've come out of this all right, you can't just turn round and dump on me.'

'You just watch me! You've got no further business here, so kindly get out of my yard. Now.'

Tanner didn't move and stood glaring at her, beside himself with rage until slowly the realization dawned that he would get no further. Suddenly he jabbed a quivering, nicotine-stained finger at her. 'This won't be the last time you'll hear from me, make no mistake about it, and if you've been covering up for Gary and hoodwinking the receivers, you'll be up to your pretty little neck in it! I'll see to that personally.'

Knocking over the chair as he spun round, he staggered out of the office and across the yard.

Annabel rushed in to see what all the shouting had been about.

'I take it that last threat was pure bluff?'

'Of course it was – at least, I hope so. I guess it all depends on what happens to the ghastly little toerag.'

Annabel chuckled. 'Whatever – it'll be worth it not to have to see or deal with him again.'

'Exactly.' Jan sniggered. 'Anyway, I've checked with Toby and he says, provided I keep the money in what they call an escrow account, I'm completely in the clear. So I think it's time to get back to real life. I think we can run Supercall at Newbury tomorrow, don't you?' She glanced at the clock on the office wall. 'We've still got enough time to declare him.'

Annabel nodded and sat down. 'He's been as sound as a bell for the last couple of weeks and he's nearly back to his best on the gallops.'

'Good. I'd like JCB to have a winner: he's been so patient he really deserves one.'

As she was returning home from Newbury the following evening, Jan reflected on how much her life had changed during the last two weeks. The removal of the pressure caused by Gary West's dilemma had left her feeling totally reborn, and the euphoria seemed to have spread throughout the yard – even, she considered, to the horses.

By anyone's standards Supercall had run a blinder. He'd had to fight every inch of the last two furlongs, but at the finishing line his superior stamina had left him a neck in front and what was more Jan knew he would improve for the run.

Johnny Carlton-Brown had been delighted but showing his usual restraint as he led the horse into the unsaddling enclosure, smiling reservedly. Not surprisingly, he hadn't brought Patrick Lamberhurst with him this time, which gave him a golden opportunity to congratulate Annabel with a long and lasting hug for the crucial role he considered she'd played in the horse's victory. He swiftly capitalized on this by asking her if he could take her out for dinner when her duties at the racecourse were over. Jan was highly amused by JCB's deftness and couldn't stop smiling as she drove Annabel's BMW back home.

After she'd swung the car from the lane onto the driveway at Edge Farm, she raced to the top of the hill, where the headlamps swept in a large arc around the parking area. It was then she glimpsed a distinctive tatty blue Morgan.

Her heart was pounding as she knew only one car like it and seeing it again unleashed such a flow of pure happiness that it flooded every other thought from her mind. But before she could give in to her emotions, she had to be entirely sure.

She sat like a statue before switching off the lights. A few seconds later she turned the ignition key and climbed out gingerly. She gently pushed the door, which closed with a clunk, and stood in the cold, dark silence.

The distant security light from the yard glimmered on the shiny black paintwork of the car, just enough to identify it.

'Annabel?' a man's voice questioned from the shadows.

'Hello, who's that?' Jan was quivering with excitement and anticipation as she tried to imitate her friend's voice.

'It's Eddie. Isn't Jan with you?'

'Eddie!? What on earth are you doing here?'

'I got into Heathrow at four o'clock. I suppose you've been at Newbury with Jan? Is she coming back in the lorry? Her car's here.'

Jan was walking slowly and hesitantly towards the dark archway under the weathervane.

'She went in the lorry,' Jan mimicked, still doing her best to sound like Annabel. She put her hand out and carefully felt for the switch that would turn on another light. 'But she's back,' she announced in her real voice and immediately flicked it on.

Eddie was transfixed, blinking for several seconds as he realized it was Jan not Annabel he'd been talking to. His mouth spread into a broad, unstoppable smile. 'Jan, you horrible woman!'

He went to rush forward, but suddenly stopped a yard in front of her.

She saw the questions in his eyes and slowly shook her head.

'No, Eddie. Not yet. It's wonderful to see you again, but it's been so long you're going to have to let me get used to the idea first!'

He nodded ruefully. 'Jan, I do understand. I wasn't expecting you to let me leap into bed with you.'

Jan stared back, still barely able to believe that it really was him standing there in front of her. A large part of her longed to move closer and envelop him. 'My God, Eddie! If only you knew what you'd put me through during the last year – leaving just when I thought it was safe to commit myself.'

He closed his eyes. 'Jan, I do know – at least, I can imagine. And I'm as sorry as you are. The whole thing was crazy and a complete waste of time . . .'

'Please, don't talk about it now, not out here,' Jan interjected quickly. 'Come up to the house and tell me what exactly's been going on.'

🐎

Matthew was slightly less cautious than Megan about Eddie Sullivan's unexpected reappearance. Once he had got over the initial surprise, he was inclined to forgive Eddie completely, begging him to tell more fantastic stories about gargantuan bush fires, kangaroos and cuddly koala bears. Jan guessed Eddie was probably making them all up, but she couldn't help smiling as she listened.

Megan had been a great deal more troubled than Matthew by Eddie's abrupt departure last spring and she looked on in silence, as if reserving judgement, while Eddie, trying to be as tactful as he could, didn't force the pace.

When Jan had finally put the children to bed, she busied herself in the kitchen, using her iron griddle pan to fry a couple of succulent steaks she had intended to use for lunch with Tony Robertson the following day.

She deliberately waited until they had sat down for their supper and an open bottle of red wine was on the table before she began to ask Eddie about what had happened in Australia.

'So how did it all work out?'

Eddie looked at her and smiled his lazy, enigmatic smile. 'I guess it worked out rather differently for each of us – for me, for Louise and for the baby.'

'For you . . . ?'

Eddie took a deep breath and leaned back in his chair. 'What can I say? I'm a father, with a really beautiful daughter I'm already very fond of, although I'm unlikely to see her more than once or twice a year. I've been taken for a huge ride by a spoiled, self-obsessed woman, who used me as an emotional crutch for the whole time she was pregnant just to keep her mother off her back. Her father was almost as bad; it suited him to have the father of his daughter's illegitimate unborn child around while she was expecting it. And he was really angry when I told him I was leaving, but I suppose in the end it made it easier for them because now they can tell everyone it was all my fault for walking out.' Eddie shrugged. 'I know the truth, though, and I really shouldn't care what they say about me, but actually I do resent being cast in the role of complete shit so they can justify Louise being a single mum.'

Jan watched every fluctuating emotion on his face, which helped her understand exactly what he was feeling.

'But what did she actually say about it?' Jan asked.

'It was just a few days after the baby was born, she was sitting up in bed feeding her when she finally confessed she'd used me. She admitted she'd only made a colossal scene when she first found she was pregnant because she wanted me around in case something went wrong; now everything was all OK she found she didn't need me. It was as cold and as simple as that. When I pointed out that she'd taken eight months out of my life, she just said, so what, I'd made a few bucks while I'd been in Oz, and I had a daughter who I could come and see whenever I wanted. Basically, she's chucked me out, though she would never ever admit that to her parents.'

Eddie leaned forward, took a gulp of wine and looked at Jan with a contorted expression on his face. 'I only went back to Oz because I felt it was the honourable thing to do.' He sighed and raised an eyebrow. 'Do you know, the day I left England, when I actually got to Heathrow, just before I went through the security check to board the plane, I was in complete agony and very nearly turned round and came back here. I wish I bloody had now.' His eyes reddened as he gazed at Jan for a moment without speaking. 'As soon as I saw Louise, I knew immediately it was never going to work out; I really don't know what attracted us to each other in the first place. I admit she's a very good-looking girl, but there's more to life than that. It's possible, after leaving you here, that I just didn't want to get on with her, I suppose. Anyway, I don't blame you for a single moment for being totally pissed off with me. I've made a prat of myself – who'd want to be mixed up with someone who could be such a complete moron?'

She reached across the table and put her hand on his. 'The trouble with you, Eddie,' Jan mused, 'is that you always did like the flash sports cars. Though I do understand – a little – and I don't think you are a total moron or you wouldn't be sitting here now. But you've got to give me time. I was completely devastated when you went, I think you develop scar tissue to cover the wounds and find different ways of dealing with the emotional trauma. And I've adjusted my feelings; if I'm going to revive them again it certainly won't happen immediately.'

'I know that,' Eddie moaned. 'I've had to do it as well, remember?' With a lot of effort he managed a strained smile. 'Anyway, give or take a few minor details, that's the whole story.'

Jan gazed at him, still wavering between the joy of seeing him and sharing the misery of the predicament he'd found himself in. 'But, Eddie, how do you possibly think you can live with that? Being a father's a serious business – it's not something you can play at, you can't leave that poor baby in limbo. They have always said that a boy can father a child but it takes a man to keep one. Which are you?'

Jan saw a hint of tears in Eddie's already bloodshot eyes and realized she had completely mistaken his bravery for bravado.

'Do you think I'm happy about it?' he asked, ruffled by her accusation. 'At least my mother's out there, I know she's not ecstatic about the way things happened, but she's chuffed to bits to have a granddaughter. You know what she's like – always dignified in a crisis – she's even managed to get on sweetly with Louise's parents and has staked her claim very positively.'

'Well, that's something, I suppose,' Jan conceded. 'Eddie, I have to confess – though it's not necessarily what I want, I've got to think of my children first and foremost – there's absolutely no way we can get together permanently until you've sorted out what's going to happen to your daughter in the future.'

Eddie sighed. 'I know that, Jan, and I'm working on it, I promise. Anyway, that's enough of my problems for now. How about you? How's your mum and dad?'

'Dad's been fine.' Jan smiled. 'He bought a pony for Matty and he's been so patient teaching him to ride, doing far better than I ever did. Mum's not so good, though. She's been back and forth to hospital having dialysis. She wouldn't go in for a scan for ages, but eventually Tony Robertson – remember him, the doctor?'

'The one who fancied you? Of course.' Eddie nodded.

'Actually, Eddie, it was a great deal more than that,' Jan said slowly. 'He's spent a lot of time with us, going out with me and the kids and helping me deal with tricky issues.' She paused and looked away. 'He's asked me to marry him.'

Eddie blinked rapidly. 'Did you say you would?' he asked huskily.

She looked back at him. 'He's still waiting for my answer,' she said guardedly.

Eddie stood up and pushed back his chair. 'Look, Jan, if you've been seriously considering it and it seems like the right thing – and I can see, with the kids, it might well be – then you must go ahead and forget about me.'

'If I think it's the right thing for us all then I will,' Jan said as calmly as she could, 'but actually we were discussing my mother.'

Eddie took a deep breath and sat down again.

'As I was saying, Tony persuaded Mum to go into hospital,' Jan continued. 'I took her myself and initially they were really worried. Still, things are a lot better now, thank God, so with a bit of luck and plenty of treatment, she should – ' Jan hesitated – 'might get better.'

'Poor old thing,' Eddie said sympathetically. 'And Megan tells me she's got a new pony that's going well.'

Despite the dreadful problems he had brought back from Australia, Jan was enjoying having Eddie with her, but she was damned if she was going to say so. Eddie seemed genuinely full of remorse that he had put her through such a prolonged period of misery, even if, in the long run, the outcome with West had been beneficial for her.

'The only thing is,' Jan said, 'I never really wanted A.D. to be such a dominant owner and now he's got ten horses in the yard.'

Eddie looked surprised. 'So what? I don't think you could get a better owner if you wrote the spec yourself. He knows what the game's all about; so far he's only sent you good horses; you know you can trust him, and what's even more important he always pays his bills on time.'

'Gee, thanks, Eddie.' Jan chuckled. 'Somehow, you always seem to make everything so much simpler than it actually is. Anyway, that's enough for now, I think you'd better sling your hook because I've had a hell of a long day and I still have to be up early and on the ball in the morning.'

Outside storm-force winds had got up and now heavy rain was beginning to lash against the windows. Eddie looked at it sullenly, then at Jan for a few moments before he slowly nodded his head. 'You're right. Luckily, I've already booked my old room at the King's Head.'

Jan smiled, relieved that Eddie hadn't tried to jump to conclusions. 'You're still welcome to come and ride out any time,' she offered with a grin, 'as long as you don't expect to be paid.'

🐎

It was only a week later as Eddie walked back into the kitchen after riding out first lot. Jan looked up smiling and thought: *It's almost like old times.*

From the other side of the room Megan watched him coolly. He still hadn't managed to persuade her to help him off with his boots, and, making a great fuss, he heaved them off with the help of the bootjack as he sniffed the aroma of frying bacon. 'That smells great. It really is marvellous to be back.'

Jan beamed back at him. 'It's great to have you riding out again and you've been so good, I've got a little present for you.'

'Oh my, a surprise!' Eddie fluted in a falsetto voice. 'What can it be?'

'Shut up, sit down quickly and I'll tell you before all the others come in.'

Eddie poured himself a mug of coffee and sat opposite her.

'I've got something that I've never ever given to anyone else before,' Jan said. 'Wait for it.' She giggled at the sight of his face. 'A real, red-hot tip.'

Eddie's eyes lit up. 'Gimme, gimme,' he demanded huskily.

'The runner we've got at Fakenham today, Holy Mist.'

'I know him, a dappled rather pretty grey horse; belongs to A.D. now.'

'Precisely. Last time he ran I felt he should have won doing triple toe loops, but Finbar screwed up and didn't see the horse right on his tail. Well, he dropped his hands half a furlong out and got beat. The winning horse's form since then has been moderate, which makes our fella's chance today look decidedly grim. It's his first run over hurdles and the starting price is forecast at sixteen to one.'

'Do you honestly think he'll win – even though he hasn't raced over jumps before?'

'Absolutely; I've never known a young horse jump so naturally; he loves it and we know he's got no phobias about the race-course.'

'But, Jan, how on earth am I going to get a decent bet on at that price? They won't do any big business at Cyril Goldstone's shops, and I haven't got time to get it set up across the chain.'

'It won't be a problem. Annabel has a friend who has an active and, I suspect, very unprofitable account with Cyril. She's already checked it out and he told her that if he asks Cyril to lay him five or even ten grand at the price published in the *Racing Post*, Cyril will take it.'

'There's still a little problem, I haven't got five, never mind ten grand.'

'I'm sure with your expertise you'll solve that one somehow.' Jan grinned. 'As long as you remember there's no such thing as a certainty, especially in jump racing, but I'm as sure as I can be that this will be my longest-priced winner this season. So I will leave it to you, do what you want, but don't breathe a word to a soul or you will completely drop me in the mire.'

'OK.' Eddie nodded. 'Thanks. But tell me, Jan, why are you doing this?'

'I'm not sure, really; but I can sense you feel I've been a bit standoffish since you got back. I guess I just want you to understand it's not about you personally, it's the entire mess you've got your-self into with that girl – I just can't forget about it. The whole problem is the children were completely shattered when they lost their father – especially Megan. The next man in my life will need to be a substantial father figure, and there's no way I would expose them to all that emotion, only to find he's disappeared again, even if it's only temporarily to visit a mysterious daughter on the other side of the world.'

Eddie looked at her bleakly, as if he could see no way out of his dilemma. He nodded slowly. 'I do understand your position, Jan, completely. I'd better leave you to it for now and go and see where I can find a few grand to put on Holy Mist. Thanks for the info anyway!'

'Eighty bloody grand!!!' Bernie spluttered down the phone to Jan. 'Are you telling me that hare-brained bloke of yours has gone and won eighty bloody thousand quid!'

'Who the hell told you, Bernie?'

'That gypsy lad of yours, Joe Paley, when I was at the races yesterday. He overheard Annabel talking about it.'

Jan made a mental note to remind her assistant that stable walls had particularly good ears, but guessed that for now no real damage had been done, provided, that is, A.D. never got wind of it.

'Well, best of luck to him, I say; but, Jan, why the hell didn't you tip me off too?'

'Bernie, I've been telling you for years, I don't do tips. Eddie works in the yard: he saw what the horse looked like, how well he was working and he knew the form.'

'But the form was bloody lousy!' Bernie argued. 'Anyway, I thought you never went in for coups and such like.'

'I don't usually, but I suppose you could say Eddie was taking advantage of the jockey's error last time out; and he'd taken the trouble to study the video of its last run.'

Which I lent him, Jan added to herself.

Bernie sighed. 'Maybe I should come and ride work for you meself, then I'd be more in the know.'

Jan laughed. 'I don't really think that's such a good idea, I doubt if we have a horse quiet enough to carry you.'

Bernie laughed too. 'Maybe not.'

'Anyway, you can do me a big favour, Bernie. Please don't tell anyone else about it, owners, lads, not anyone.'

'All right, Jan, I promise.'

Jan put the phone down, praying that she could trust him.

🐎

Jan was at the bank in Broadway, paying in a cheque she had just received from the developers for the purchase of Olwen's bungalow, together with the right of access from the road to the highly sought-after buildings and the large farmhouse. She was also making a deposit in Eddie's account – the cheque Annabel had brought round for him the night before – since Cyril Goldstone's office had already settled her friend's account.

Jan was pleased that she had been able to help Eddie out of a large financial hole, but in some ways she was already regretting it. She was extremely concerned that A.D. might get to hear about Eddie's good fortune and demand an explanation. Jan knew that A.D. would take the view if Eddie was so positive the horse would win then she must have known as well. And if that was the case, since he owned the horse, he should certainly have been 'on' it too.

Jan had already told Eddie that she would never ever give him a tip like that again, but she completely understood his burning desire to get even with Goldstone for what the crooked bookie had done to him at Aintree. At least the eighty thousand pounds went some way to satisfying that desire, as well as giving Eddie some critically needed funds.

She was just leaving the Cotswold stone building which housed the bank when she found herself face to face with Tony Robertson. Instinctively, she closed her eyes in a desperate attempt to avoid blushing and looking guilty.

'Jan? What on earth's the matter?' he asked.

She opened them, blinking. 'Oh, Tony. I'm so sorry, I've got rather a lot on my mind, that's all.'

'Jan, what's been going on? I've hardly heard a word from you since the night you got back from Ireland, and then when you can-celled Sunday lunch at the last minute two weeks ago I thought . . .'

Jan glanced at the people bustling in and out of the bank and along the High Street. 'Tony, do you really think this is the best place for a discussion?' she asked. And felt shaken by his obvious distress.

The doctor looked around him miserably and nodded. 'Have you got time for a cup of coffee?'

'No, not really,' Jan said quickly. 'I'm a bit pushed at the moment but I'll have one with you anyway.'

The doctor looked desolate. 'Oh, it doesn't matter,' he said dejectedly. 'Eddie Sullivan's back, isn't he?'

Jan nodded vaguely.

'Not again,' Tony added with a hint of bitterness.

'I'm really sorry, Tony.'

He shrugged. 'What have you got to be sorry about? I knew the score when we were at Annabel's engagement party, the night I asked you to marry me. I can remember telling you how beautiful women often go for shits.'

'Tony, that's not altogether fair. Eddie may be a bit irresponsible, but he's certainly not a shit . . .' she paused '. . . anyway I'm not a beautiful woman.'

'Hmm,' Tony grunted. He opened his mouth to speak and changed his mind; turning sharply, he marched off and disappeared up the High Street, leaving Jan gazing at the ground.

A large part of her wanted to run after him, to put her arms around him and mother him. She sighed – he didn't want a mother, she knew that for certain, he wanted a lover. And so did she.

27

At the end of February Jan confirmed to the press that, barring accidents, Magic Maestro, now owned by Mr A.D. O'Hagan, would definitely be running in the Cathcart; it was a two-and-a-half-mile chase, worth £30,000 in prize money and held on the third day of the Cheltenham Festival.

On the first Sunday in March Jan arranged to take Eddie and the children to her parents for lunch.

A few crocuses still bloomed in the grass verges at the small farmhouse, and the newly born lambs of the ewes Reg kept on the meadow pasture with Rocket bleated to their mothers as they skipped about in spring sunshine beneath a crisp blue sky.

Reg was almost as excited as his daughter at the prospect of attending the Festival with a runner. Jan had brought over a videotape of Magic Maestro's last run especially for him to look at, and he insisted on viewing it the moment they arrived.

Jan and Eddie sat and scrutinized the tape with him while Mary, bravely denying any discomfort she had from her kidneys, asked the children to lend a hand in the kitchen.

'He's not as big as you usually like 'em, Jan,' Reg observed when Magic Maestro first appeared on screen.

'No,' she agreed, 'but he is very muscular and probably looks smaller because he's short-coupled, which I like in a horse.'

The eight-year-old gelding, who had lost his novice status when he won in Ireland the previous year, was a light bay in colour with a white sock on his foreleg.

'He's probably not the most elegant horse I've ever seen,' Eddie chipped in, 'but he's very workmanlike.'

'You can see that he runs a bit like that Jack Russell you used to have, Dad,' Jan teased.

'Maybe he does, but he's a tidy jumper all right,' Reg grunted with a nod as they watched the horse fly the water at Newbury with plenty of room to spare on touchdown.

After they had watched the whole race, Reg turned to Jan. 'I know he's won over the same course and distance as the Cathcart, but will he still have the same pilot on board at Cheltenham?'

Jan made a face. 'Virginia's running a real no-hoper and I can't help thinking she's doing it just to stop Finbar riding ours.'

'She wouldn't be so daft, would she?' Reg asked.

'I wouldn't bet against it. Maybe the owner's insisting on it, though,' Jan continued thoughtfully, 'but I can't have Murty either, so I'll just have to wait and see who's available when some of the other horses drop out.'

'Pity you can't run that Miller's Lodge in the Cathcart. He won it last year, didn't he?'

'Yes, but he's not eligible as he's in his third season over fences and he won in his first year.'

'That's the only decent race Virginia's ever won, ain't it,' Reg said thoughtfully, 'and now you've got the horse. No wonder she's got it in for you.'

Jan shook her head. 'Maybe, but she's never really said anything, so I really don't know what her problem is – it's been going on for years.'

'Ah well, the main thing is it's her problem, not yours,' Reg declared philosophically. 'Now let's go and have a look at Rocket.' He turned to Eddie. 'You said you wanted to see him, didn't you?'

'Yes, please. You must show me how Matty's getting on.'

Reg didn't need any encouragement. 'I was going to anyway. I reckon he's really taken to it.'

'Dad, don't you rub it in.' Jan laughed and turned to Eddie. 'He can't help bragging, he's chuffed to bits because when I tried to teach Matty the little horror just ran off and hid under the table.'

'I know,' Eddie grinned. 'I saw him do it dozens of times.'

Reg led them from the house through his immaculate vegetable garden, already finely raked and prepared for the neat rows of seedling, he would be planting out soon. Beyond the gate into the paddock, Rocket was grazing on his own, well away from the ewes and their lambs. Looking up, he immediately spotted Reg and whinnied, then started to trot over to check what titbit he was going to receive.

'He certainly knows which side his bread's buttered,' Jan said with a chuckle full of admiration for her father's natural empathy with horses.

They fondled the pony as Reg fed him the bits of carrot he had secreted in his pocket.

As they turned and headed back towards the house, the old man pronounced, 'I see Harold Powell's got that good horse running at Cheltenham – the one you had a win with at Ludlow a few years back.'

Jan gritted her teeth at the very mention of Powell's name. 'Yes, I noticed. I hope he doesn't intend crossing my path.'

'He got off that case then, didn't he?'

'I'm afraid so. He claimed he had no idea that strychnine was in the jars and he never asked his men to chuck them in the well either. His men said they had no idea what the stuff was and thought they were just dealing with some old cider bottles as they were so dirty and didn't have any labels on them either.'

'Do you believe 'em?'

Jan took a deep breath. 'I suppose I don't really have a choice. Anyway after that he had no choice about selling the ground and the buildings, there was so much bad feeling in the district. He had to take a big loss on it in the end.'

'Poor old Olwen. I hope she didn't suffer.'

'They say it can be extremely painful, but when I found her I have to say she looked quite peaceful.'

'Well, let's hope that bloody Harold Powell's horse doesn't do any good.'

'Oh, I don't know, Dad. Life's too short to carry grudges.'

On the way back to Edge, Eddie's mobile beeped, indicating he had a recorded message. He reached into the side pocket of the car to grab the phone and pressed it tightly to his ear. When he'd finished listening to it, Jan could sense by his flushed appearance he had something he was burning to tell her, but was loath to discuss it with Megan and Mattie in the car.

As soon as they arrived back at the yard and the children were haring off up to the house, Jan turned towards him. 'What is it, Eddie? What's happened? Come on, spit it out.'

'That message I picked up on my mobile, as we were leaving Riscombe, it was from my mother.'

'And?' Jan asked warily, knowing his mother's current obsession.

'It was a bit garbled, so don't get your hopes up, but . . .'

'Eddie,' Jan interrupted, 'please don't give me some half-baked story if this is about your daughter. Ring your mum back right now and see what's going on.'

Eddie nodded. 'OK, fine.'

Jan sighed, leant back in the car seat and stared vaguely in the direction of her buildings, making a mental note of what she needed to do. Eddie sat beside her and punched the long number onto his keypad, then checked it carefully before placing the phone to his ear. 'It's the middle of the night over there,' he said, turning to Jan, 'but she won't mind. Oh, hello, Mum; it's Eddie.'

Jan watched anxiously for the next few minutes as Eddie's expression swung from restraint to relief, followed by doubt, then revived hope as he said his final goodbye. He looked at Jan apprehensively. 'Still don't get your hopes up!' He shook his head to discourage her from uncalled-for optimism.

'Oh for Christ's sake, get on with it!' Jan snapped. 'What did she say?'

'OK, don't get your knickers in a twist. She said last week she treated herself to a session at Minerick's, the top crimper in Sydney. The poor old thing's trying to be so restrained with Dad being on the skids. Well, this salon happens to be the one Louise uses, which is not surprising; anyway, the girls were gossiping about her without realizing Mum had any connection. They were saying Louise has had this baby and nobody really knows who the father is because she'd been seen around with quite a few guys besides Eddie what's his name. I'd never met them, you see, I was away half the time, trying to drum up some antiques deals.'

Jan couldn't help feeling roused by the tale and where it might be leading, but she didn't interrupt.

'Mum, cool as a cucumber, managed to wheedle a bit more from them. Of course, a lot of what they'd heard was third hand – but Louise is someone who gets talked about a great deal in Sydney – so Mum came away fairly convinced that the baby's not mine. She was devastated and went straight up to Vaucluse to see Lou's parents, and apparently she's persuaded them to have the baby DNA-tested to establish who the real father is. She suggested it was far better to sort it out now rather than later in the child's life when it could be a lot more embarrassing. Apparently they were quite calm about it all; as it was, they already had an inkling it might not be mine.'

'Oh, Eddie! This is so awful!'

'Awful?' Eddie exclaimed. 'What do you mean awful? Now I won't have any commitments to the baby or to Louise.'

'But, Eddie, you're already committed. I can tell you're proud of her; you may not have realized it, but you've already bonded with the poor mite.'

'Obviously, I think she's a beautiful little girl because she is, but if she's not mine . . . well, that's another matter.'

'I bet it won't be that simple, Eddie, not after what you've been through with Louise. After all, you've already given her six months of your life before the birth of this baby.'

'OK, Jan, maybe that was all a complete waste of time, it doesn't matter any more. As from now, it's all in the past and there's absolutely nothing I can do about it, so I'm not going to keep harping.'

Jan stared at him transfixed for a few moments. 'Eddie, before you decide to go along with your mother's plan, perhaps you should take a bit of time to think about it. Firstly, you've got to decide if you really want to go through with this. I mean, suppose she is your daughter? And if you've already half decided she isn't, it's bound to make a huge difference to your feelings for her.'

Eddie puckered his face in bemusement. 'I don't know about that, maybe – I suppose it might, but so what? I'll just have to readjust, she'll never need to know.'

'Well, I think it would always be there as a barrier between you,' Jan insisted. 'Now I almost wish the possibility of her being someone else's had never been raised.'

'At the same time, Jan,' Eddie interrupted, 'being pragmatic about the situation, you've got to admit that it will make things a whole lot easier for us if I haven't got a daughter on the other side of the world. But you're right, she could quite easily be mine, so we'll have to wait and see what happens next.'

'When's this test going to take place?'

'Mum wasn't too sure. Over the next couple of weeks, I expect. Apparently I've got to send them a smear from the inside of my mouth, certified by a doctor over here.' Eddie screwed up his face.

'Well, that's better than a bottle of blood – or anything else, for that matter,' Jan observed.

'Look, Jan, I understand what you're saying, but this is my problem and I'll have to deal with it. Yes, I was already getting attached to the lovely little soul. I know that she's going to be such a beautiful child and that's why I thought she might possibly be mine.'

'Eddie, you pig!' Jan chided. 'Your vanity's going to get you into very serious trouble one of these days.'

It was less than three weeks later that Jan was crudely reminded of the conversation she had had with Reg about Harold Powell and she now found herself less able to forgive the crooked auctioneer.

On the day his horse was running in the Cathcart, A.D. O'Hagan, in a huge display of confidence, paid well over the odds for the largest box he could obtain. He had invited his old friends from Kerry, some business associates and most of Jan's other owners, as well as her parents.

During lunch there was an intense buzz of excitement amongst the guests, but Jan was so dreadfully tense she could barely eat.

Eddie was in his element acting as the master of ceremonies; teasing Annabel and Johnny Carlton-Brown, and keeping the group entertained, he appeared to be on more relaxed terms with A.D. than Jan had ever been. As the time for the race approached Eddie was still in full flow, Jan smiled, then glanced at the clock on the magnolia-painted wall and slipped away.

Harold Powell was standing directly in front of her blocking the path from the weighing room to the saddling boxes. He was dressed impeccably in a green tweed suit, well-polished brogues and a brown trilby. His dark eyes glowered red and were filled with venom.

'Jan Hardy, I hope you're fucking proud of yourself,' he growled with a menacing edge to his voice.

'Harold, please. I haven't got time to deal with this right now.'

'No? I bet you haven't. Not when you've just ruined a man's career? And wrecked his marriage?'

'Harold, whatever it is you've done, everything that's happened since is all down to you. I never got involved, you know that.'

He stared at her, and although there was room to squeeze past, she found herself transfixed by his gaze.

'I hope you rot in sodding hell, Jan Hardy. I gave you every bit of support I could when you started in this game, but now you're getting nearer the top, you think folk like us are just dispensable. Well, you can't treat people like that, you'll see; you won't get away with it, mark my words. You'll get what's coming to you.'

Jan stared at him in shock and disbelief. How after all the deception and vindictiveness she had suffered could he possibly see himself as the victim? It was incredible. And yet his vociferousness carried great conviction.

She forced herself to turn away and break eye contact with him, then taking a deep breath she clenched her fists as tightly as possible and quickly walked away. *Damn it*, she said to herself as all the euphoria of the last few hours quickly disappeared; she swallowed as a feeling of nausea tried to consume her.

She shook her head. Why had this man turned up today, of all days, when she was saddling her first Festival runner, when everything else in her life was going so right for a change?

The confrontation had left a really bitter taste which she struggled to dispel, even with all the excitement and the concentration she needed to prepare her horse for his Festival debut.

'What on earth's the matter, Jan?' Annabel asked. 'You look as if you've just seen a ghost.'

'Well, I have, sort of. That bastard Harold Powell's here and you're not going to believe this, he had the nerve to waylay me and tell *me* I'd ruined his life.'

'My God, Jan! How the hell . . .'

'I tell you, there was such viciousness in his eyes I almost believed him myself.'

'How horrible! But listen, you can't even think about that now! Just look at our beautiful horse,' she added proudly as Joe Paley led the Magic Maestro into one of the saddling boxes.

Jan grinned. 'I don't know if I would describe him as beautiful, but he's looking great. Well done, Joe, you've done a brilliant job.'

The young man beamed so broadly it looked as if his face would split. Jan thanked her good sense, not for the first time, that she had given the lad a second chance following Cyril Goldstone's corruption of him at Aintree two years ago.

'He's in some order, Mrs H. He knows what's on and he's raring to go. Bloody good job we got Finbar back on board – him knowing the 'oss so well an' all.'

'I bet Virginia's as sick as a flock of parrots her horse couldn't be here. Right, enough of that. Let's get on with it,' Jan said, picking up the saddle, 'or we'll be late getting this show on the road.'

🐎

Reg Pritchard squeezed alongside Jan on the balcony of the box, and was pressed up against the concrete balustrade by the enthusiasm of A.D.'s guests.

'By God, you were right, Jan. That horse runs just like a terrier after a rat.'

Out on the track Finbar Howlett was riding a race he would remember for the rest of his life. Knowing the Magic Maestro's ability to win was on stamina rather than speed, he had managed to settle him in a fluctuating position close to the leaders most of the way round, making good use of the ground he made at every fence and barely letting him off the bridle.

He only gave the Magic Maestro his head when they had pinged the fence at the bottom of the hill before the turn into the home straight with just two left to jump, cunningly staying a few lengths off the three up front.

Halfway round the bend, Finbar whipped up the inside and passed two of the runners. Seconds later Magic Maestro flew the second last and landed alongside the leader.

'Hold him steady, by God,' Reg Pritchard bellowed. He turned to Jan with his eyes sparkling like diamonds. 'That other horse has had enough, he's done for. Look, he's beginning to wander!'

Finbar, riding as short as any jockey over jumps, crouched low over his horse's withers as they forged relentlessly towards the last, reaching it half a length ahead of their rival.

In his eagerness, the Magic Maestro took off a shade too early and dragged his hind legs through the fence. He sprawled on landing and the crowd let out a sharp groan. For a microsecond Jan thought it was all over. But the horse didn't want to go down and quickly regained his balance.

Finbar leaned right back in his saddle to help the horse recover and just two strides later the Magic Maestro regained his momentum and stretched out courageously towards the winning post.

Somewhere out of the blue a new challenger attacked; just a length and a half behind he had landed full of running and was gaining with every stride.

Finbar crouched even lower, punching the reins back and forth like pistons above the horse's plaited mane. The noise from the huge Cheltenham crowd was reaching a crescendo.

At the line, the Magic Maestro was no more than a neck in front. But it was enough.

Jan's legs went weak and her head was spinning. She thought

she was going to faint while her father was going ballistic and cheered himself hoarse. Suddenly she heard A.D.'s voice, which seemed to be coming from the other side of Cleeve Hill.

'Thank you, Jan,' it was saying. 'That was one of the best wins I ever saw.'

She turned and silently acknowledged his congratulations with tears streaming down her face. A.D. gently wrapped his arms around her and gave her a hug. She hardly noticed the change when a moment later Eddie was holding her and kissing away the tears.

As Finbar rode the horse back up the walkway to the illustrious winners' enclosure, A.D.'s party hurtled down the stairs before rushing to greet him. The horse and jockey jogged through the crowd, cheered all the way to the number one position in the unsaddling enclosure, where they received an irrepressible welcome for a great display of classic Cheltenham courage.

The whole team were beaming, as each individual stepped forward to receive their trophy. For Jan it was the most magical moment of her whole life, and when she caught sight of Mary and Reg crammed up against the rail of the paddock, she was overwhelmed by the love she saw there.

But no one was more proud than Joe Paley, as he led his charge away marching like a soldier.

Back in A.D.'s box, as the champagne flowed, Eddie touched Jan lightly on the arm.

'You have as much of this as you like. I'll drive home. After all, it is your day.'

She smiled fondly at him. It was as if he understood that for once she felt like letting her hair down to celebrate the biggest race she'd ever won in Great Britain, and to exorcize the dreadful memory of Harold Powell's threats.

Eddie nudged her gently. 'Look, over there!' He was nodding at Annabel. 'I think you may be in danger of losing your assistant again.'

Jan peered across the crowded room to where Annabel and Johnny Carlton-Brown were standing overly close to one another, their faces almost touching. Bel had her long slender arms draped around his neck.

'Oh no.' Jan giggled. 'I thought Johnny was too keen on his horses to risk upsetting the equilibrium at Edge Farm.'

❧

It was rather late and pitch black in the almost empty trainers' car park, as Eddie opened the low door of the Morgan for Jan to climb into the passenger seat.

Jan watched affectionately as he walked around the front of the car. Opening the door, he stuffed his Barbour into the tiny space at the back, then dropped into his seat and strapped himself in.

'You haven't had too much bubbly, have you, Eddie?' she questioned.

'I've hardly had any – I didn't need another fix after watching that race.' He shook his head, still awestruck by the day's events.

'I mean would you pass a breathalyser?'

'Jan, I promise, I've only had a gnat's bladderful. I swear I'm as alcohol free as the pope in Lent.'

He turned on the ignition and the old sports car eventually sprang into life. Gently they rattled out of the car park.

As they drove slowly through the last of the race traffic on the edge of town, Eddie's mobile phone chirruped in the pocket of his coat.

'Can you answer that for me?' he asked.

Jan fumbled behind the seat and found the coat, which had got well and truly tangled up with the strap of Eddie's binocular case and the seat runners. As she tugged to release it, the chirruping ceased.

'Oh hell!' Eddie said. 'It looks like you've missed it.'

'Don't fret. It's probably just someone ringing to congratulate you.'

'Congratulate *me*?' Eddie asked. 'What for?'

'For giving me so much support and telling me not to panic

when everything seems to be getting on top of me,' Jan smiled warmly.

But Eddie wasn't to be pacified. He hated missing calls. 'Whoever it was may have left a message. So see if you can get the bloody thing out and have a look.'

After a further tussle, Jan heaved the coat clear and pulled the phone from an inside pocket.

'You were right. Do you want me to listen?'

Eddie grinned. 'You know I don't have any more secrets from you.'

Jan called the message number and waited until she heard a voice which was instantly familiar, although she hadn't heard it for nearly two years.

'Hello, Ed. It's Mum here. Sorry to miss you, I saw you did brilliantly at Cheltenham today. Well done, lots of love to Jan. And by the way, I've got some very important news. Give me a ring as soon as you get a chance.'

Jan waited until another voice said, 'End of messages.' She stared at the phone in disbelief.

'That was your mother, saying well done and she's got some important news for you.'

Eddie jerked his head round to stare at her. 'And?' he asked.

'And nothing. That's all she said.'

'Did it sound like good or bad news?'

'I really don't know. I couldn't tell.'

'Oh shit! That's just typical of her. She only ever wants to discuss things face to face. Get her back, quick. Do a return call.'

Jan's hand was shaking as she pushed the buttons.

She heard the connection being made, and the universally frustrating sound of a busy line.

'Hell!' she gasped. 'She's engaged now.'

'It's about five in the morning out there. She must be trying to get hold of me on another number. Best leave it until we get home,' Eddie continued philosophically. 'Whatever it is, it's not going to change between now and then.'

🐎

A quarter of an hour later the car was spluttering its way up Cleeve Hill.

'Bloody hell, Jan, what a day!' Eddie exploded gleefully for the third time since they'd left the course. 'Can you Adam and Eve it? I never thought I'd experience a day like that. I reckon this must be about as good as it gets! By the way, I bloody love you, Jan Hardy!'

'So, you've said – about ten times and I love you too, Eddie. But right now I'm dying to get home and see the kids and to hear what your mother's got to say. Can we crack on a bit?' Jan said impatiently. 'I thought this was supposed to be a sports car.'

'But she's a very old sports car, and not quite as frisky as she used to be. Good God!' he exclaimed suddenly, peering into his offside wing mirror. 'What the hell's this silly bastard trying to do?'

As he spoke, a pair of headlights dazzled him from behind. A split second later a Range Rover surged past them at full throttle.

'Eddie, Eddie! Look out!'

The car coming down the hill had nowhere to go. Its headlights suddenly veered across the road, glaring straight at Eddie's eyes, blinding him.

They heard a massive grinding followed by an earth-shattering bang.

Suddenly the whole world went black.

🐎

As Jan slowly came to, everything was in complete darkness. She wondered where she was; how long she had been there.

She tried to move. Her legs were trapped. Frantically, responding to some half-remembered advice, Jan wriggled her toes and felt them move inside her shoes.

She listened. There was a slight hissing noise somewhere in front and a faint whine as the wind whipped through the ill-fitting canvas hood. From a long way off the two-tone wail of a siren was carried up on the breeze. She vaguely remembered the police car emerging from the mist on the hills above Olwen's bungalow.

Now, casting her mind back, she remembered. Eddie was driving. He'd just told her he loved her.

Suddenly a huge wave of dread washed over her. She reached out and started to sob as she fumbled in the blackness.

'Eddie, please help me! I'm trapped!' Finding his hand, she squeezed it. 'Please say something . . . Eddie!'